FULL
DRESSOUT

FULL DRESSOUT

Craig A. Kelley

To order additional copies of this book, contact:
Xlibris Corporation
1-888-795-4274
www.Xlibris.com
Orders@Xlibris.com

PROLOGUE

3 SEPTEMBER, 1957
EAST BOSTON, MASSACHUSETTS

The box itself was innocuous, measuring only eighteen inches long by eight inches wide by ten inches high. Weighing just under twenty pounds and built out of thick plywood banded by iron straps, it was the sort of box that defines the term "solid." In the forgotten corner of someone's basement, it would have been the type of container that holds old horseshoes, bent nails and used paint brushes. Tightly strapped down in the back of the flatbed truck and stamped "Fragile" in large, bright yellow letters on each side, it clearly held something else, something far more threatening than household hardware scraps.

Nestled securely inside the box, a dozen metallic spheres jiggled only slightly as the flatbed hit a large pothole. Exactly 3.5 inches in diameter and packed with seven ounces of high explosives, each sphere represented the culmination of months of secret research at the Army's Rock Island Arsenal. When detonated, they would have an effective casualty radius, called an ECR by the Army's ordnance experts, of over twenty-five feet. In civilian terms, these experts would explain, that meant that anyone standing within twenty-five feet when one of these deadly globes exploded would have a fifty-percent chance of being completely shredded on the spot. Because no weapon system is perfect, they'd add with a smile, the other fifty percent would only be partially shredded.

Even more impressive to these experts, and to the civilian technicians who had ordered them, was the spheres' permeability.

While other fragmentation grenades had a smooth metal skin that would not accept chemical coatings, these spheres could be treated with a variety of substances that would volatize into the air when the grenade exploded. If everything went properly, the program managers hoped that these spheres would provide US special tactics forces with a combined chemical and shrapnel weapon for quick strike operations. Dipped into the right chemical mixture, the experts estimated that the fatality percentage for these spheres would be one hundred percent for anyone within fifty feet. For people worried about body counts and unit casualty ratios, these new grenades could provide a significant battlefield advantage.

Knowing nothing about his cargo's military specifications, the truck's driver, his face largely concealed behind a bushy beard stained with chewing tobacco, carefully snaked his way through Maverick Square's late-night revelers and onto Sumner Street, stopping in front of a drab, one story brick building ringed by a chain fence. Climbing down from the cab, his joints somewhat stiff after the long ride, he spat a squirt of tobacco juice onto the already stained pavement and then walked around the back of his truck to undo the canvas straps holding down his cargo. By the time he had finished wrestling the box out of its straps and down to the ground, two men had come through the fence to sign for it and take it inside. Terse and businesslike, they ignored the driver's attempts at small talk and soon the man was left alone in the street standing by his now empty truck.

"Shit," he said, without feeling, "just sheee-it." The return trip to Maryland's Aberdeen Proving Grounds was long and he would have welcomed a cup of coffee before hitting the road. That never happened, of course, not with these guys. They came and went like silent gnomes, never offering coffee, never asking how his trip had been, never wishing him well. He'd been making shipments to this small research facility for over a year and he had yet to exchange two complete sentences with anyone on this end of the run. "Shee-it," he said once more, then he spit a final gob of tobacco towards the fence, climbed up into the cab and drove slowly down the street.

16 SEPTEMBER, 1995
EAST BOSTON, MASSACHUSETTS

Don Green turned on his flashlight and directed the beam towards the closed door in the corner of the basement. "There it is," he told his partner in a strong Boston accent. "I don't know how long it's been shut up like this, but judging from the rust on the lock, it's been quite a while."

"Yeah, it looks older than dirt," responded Frank Silot in a voice that was raspy from too many cigarettes. "Let's chop it and see what we've got. We need to be ready for a walk-through this afternoon and we don't have time to waste." Silot had reason to be concerned about timing. The building, although unassuming in appearance, was on a piece of property destined to become a key part of Logan Airport's next major expansion. The MassPort Authority was willing to pay top dollar for it but was unwilling to do so without a site visit to make sure the structure was clean. Silot and Green had done the same when they had purchased the building three weeks earlier, but a set of heavy metal shelves had hidden the door. Foolishly, the two men had not thought to return for a site check when the former owners had removed the shelves just before transferring title. That was an oversight they would rectify now, before MassPort found any surprises that could kill the deal.

"Hand me the cutters, would you?" requested Green, holding his hand out expectantly. A larger version of his slightly built partner, Green was especially excited about closing this deal. It would be, he thought, a signal to Boston's real estate community that he had become one of its major players, not to mention his ticket to a large house in one of Boston's nicer suburbs. He took the bolt cutters in his powerful hands, callused from years of swinging a hammer when he had worked the construction end of the real estate business, and easily chopped through the stainless steel padlock that sealed the door in question.

The lock cut, Frank seized the handle and pulled with all the might that his thin frame could muster. Reluctantly, its hinges squeaking like a tortured rat, the door swung open, revealing a dark, damp room the size of a large broom closet. Cobwebs brushed against Frank's face as he peered in.

"Shine a light in here, Don, it's black as the Ace of spades."

The flashlight's beam cut through the room's dank air, highlighting the forest of cobwebs that dangled from the ceiling and walls. Small mounds of crumbled mortar dotted the floor where it met the exterior wall, evidence of the wet basement expected in a sump room.

"Jeesh," said Green, "it looks like a room out of *Dracula* or something. No wonder they forgot about it."

"Hey, what's that?" asked Frank sharply as the beam illuminated a medium sized box at the base of the far wall, the word "Fragile" stamped in fading yellow paint faintly visible through multiple layers of grime.

"I guess we still have some cleaning up to do," responded Green stepping quickly across the room. "Let's see what those jerks forgot."

Ten minutes later, Green and Silot stood in the warm sun that soaked the building's entranceway. It was a pleasant change after the basement's tomb-like atmosphere but the warmth failed to remove the glum expressions from their faces.

"This isn't good," said Green. "What the hell do we do now?"

"Why don't we just call the police?" asked Frank, searching for an easy answer. "They're trained in bomb disposal. They'll know what to do."

"No, I don't think that'd work too well." Green's voice was heavy with despair. He could see his great real estate deal slipping quickly down the toilet. "By the time the cops get here with their bomb team they'd have half the Boston Fire Department on site too. Then they'd probably want to search the entire building again and again just to make sure there's nothing else here. And the construction company would probably want to do the same thing.

"And then some local activist would jump in." Green exaggerated his pronunciation of *activist* to indicate his distaste for the breed. "There are more than a few folks who'd love to stop any airport growth and this box would give them a nice stone to throw. We don't need some irate mother screaming about the expansion's being built on top of forgotten bombs."

"Can't we just give them back to the people who sold us the building? It's their box." Frank still wanted an easy out.

"Be serious." Green's voice was harsh. "The bankruptcy court was right behind us when we bought this building. Those guys aren't around anymore. By the time we could figure out who was responsible and how to get out of it, we'd be knee deep in bankruptcy court ourselves.

"No," Green sighed heavily. "If we want the deal to work, we'll have to take care of this ourselves."

"What the hell are *we* going to do with these things?" Frank asked. "I don't know the first thing about bomb disposal."

"Relax." Green sounded stronger now, more confident as he decided on a course of action. "It's not that big a deal. Look around you. What do you see?"

Frank squinted into the morning sun, his face creasing into a series of frowns. "Not much. Some buildings, a few cars, a couple of dozers, some parking lots. Nothing that makes any difference to me."

"Look closer," Green urged. "You're missing the obvious."

"Seagulls? Birdshit? What?" Impatience filled Silot's voice.

"Dumpsters, pal. I can count five of them from right here. And that's just the construction bins, never mind the trash boxes. Five dumpsters chalk full of building debris, just like the debris they're going to cart out of this place when they rip it down."

"So?"

"So you give me fifteen minutes and nobody's going to have to worry about that box downstairs anymore. Zippo! Gone! Off to be buried in some landfill someplace far away for the next thousand years. The bomb squad couldn't make it any safer if they tried."

"Jesus, Don, are you sure we want to do that? It sounds dangerous. And what if someone sees you and calls the cops? Then we'd be in even deeper shit." Frank was still concerned. He didn't know much about bombs. "What if they go off or something. Someone might get hurt."

"Don't worry about it. These are grenades. They don't just blow up, you've got to pull the pin first. And no one's going to be dumb enough to do that." Green used his most reassuring voice, the one usually reserved for his wife when she worried about whether they would ever move from their crowded apartment. "No one's going to notice one more box going into one of those dumpsters, and then they'll be gone forever. And even if someone finds them, there's no way they'll be able to track them back to us, since they'll be in someone else's dumpster. It's the only thing to do, Frank. No one's going to get hurt. Trust me on this one, unless you have a better idea."

Frank Silot was silent. He did not have a better idea.

2002

3 JANUARY
NANTUCKET, MASSACHUSETTS

The fishing boat rocked gently in the ocean swells, its motor making a soft thunking sound that quickly disappeared in the inky darkness of the moonless night. As dark as the surrounding waters, the vessel was coated in a sheath of ice from the ocean spray, forcing the two men on board to climb cautiously about its decks. The larger of the two cursed softly as a dash of spray whiffed over the gunnel and into the cockpit, splashing him in the face. Although he was about to dive into the frigid waters and was equipped accordingly in a heavy duty dry suit, he still did not relish the thought of spending the next forty-five minutes exposed to this hostile environment.

"Are you sure you don't want to just hump it in over land?" asked the smaller man, feeling his companion shiver as he hoisted a SCUBA tank onto his back. "It'd be a hell of a lot easier. In and out. We could get the box in place in less than fifteen minutes."

"No way!" The big man's voice combined the authority of command with an underlying sense of impatience. "We've gone over this before. If we go overland, someone will notice the vehicle, or they'll see the tracks, or we'll get pulled over by the local cops for driving too slowly. A million things could happen and all of them would be bad. This way, all we've got to worry about is my freezing to death." He slapped his huge hands together for emphasis and snorted derisively at his own gallows humor. Clearly he didn't think his freezing to death was a possibility. "Any traces we leave will be gone by morning, no one's going to report a suspicious vehicle parked by the beach, no one's going to notice a thing. Come spring, the beach'll look just like it did when God made it. We might not be doing things the easy way, but it's a hell of a lot safer."

"Okay, bossman. You're the one playing seal." The second man waited as the SCUBA diver gingerly lowered himself over the side, then he hoisted a medium sized box out of the boat's cabin and let it carefully down into the water beside the diver. A flurry of small splashes and both the diver and box were out of sight, headed for the beach a hundred yards away.

24 MARCH
NANTUCKET, MASSACHUSETTS

On the far side of the dunes, a powerful spring storm raged wildly up and down the island's coast. Huge waves, pushed by gale force winds roaring furiously over the Atlantic's waters, smashed violently against the beach, robbing the once secure dunes of their protective sand with the efficiency of a hundred steam shovels.

The box shuddered as a wave battered the dune in which it had been shallowly buried months before. Then it shuddered again as another, even larger wave broke over the sandy mound. Salt water flowed freely through the box's holes, between the spheres and then back out towards the sea again, becoming part of the next wave and continuing the ocean's furious assault.

Sucked forward by the force of a retreating wave, the box slid partially out of its hole, exposing itself to the open air for the first time in months. Again and again, waves rolled around the plywood container, rocking it back and forth against the dune but never quite working it free of the island's grasp.

Eventually the sea gave up its attack and retreated for good, leaving behind a beach littered with driftwood and an island that was smaller by several thousand cubic yards of sand. As the clouds thinned and then disappeared, the moon shone over the island with increasing intensity, catching the rusty metal of the box's old hinges in its ghostly gleam.

CHAPTER I

As geological accidents go, Nantucket is a relatively fortuitous one. Sculpted out of Atlantic Ocean sand deposits by massive glaciers over 10,000 years ago, the crescent shaped island measures roughly 16 miles by 8 miles, with a maximum elevation of 124 feet above sea level. Its sandy soils are covered with scrub oak and blueberries, while its miles and miles of beaches are famous for swimming, sun bathing and surf casting. The quaint village of Nantucket, the backdrop for countless family pictures, combines with the island's rich nautical heritage to attract boaters and sightseers.

Unfortunately for the Islanders, as the 11,000 locals are known, the sand and ocean waves that make their home so idyllic do not come without costs. Every year the island becomes smaller and smaller as fierce storms, commonly called "Nor 'Easters," batter its northern shores, scouring sand away from the beaches, undermining roads and washing away what once were beautifully situated vacation homes. Yet, despite this ceaseless erosion there has always been enough of Nantucket to serve the natives, and there continues to be enough of the island to make it a popular vacation destination for huge numbers of the work-weary.

Julia Gunder wasn't worried about the effects of the previous night's storm on the island's size, however. Unlike Senator Jackson, whose palatial summer home was just a few hundred feet away, her house, a modest three-bedroom cape, was almost a mile from the ocean. Absent the Antarctic ice cap melting, her house wasn't falling into the sea any time soon. For Julia, a nature photographer, the storm offered another opportunity to snap pictures of the fearsome beauty to be found in the wreckage it had left. New driftwood formations, outlandishly sculpted dunes, precariously carved cliffs and the occasional beached marine animal were subjects for her talented lens. Opportunities like this, when the beaches were deserted, their harsh charms standing out in stark contrast against the lack of humans normally associated with island shots, were few and far between. Julia wasn't going to let this chance escape.

It wasn't as easy as she had hoped, though. Her ex-husband was supposed to have had the kids this weekend. Not surprisingly, he had called at the last moment, saying something had come up and could she watch them. She'd sighed silently, but hadn't made a big deal out of it. She never did. It was just the way he was. That'd been one of the reasons she'd filed for divorce. She'd just gotten too frustrated with the missed dinners, the cancelled weekend plans, and the forgotten school plays. When her ex set his mind on doing something, it got done. Unfortunately, he had rarely set his mind on being with his wife and kids, or even, it seemed at times, on communicating with them. Once they were divorced, she had hoped he'd make more time for the girls, but he still always seemed to find something else that he just had to do. It was his nature.

Julia smiled wistfully. She still loved him, despite his faults, but she couldn't stay married to him. She wasn't sure who could. To the best of her knowledge, he hadn't had a serious relationship in the almost two years they'd been divorced. On an island as small as Nantucket, no relationship stayed secret for long and, with a remarkable feeling of detachment, she'd followed second hand accounts of his summer flings with tourists and his off-Island romance with a Cape Cod schoolteacher. None of them had amounted to much. The girls had never even heard him refer to another woman, much less been introduced to a romantic interest. It was sort of sad, actually, Julia thought. A mid-thirties male with three kids and an ex-wife wasn't the world's best catch. Add the inability to focus on the emotional aspects of a relationship and it spelled doom once the glow of the first kiss wore off.

Julia shrugged philosophically. That was his problem, except when he asked her to take the kids. She looked at her watch. They'd been out on scenic Dionis Beach for almost two hours now, the fierce post storm wind whipping the sand against them like small pieces of buckshot. The pictures she'd taken were going to be fantastic, she knew, but the kids must be bordering on freezing. Even on the islands, early spring was not a warm time of year and the wind wasn't making it any easier to stay outside. She was pleasantly surprised that they'd lasted as long as they had. Eight-year old twins and a toddler just pushing two and a half weren't the easiest companions to have on a trip like this.

Still, they were good kids and the twins had learned to accept their mom's outdoor activities as part of having her as a mother. If they wanted to be with her, or if they had no choice, they had to accept being outside. Over time they'd come to enjoy it and the older girls took pride in seeing their mom at work. Katie, always a bundle of energy, just wanted to be with her big sisters, helpfully interfering in whatever it was they were doing as only a young child can.

There was a practical side to making sure nothing got in the way of her shoots, of course. While her ex's child support payments helped pay some of the bills, Nantucket wasn't a cheap place to live under the best of circumstances. If Julia couldn't keep up a steady stream of income from her photography, it wasn't clear how long they could afford to stay on the Island, where at least they saw some of their dad.

All in all, Julia thought, it wasn't a bad way to raise kids, especially girls. They'd see that their mother had a real job, that she produced something people paid good money for. They'd take that knowledge with them through life, knowing that a woman could put food on the table every bit as well as a man. It was, she'd decided, far better than the annual "take your daughter to work" day espoused by so many professionals in more traditional office jobs.

From the other side of the sand dune a chorus of young voices rose over the roaring wind, bringing Julia's thoughts back to earth.

"Mom, come here. Look what we found."

Julia groaned. When the twins began asking her to join them, it was usually pretty certain that they wanted to call it quits. She wouldn't get any more shots that morning unless she was prepared to hear them scream, holler and, eventually, bicker. A particularly strong gust of wind made her stagger sideways, the flying sand stinging against her cheek. It probably was about time to pack it in anyway, she decided. If the photos she already had weren't enough, that was just too bad.

Brushing her shoulder length blond hair off of her face, Julia knelt down and unzipped her camera bag. Her slender fingers, delicate looking but as strong and graceful as the rest of her, worked automatically as they disassembled the Nikon and tucked it gently into the bag's various nooks and crannies. The camera secure, Julia stood and, ignoring the powerful wind that buffeted her lithe frame, began trudging up the dune towards her daughters.

Sarah and Tracy bounced up the dune as quickly as possible, shouting happily into the wind that roared in over the ocean. Behind them, their little sister Katie, bundled in a bulky jacket, a brightly colored scarf and a fleece hat with tie-down earflaps, stumbled determinedly in their tracks. Wherever the older girls went, Katie was sure to follow like a cheerful shadow, always trying to be one of the crowd no matter what the activity. For the most part, this attachment ran both ways, and the twins doted on the little girl as much as their eight-year old attention spans would allow.

Identical twins, born only a few minutes apart, Sarah and Tracy were average in height and weight for their ages. With the same taste in clothes and similar hairstyles, even their father had begun having trouble telling them apart. Katie, though not yet three, was already beginning to look and act like a miniature version of her sisters, making up in enthusiasm and sheer joy of living what she lacked in stature and experience.

Native islanders, the older girls loved exploring the vast seas of sand dunes that made up their world. While they might complain to their mom about having to spend time out on the beaches, that was just for form. In reality, they were thrilled. Every dune was a new kingdom to explore and every wave carried new aquatic treasures. Generally, all they ever found during their explorations were old bottles, pieces of clothing and driftwood, but from time to time the sea gave them a real treasure.

Today was one of those times.

Tucked under a near-dead juniper bush on the far side of the dune, mostly buried in the sand, Tracy had spotted the corner of what looked like a treasure chest.

"Check it out," cried her twin sister, "Maybe it's Blackbeard's gold!" They'd been studying New World pirates in school and rumors of hidden pirate loot filled the playground at recess.

"Cool! Let's dig it up."

The two girls fell to their knees by the bush and feverishly began to scoop away the sand with their hands. Whatever it was, this promised to be their most interesting find ever. They'd never found a real buried chest before. Eager to help, Katie, her fleece-covered head bobbing purposefully on her sturdy shoulders, pushed her way between her sisters and poked enthusiastically at an exposed piece of wood with a small stick she'd plucked from the sand.

Calling to their mother to join them, Sarah and Tracy continued to enlarge the depression until an entire side of the object was in view. About the size of an extra large briefcase, the box had metal edges and hinges with plywood sides. The metal was rusted and the plywood was just about gone in spots, but, judging from its weight as they tugged, the girls could tell it was full of something.

"Mom, come here now!" shrieked Tracy, adding a softer "this would make a great picture," as she peeled back a strip of plywood to get a better look inside.

"Oh wow, this is wild," gushed her sister. "It's full of little balls." She reached through the hole in the box and grabbed one of the solid metal spheres. "I wonder what they are." She passed the sphere to Tracy and reached in for another one.

"Can't you little vixens let a lady take a picture in peace?" Julia broke in playfully from the top of the dune. Then a slightly softer "What on earth are you doing? What is that thing and where did you find it?"

"Oh Mom, this is cool," said Sarah proudly, turning to show her mother her new trophy. "The box is full of them, whatever they are."

"Oh my God!" gasped her mother, turning white with shock. "Tracy! Sarah! Put those down and get away from there, both of you! Katie, come here now!"

"Jeez, Mom, what's the big deal?" asked Sarah, a frown on her normally smiling face. "They're just balls with little rings attached." Still, Mom was Mom and Sarah recognized that tone of voice. She put the sphere in the sand by her feet and reached across the box to take back the one she had given her twin sister.

CHAPTER II

Walt Crawler flicked his right thumb forward and grunted in satisfaction as his hyperglide chain slid smoothly onto his bike's largest front sprocket. A wildlife biologist for the Massachusetts Department of Fisheries, Wildlife and Environmental Law Enforcement, Walt's chief after-work passion was mountain bike racing. When he wasn't conducting fish counts or measuring saline levels, he was usually on his bike, tearing around whatever backcountry trails he could find. He wasn't quite good enough to be a professional, but he was good enough to nip at the pros' heels from time to time. He hoped that this race would be one of those times.

Touching his brakes lightly, Walt brought his Cannondale Super VDH Active 4000 to a complete stop, balancing himself in a perfect track stand as he waited for the race to start. He was lucky to be here, he knew. While his trial times hadn't been as strong as he'd hoped, they'd been good enough to make him the next in line when the Department's mountain bike team captain had broken his clavicle in a five bike pileup the week before. The team had asked Walt to join them and he was determined not to let them down. If the team won, or even finished in the top five, he could count on spending the next several months being shuttled to races around the country courtesy of a variety of corporate sponsors. Living on the relatively remote island of Nantucket, the opportunity to catch more major races was something Walt had dreamed about in past seasons.

Walt glanced at his watch. It was only a few moments before the posted starting time. Even as he turned his eyes forward, the announcer barked a 30-second warning over the loudspeaker and Walt forced himself to focus. For the next forty-five minutes, give or take a few seconds, he would have time to think of nothing but the trail in front of him, his fellow racers and how his bike was handling. How he got into the race would be as irrelevant as the throbbing pain he'd feel in his lungs when he topped the course's hills. To think about anything but the race, to be at all bothered by the pain of the ride, would be to lose.

The five second warning sounded, then three, two, one and the starter's gun barked and two hundred riders began hurtling over a mixture of mud, ice and dirt on a trail that would have been challenging just to walk. Out of the saddle, his legs pumping like iron pistons, Walt stayed close to the bike in front of him. Until the field thinned out a bit, the best thing to do was just to charge forward as fast as possible. A moment's hesitation and a whole line of cyclists would bluff their way in front of him. By riding aggressively and staying tight in the pack, Walt was sending his competitors the same message they were sending him–get in my way and I'll run you down. Of course, running someone down on a bike could be just as disastrous for the runner as the runnee. Walt's presence on the team was testament to that. But it was still paramount to push one's right of way. Otherwise, a race was just one more ride in the woods.

By the three mile mark, the crowd of cyclists had thinned considerably. Though more than one had fallen victim to the treacherous trail, the majority simply lacked the strength and stamina to keep up with the leaders. Twelve riders back from the front, Walt was pleased with his position. Two of his teammates were ahead of him and the third just a few places behind. If they could keep it up, they'd have a very respectable showing.

Walt snapped at himself to focus. One slip and he'd be tumbling off the trail, the team's hopes finished. Through the increasing pains in his thighs and the pounding in his chest, he forced himself to concentrate on how the riders in front of him were handling the trail. Where the soft spots were, who was taking the corners too loosely, whose gears were sticking, these were the little things that could help him move up through the tight group of race leaders.

The four mile mark passed, then the five and the six without any significant changes in the front pack. Walt could feel himself beginning to drag a bit longer on the uphills, his fingers were clumsier on the hydraulic brakes and his arms were too loose over the handlebars. If he hadn't known the other riders were suffering the same fatigue, he would have been worried. In a pack this tight, at the end it became a question of who could handle the most pain. Through the mud that had spattered all over his face, Walt grimaced happily. If there was one thing he could handle, it was pain. He tucked further over his handlebars and dug deep inside himself to battle up another hill, passing two riders in the process.

Bouncing over the hill's rocky top, Walt settled his weight behind his seat, bringing himself as close to his rear tire as possible without actually making contact. Getting low enough on the downhills to have a good center of gravity while at the same time maintaining control of the bike was essential to successful mountain bike racing. If he did it right, he'd hardly have to touch the brakes.

At the bottom of the hill, Walt shifted to a higher gear and stood on his pedals. The rider in front of him was taking the turns wide. By cutting inside at the next turn, Walt could pick up another place. After that he'd probably be hard-pressed to move further ahead, but he should be able to hang on to what he had. And, in this crowd, finishing ninth was nothing to sneeze at.

Walt was directly behind the other cyclist as they made it to the curve. When the other rider swung wide through the turn, Walt powered down on his pedals and cut inside, bulling ahead just as he'd done at the start of the race. Now it was just brute force and nerves. He'd already made his decision. His opponent would only have a moment to tighten his turn and try to cut him off, but he'd have to be willing to call Walt's bluff if it came to a possible collision. Walt knew there was no bluff. He'd either pass this man on the inside or, if the other cyclist tried to head him off, they'd knock each other into a mess of bikes and bodies tumbling down the trail. At times like this, mountain bike racing was not for the faint hearted.

His eyes on the trail, Walt pulled even with the other rider. A muddy face turned towards him then looked back at the trail. Walt felt a surge of elation. His opponent was going to try and beat him on the outside of a curve. With the increased distance on the turn's outside, it couldn't be done and Walt steadily drew ahead. When he hit the bottom of the course's final hill, he had a full bike length on his opponent, a lead he was determined to keep despite the almost crippling pain in every part of his body.

Topping the hill, Walt settled back over the rear tire, confident that his handling skills would allow him to rest on the downhill and save enough energy to fight off any last minute challenges by the riders behind him. He squeezed his rear brake gently to cushion the impact of a series of large rocks sprayed across the path, then rose up to bunny-hop over a fallen log. Behind him Walt could hear bouncing rocks as the cyclist he'd just passed negotiated the same obstacles, staying right on his heels. It would be a close finish.

By the time he reached the bottom of the hill, Walt figured he was doing at least twenty-five miles an hour. He never raced with his odometer on because he found it too distracting, but after years of riding he'd become very good at estimating his speeds. He could have gone down the hill much faster, but he knew that the sharp turn at the bottom would be impossible to handle at high speed. As it was, he'd have to brake heavily to keep from overshooting the bend and doing a header into the trees.

Maintaining pressure on his rear brake, Walt rose back over his handlebars and clamped down hard on his front brake with his left hand, simultaneously veering left and turning the front tire. But his left hand felt no resistance as he pulled the brake lever and Walt's heart jumped to his throat. His front hydraulics must have broken. Capable of producing massive stopping power with a two fingered squeeze, hydraulic brakes were state of the art for mountain bike racers. If the system lost its integrity, however, and the hydraulic fluid leaked out, they couldn't stop a child's tricycle.

From the complete lack of resistance in his brakes, Walt knew he'd suffered a catastrophic failure. One of the branches he'd snapped through must have torn a hole in his lines and he'd been leaking fluid ever since. Even though he knew it was useless, he tried compensating by hitting his rear brakes as hard as possible. But rear brakes just control and stabilize; the front brakes have all the stopping power. Walt wasn't going to make the turn. The best he could do was to try to control his fall.

The next few seconds flowed by as if in slow motion. Walt felt his front tire slide on a pile of leaves as he passed over the edge of the trail, then his whole body jolted back as the wheel hit a large rock and buckled. Instinctively tucking his head down against his chest, Walt flipped with his bike and crashed through the thick underbrush like a small avalanche. He landed heavily on his back, the mangled bike still attached to his body by the clip on his right pedal like a ski attached to a fallen slalom racer by its safety binding. Black dots swam randomly back and forth in front of his eyes, and, for a moment, Walt thought he would pass out from shock. Then the pain of his landing hit him like a tidal wave and, turning his head to the side, he began to vomit.

Walt was still dry heaving when the course safety staff stationed at the turn reached him. With practiced expertise they knelt beside him, flashing lights into his eyes and probing his fingers and toes with sharp picks.

"It's okay, Buddy," said a wiry man with a neatly trimmed mustache. "That was a nasty spill. How do you feel?"

It was a pointless question, Walt knew. All the man wanted was to get a response, to know if he could speak. "Like shit," he grunted, then dry-heaved again.

"Can you feel the needle?" asked the wiry man as his partner probed Walt's extremities.

"Yeah, I can feel it," Walt wheezed.

"Wiggle your toes and fingers for me? Okay, now follow my light." The medic waved his penlight and smiled as Walt's eyes tracked it. "Good. Now where do you hurt?"

Walt grimaced. "Where don't I hurt?"

The medic smiled. A sense of humor was a good sign. He began to tap Walt's arms and legs gently. "Anything hurt more than anything else?"

"No." Walt grimaced again. He heard a bunch of riders pass on the trail over his head and thought of his lost place. His team wouldn't go anywhere notable this summer. "Just my pride, I guess." He struggled to a sitting position and looked ruefully at his mangled bike. "I guess I'm out of this race, huh?"

The second medic, a cherubic-looking male barely out of his teens, reached over and gently unsnapped Walt's helmet. He pointed to a large gash on its side, saying "You're lucky you're just out of this race. That was one heck of a spill." He frowned at Walt's bike. "Your hydraulics go on you?" It was more a statement than a question.

"Yeah. Picked a hell of a time, too."

"They always do," replied the young man.

"Murphy's law," added his partner. "It'll bite you in the ass every time."

"Fuckin' Murphy," Walt said as the two medics helped him gently to his feet.

"It's worse than that," said the younger medic as he leaned down and picked up Walt's bicycle.

"It gets worse?" asked Walt, taking his bike and speculatively spinning the crumpled front tire. It completed a quarter revolution before the bent rim bound securely against the brake pads. "I'm not sure how it can."

"You forget," the medic said gravely, "Murphy was an optimist."

Walt hobbled to the finish line with his bike hoisted on his shoulder. His entire body ached and sweat stung at countless scratches and minor cuts, but the younger medic had been right. He was lucky to be walking. He'd rest a few days, but he'd be back in the saddle by the end of the week. Maybe he could take his older girls riding on the Cape's Trail of Tears. Falls, big and little, were just another part of racing. If he let them get to him, he'd lose his nerve and his racing days would be over. He wasn't willing to let go of that part of his life yet.

"Hey, Walt, over here!" a burley man hollered from the crowd of cyclists milling by the podium. He detached himself from the people he was talking with and rushed over to his limping friend. "Man, you look like shit," Walt's co-worker, Lewis James, commented enthusiastically. "And your bike looks like it just lost a war. But at least you're walking." Lew had been racing for years. To him, any fall you walked away from was a good fall, no matter how bad you looked.

It was hard to hold a smile, but Walt managed it. In addition to his bodily injuries, his wallet was going to take a major pounding. It would probably cost him over a thousand bucks to put his bike back together. After taxes, mortgage payments, day to day living expenses and a hefty child support bill, that kind of money wouldn't come easily. But all of that was his problem, not his teammates'. It was bad enough he had cost them a competitive season. He wouldn't burden them with his financial woes, too. They were happy he was walking. That was enough.

"Your brakes didn't hold, huh?" Another of Walt's teammates and co-workers, an administrator from the Department's Boston headquarters, hurried up. He looked at Walt's waxen face. "Are you feeling okay?"

"Yeah, Sam, I'm okay. I look worse than I feel." Walt lied, knowing that his friends wouldn't believe it but not wanting them to worry about him. "The hydraulics blew on the last downhill. I didn't make the turn and that was that. I'm sorry, I guess that kind of shoots the team's chances to move up."

It was an athlete's apology. It could have happened to anyone, but it had happened to Walt and he felt responsible.

"Don't worry, Walt," James tapped Walt gently on the shoulder. "You're walking. That's what counts. There's always another race."

"Not today, though." Walt felt better. Apology offered, apology accepted, time to move on. "Let me put this high tech junk heap in my car. I'll pop some ibuprofen and join you." Walt knew from experience that downing some pain relievers immediately after a fall would significantly ease his future stiffness.

"Okay, Buddy. See you in a few." The two men turned back to the crowd as Walt continued on to the parking lot.

Reaching his car, Walt opened the door and was greeted by a loud buzzing sound. He'd forgotten to turn off his pager. He ignored the noise, instead disassembling his bike and putting it on the folded down back seat. No matter how badly his bike might have failed him, he always attended to his equipment first. His bike safely stowed, Walt rummaged through the glove compartment and pulled out a pill bottle. Unscrewing the top, he popped several of the small capsules into his mouth, swallowing them without water. Then he fished behind the passenger's seat for the towel and water bottle he kept there. He'd never make himself ballroom pretty, but a few moments with the water and towel would clean up most of the mud, blood and vomit that flecked his body. Maybe then he'd start feeling human again.

When his sponge bath was complete, Walt looked at himself in the sideview mirror. His black hair, almost shoulder length, was matted with sweat and his blue eyes still looked a bit dazed from the fall. His arms and legs, powerfully built from years of mountain biking, were scratched and bleeding but there were no cuts that wouldn't scab over in an hour or so. He'd taken a sharp jab from a branch on his right side, but that, too, was more painful than serious. His cheeks were filling back up with their normal color and Walt grinned, checking his white, even teeth. Nothing seemed out of place. For a thirty-six year old guy who'd just taken a major tumble, he didn't look half bad.

Walt straightened to his full five feet ten inches and flexed his arms over his head to help ward off some of the impending stiffness. All in all, everything seemed to work but his bicycle. It could have been worse. He put the water bottle to his lips and emptied it. After tossing the towel and empty bottle back in his car, he picked up his beeper and shut the sound off. Then he looked at the display and frowned. It was Jeff Tillison's office number. Jeff, a Nantucket police detective, had been Walt's best friend for as long as he could remember, but he'd never before called Walt's beeper. The three digit code following Tillison's phone number gave Walt even more reason for concern: 666, his office's shorthand for extremely urgent.

Walt opened the glove compartment and pulled out his cellular phone. He forgot his recent fall as he punched in the numbers, anxious as to why Jeff would need to get in touch with him so urgently on a Saturday morning. He'd logged off the Department's Hazardous Incident Response Team the previous afternoon and, as far as he knew, there'd been no special fishing boat checks or seal tagging operations planned over the weekend that would require his attention. It was possible that someone had brought in a load of illegal fish or had found some buried hazardous waste, but Jeff wouldn't have called him for that. There were other people on the island who could handle those things in Walt's absence.

The phone rang and Walt forced himself to stop speculating on the reasons for the call, forced his mind away from the thoughts that run through every father's mind when an unexpected call comes in: was it the kids? Jeff would tell him soon enough.

"Tillison here." The detective's voice was deep and slightly raspy, and he spoke with a measured cadence that was noticeable even in the short greeting.

"Jeff, Walt here. What's going on?"

"Jesus, Walt. Where've you been, man? I've been trying to get ahold of you for hours."

"I'm at a bike race in Connecticut. Just about cracked my noggin, too," Walt added. "It's a good thing state employees have thick skulls. Why, what's up?"

"There's no easy way to tell you this so I'm just going to lay it on the line. Are you driving right now?"

"No, I'm in the parking lot." Walt felt nauseous again, just as he had after taking his fall. His knees turned rubbery and he sagged back against his car for support. He opened his mouth to speak but no words came out. What the hell was Tillison talking about?

"Walt, it's your girls, and Julia, too. There's been an accident." Tillison stopped speaking, waiting for Walt to respond.

"An accident?" Walt put his free hand on the car's sideview mirror and pushed himself upward as bile rose in his throat. "What kind of accident? How are they?" His mind screamed with more questions but he couldn't put them into words.

"They found some sort of chemical bomb back in the dunes at Dionis Beach and it exploded on them. Julia's dead, Walt, and so are the twins. Katie's alive, but she must have got a dose of chemicals. She's in a coma right now. They flew her up to the Mass General Hospital. I'm sorry as hell about this, Walt." Despite the clear connection, the detective's voice sounded shaky over the phone. "Sorry as hell."

Walt's knees gave way and he slid slowly to the ground, the back of his bike jersey leaving a muddy smear down the side of his car. "You're shitting me, Jeff. Tell me this is all a sick joke." Walt's voice sounded impossibly small and distant to his own ears. He knew it wasn't a joke. Tillison never joked much and he was far too good a detective to be mistaken on an issue like this.

"I'm sorry. I wish it were a joke, but it's not. Can I send someone to pick you up? Who are you with?"

"I'm with some guys from the Department, but I drove out on my own. I can get myself home." Walt's ears were roaring. His girls were dead, in the hospital! It couldn't be. He heard Tillison speaking again as if from inside a tunnel.

"Where exactly are you?"

"At Cockaponsett State Forest in Connecticut. About thirty miles south of Hartford."

"Here's what we're going to do. Hang on a minute." There were some muffled voices in the background and then Tillison was back on the line. "Walt, we're on line with the Connecticut State Police right now. They'll send a car for you and take you to the Mass Line. We'll have a Massachusetts state trooper pick you up there and drive you straight to the Mass General. You'll be with Katie in less than two hours. What do you say?" Tillison's voice was much firmer now, sounding more like a police officer than a friend. He didn't want Walt to say no.

"Yeah, okay. That'd be fine, Jeff." Incongruously, Walt was suddenly aware of the cold ground chilling his butt. "I'll be at the entrance to the park."

"Wait, Walt, don't…"

Walt pressed the power button and the line went dead. His head was pounding and black dots swam back and forth before his eyes as they had after his recent fall. Julia and the twins, dead. His little Katie in the hospital. Oh God, it couldn't be true, it just couldn't. A long, low, guttural moan escaped his lips and the black dots swam closer and closer together until, finally, there was just blackness.

When he came to, Walt saw his teammates gathered anxiously around him as James and a beefy Connecticut State Trooper splashed water on his face.

"Christ, Walt, I'm so sorry," said James, "Trooper Jenkin's told us what's going on. What can we do to help?"

Walt looked around him blankly and began to struggle to his feet. James extended an arm to help pull him up, but Walt shrugged it off. "I'm fine," he said mechanically, not caring if anyone believed him or not. He wasn't fine. He'd never fainted before in his life. His stomach was roiling furiously, bitter with the bile from his earlier vomiting and the horrible news from Tillison. His body ached from the fall and his mind still couldn't comprehend the fact that his world had just ended. But, instinctively, Walt never showed anything but a flint-like exterior to anyone. "I'm fine," he said again. Turning towards the Trooper, he asked, "Are you my ride?"

"Yes, sir. Do you need medical attention first?"

"No, I'm fine. Just get me to my daughter."

The circle of cyclists parted slightly as Walt hobbled towards the police car, followed by James carrying the overnight bag he'd taken from Walt's car.

"Make sure this goes with him," he instructed the trooper, placing the bag in the front seat. "And don't worry about your car, Walt," he continued in as comforting a voice as he could manage, "we'll get it home for you. Let us know what else we can do, okay?"

Walt didn't reply and, lights flashing and siren blaring, the police car sped out of the Park's drive.

At the state line, Walt switched over to a Massachusetts State Police car and continued his trip. The Trooper driving Walt tried briefly to engage his passenger, recognized it was a futile effort and drove the rest of the trip without speaking, the silence inside the car magnified by the shrieking siren overhead. As they passed through the Boston tollbooths, the Trooper radioed ahead. When he stopped in front of the hospital's main entrance, a thin man waiting at the curb opened the door, helped Walt out and then picked up Walt's small overnight bag.

"Mr. Crawler," the man said gently, "I'm Dr. Bocall from the MGH pediatric toxicology group. Katie's under my care. I can't tell you how sorry I am about this." He held Walt gently by the right arm and guided him into the hospital's lobby. "Can I get you anything. Coffee, a glass of water, maybe?"

"No, thank you." These were the first words he'd uttered since leaving Cockaponsett State Forest and Walt's voice was thick and heavy as if with disuse. "I just want to see my daughter."

"Yes, yes, of course. Please, follow me," the doctor bobbed his head self-consciously and led Walt onto an elevator. When the doors shut behind them, Dr. Bocall turned back to Walt and cleared his throat awkwardly. "I'm not sure how to best put this, Walt. How much has anyone told you about what happened?"

"Just that there was an explosion. Julia and the twins are dead. And Katie got a dose of poison of some sort and was sent up here in a coma." Walt had refused to talk with Tillison during the drive to Boston. He'd felt he already knew too much, more than he could handle. He'd wanted no new information until he could assimilate it.

"That's essentially it." The doctor wasn't fooled by Walt's no-nonsense tone. As a doctor, he'd seen shock do that to other parents. "It might help to know that Julia and the twins died instantly from the blast," he said. "Katie didn't get hit by any shrapnel but she was already unconscious when response personnel got on the scene, maybe fifteen minutes after the explosion. They called for a life flight immediately and she was here within an hour. Initially we thought she was suffering from the concussive effects of the blast. Even without shrapnel, explosions can create deadly shockwaves." The elevator stopped and Dr. Bocall fell silent until he'd taken Walt into the small, windowless room that was his office.

"But these were relatively small grenades," the doctor began again, motioning to Walt to sit down in one of the room's two chairs. "A box of them had been exposed by the ocean and somehow one of the girls, or maybe Julia, set one off in an open area. Katie was obviously shielded from the blast by her mother or one of the twins, so a concussion didn't make sense. Then a few of the response personnel, two cops, a fire fighter and an EMT, started feeling nauseous. Dizzy. Sweating. One or two of them started to vomit, had trouble breathing, extremely constricted airways. The response coordinator figured it must be a chemical of some sort. It was probably too dissipated by the strong winds over the beach to result in immediate death or long-term injury, but it was dangerous all the same.

"Because of the mixture of grenades and chemicals, he pulled all his response people out and asked the Defense Department to send in its Special Chemical Operations Team. I'm afraid he had to leave Julia and your girls at the site until more qualified experts could take over." Doctor Bocall coughed slightly to ease the tension. No one was ever comfortable leaving bodies on site. Closure never really started until a medical examiner pronounced a loved one dead. Until then, there was always hope. He waited for Walt to respond and, seeing nothing, continued. "The next thing the coordinator did was to call here and let the hospital know of the potential for chemical poisoning. That's when I got involved. I ran a few tests and I'm certain Katie's suffering from some sort of chemical exposure. What it is, I can't tell. We're still running tests. Hopefully we'll learn something definite soon."

"I want to see Katie now," Walt stated flatly, not giving any indication that he had understood the doctor's monologue or not.

"Of course, Walt, but you understand she's been poisoned with something. She's not going to..."

"Doctor," Walt interrupted in a quiet but forceful voice, "I appreciate your talking with me. I know it can't be easy. But you don't have to tell me any more. I've been involved with hazardous incident response operations for years. I know far too well what chemical exposure can do to someone. I'd like to see my daughter now."

Dr. Bocall blinked in surprise. No one had told him about Walt's background. "Katie's straight down the hall, last door on the right. Do you want me to go with you?"

"No thank you, I'd just as soon be alone." Hoisting his bag over his shoulder, Walt left the Doctor's sterile office and passed through the equally sterile waiting room into the hall. The hospital's unique version of silence, the hushed voices of patients, the irregular beep of monitoring equipment, the overarching hum of the air handling equipment, struck him like a physical object as he walked towards his daughter's room, magnifying the tragedy that had just befallen him. Julia was dead. Sarah and Tracy were dead. Katie was here, sick in the hospital. It was too much and, as it had when Jeff had first told him the news, the enormity of the disaster once more threatened to overwhelm him. With trembling arms, Walt reached out to the handrail that ran the length of the hall and steadied himself, concentrating on his breathing until he felt he could go on. He knew Dr. Bocall was watching him, as were the nurses, but no one offered assistance. They realized he wanted to do this by himself, that he had to prove he could control something.

Walt finally reached Katie's room and, taking a deep breath to brace his nerves, opened the door and stepped in.

Looking like a lifeless doll propped up on the hospital bed, Katie lay with open, unseeing eyes, tethered to a vast array of life support equipment by a veritable maze of tubes. In a vain attempt to somehow humanize the scene, someone had tucked a small teddy bear by the little girl's head. Walt stood by the end of the bed for what seemed like eternity and the blink of an eye at the same time. This was his little Katie, this unmoving, unseeing, chalk white creature on the bed. His eyes brimmed and then overflowed with tears. Katie had always been so vibrant, so happy and so outgoing, excited by everything and everyone around her. This couldn't be her on the bed, it just couldn't. Lost in his reverie, he didn't notice the door open behind him.

"Are you all right, Walt?" It was Doctor Bocall.

When Walt didn't answer, the doctor repeated himself as gently as he could.

"You know something, Doctor," Walt finally replied in a conversational tone, "it's weird. In my job I've seen people drowned, blown up, poisoned, burned and crushed in boating accidents. Hell, one time I even saw a guy get crushed to death by a bluefin tuna. He was posing with the fish, it was a big sunofabitch, must have gone 800 pounds, and the line holding the fish broke. The damn tuna fell right on top of him. I wouldn't have believed it except my boat was only about sixty feet away. I was waiting to get some stomach content samples for a study I was doing." Walt paused for breath. "Anyway, sometimes I sit at home and catalogue all the bad things I've seen happen to people. It's a little game I play to keep it impersonal, to help distance myself from this stuff. You know how it is, you think too much about something and your mind gets in the way of your actions. I can't let that happen on a response operation, just like a fireman or a cop can't let the brutal edge of their work get to them.

"But all those things always happened to strangers. Never a friend. Never even an acquaintance. I guess I hang around with safe people. But now it's my family. That changes things. It's not some stranger lying in that bed, it's my little girl. And I can't do a goddamned thing for her." Walt's voice was bitter now and tears streaked his cheeks.

"I can't imagine," Dr. Bocall said consolingly. "Even the thickest of skins can only handle so much. To have such a thing happen to the ones you love the most would devastate anyone." There was a break in the conversation and then the Doctor continued. "As you know, Walt, the situation's fairly bleak. Katie's stabilized right now. We'd like to put her on a stimulus program to keep her muscles from atrophying too much and, maybe, to jar her out of the coma. It's a long shot but it's non-invasive and there's not much else we can do right now. Until we know what is poisoning her, we're cautious of trying chemical antidotes. That would be playing with fire. If we got the wrong antidote, or the wrong amount, we would just make things worse. For the stimulus program, what we do is attach electrodes at various parts of her body and send programmed electric shocks through her muscles."

"You want a consent?" interrupted Walt.

"Excuse me?"

"You've got nothing else you can do, so you're hoping the electrodes will at least keep her as healthy as possible. It makes sense, but you can't do anything to Katie without parental consent anymore. So you want a consent form."

"Of course," Dr. Bocall stammered, taken off guard by Walt's bluntness. "Now that Katie's been stabilized, there's no longer an emergency. You'll need to approve everything we do."

"You've got consent forms?"

"Right here," the doctor pulled a clipboard from a basket at the end of the bed and stood, dumbfounded, as Walt swiftly scanned the pages and signed the documents without question. "You don't want to learn more about what we're planning, what the options are?" he asked.

"No, Doctor, I know everything I can understand right now. My daughter is poisoned and you're the expert in childhood poisoning. My getting in your way isn't going to help her at all." Walt picked up his bag and turned towards the door.

"You don't want to stay?" Dr. Bocall couldn't keep the surprise from his voice. Never, in his considerable history, had a father had such a brief visit with an incapacitated child.

Walt stopped and looked back at the doctor. "I can't do anything here, doctor," he explained in a voice that was deadly calm. "The best thing I can do is to go back to Nantucket and try to find whatever's poisoning Katie." Walt couldn't bring himself to mention the other reason he was so eager to get back to the Island. The bodies of the twins and Julia were still there. Depending on how quickly SCOT, the Pentagon's Special Chemical Operations Team, was moving, the bodies could still be on the beach. Having responded to fatal chemical releases,

Walt knew that, while a team would act quickly to remove the injured, usually they'd leave bodies where they were until the threat was entirely neutralized. Even if they had taken the bodies off site, they'd be at the Island's Medical Examiner's Office. Either way, he had to see for himself.

"Wait a moment," cried the Doctor, catching up to Walt and thrusting a card into his hand, "here's my office number and my home phone. Call me anytime, okay?"

"Okay, Doctor." Walt held the Doctor's eyes for a moment before turning away. "And thanks."

Leaving the hospital, Walt was surprised to find the same State Trooper who dropped him off waiting at the curb. The Trooper waved him over and opened up the cruiser's door.

"Detective Tillison must know you pretty well," explained the officer. "He said you wouldn't be long. He's got a Cape Air charter on standby at Logan and will meet you himself on the Island."

"Thank you, Officer. You're very kind," Walt replied as he got in the car. For the first time since he'd learned the news about his family, he didn't feel terrifyingly alone. Jeff Tillison was a good man to have as a friend.

CHAPTER III

Before the plane's propellers had stopped spinning, Walt was hurrying across the tarmac to a waiting police Bronco. He'd washed and put on clean clothes at the airport lavatory, although it hadn't made him feel much better. He tossed his bag in the back, climbed up into the cab and extended his right hand to the driver. "Thanks, Jeff," he said in a husky voice, in itself more emotion than he usually displayed to anyone.

"No problem, Walt. It's the least I can do."

Walt looked at his friend. Jeff Tillison and Walt had both grown up on the island, fishing, hunting and going to school together. Jeff had even been Walt's best man, and he had maintained an easy friendship with both sides of the couple since their divorce. That he shared some of Walt's grief was evident in his red and puffy eyes.

Beyond Jeff, the control tower of the small, though busy, island airport stood against the clear blue sky. Walt had seen this view a thousand times, and it always made him feel comfortably at home, safe back in his little island paradise. This time was different, though. Now the tower stood out like an exclamation point, marking the end of one part of his life and signaling the start of something new. Something new, alone and terribly sad.

"What do you have for me?" Walt was true to form. The task at hand was what he'd talk about. He'd known Tillison would know what to do without instructions.

"I cleared out your locker. It's all back there." Tillison waved his right arm towards the back of the truck. Unlike Walt, Tillison's skin was surprisingly white, evidence of the scant amount of time the man spent outside. Where Walt's youthful passion for fishing, biking and other outdoor sports had continued beyond his childhood, Tillison had become bewitched by the historical side of Nantucket, diving into its history of whaling ships, farms and railroads with ever increasing enthusiasm. It was his unmatched knowledge of the Island and its history, his almost sixth sense about how all the pieces made a whole, that made him such an extraordinary detective. Regardless of what happened on Nantucket, if Detective Jeffery Tillison wanted to know any of the who, what, when, where, and why involved, he probably could.

Tillison started the engine and put the truck in gear. There was no need to turn on the flashing lights, for on an island as small as Nantucket, no point was more than a 20 minute drive from any other in the off-season. "It's all there," he repeated, "Your mask, oversuit, a couple of tyvek suits, three tanks, regulator, the works. Whatever the SCOT's working in out there, you'll be able to mix and match."

"Do you know what the SCOT's in?"

"When I left to pick you up, they were still in Level A, full dressout." The most protective state of response operations, full dressout required a full body suit of heavy plastic with a clear face visor and room for a back-mounted, self-contained air supply system. In Level A, the only part of a responder's equipment exposed to open air was the exterior of the suit. Absent a puncture of some sort, or saturation of the suit, it offered total protection to the wearer.

"What else is going on out there?" Walt asked while trying to digest this new information. If they were staying in Level A, that meant they still considered the site high risk. It was very unlikely the bodies would be removed until the risk had been reduced.

"It's tough to tell. The SCOT flew in around the time I talked with you. They ran some quick tests of some sort and determined that the threat was limited to the immediate blast site. They've got that whole area taped off now, and they had us post a couple of cops to control access. Once they got organized, they went right to work. They seem pretty sharp." Walt could hear the grudging admiration in Tillison's voice. Like any Islander, the detective had a healthy skepticism of outsiders, especially those who came in as experts and started to run things. "A guy called Charlie Laste is the head honcho, but the actual work seems mostly to be done by a man named Adam Branson. Ever hear of either of them?"

Walt shook his head no. He'd read about the SCOT in some professional magazines and he'd heard the team mentioned at conferences, but he didn't know much about it. Hazardous incident response experts, capable of operating under astoundingly difficult and dangerous conditions, the members of the SCOT were a small, top-secret group. They were called on to carry out tough response operations, did their jobs and then left.

"Laste seems okay," Tillison summarized. "Doesn't say a hell of a lot but seems to know his stuff. He's the one that runs interference with the locals. Branson's probably just as competent, but he comes across as one mean son of a bitch. Huge, too. Wouldn't want to run into him in a dark alley." Over six feet tall and barely tipping the scales at 145 pounds, Tillison wouldn't want to run into anyone in a dark alley.

"No locals are allowed on site?" Walt asked.

"None. The SCOT's a pretty secretive bunch. They put a big tarp over the blast sight and ran mesh fencing across the high ground. No one's going to see what's going on, much less take a picture of the area, without Laste's say so. I don't know what the hell they'll do when you show up. Branson'll probably blow a gasket. He's a control freak, that one."

"Everything's at the site?" Despite his professional exposure to similar situations, Walt couldn't bring himself to say 'bodies.' The word was too devastatingly final.

"You mean . . ." Tillison probed.

"Julia and the girls."

"They're still there, Walt." Tillison paused, then exploded, "Christ there're times when life sucks!" He punched the dashboard in anger, then collected himself. "Are you sure you really want to go on site? I've heard it's ugly."

"Wouldn't you?" Walt responded with a question. When Tillison didn't answer, he continued. "It's my family, Jeff. I was away this weekend instead of being with the girls. They needed me and I was off biking, and they got hurt. I'm not going to shield myself from what happened to them no matter how ugly it is."

"Jesus, Walt, you can't blame yourself," Tillison began.

"No," interrupted Walt angrily, "then who can I blame? Shit like this doesn't just happen. It's not every day your family gets wiped out by some strange bomb. Someone, at some point, put that bomb there. You find me that person and the coroner will have one more body to examine, but right now I'm the only person I know of who could have made things turn out differently. If I'd been with my girls, they'd have been safe. So don't tell me who to blame."

Walt lapsed into silence for a few miles, then broke it with a question. "So, what has the SCOT been telling people?"

"Not a hell of a lot, actually. They're pretty close mouthed. They think the site's probably not an immediate threat. The folks that got sick, it was the Holmes brothers and Jessie Holger that got it the worst, are still in the hospital, of course, but just for observation. They seem to have recovered completely. Charlie Laste said the wind must have dispersed the chemical to the point of being safe soon after those guys got sick. The wind had probably already dispersed it quite a bit in the fifteen minutes between the blast and when the responders arrived onsite. That's why they didn't go down too hard. The SCOT has its own portable laboratory out there and they've done a bunch of tests. So far they've found nothing unusual in the air or on the ground."

"Are they still saying it was chemical grenades?"

"Yeah. Dr. Bocall tell you that?"

"Uh-huh."

"He seemed pretty sharp. I told him everything we knew, hoping it might help him with Katie. But I don't think it's done much.

"It hasn't." Walt's voice was as even as if they were discussing the weather, but the fire in his eyes betrayed his raging emotions.

"Everything I told him still holds up. Katie was shielded from shrapnel by either Julia or one of the twins. We'll never know exactly who. The SCOT's already found the grenades, or at least one box of 'em. They're trying to learn more about them before actually moving them but there's not much hope. I guess there're no lot numbers or any other identification on the grenades or the box. Could be just about anything.

"They're sweeping the whole area with metal detectors to make sure there are no other bombs out there. Once they've done that, whether they know any more about the grenades or not, they'll pack up what they've found. If things go according to plan, then the site becomes ours."

"Any idea when they'll remove the bodies?" Using the word bodies was like pounding nails into a coffin. "Bodies" made it real, final, inescapable, sending fresh jolts of nausea through Walt's stomach. Despite Jeff's presence next to him, he was once again alone.

"If all goes according to plan, sometime before they shut down for the night." Tillison checked his watch. "That ought to be within the next three hours or so. You'll be there by the site at least. Whether Laste and Branson will actually let you on is another question."

"Don't worry. They'll let me on." Walt had picked his course of action. If anyone tried to stop him, he'd bring everything down in a gigantic crash before he'd be bluffed away.

CHAPTER IV

Tillison coasted the truck through a small gap in the barrier tape around the blast site and looked at Walt. "Here you are," he said with forced enthusiasm, "good luck."

Before Walt could reply, a member of the SCOT was next to his door. "Wait a minute, partner, this here's a secured zone." The man peered through the windshield at Tillison and his mouth grew taut. "What's going on here, Detective? I've already told you to stay out." A big redheaded man with a massive head and matching hands, Adam Branson was second in command of the SCOT, its operational chief. He was not used to having his decisions questioned, much less ignored.

"You have a visitor, Adam. Thought I'd deliver him personally." Tillison didn't bother to look at Branson, instead keeping his eyes focused on an invisible point someplace on the dune in front of him. This was Walt's fight, although Tillison would jump in if needed.

"I'm Walt Crawler." Taking his cue from the tension between Tillison and Branson, Walt didn't bother to extend his hand. "I'd like access to this site."

"Absolutely not!" replied Branson, his entire face taut now. "This site is secured. The detective knows that. No one's allowed on unless I say so. And I say no."

Walt shrugged his shoulders resignedly. He'd known it would play out this way. He'd dealt with Branson's type before. "Where's your boss?"

"What?"

"Charlie Laste. The guy in charge here. Where is he?"

"Why"

"Because he's the one who makes these decisions and he's going to decide to let me on."

"And just how the fuck do you know that?" Branson moved closer to Walt as if to intimidate the smaller man with his large bulk.

"Because the bodies you have inside this fence are my ex-wife and my two daughters." Walt pushed on without waiting for that fact to sink in, "Because I'm a wildlife biologist for the Massachusetts Department of Wildlife, Fisheries and Law Enforcement and you've just had a major release of unknown chemicals in the middle of a prime natural resource area. And, finally, because as a senior member of the Department's hazardous materials response group, I've got the qualifications and equipment to help with your response. Now get me your boss or I'll go get him myself."

Branson's shoulders bunched up in anger. He wasn't used to having people push their way through him and his natural response was to push back. "You try getting anyone and you'll wish you hadn't. Family or no family."

Tillison took his eyes off the dune and looked Branson full in the face. "Adam, I've been trying to give you the benefit of the doubt since you got here," he said through the open passenger's window, "but you've gone too far now." He reached down to the truck's dash and all at once the site came alive with shrilling sirens and flashing lights. "This ought to get Mr. Laste down here, don't you think?" His hand stayed hidden below the dashboard as if reaching for something else. "Try and turn this racket off, Adam, and you'll be running the rest of the response out of a nice jail cell." He smiled without mirth at the redheaded man. "Oh yeah, just so you can't say I didn't warn you. Everything being said from here on out is getting radioed back to my office where it may be taped. Comprendez?"

"Asshole," Branson muttered, starting to walk around Walt to Tillison's side of the truck.

"Adam," a voice shouted above the din, "what's going on here?"

"This is Walt Crawler, Mr. Laste," Tillison spoke over the truck's PA system, "He has full response qualifications and it's his ex-wife and girls who were the casualties here earlier. He'd like to get onto this site."

Branson stopped in his tracks. "Fucking asshole," he muttered again. "Wait here," he said to Walt in a voice laced with anger. "And Detective, you can turn all that crap off now. You've made your point." Motioning for his boss to join him, Branson walked a short distance from the truck to have a private conference.

"I see Mr. Crawler has made it." Laste's voice was perfectly calm as he looked up into Branson's angry eyes.

"Excuse me?" Branson's face expressed his surprise. "You knew this jerk was going to show up?"

"Of course. I didn't realize he'd be here this quickly, though, or I would have given you a warning. He's the ex-husband of the dead woman and the girls' father. Runs the local fish and wildlife's response team." Laste noted these facts with the precision of a man who'd been expecting this event for ages.

"You knew all that and didn't tell me?" Branson clenched and unclenched his fists violently.

"I'm sorry, Adam. I was going to, but I got waylaid by the fire chief. I only found out myself thirty minutes ago." Laste seemed unimpressed by his subordinate's display of anger.

"Well, I don't care who he is. I still don't want him on the site." Behind his rage, Branson sounded petulant. He didn't like being kept out of the loop. "He's a security risk."

"Of course you don't want him. I don't either. But we don't have much choice."

"We don't?" Branson's voice was one of total bafflement.

"Mr. Crawler has solid credentials. He called his boss about an hour ago and she faxed us his training records. She wants him on site and, for some reason I don't know, she's got more power than you'd expect from a local wildlife department head. The word's come down from on high to humor her. Absent a real risk, we can't keep Mr. Crawler out. Since we've got the threat contained, he should be safe enough on site."

"You're serious?" Branson rocked his big body back and forth on the balls of his feet like a wrestler getting ready to charge.

"Yes. I know this bothers you, Adam," Laste was a master of the understatement, "but it's for the best. Otherwise it starts to look like we're hiding things and then it becomes a competency issue. Just assign someone to him whenever he's on this side of the tape to keep him out of trouble."

Branson slumped in defeat. "Okay," he growled, "but I still don't like it. And if he screws up, he's gone. No matter what his boss says." He turned abruptly on his heels and stalked back to the police truck. Gesturing roughly towards Walt, he growled, "Crawler, grab your gear and go around to the other side of the response van over there," he pointed to a squat vehicle a hundred feet away. "I'll have one of my team members check you out. If your gear isn't up to snuff or if you don't know how to use it well enough, I'll bounce you back out before you can say 'boo.' And you," Branson glared at Tillison, who seemed oblivious to the big man's existence, "don't let me catch you inside this fence again. You may be a cop outside, but in here I run the show."

"Whatever, Adam. Whatever." Tillison waited until Walt had removed all his gear from the truck then, flashing the lights and sounding the siren again, he backed through the security tape and headed towards town.

Alone inside the response van, Branson took a deep breath and counted to ten. He was annoyed with himself for letting both the detective and Crawler get under his skin. In hindsight, Crawler's request wasn't unreasonable, but, all the same, allowing him on site was an enormous risk with little corresponding benefit. Plus, Tillison could be a real flaming asshole. Reviewing the exchange in his mind, he could see that Tillison had been needling him intentionally since the SCOT first showed up, pushing all the right buttons, just trying to find a chink in his take-charge armor. People like Tillison did that sort of stuff because they resented the Feds coming in and taking over their show. Still, it had been stupid to have gotten so upset, blowing the whole thing out of proportion. There was a lot at stake here and getting mad over extraneous issues would only undermine his abilities to tackle the real problems.

That had always been his problem, letting his temper get out of hand. That's why he needed a Charlie Laste, even though it meant always staying number two. Men of his ilk never rose to be top dog in a bureaucracy, Branson thought, because they lacked the fundamental skill of being able to kiss ass. He could kick ass all day long, but the big redhead knew he'd never learn to kiss it.

He unwrapped a stick of gum and slowly, reflectively, began to chew on it. Branson had given up smoking years before, but at times his former two pack a day habit reasserted itself and had to be assuaged with massive amounts of spearmint gum. It was always Wrigley's, just like on the commercials.

In his early fifties, Branson was a big-boned, beefy man with huge hands and an open-looking face that concealed a cunning mind. Conveying an image of pure energy, he was the heart and soul of the SCOT, finding and training new team members, developing response procedures, and running drills. The team, with its highly trained and uniquely qualified members, was his baby and he fought vigorously every attempt to limit his control over it. Tell me what you want done, he'd told Laste time and time again, but don't tell me how to do it. In an informal arrangement, Laste handled the strategic and political stuff, joining the team on high profile responses where Branson's temper would be a liability, and Branson got down in the weeds where he was happiest and most effective.

So far, things had worked fine. With top notch equipment, a portable laboratory complete with the most modern chemical identification equipment available and the ability to call in a variety of non-SCOT support systems, his men could handle just about anything. Containing a chemical release, disarming explosives, testing drums, overpacking hazardous waste for transport or stabilizing and securing an area for future work were run of the mill operations for the men of the SCOT. They'd done it all, and they'd done it with uniform success.

Only ten of the twelve were men, actually, but even in public Branson rarely referred to any member of his team as a woman. Anyone with the guts, the skills, the strength, in short, the *cojones*, to be on the team was a man in Branson's book regardless of their physiological makeup. Far from being offended by this sort of chauvinism, the two women considered it a sort of compliment. Theirs was a man's world and the fact that they excelled in it, they argued, was another boost for women's equality. Regardless of sex, in these twelve individuals, Branson knew, rested virtually all the knowledge of hazardous chemicals, chemical weapons, delivery systems and response options in the world.

Perhaps as important as their specific chemical expertise, these people were pragmatic. Even the younger ones knew that the ends sometimes justified the means. They all understood that time spent splitting ethical hairs could be the difference between a successful response operation and a failed one, between a subway system full of bodies and one that kept running on schedule. If special concerns arose, such as locating specific information in a sealed database, getting access to a locked facility or asking tough people tough questions, the SCOT had no compunctions about how to get the job done. Branson knew that the post-Cold War world society would frown on some of the skills the team members had. He also knew that the frowning would turn to praise when those same skills prevented a chemical disaster.

He thought about the first operation the team had carried out. A recycling company in Massachusetts had set off some explosives while sorting building debris. The State Police bomb squad had arrived on site but had backed off when two members of the squad started to vomit for unknown reasons. The local fire department's Hazardous Response Operations Team took some air samples and discovered an unknown chemical pollutant was responsible for the troopers' illnesses. While the bomb squad could handle any explosives that might have remained on the site and the fire department could deal with hazardous contaminants, neither could do both safely so they had looked to the Pentagon for help. To the Strategic Chemical Operations Team in particular.

The team had flown from its headquarters in Washington, DC up to the recycling facility in two Army helicopters on loan from Fort Belvoir and had quickly taken charge of the response operation. A box of chemical grenades had somehow gotten mixed in with a dumpster full of building rubble. When run over by one of the facility's bulldozers, the box had broken open and one of the grenades, crushed by the dozer's heavy treads, had exploded and discharged its chemicals into the air. Dressed in their oversized chemical response suits with attached air tanks, the team had gone over the rest of the rubble with a fine toothed comb. After safely removing eleven intact grenades and determining, through extensive testing in the portable laboratory, that the chemicals from the first one had completely dissipated, Branson had declared the site safe.

No one had ever asked to see the grenades.

Statistical probability, Laste told his superiors over and over after the recycling facility response. Chemical disasters were going to happen again and again and again, by accident or on purpose, and the nation couldn't afford not to be ready. He'd made sure to describe other similar incidents as well, such as the cache of World War I chemical shells found at a residential construction site on a quiet cul de sac just a few miles from the White House or the nerve gas poured into the Tokyo subway system by religious fanatics. Whether it was old, haphazardly discarded chemical munitions or modern, terrorist fueled chemical attacks, the danger, Laste always made crystal clear, was unmistakable and quite real. In short order, the SCOT had become indispensable and he and Branson had been given virtual carte blanche to run it as they wished.

Branson looked through the van's windshield towards the dunes where the bodies of Walt Crawler's family still lay, crudely covered with plain white sheets. He had been a bit hard on the guy, but a secure site was supposed to be completely secure. That meant one hundred percent. Laste, of all people should have understood that. Still, it must be hell, what the dad was going through. Life was such a temporary, fragile thing. And to die so young . . . He shook the thought from his mind. He couldn't afford to feel personal about casualties. They were unavoidable. Statistical probabilities.

He looked at his watch and frowned. It was time for him to suit up and help with the site sweep. Like any good leader, he knew he had to spend some time on the front lines doing the dirty work. He didn't particularly like getting suited up into full dressout, he always felt terribly confined in the cumbersome plastic suits, but it was important to show his troops that he wasn't asking them to do anything he wouldn't do himself. With 35 pound self-contained breathing apparatuses strapped on their backs and wearing the big white moon suits like huge outer shells, the team would be lucky to get 30 minutes out of one run before they'd have to get some air and cool off. And every time they left the immediate response area, they had to go through the decontamination line, slowing things down even more. On top of that, the standby team couldn't go in until the exiting team was ready to provide backup.

To keep the team focused, Branson constantly reminded them of an incident in San Diego in 1983 where two kids had been killed by an old artillery shell no one had found before developers turned an old range into a housing development. Professionals had swept that range twice, and still missed the shell. Branson didn't want that happening at any site his team swept, so he told the same story again and again. They understood his point. They were, after all, response experts.

Branson left the van and went up to the decon line, walking with the confidence of a king surveying his realm. He loved that part of the job, the power, the complete authority over events. Laste might be the man the Pentagon thought was in charge, but, once on site, it was Branson who ran the operation. Perhaps that was why Crawler's being allowed on the site stung as it did. For the first time, Branson had been overruled during an operation.

And that damned Tillison, goading him right on the site itself. The cop probably couldn't find his own asshole with both hands and a roadmap. Branson should have put him in a decon suit just to see how long the skinny prick would have toughed it out before breaking. He liked doing that, letting people who knew nothing of the program talk their way into working in the suits and then standing back and watching them crack. With the arrogant ones like Tillison, it was especially gratifying, but there was too much at stake here to justify such entertainment.

"Hey bossman, your time's coming up, huh?" a wiry Texan remarked as Branson stepped up to the line of suits. Everyone on the team, except Laste, referred to Branson as "boss" or "bossman."

"Yeah, Rodriquez, someone has to show apes like you how to do this stuff. I don't want to be here forever waiting for you guys to finish. Find anything new?"

"Not much," the Texan's voice was matter of fact. "Besides the grenades and the bodies, all we've turned up so far are bottle caps, some shrapnel, fishing gear and the like."

"That's probably it, but you know what they say."

"Better safe than sorry," Rodriquez responded automatically. They'd had this discussion before. He flexed a wiry right arm and gave his solid biceps a tender kiss. Despite his slender build, the Texan was a devoted body builder who took great pride in his considerable strength. Years before, when he hadn't been in a job where secrecy was a byword, he'd made significant amounts of money by challenging men twice his size to arm wrestling matches. He'd lost only once. He rarely lost at anything. That was just one of the reasons Branson had picked him for the team. Neither the SCOT nor Branson had room for losers of any sort.

Rodriquez pulled a tank out from a large metal rack and checked its regulator. "This one's full," he said as he helped the larger man get suited up. While it was possible to suit up solo, having an assistant made the task much easier. For now, being that assistant was Rodriquez' duty and, dressed in jeans and a light overcoat, he was enjoying this more relaxed backup role. Hooking up the clasps to the tank, the Texan leaned his head towards Branson's ear and muttered something softly in Spanish.

"I know," replied Branson, also in Spanish, "who could have figured this much erosion. It was a risk we took. Now we'll just have to deal the hand we've been dealt." He smiled without humor. "Murphy wins another one."

Once suited up, Branson began to plod up the path that led over the sand dune towards the blast site. Moving ponderously in his chemical protection suit and feeling more like the Pillsbury Dough Boy than a highly trained chemical warrior, Branson waddled past the orange caution tape and through the decon line. He didn't like the fact that the huge suits made him feel fat rather than powerful, robbing him of some of his dignity and command presence. It was tough to feel in charge while wearing one.

From inside the suit, Branson peered through the suit's clear plastic visor, sucking greedily on his forced air. Despite years of carrying out such response operations, he always went through air like crazy in Level A. Already some condensation was forming on the visor, cutting down his narrow field of vision, turning the Nantucket scenery into a long, darkening tunnel. Ahead of him, he spotted another figure, looking like an overgrown marshmallow with legs as it waited for him to cross into the exclusion zone.

When he got next to it, the figure leaned up close. Even though Branson knew the man was shouting as loudly as he could, his voice still sounded muffled and distant, almost drowned out by the noise of Branson's own breathing. They had radio headsets they could use if they wanted, but it was usually easier to shout if someone was close enough.

"Glad to see you out here, boss. We were beginning to think you'd decided to go babe watching on the local beaches instead of earning your living like a real man."

Branson knew the man, a heavy-set weightlifter named George Burks, was smiling inside his suit. As always, Branson had been conducting more sweeps than anyone else on the team. "Thanks, George," he shouted back, "but all the girls I met did nothing but ask about you. It got depressing."

"Everyone's got that problem, boss. I guess it's just tough not to be me." Burks turned and Branson followed him towards a large plastic tarp that fluttered over the sand like a picnic tent. Setting up the tarp had been one of the first things the team had done. While the yellow tape would keep prying eyes away on ground level, nothing would keep reporters from flying over the site with high resolution cameras and Branson wanted the public record on this incident to be limited to what he and Laste chose to put in it.

As he waddled behind Burks, Branson wondered where Crawler was. The biologist could observe from a distance, Branson had decided, but no hands-on stuff and always with a SCOT member assigned to him. These limitations didn't make Branson any happier with the situation, but it was the best he could do. Despite his anger, Branson hoped he wouldn't run into Crawler by the blast site. He'd watched too many grown men grieve for destroyed families. Here it would feel especially awkward.

Slowly, Branson and Burks hiked up the dune, two oversized figures stumbling every now and then in the loose sand. Eventually reaching the top, they paused to catch their breath.

From the summit, Branson could see miles of sandy beach, the white foam of crashing waves speckling the beige sand. It wouldn't be a bad place at all, he thought, if he had come on vacation. As it was, the business at hand stripped the scenery of much of its glory.

Branson felt a tug on his arm, and turned gracelessly to his left. Another suited figure held up a metal detector. Unlike most detectors, which alerted the operator to underground metal via a change in the tone heard over a pair of earphones, this device had an arrow meter on its handle that allowed it to be used without having to put equipment underneath the response suits. When the arrow pegged, there was metal in the detection zone. Within the rope lines that cut the blast site into grids, a variety of flags marked spots where the arrow had already pegged. Some of the flags were still red, indicating the hazard had not been identified yet and further investigation would be required once the initial sweep had been completed. Branson knew the risk of another incident was virtually non-existent, but the SCOT could not afford to develop a habit of shortcuts. They'd treat each flag as a threat until proven otherwise.

The big man took the proffered detector and moved to a grid that lacked any flags. Behind him, Burks stood with a box of flags and sharp wooden sticks at the ready. After the detector registered a hit, Branson would gently poke through the sand to see if he could identify it as a possible threat or a definite non-hazard. Each type of item, including unknowns, got its own colored flag. When all the grids had been swept, they'd come back to check the unknowns and the threats. The key to success in an operation like this was being absolutely, one hundred percent thorough. It was tough, boring work, where even a small mistake could be deadly. It was here where the team earned its pay.

Almost immediately, Branson saw the arrow on his detector peg to the far right. A hit. He stepped backwards, swinging the detector in slow arcs over the sand to trace a rough outline of the hidden object. It was about the size of a silver dollar. When he was through with the detector he took a wooden stick from Burks' box, dropped softly to his knees and began to probe the sand. The stick went in two inches and stopped. He moved it over slightly and probed again. Once more, the stake penetrated about two inches into the sand. Branson repeated this procedure again and again, his vision increasingly blurred by the condensation inside his suit and his breath sniffled by the sweat dripping off his nose. Soon he had outlined the entire object. It was exactly the size of a silver dollar.

With one spade-like hand, Branson began scooping the sand away from the item he had found. As the sand cleared, he saw a medallion and chain. He reached in with one of the sticks, hooked the chain and held it up for inspection. It was still shiny and fairly new looking, indicating it hadn't been in the sand for long. He swung around, the medallion glinting as it caught the last of the afternoon light. "Hey George," he yelled, "take a look at this."

Another gloved hand, moving with a speed that was uncommon in response suits, shot out from behind Branson and yanked the medallion from the stick. Branson lurched to his feet and spun around as quickly as the cumbersome equipment would let him. "Who the fuck let you up here?" he bellowed, recognizing Walt's face inside the suit holding the medallion. "Givens," he hollered at the SCOT member behind Walt, "what the hell's he doing here? He's supposed to stay in an observer status, not get right on my ass."

As Branson paused to catch his breath, Walt leaned forward so the two men's visors were almost touching. He swung the medallion in the small space between their faces. "See this?" he asked, he voice losing none of its intensity despite the plastic shell enclosing his body.

"Of course. What of it?"

"It was Julia's." The medallion swung rhythmically on its chain. "There's pieces of my family scattered all over this site and there's no way in hell you're keeping me on the sidelines. I'll go where I want, when I want. If it's got something to do with my family and what happened to them, I'm going to be there. If you've got a problem with that, try kicking me out. I'll create more problems for you than you ever thought possible." The medallion disappeared into the glove. "Now why don't you go back to seeing what else you can find before you use all your air up."

Branson trembled with anger and the blood rushed to his face. Instinctively he dropped into a crouch, flexing his knees as he prepared for the short, brutal struggle that so often took place when he felt such emotion. As quickly as it rose, however, he forced the anger down. Fighting with Crawler, especially while wearing the awkward response suits, would be the worst mistake he could make. All Branson wanted was for this event to end and for the eyes of the world to start looking someplace else. A confrontation with Crawler, especially a physical one where the biologist would almost certainly get maimed, would just focus even more attention on the operation. Crawler would win this round, too.

"Okay," Branson spoke deliberately, his voice choked with anger, "but don't get so fucking close. It's dangerous enough out here without you sneaking up on people." He shot a withering look at Givens, the failed watchdog who had let Crawler force his way up the dune, then picked up the metal detector and, slowly and methodically, starting sweeping the grid again.

Five hours later, long after their scheduled stop time, Branson finished the last of his series of backup, decon and sweeping assignments. Crawler had been on his ass the whole time, but, after that first confrontation, Branson had ignored him. It was just like the stunt Tillison had pulled, trying to rattle him just to find the weak spots. If he tried, Branson could even sympathize with the Islander. Most of his family was dead and his youngest daughter was hooked up to life support, waiting for an antidote Branson knew the doctors would never find. It was a wonder the man could even function at all, much less operate relatively effectively in full response gear. In any other situation, Crawler would have won Branson's admiration for his ability to focus despite such a tragedy. Here, however, that attribute posed something of a threat.

After passing through the decon line, with its soapy water and car wash scrubs, for the final time, Branson shucked off his response gear and headed back to the response trailer. The site had been thoroughly swept and he no longer cared all that much where Crawler went, as long as he eventually went away. In all probability, Branson thought, the Islander would accompany the bodies to the morgue and then start making the funeral arrangements. There was little he'd gain from hanging around the SCOT any longer.

Alone in the trailer, Branson took a beer from a small fridge, hooked his legs around a heavily built stool and sat down. He looked at the beer bottle speculatively, thinking of the road that had brought him to this place in his life. He'd been born overseas, in Germany, the son of an Army helicopter pilot. Most of his youth had been spent shuttling between overseas military bases: Korea, the Panama Canal, Germany, all in a constantly repeating cycle. Even forty years later, the list of places he'd lived as a child seemed endless. Despite the travelling, Branson had loved the military part of his world and had stayed in it long beyond his childhood. He relished commanding soldiers and cherished the pride he felt for his country when he watched the brightly colored flag snapping on the parade deck. It had seemed, at times, that the Army had been created just for him, a special world whose secrets he had mastered.

He'd learned the hard way that he'd been wrong. And he'd never forget it.

Or forgive it.

CHAPTER V

28 MARCH
NANTUCKET, MASSACHUSETTS

Charlie Laste, facing a battery of microphones, squinted into the morning sun and looked over the makeshift podium at the crowd of reporters assembled to hear his briefing. In the back of the group he could see Walt Crawler standing next to his detective friend, their heads tilted towards each other as they talked. Laste shivered slightly in the cool spring breeze. He wished the SCOT could just pack up and head home, but things were never that simple. The press and the locals all wanted closure. This operation had turned their island into something of a circus and the locals needed some final answers before the big top came down. Making those speeches was Laste's job.

"Good morning, ladies and gentlemen," he began. "First, let me thank you all for your patience over the last few days. I know we haven't been flooding you with information, but we wanted to avoid speculation until we were certain about what we'd run into. Your understanding has been critical to our being able to carry out our mission in a safe, effective manner."

Laste knew he was laying it on thick, but that was expected. He'd give them nothing but positive thoughts and some good, solid statements about how the situation was under control and his team had performed well. Staying positive was a trick he'd learned in one of his many communications seminars and he was a master at it.

"While we are all still shocked by the sudden and tragic deaths of Ms. Gunder and her daughters and extend our prayers for young Katie's recovery and our sympathy to Mr. Crawler," here Laste paused appropriately, biting his lip and looking down like a man who really cared, "I am pleased to report that the men and women of the Defense Department's Strategic Chemical Operations Team have thoroughly searched the incident area and have found no other hazards of any sort, explosive or otherwise.

"Additionally, I am pleased to let you know that, after extensive testing of soil and sand samples from the blast site, as well as tests of all the pieces of shrapnel we found, we have positively determined that there is no further chemical contamination at this site. As you can see, if you look over the dune, the SCOT is packing up its equipment and is getting ready to turn the site over to local authorities.

"At this point, it seems that the explosion was caused by a box of Cold War-era chemical grenades that somehow was dumped here. Ms. Gunder or one of the girls uncovered and handled one of the grenades and it went off with tragic results.

"While we're not certain how these particular grenades came to this spot, I should note that military ordinance of various sorts has been in use in this area for decades.

"For example, from 1942-1996 the Navy had a practice bombing range about 20 miles south-west of here, on No Mans Land Island just off of Martha's Vineyard. German submarines plied these waters shortly after our entry into the Second World War and even sank ships right outside of Boston harbor. Further, military units have held exercises on Cape Cod and the islands since at least the turn of Century. During World War Two, for example, the Eastern Seaboard was littered with military camps and ranges that would be difficult to precisely locate today.

"Despite the mystery of how these grenades wound up here, it is important to remember that we have found no evidence of any other explosive devices within a quarter mile of this site, indicating that these particular devices were a terrible fluke, but not something that should negatively impact future activities in the area.

"The other important thing to remember is that humans have been making explosive devices for centuries. No matter how careful we are there will always be a few bombs, rockets or shells that remain unexploded in the ground. They'll sit there forever, generally causing no harm to anyone, but they're still very dangerous and can go off with little provocation. Merely picking up an old rocket may be enough to set off its detonator, with the same disastrous results we've seen here. People who find old explosives should never, ever, touch them under any circumstances, no matter how nice a memento it might make on their desk or in their den. The only people who should ever touch such dangerous items are properly trained authorities.

"I would now like to take a moment to thank the men and women who make up the Pentagon's Strategic Chemical Operations Team. We've given you a variety of briefs on how they do their work and what their overall mission is, but I'm not sure any of us can appreciate their efforts until we've spent two or three days in those protective suits, going over an area inch by inch looking for something so lethal that even the smallest mistake could be deadly.

"Fortunately, the SCOT found no remaining dangers beyond the box of grenades and their hazard handling skills were not put to the extreme test this time. I truly hope that they never are. Nevertheless, it should be a comfort to all of us that such dedicated and trained professionals stand ready to respond at a moment's notice to incidents such as this."

After a short question and answer period, during which time he repeated his mantra of "trained and skilled professionals" half a dozen times but never directly answered a question, Laste closed the conference. The click of cameras increased to a crescendo as he stepped away from the podium and went back to his van.

CHAPTER VI

Walt turned as the footsteps halted outside his office door. His eyes went to the twenty-four hour clock on his wall. Nineteen-thirty. Who the hell else would be here this late? Whoever it was knocked loudly on the door and then waited silently. Walt's eyes shifted to the framed picture in his hand and the half-full box perched on his chair. "Oh fuck," he said softly, putting the picture face down on his desk. Raising his voice he called, "It's unlocked. Come on in."

The door swung slowly open and a short, immensely fat woman walked, almost rolled, into the office. "Good evening, Walt," said Janice Rago in a kind voice, "you're working late."

Walt looked at his boss with no expression on his face. He both liked Janice personally and respected her professionally. A leading national authority on marine fisheries, she had taught Walt a lot about ocean ecosystems in the four years since she had come to the Island. At the same time, she understood his emotional walls and, without becoming overly solicitous, had been of great comfort during the toughest months of his divorce. He realized with some surprise that he'd been avoiding her since the funeral services three days earlier when Julia and the twins had been laid to rest. But he'd been planning on talking with her the next morning anyway, so he might as well do it now.

"I'm on leave, Janice." She knew that. "Just cleaning up is all. But please, take a seat." He pointed to a chair near the door, and then sat in another by his desk.

"How are you doing, Walt? How's Katie?" Janice's voice was deceptively high pitched for such a big, competent woman. Walt loved seeing the look on men's faces when they first met her after working together over the phone. Her voice would have been ideal for a squeaky sixteen year-old but it didn't fit such a competent bureaucrat.

"Katie's the same. I was up there this afternoon. Absolutely no change. The doctor says she could stay that way indefinitely."

"And you?"

"Me? I'm fine, I guess. As fine as I can be."

"What are you doing?" Janice appeared comfortably settled in her chair, unconcerned about going anywhere else at that moment.

"Oh, just straightening out my desk."

Janice looked around the small office, noting several newly emptied shelves and the surprisingly clear desktop. She let the silence hang in the air between them for a few moments before probing again. "The place looks a little different, barren somehow. Are you doing something with all your pictures?" She'd guessed what was in the box.

Walt's body tensed and then sagged. Janice was a good friend. He couldn't hold it in forever. It was getting to be too much. "I'm putting them away for a while." He stood and walked over to the door, shut it and began slowly pacing the office.

Janice watched him silently, waiting for him to decide the moment was right.

"I guess it's just the way I am." Walt had stopped pacing and was gazing out the window at the dark street below. "I've always done that when part of my life's over. Box it up. Move it out of the way. Don't think about it anymore. Don't let it bother me.

"I think that's why Julia left." The words were starting to come out in a flood after so many years of being unsaid. "She never accepted my tendency to focus on the real, the tangible. She never accepted it and I never changed. I taught her how to fish, rebuilt a sailboat with her, took the kids on some amazing bike trips, did all sorts of fun things. But it was all action—biking, fishing, sailing. All doing. Never talking. Even after six years of marriage, she had to prod me to get an 'I love you.' Three little words, but I had so much trouble saying them. There was never any doubt that I loved her, but she needed to hear it. Instead, she got Mr. Action.

"When something happened, I'd deal with the physical aspects of it. My mom and dad died in an auto accident. I boxed up all their stuff, settled the estate, sold the house, but never talked to Julia about how I *felt* about it.

"I never talked to her about how I *felt* about anything. Personally, I could tell her how I felt about using treble-hooked spoons for bluefish or how I felt about the potential poisoning of waterfowl from lead birdshot deposited in the water. But I couldn't tell her how I *felt* about us.

"The closest I ever came was agreeing to have a third child. I guess I knew our marriage was in trouble. Katie was supposed to help bring us together." Walt snorted derisively. "As if a child is some sort of human super-glue. Maybe it worked for a while, I don't know, but it didn't work for long. I still couldn't talk about anything internal. Julia called me emotionally constipated. She was right, too. Box things up, focus on the physical and move on. I didn't mean for it to hurt her, but I'm sure it did. Eventually she couldn't take it anymore and we separated. Hell, I couldn't even talk about our divorce with her." He laughed mirthlessly. "I boxed all that up, too. My basement's full of boxed-up memories I never open." He pulled the silver medallion and chain he'd taken from Branson out of a nearby box, bounced it lightly in his hand and then let is slip through his fingers back into the box. "I just add to them every once in a while."

"So, you're packing all your pictures away?" Janice asked, sadness evident in her squeaky voice.

"No. Not Katie's. She's still with me." Walt dabbed at his eyes and was relieved when Janice said nothing. "But you didn't come here to talk about my house cleaning habits." He looked directly at his boss. "What gives?" Even after baring his soul, Walt was still direct and to the point.

Janice met his gaze. "It's work, Walt."

"I'm on leave."

"You'll want this."

They'd done variations of this dance dozens of times. Walt could never say 'no' to a new mission. It was in his nature, something new to focus on. Julia hadn't ever complained, but Walt thought it had helped lead to the divorce.

"Fill me in." He'd listen politely. Then he'd say no. He had other plans, but he needed Janice's help and didn't want to irritate her first.

"You know Shipwreck Rocks, right?"

"Of course." Every fisherman on the Island knew the Rocks. They poked up a few feet above high tide off of Dionis Beach, half a mile from where Julia and the twins had died. "Why?"

"I got a call about an hour ago from Bobby Myers. You know him?"

Walt nodded affirmatively. Bobby worked for the Steamship Authority and spent most of his off-time fishing. Anyone who took the ferry more than a few times a year would eventually be cornered by Myers and learn everything there was to know about bluefish and stripers.

"Bobby went out to the Rocks this afternoon to drown some worms. Nothing's running, he was just killing time. But when he got out to the Rocks, he noticed something odd."

Something odd a half mile from the blast site. Walt was all ears. Maybe he wouldn't say no after all.

"You know the Rocks, they're always full of birds. A fisherman shows up and they're all over him, hoping for a handout or the entrails from the cleaned fish. But nothing flew out to greet Bobby. The sky was empty. That struck him as strange so he motored closer to get a better view. The Rocks were full of birds, but none of them were flying. They all looked like they were dead or sick. Bobby didn't waste any more time. He turned right around and scooted back to the harbor. As soon as he got in, he called Jimmy Mack, the harbor master. I don't know why, but that's who he called. Jimmy called here and, because I was working late, the phone bounced over to me."

Walt nodded. He'd forwarded all of his calls directly to his voicemail system. At some point he'd start worrying about picking up his messages.

"You're the only wildlife biologist in the office, Walt. Something's made those birds sick and we need to find out what it is. I could ask the Staties or the Coast Guard to go out and pick up a few specimens, but they don't have your experience with wildlife. They may miss evidence that you would notice. Which birds are sicker than others, if they've lost feathers. Stuff like that."

"And you want me to go now, in the dark?"

"It's been three hours since Bobby saw them, Walt. If we wait until daylight, it'll be almost twelve more hours. Every minute that passes makes it less likely we'll recognize all the clues that are there now. The birds'll probably all be dead by then, if they're not already. A freak wave might wash the Rocks clean. Who knows what'll happen. We need to go out there now.

"And, Walt," Janice rose out of her chair for the clincher Walt knew was coming. "I'm not trying to read anything into this, so take it with a grain of salt. But the Rocks are only a half mile from where Julia and the girls…from where the blast occurred." Even Janice couldn't bring herself to speak about the deaths directly. "We know there were chemicals involved and now we've got a bunch of sick or dead birds. There might be nothing to it, but the wind was blowing in that direction."

"What are we going to do with the birds?" By using 'we,' Walt was giving Janice his answer.

"Scoot 'em over to your buddy Harley at Woods Hole. I've already talked with him. He'll have the lab open. I'll call him at home once you're on your way."

Walt had to smile. "You don't miss much, do you, Janice?"

"No. I can't afford to with people like you to keep me on my toes."

"I can't go out there and do this alone at night, you know."

"You won't have to. When I saw your light was on, I called Detective Tillison before coming here. He'll meet you at the city docks in half an hour!"

Walt's smile turned into a full-fledged grin and he shook his head in admiration. He thought he could focus, but next to Janice, he was simple-minded. "I was going to come talk to you, too, Janice. Except I was going to do it tomorrow morning."

"What about?" Janice had sat back down again, overflowing around the chair's armrest.

"I want to get put on Laste's response team for three months." No sense in beating around the bush.

"Is that all?" Janice appeared unfazed.

"Not entirely. I want to start a week from Monday."

"You're serious."

"Absolutely."

"Why?" It was like Janice not to say 'no' immediately. She'd fish around a bit to help her decide.

"Six days ago, I lost just about everything that meant anything to me. One day they're all alive and then, boom, the twins and Julia are dead and Katie's comatose in the hospital.

"I couldn't have told you before all this shit happened. I didn't realize it myself, but Julia was right. I was emotionally constipated. I probably still am. I couldn't connect with my feelings, couldn't tell Julia that I loved her. I always had to hide behind something physical like my job, or fishing, or bike racing. Towards the end of my marriage, I even started spending a lot of time at the horse races with Harley. I guess I was looking for some sort of thrill I couldn't find at home. Julia looked for intimacy and I always found someplace else to go. It's a wonder she put up with me as long as she did."

Walt had started pacing again. "You know, I was supposed to have custody of the kids last weekend. That's the way we had it arranged. She had them during the week and we split weekends. One weekend with me, one with Julia. Except I always had reasons to avoid my custody times. Probably half the time I was supposed to have the kids, I was out of town or otherwise busy. Usually it was work." He wanted to remind Janice she owed him. "I thought it was important to improve my hazardous response qualifications, thought I could help people and I did. I thought it was important to go out on the trawlers to get fish counts. And it was. I thought it was important to map weekend use areas within our wildlife refuges and that, too, was true. Everything was important. All of it. But a lot of that work came at the cost of time with my family. Julia always took the kids without a word of complaint or criticism. And the kids never said anything, so I never thought it made that much difference. Everyone seemed happy enough.

"Except last weekend." Walt paused, then his face twisted and his voice became raspy as he started speaking again. "The kids were supposed to be with me. We should have been fishing or working on the boat or even just hanging out. They should have been safe with me, but I had a chance to bike on the Department's team and, like I did all the time, I asked Julia to take the kids for the weekend. She said fine, she'd take 'em on a photo shoot.

"That's why the kids were on the beach, playing in the dunes. Because I couldn't find time for them. That's why the bomb went off."

"Walt, you can't blame yourself," Janice started to comfort him.

"Let me finish, please, Janice." Walt's tone was sharp. "If I'd found the time for my kids, if they'd been more important to me than a bike race, they'd all be okay now. Whether I'm blaming myself or not is irrelevant. What I've told you is fact. It happened. The issue has now become, where do I go from here?

"Janice," Walt's voice dropped and his tone softened, "I've spent most of the past week, when I wasn't up in Boston, looking through every old response file, illegal dumping report and landfill filing I could find for Nantucket, hoping somewhere, somehow, I could find a link to the blast. I came up with zip, nothing. We have no information at all on what those grenades were doing there or what poisons they contained. We're no closer to finding an antidote for Katie than we were six days ago.

"I can't do anything about Julia and the twins anymore." Walt was using his internal system of boxed emotions again, focusing on the physical, the immediate, "but Katie's still alive. As long as she's alive, there's hope for her. But not without new information on the blast, on what's poisoning her. And the only possible source of info we have is Laste's response team. They took samples from the site. Someplace in their data, in their files somewhere, maybe there's information that could help Katie. If I'm with them, I can look."

"Are you implying the Feds are hiding something?" Janice arched her eyebrows. She had little patience for conspiracy theories.

"No, not at all. The Pentagon's claiming national security interests and won't release any information on the grenades the SCOT picked up, except to say that each grenade had a different chemical poison so any data they could give us would be useless in determining an antidote for Katie. I guess that makes sense. But the SCOT might not be aware of all the information they have. They might be overlooking something relevant from their meter readings or gas chromatography tests or something. You look for different things when you review data during a response situation than you do when you're looking for an antidote for your little girl. You've got different concerns.

"Hey, I know I'm looking for a needle in a haystack. A needle that might not even exist. But I've got to look." Walt took a deep breath and his voice got lower, almost pleading. "I haven't been there much for Katie, especially when it counted. This is my last chance. I've got to be there for her now. She's got no one else."

"I don't know, Walt." Janice looked uncomfortable. "It's almost as if you're asking me to plant a mole on the Pentagon's response team."

Walt walked over to his desk and opened up the center drawer. He reached inside and handed Janice a small white paper bag. "Open it up," he encouraged her.

With a quizzical look on her face, Janice unfolded the bag and pulled out an ornate cardboard box.

"Open that up, too," said Walt.

Janice complied and pulled out a small silver spoon. "To Katie," she read the inscription, "the world's most wonderful three-year old. Love, Daddy."

"She doesn't turn three for another five months, but I jumped the gun a bit and got the spoon engraved anyway. Actually," Walt looked embarrassed, "I had it engraved two months ago. I liked having it around. It made me feel more involved in her life somehow.

"I want to give Katie that spoon, Janice. I want to give it to her and have her say 'Thank you, Daddy' more than I've ever wanted anything else in my life. But unless we find an antidote, I doubt that's going to happen. I can still give it to her, of course, but she won't say a thing." Walt gently took the spoon from Janice's hand and placed it on a shelf. "I need your help, Janice, please." The desperation was clear in Walt's voice. He had no place else to go.

Janice's expression softened. "How are we going to get you on? That big guy, Brudson or Bulsom or whatever his name was, threw a real shit-fit when we stuck you with him before. And that was on your island, with your family involved. I don't know how we'll get him to agree to having you in his office for three months."

Walt smiled. He'd gotten past the hard part. "Janice, you're a most high muckety-muck and you know people who are even more most high. Pull some strings." Walt had already thought this one out. "Tell them the blast has really got you scared. That's certainly true enough. Tell them that you're worried you'll have a repeat event someday and you want more in-house expertise. With my professional background, I'm a natural fit. They'll give you a hard time, of course, but I've made life easy for you." Walt handed his boss a small manila folder. "Although I didn't do an exhaustive search, I did find some good information on the threat we face. In the past six months alone, just on Cape Cod and the Islands, people have dug up grenades in their gardens, found explosives when putting in fenceposts and stumbled over bombs on the beach. Just like Julia and the girls." Walt forced down the lump in his throat and continued on.

"On top of that, the state's turning most of the MMR," Walt used the local shorthand term for the huge Massachusetts Military Reservation that straddled the Cape, "into a wildlife refuge. Bombs and chemical waste," the MMR was infamous for poisoning Cape Cod's drinking water from its many ranges and dump sites, "alongside birds and bunnies. The perfect mix for sending someone with my qualifications to Charlie Laste and his bruiser sidekick for a few months. I don't see how they can say no."

There was silence as Janice thought for a few moments, slowly leafing through the news clippings Walt had given her.

"You make a strong case for your plan, Mr. Crawler," she said with mock gravity. "I'll see what I can do." Those with any experience working with Janice knew that meant she'd get it done. "Now do you think you can go meet Jeff?"

"I'm on my way." Walt picked up the spoon from the shelf and put it in his pocket. "I'll drop the birds off with Harley and then head back up to the hospital. You'll be able to reach me in Katie's room." Walt handed Janice a slip of paper with the number on it. "Once you've given me the details, I'll schlep down to DC. I'm already packed and ready to go."

"You'll keep me posted?"

"Certainly."

"And Katie?"

"I'll fly up to visit her when I can. I'd rather stay by her side, but that wouldn't be any help at all. For the next few months she'll have to be on her own." Walt's face took on a sour, bitter look. "The doctors think she's stabilized okay, but they can't do anything for her besides give her electric shock treatments to keep her muscles from atrophying too much. They haven't given me a definite time frame, but I'm sure they can only do this for a while before being in a coma starts having a permanent effect on Katie. The longer she spends in the hospital, the worse her chances are. I've got to do everything I can to get her out as soon as possible."

Janice looked closely at his tired, tear stained face. "And I'll do whatever I can to help you, Walt. All you have to do is ask."

"Hey, Walt," Tillison's greeting was as casual as if trips like this occurred every day. That they only went out on a boat together a few times a year, the detective spending his limited free time in the Whaling Museum rather than on the water, warranted no comment.

"Hi, Jeff. Are we ready to go?"

"I think so. We've got specimen bags, crabbing nets, ice, hip waders, protective masks and gloves and some good flashlights. I've topped off the gas, checked the radio and," Tillison displayed a large paperbag with a flourish, "I even brought you dinner— pastrami on rye, no mayo, and a six-pack of Ipswich Ale."

"You are a gem, Jeff, an absolute gem." Walt climbed into the Boston Whaler and uncleated the mooring lines as his friend started the engine. Once they were moving through the harbor, he sat by Jeff at the command console and opened up the bag. The sandwiches were still warm.

"I appreciate your help, Jeff."

"It's nothing, Walt. Too dangerous for someone to do alone this late at night. Janice said you'd need help. I figured it might as well be me." The detective pushed the throttle forward as they cleared the breakwater, then pulled two bottles out of the bag, popped the tops on an opener mounted by the wheel and handed one to Walt. "Besides, I thought it would be nice to talk for a while with nothing to distract us."

"Nothing besides picking up a bunch of dead and dying birds, you mean," Walt corrected.

"Besides that," Jeff said agreeably. "Like why Janice wanted you to go out here anyway? You're supposed to be on leave."

"I was in the office. That's one reason. But mostly because she wanted it done right, I suppose."

"Done right?"

"Yes, done right. This isn't simple stuff. Let's look at it from an angle you, as a detective, can appreciate. We don't have a bird kill, we have a mystery. The mystery just happens to be *why we have a bird kill?* The same way you pick up clues to solve a murder-gloves, blood samples, footprints, hair follicles and so forth-I'm going to pick up clues to help us solve this mystery. But you've got to understand the nature of the clues before you can collect them.

"We need to get specimens from each species out there. We need males and females, young and old, sick and dead and even healthy, if we can find healthy birds out there. We need to know how the birds are grouped, if they've molted, if anything unique is floating in the water. There's a whole host of things I'll notice that you wouldn't because I understand birds, and wildlife in general, better than you do. Then, when Harley starts to get information on stomach contents, blood cell counts and things like that, I'll be better able to fit the pieces together.

"Of course, there's no guarantee we'll solve this mystery. But the more clues we have and the better we understand them, the more likely it is that we'll figure this out. Or, if it stays a mystery, we may find matches with other bird or animal kills somewhere else that could help connect things."

"I guess that'd be a serial murderer analogy," Tillison interjected dryly.

"More or less," Walt responded. "It all revolves around correctly collecting and interpreting clues. That's why Janice asked me. If I hadn't been around, she probably would have taken a gamble with the Coast Guard because they have some, albeit minimal, wildlife management experience. But there would be more holes in our bird kill puzzle."

Tillison pondered Walt's explanation in silence for a few moments, his body rocking gently with the bouncing of the boat as it skimmed over the waves. Although the detective now spent little time on the water, he'd held onto the boat handling skills he'd learned as a youngster. Jeff finished his beer and popped the top off another. A man of precise habits, he never had more than two beers a night, but rarely had fewer.

"That's a good explanation, Walt. I almost bought it." Tillison took his eyes off the spotlight cutting a hole in the darkness ahead of them and focused a laser-like look on his companion. That look was one of the many traits that made him such a good detective and, even after knowing Jeff for over thirty years, it could still rattle Walt. "It's the location, though, that's really the reason you're out here. The rest is just window dressing to keep from sounding paranoid, isn't it." Jeff looked forward again, leaving Walt to work out an answer unharassed.

Another few minutes passed, the silence broken only by the steady chugging of the engine and the slap-slap as the bow broke through the slight swells. "I should have known I couldn't slip anything by you, Jeff," Walt finally said. "You're right. It's a long shot, but if I didn't think there might be some connection between those birds and the blast, someone else would be making this trip."

"It is a reach, though, isn't it." Tillison was talking like a friend, not a detective. "I mean, the Rocks are a half mile off shore. The wind was blowing like hell last Saturday and we know for a fact the birds were fine yesterday." Like any good cop, Tillison had checked a few sources before leaving his office to join Walt. "If they'd died Sunday, or had been roosting on the beach when the grenade went off or if the wind hadn't been strong enough to disperse the contaminants so quickly, then maybe I'd agree with you. But with what we've know, it's a reach."

"Those points are all clues, too," Walt acknowledged. "The wind, the time of death, where the birds were. Somehow all that information fits with everything else to make the pieces come together. Maybe it's just a coincidence, but as long as there's a chance that it might help find an antidote for Katie, then I'm going to chase it down until I find an answer or reach a dead end."

"I'd do the same thing," Tillison said approvingly. "And you know, if you ever need any help…" He let the sentence drift off, his meaning clear.

"There's something else, too, Jeff. Something I haven't told anyone." Walt spoke slowly, deliberately. He was going onto thin ice and he didn't want Tillison to dismiss him out of hand. "I spent Saturday night and all day Sunday with Laste and his team. I mostly observed because they have a pretty set routine to their work, but I got a funny feeling about the whole thing.

"Branson would rather have had a root canal than to have had me on the site. In fact, everyone gave me a major cold shoulder, like they'd been coached to ignore me. I'd expected some discomfort and maybe embarrassment given the circumstances, but this went beyond that. At one point, Branson found that silver medallion Julia used to wear and was waving it around on a stick. I took it from him and I thought the guy was going to go catatonic. Even through our response suits I could see he was almost out of control. I really thought he was going to attack me. Christ, it was my family that got destroyed, you'd think I'd be the one going nuts. The guy's just too excessive. It stinks of something."

"You think they're hiding something?" Tillison asked, unknowingly echoing Janice's earlier question.

"I don't know what I think, Jeff." Walt finished his beer and dug through the bag for another one. "I'm getting opconned to Laste's team for three months starting a week from Monday." He shifted the discussion without preamble.

"You're what?" Tillison's eyes were back on Walt.

"I'm going to spend the next three months with the SCOT."

"How'd you manage that? You had enough trouble getting near the team last Saturday."

"Janice is connected. She's going to make it happen. If it might help find an antidote for Katie, she's willing to go to bat for me."

Tillison cut the throttle back until the boat had slowed to a quiet crawl through the dark night. "Just between you and me, I've got a weird feeling about the SCOT's response operation, too," he said softly as if thinking aloud. He took his hands off the wheel and curled both of them around his beer bottle as if he were trying to warm it. "After Laste cleared the site, us regular joes were allowed on. On behalf of the police department, I was the first person in. It made sense. There was an explosion. People were hurt. I'm a detective. We can't rule anything out at the start, no matter what the Feds might tell us. So I looked at the site like it was a potential crime scene, just like you're going to look at the birds. Tried to see what looked strange, what was out of place. And you know what I found?"

"What?"

"Nothing."

"Nothing?"

"That's right. Nothing." Tillison sat back and took a pull from his beer in satisfaction.

Walt huddled deeper into his jacket as the cold ocean air finally began to eat at him. "Nothing?" he repeated again, confusion filling his voice.

"Don't you get it?" Tillison leaned forward again.

"Honestly, no, I don't"

"Think about it. There were a dozen people in full chemical response suits, probably the most awkward thing you can wear and still move around in, poking all over that site with metal detectors, probes, tubes and God knows what else."

"So?" Walt asked, trying in vain to understand Tillison's point.

"But when I got on the site, it looked just like any other patch of beach, not one where a fatal explosion just took place. It was subtle and I couldn't prove it in court, but my gut tells me the site was reconstructed."

Walt's stomach lurched and he almost coughed up the beer he'd just swallowed. "They altered the site?!" It was inconceivable. "Why would anyone want to do that?"

"I don't know why, Walt. And like I said, it's more of a gut feeling than anything else. But stuff that should have been uncovered after all that activity-grass roots, shells, pebbles-was buried just like normal. Twigs, dead branches, even the damned bird feathers looked almost exactly the same at the site as they did on a patch of dunes a hundred yards away that I used for comparison. It just doesn't add up."

"So you're saying there's a cover-up?"

"Like you, I don't know exactly what I'm saying. Maybe I'm reading too much into something minor, but it bears consideration." Tillison pushed the throttle forward again and the boat shifted gears. "Do you know much about World War II?" he asked.

"No. Not really." Walt was surprised by the question.

"Well, the Japanese had these special weapons that they used against us. Basically, they were bombs in balloons, sent up into the jetstream and detonated over the Pacific Northwest to start forest fires, scare people and generally raise havoc. The Pentagon knew of these balloon bombs, but they didn't want the Japanese to know they knew, so the military clamped a news blackout down on the whole thing. That wouldn't have been an issue, except someplace in Oregon a preacher was out picnicking with his family and they found one of these bombs. Problem was, they didn't know what it was, because the Pentagon wasn't letting anyone know what was going on. So this family picks up the balloon bomb to check it out and, boom, just like that, they're dead."

"Like what happened to my family?" Walt's stomach lurched again.

"I'm not saying that, Walt. I'm just saying the Feds aren't always up front about stuff. I'm sure they have their reasons. Maybe, from the big picture perspective, they made the right decision to be quiet about the balloons. After all, they had a major war to fight. But in the short term, some people can pay a hell of a price for the government's penchant for secrecy."

The boat's powerful searchlight picked out a blob of rocks poking up through the water and Tillison fell quiet. A variety of formless shapes dotted the boulders and a few more bobbed with the rise and fall of the water. Nothing looked alive. The detective put the boat in neutral and they coasted towards the rocks. "One last thing, Walt," Jeff said as his friend readied the nets and bags they would use to pick up their specimens for Harley.

"What's that?" Walt's mind was whirring with the information Tillison had just given him and he found comfort in the familiar feel of the tools he was getting ready to employ. As always, he noted wryly to himself, he was taking refuge in the physical, the real, the immediate.

"On the off chance something might be amiss here, you be careful." Tillison's tone was serious. "The Feds have long arms and sometimes they have strange attitudes. By going down to the SCOT's office, you just might be sticking your head in the lion's mouth. Don't take anything for granted and stay in touch. Okay?"

"Okay." Walt flashed his friend a smile. "Now let's get us some birds."

Walt had finished the last of the six-pack by the time Tillison slid the Whaler into the harbor at the Woods Hole Oceanographic Research Center in Falmouth. Although he wasn't much of a drinker, his mind felt painfully clear and unimpaired by the alcohol as he considered the implications of what his detective friend had just told him. Cover-ups? Conspiracies? Or just coincidence and a strong case of Island paranoia? Who the hell knew.

He checked his watch. Just after midnight. Around him, the dark hulks of moored boats loomed against the backdrop of streetlights along the shore. Above the dull throb of the boat's engine, the thin sound of halyards slapping against aluminum masts set a peaceful scene that was completely at odds with the maelstrom of emotions he was experiencing. Everything about the harbor seemed so quiet and sleepy, but Walt couldn't help but wonder what horrible truths lay hidden out there. Hidden like the grenades, just waiting to explode.

"Ahoy, Maties. Throw me a line and I'll rescue you." Harley's voice boomed out from the Institute's docks.

Despite his morbid reverie, Walt smiled. His big friend's irreverent, almost flippant, attitude extended to everything but his work. Waking people sleeping in their yachts this early in the boating season wasn't even close to one of Harley's concerns.

"Catch, Buddy," he responded in a softer voice, tossing Harley a line. "And try not to wake up the whole harbor, okay?"

"Whatever. It's too early to sleep anyway." No one quite knew when Harley slept. Something of a mad scientist at work, he was one of the East Coast's leading marine toxicologists with a professional reputation so solid that even the most straight-laced donors to the Institute preferred to look the other way at his off-work activities.

Big, almost huge, Harley, born Ross Mitchell but called Harley by nearly everyone who knew him, looked and acted the part of a veteran motorcycle gang member. A born rebel, however, he took great pains to affirm his independence from any known groups. With his clean-shaven head, tree-trunk like arms and massive fists, Harley could, and often did, hold his own in a barroom brawl and Walt had learned to be careful when approaching his friend during a drinking spree. Unmarried, Harley's collection of bikes had taken over the physical and emotional space most men devote to their families, with pictures of them displayed on his walls and parts of whatever bike he was putting together scattered throughout his house.

Besides his work and his motorcycles, Harley's only other passion was playing the horses. Over the years, Walt had been on more than a few racing trips with his big friend, riding "bitch," as Harley called the backseat of his bike. Because the big biker was pathologically afraid of flying, much to Walt's amusement, their trips never strayed far from home, but regardless of the distance, a trip with Harley was always interesting.

Harley extended a hand and lifted Walt out of the boat as easily as if he were a small child. "How're you doing, Bud?" he asked in an uncharacteristically tender voice. "Still hanging in there?"

"Still hanging, Harley. Don't know if it's in there or not."

"It's the shits, Walt. The absolute shits." Harley paused and then engulfed the smaller man in a smothering bearhug. "I feel for you, man." He released Walt abruptly. "How's Katie?"

"The same. The doctor says not to expect much any time soon."

"Shit." Harley's whole body emphasized the word.

"Hi, Harley, how's it going?" Tillison had tied up the Whaler's stern and climbed up on the dock.

"It's going okay, detective." Harley extended his right hand for a cautious handshake. He knew Walt and Tillison were good friends and he'd even helped the police officer on a few occasions, but Harley's numerous brushes with the law made him skittish of anyone who carried a badge. "Still sucks about Julia and the kids."

"Yeah, it does." Tillison disengaged his hand from Harley's monster palm and pointed towards the boat. "We've got a lot of work for you here, Harley. It's good of you to take it at such short notice." The police officer in him had trouble pegging people of Harley's ilk. Brilliant, hard-working, stubborn and erratic as hell, one never knew what lay below the surface of such a walking contradiction.

Harley's file was, to put it mildly, quite colorful for a man in his position. Honorably discharged from the Army, Harley had spent four years as an intelligence officer, something Tillison always had trouble envisioning. Since then, the biker had gone back to school, embraced a counter-culture lifestyle and established a lengthy, if not too serious, list of criminal offenses. A slew of drunk and disorderly charges, three assault and battery arrests, one DUI, two aggravated assaults and countless disturbing the peace complaints. But there were no felony convictions and only occasional jail time. Mostly the charges were either dropped or pled and there were no drug crimes, no sexual charges and no apparent links to any other more serious crimes or criminal groups. Though he was still something of an unpredictable powder keg, the vast majority of Harley's rap sheet had been created years before and the big biker appeared to have calmed down recently.

The toxicologist picked up one of the sample bags and bounced it in his big hands. He smiled, the mad scientist looking forward to another night alone in the lab. "This is what I do best, detective, and I'm just glad I can be of service." Out of deference to Walt, Harley's voice held no touch of sarcasm. "I brought down a cart for the samples. Let's start loading it up."

It took the three men almost ten minutes to unload all the bird specimens, water samples, rocks, seaweed, living and dead barnacles, clams and other things Walt and Tillison had collected from the Rocks. As they worked, Harley's eyes kept darting to the ever increasing pile in his cart. When it was finally loaded, he sighed. "You're asking for a lot, Walt. It'll take some time."

"I understand that, Harley. I wish I could give you more to go on but I don't want to rule anything out and I don't want to prejudice your lab work. It'll be better if you start with a blank slate."

"Well, it can't get much blanker. You guys want to come up to the lab?"

Tillison shot Walt a glance. "Not me, thanks. It's getting late and I still need to get home."

"Walt?"

"No thanks. I'm going to take a cab over to Hyannis to pick up my car. Then I'm headed back up to the hospital."

"Okay. I'll call you when I find out something."

Walt handed his friend a slip of paper similar to the one he'd given Janice. "You'd probably do best trying this number for the next week or so." He stuck out his hand to Tillison. "Thanks for the help, Jeff. Have a safe trip home."

"You too, Walt. And remember what I said. Stay in touch."

When the first rays of daylight began filtering their way into Katie's hospital room, they found Walt Crawler asleep in a chair, his head resting on the room's table and his hands cradling a small silver spoon.

Adam Branson was upset. Beyond upset. He was livid. "I don't want him coming in here," he said for the umpteenth time. "It's a major security risk."

"I understand that, Adam," Laste's voice oozed patience, "but the choice isn't ours. Somehow Mr. Crawler has enough juice to have the Secretary of Defense himself direct us to accept him. As much as we'd like to, we can't very well say no."

"I still don't like it," Branson repeated doggedly. "I don't care what anyone says, he's here to snoop about the Nantucket blast. I know it, you know it, he knows it and the Secretary must know it. And I don't like snoops."

"You're right, Adam." Ever a pragmatist, Laste knew they were stuck with the decision. The question now was how to make the best of it. "But his cover story's perfect–solid response credentials, a definite threat throughout Cape Cod and the Islands, a career in wildlife management. We can't say no just because we don't like it. Or him," Laste noted, remembering the sparks between Crawler and Branson.

"How the hell'd he get a clearance so quickly?" Branson was a fanatic about team security. Amongst themselves, security was fairly lax, but to the outside world he made sure the team presented an impenetrable wall. Bios were sanitized, pictures avoided, addresses concealed. To have a stranger forced into their midst threatened the integrity of his entire security system.

"I told you, he's got juice. I did manage to tailor his security access, however." This had been the Secretary's one concession to Laste's long list of objections when told Crawler would be joining his team for three months. "He's not to have his own password into the office. He is **never** to touch one of our computers and all personnel files are one hundred percent off limits. That way, at least, he won't be poking around without supervision."

"Are you going to assign someone to him?"

"Yeah. I was thinking of Pryor. He's single and closed-mouthed." The latter criteria was probably the most important. The World War Two motto–"Loose lips sink ships"–still rang true for the SCOT.

Branson thought it over for a few moments. "I hope we're getting something out of all this," he growled, not willing to take defeat graciously.

"Well, now that you mention it," Laste never gave something for nothing, "having an outsider stuck in the middle of the team highlights the need for different operational clearances. Crawler's just the first 'observer' we'll get stuck with. So the Secretary gave us another one point five million to design a system to manage long-term visitors without risking security breaches."

"One point five mil?" Branson knew it wouldn't cost a third of that amount.

"One point five mil. Annually."

"I still don't like it," Branson said once more, in a tone that wasn't quite as gruff.

"Neither do I, Adam. But at least there's a silver lining."

CHAPTER VII

5 APRIL
WOODS HOLE, MASSACHUSETTS

On his way to DC, Walt slipped off Route 95 and wound down Route 6 to the Woods Hole Oceanographic Institute. Harley had finally called the night before, not saying much besides the fact that they should get together. It was unlike the toxicologist to be so taciturn about his work, and the unusual behavior, added to Jeff Tillison's thoughts about the beach reconstruction, was troubling. Nothing, thought Walt as he fiddled with the car radio, was normal anymore.

Harley was sitting in a ratty old swivel chair on the back loading dock when Walt pulled in. Despite a series of no-smoking and flammable signs posted all over the dock, the big biker was happily puffing on one of the longest cigars Walt had ever seen. With his feet resting on a battered motorcycle frame and the loading dock littered with cast-off office furniture, all Harley needed was a banjo to look like a Cape Cod version of *Deliverance*. "I'm glad you could make it, Walt," Harley said between puffs, watching with an expressionless face as Walt vaulted up onto the dock. "Sorry it took me so long to get back to you."

Walt looked at him closely. Usually Harley was much more animated than this. At the very least, he would have expected his friend to stand up to greet him, but instead Harley just rocked slowly back and forth, steadily puffing on his cigar.

"Have a seat," Harley offered, patting another, equally ratty, chair next to him. Walt grimaced as he got a face full of cigar smoke, then he pulled the chair upwind of the cigar and sat down.

The chair's worn out springs pressed through the seat's fabric and Walt hoped he wouldn't be sitting for long. Still, it was Harley's show and he'd play it out in his uniquely eccentric way.

"How's Katie?" Harley asked when Walt was settled.

"Same. No better, no worse." Walt felt no need to elaborate. Harley was, after all, a toxicologist. He probably understood what Katie was going through better than Walt did. "Have you found something that might help her?" Walt asked, even though he knew the answer was no. Harley would have been much more animated if he were closer to finding an antidote for the little girl. Still, Harley had something on his mind, but he clearly wanted Walt to poke around a bit first. It fit his mad scientist image.

"Not exactly that will help her," replied Harley, looking pleased with himself.

Before he could stop it, Walt's patience snapped. Having just left his daughter, looking like a life-size ragdoll in her hospital bed, he was in no mood for Harley's games. "Then exactly what the fuck have you found?" he asked in a voice so intense that Harley stopped rocking in his chair. "I've got a two and a half year old girl on life support seventy miles from here who would be very interested in finding out. If, of course, she could speak."

"Jesus, Walt. I'm sorry. I wasn't thinking. Christ, I can be an asshole sometimes," Harley looked down at his feet, "It's just that I'm chewing on something really interesting."

"What've you got?" Walt was to the point. There was no use in spending forever exchanging sorries.

"Well, you and your Detective Tillison gave me a pile of work last week." Harley wasn't complaining, he was just setting the stage.

"Yeah, I know. It took quite a while to collect it all."

"You told me to assume nothing, so I started at ground zero. Did every scan I could think of on the blood, tissue, feathers, everything. Checked the water for pH imbalances, sliced up the barnacles and scoped them, grew cultures, did the whole nine yards, and you know what I found?"

Walt was experiencing déjà vu. He remembered his conversation with Jeff Tillison about the dunes. "Nothing."

Harley removed the cigar from his mouth. "Excuse me?"

"You found nothing. Well, almost nothing. The water was fine. The barnacles, seaweed and rock scrapings were all normal, even the dead birds seemed clean."

"How did you know?" Harley looked disappointed.

"Because if you'd found something that easily, you'd have told me over the phone, not out here on the dock. You found nothing at all, at first. But when you dug deeper, you found a common thread which proves your brilliance, which is why you wanted to talk face-to-face."

Walt was still thinking about Jeff's story about the altered dunes. "It's nothing anyone else could have found, but you dug deeper and came up with something. What is it?"

Harley sat back in his chair. "There's something strange going on here, isn't there?" His eyes gleamed. "What is it?" Harley loved conspiracies.

"I don't know, Harley. Even what I do know, I'm not sure of. I don't want to prejudice your scientific mind, though, so I'd rather not tell you until I'm a bit more certain."

Harley nodded his head. After his earlier faux pas, he was eager to accommodate. "When my first round of tests all came up nil, I was confused. I had a bunch of dead birds and not a clue as to why they died. No weird cell counts to indicate an infection, no poisons in the blood or the stomach that I could detect, no viruses or bacterial infections. Nada.

"A lot of times, if it's not a disease, you'll get cross species kills. You know, like the Sandoz chemical spill in Switzerland in 1986. It decimated all sorts of life in the Rhine River for miles and miles and miles. Fish, eels, snails. Just about everything. And here, we had dead birds and a few dead barnacles, so I knew it was cross-species. But only a few off the barnacles died, and none of the seaweed or clams did."

"Well, that's not too surprising, is it?" Walt interjected. "If it were airborne, it would primarily get the birds."

"True, in a sense, but nothing is ever just airborne. Pollutants precipitate out, settle into the water, onto the rocks, or, more to the point, onto the barnacles. I checked your collection notes against the tide tables. You keep very thorough notes, by the way." Harley appreciated professionalism in others.

"Thanks. It usually comes back to haunt me when I'm sloppy."

"You collected those barnacles at high tide. You even went a few feet under water for some samples."

"So."

"So, unlike the barnacles lower down, the top barnacles would not have been covered by water for extended periods of time. They would have been exposed to a lot of air between tides. Poisons in the air should have affected them, too."

"I guess. Depending on the poison."

"Exactly. Depending on the poison. And I was right. The very top barnacles were dead. But the deeper barnacles, the ones covered with water longer and exposed to less air, were alive and the clams, all of which came from further below the high tide level, were alive. So, with nothing showing positive, I did what you told me not to do. I started making assumptions. Like the good scientist I am, I took stock of the facts I knew. The birds and the top barnacles had died, the lower barnacles and clams were alive, there'd been a chemical release six days earlier a half mile upwind and some people may have suffered respiratory problems.

"I took those facts and I made a model out of them. My model was based on the assumption that the same chemicals released by the blast were the ones that killed the birds. My model also said that the chemicals from the blast killed only the birds and the upper barnacles because they broke down in salt water. Maybe they break down in any water, but they certainly do in salt water. My model further said it was a chemical that mainly attacks the respiratory system with an impact on other mucus membranes, much like mustard gas or chlorine gas used in World War One. And, finally, my model said it took these birds six days to die because the chemical affects them differently than it does people. I have no idea when the barnacles died so I could only use the fact that some died and some lived in my model. When I finally put all my model pieces together, you know what I figured out?"

"Saliva." Walt's mouth was dry as he took Harley's analysis to its logical conclusion.

"Excuse me?" The cigar came out of Harley's mouth again.

"The chemical, whatever it is, reacts in salt water and breaks down." Walt spoke rapidly excited by this new discovery. "In the human respiratory system or the human mouth, bodily fluids like saliva break down the chemical. In the process of breaking down, wherever that breakdown occurs, the chemical does its damage. With the deeper barnacles and clams, there was so much water slapping around that the chemical broke down and was washed away before it could kill them.

"Katie was knocked unconscious by the blast. Maybe her mouth was shut, and, with the wind blowing like it was, only a tiny bit of the chemical entered her nostrils. Not enough to kill her, but enough to put her under."

Harley was watching Walt like a professor following a prized student.

"But birds don't have saliva," Walt continued. "Everything about them needs to be light to allow them to fly, so they hardly have any bodily fluids at all. They inhaled the chemicals, but the breakdown, and the resulting damage, was very, very slow. Maybe faster in ones that drank more water, but still very slow overall. Evidently breakdown has to occur in some sort of mucus membrane or some other wet, internal body part like the head of a barnacle. Wet feathers don't provide an adequate exposure pathway for this stuff."

"Walt," Harley's face glowed, "you are very, very sharp."

"But not as sharp as you because you've got one more thing for me."

"I do?" Harley pretended to be surprised.

"What was the chemical, Harley?" Walt's tone of voice was slipping back into the *don't fuck with me* range.

"I can't tell you exactly what it is, Walt, because I don't know. I did some precipitate tests on the roofs of a few of the birds' mouths and some other relatively dry spots and I found something called methyl ethyl chlorinate."

"Methyl ethyl what?"

"Methyl ethyl chlorinate. Don't bother trying to find an MSDS sheet on it. One doesn't exist." Material Safety Data Sheets, called MSDS sheets in the trade, listed the harmful characteristics and suggested precautionary measures for all manufactured chemicals, or at least they were supposed to. "Officially, Walt, the chemical doesn't exist. No one is supposed to make stuff this deadly any more. If I weren't a toxicologist with an extensive, and top secret, history of dealing with shadowy chemicals, I wouldn't even know about it. But it was in your birds."

"So where do we go from here? Can this help Katie?" Walt was suddenly full of hope.

"I'm afraid it's not quite that easy, Walt. Methyl ethyl chlorinate was only part of the chemical equation. While it can be used on its own, that's not the preferred method of employment. Generally, you're supposed to mix it with other chemicals to maximize its effect or to conceal its use, make it look like another poison. Unfortunately, I have no clue what these other chemicals might be. We'll need to plug that data gap before we can go experimenting with antidotes."

"Shit." Walt slumped like a punctured balloon.

"But I *can* tell you something definite." Harley dropped the remainder of his cigar on the dock and ground it to pieces with his toe.

"What's that?" Walt perked up again.

"Methyl ethyl chlorinate wasn't even invented until 1989, much less used in chemical weapons."

"So?"

"The grenades the SCOT found on the beach?"

"Yeah."

"They all dated from 1957." Harley leaned back and crossed his arms in triumph.

"Oh shit. You mean . . ." Walt's voice faded away as comprehension dawned in his eyes.

"It wasn't those grenades that destroyed your family, Walt. There was something else in the dunes. Something no older than 1989."

CHAPTER VIII

Walt knocked on Laste's door and waited respectfully outside until told to come in. He opened the heavy oak door and entered the director of the SCOT's corner office, noting its understated but tasteful décor. As a government bureaucrat himself, he'd seen enough pressboard, fake cherry and worn out carpets to last a life time, but Laste's office looked more like a high quality law firm than any government set-up Walt had ever seen. Perhaps, he thought before his eyes went to the man behind the desk, this was how the upper crust lived inside the beltway. It made sense. Someone had to figure out a way to spend the budget surplus.

"Welcome, Walt," Laste rose to his feet and extended a well-manicured hand towards the biologist. "I'm glad you could find time to see me. I understand Adam is keeping you busy right now."

Laste was, Walt thought, somewhat like his office. Understated. Busy was not an accurate description of what Branson had him doing. Any odd task that hadn't been important enough for anyone to bother with since the SCOT's inception had suddenly become a priority for Walt to complete as soon as possible. Less than a week into his special assignment and he was already being run ragged, making copies of topographic maps, putting together contact lists and alphabetizing files. It was tedious, boring work, designed to annoy him. Still, he was in the office, gaining access to materials and people he couldn't find anywhere else. As long as it might help his daughter, Branson would never be able to wear him out.

"Busy is one word for it, Mr. Laste," he said in a light tone as the two men shook hands and Laste sat down, "but I'm glad to be here all the same."

"And we're glad to have you." Laste was very smooth. No one was glad to have Walt on the Team. The week's wait before this interview was a not so subtle indication of that. "I would like to take this opportunity to extend a personal expression of sympathy to you about the fate of your ex-wife and children," Laste locked his hands together and rested his chin on his two forefingers. "It's admirable that anyone can focus on work after such a tragedy."

Translation, Walt thought: we're stuck with you and can't do anything about it and, on top of that, we know you're here to snoop. "Life goes on," he replied gamely, wondering if Laste would ever invite him to sit down, "it's not going to help anyone for me just to hang around and mope."

"No, moping's never done anyone any good," Laste agreed, "action's the cure." He stroked his chin reflectively. "I'll be blunt with you, Walt," he said as if about to pass on a great revelation, "it's clear why you're here. You're looking for something we might have missed on Nantucket, some scrap of evidence that might help your daughter recover from her horrible accident. That's understandable. In fact, it's admirable. Any father would want to do the same. And I want to make sure we help you as much as we can. But I can't sacrifice SCOT's security to further your search. We run a tight ship here. You're the first non-SCOT member to be on this side of the door. We don't have a published roster and you'd find it nearly impossible to ascertain any of our members' names and addresses if you were on the outside trying to get in. Sort of like a chemical response team equivalent of Delta Force. We value our secrecy. It helps us get our work done safely and efficiently. And we can't loose that no matter how much we might want to help you.

"And I'll be honest about something else." Another revelation. "Not everyone is glad that you're here. As you've probably guessed, Adam would rather cut off his right nut than let you in his office." The analogy sounded crude coming from Laste. "He's very protective of the SCOT. I'm in charge of the big picture, but Adam's the guy who runs the show from day to day. Having you come aboard on such short notice has really thrown a wrench in the very tightly constructed program that he's developed. I apologize if he seems a bit brusque," another understatement, "but to Adam this is much more than a job. I've talked to him about it, but you can't teach an old dog new tricks. Nor, I'm afraid, can you teach those same tricks to some of his pups."

That explained his desk, Walt thought. A sheet of plywood on top of some filing cabinets three steps from the bathroom. He didn't even have his own phone. Another not-so subtle message about how the SCOT felt about him.

"I've instructed my team to be of assistance where possible," continued Laste, "and to consult me when unsure of what they should do. I haven't told them to be friendly. Please don't take it personally," a set of perfectly straight teeth flashed for a second, "we're just trying to keep things on a professional level."

Walt wondered if Laste had ever seen his own daughter lying in a coma. He looked around the office for pictures of the man's family but found none. Maybe the man didn't have a family. "Sure, professional. I understand." Translation: I'll do whatever I can to find any useful information, but we'll all try to be polite about it. "Is that it?" Laste didn't look as if he wanted to chat any longer.

"Yes, that's all," Laste responded, "I just wanted to let you know where things stand. And, on a personal note, to let you know I'll do what I can to help you out." He passed Walt a piece of paper. "Here are my home and beeper numbers. If you're having trouble, call me anytime. Okay?"

Translation, thought Walt again: I don't want whoever forced you on me to claim I'm not being cooperative, but don't even think of calling. "Okay," he managed a cheerful smile, sticking the paper in his dayplanner. "Thanks for taking the time to talk with me. Now I guess I'd better get back to work."

"That's probably a good idea," said Laste as Walt turned to go, "Adam hates slackers." He smiled enigmatically and directed his attention toward a stack of papers on his desk, Walt's problems already forgotten as he tackled some other big picture issue.

His interview with Laste hadn't been particularly surprising, Walt decided as he left the SCOT chief's office. He hadn't expected the men and women of the team to greet him with open arms. Yet, while no one seemed happy to see him there and he was stuck with massive amounts of scut work, he was actually pleasantly surprised at his freedom of movement. He wasn't allowed in the office suite or in any other SCOT area alone. He didn't have a phone and he had to use his own laptop to access his email and the internet. He couldn't touch the team's computers and none of them were going to invite him over for dinner. But his questions were generally answered in great detail. His access to operational files, while always observed by a SCOT member, was nearly unrestricted and his participation in training exercises was actually encouraged. In many ways, despite the cold shoulders, he was just another member of the team.

In fact, Walt remembered as he left Laste's office, he was supposed to be at a planning meeting with the SCOT at that very moment. He lengthened his stride and arrived at the SCOT's situation room just as Branson began to describe a training scenario. For almost an hour, Walt took notes as the SCOT's second in command sketched out the exercise. Then, along with the rest of the Team, he crowded around the easel on which a map of the exercise area was displayed. Walt looked at the map carefully and then reviewed his notes while the SCOT members peppered their leader with technical questions. When there was a break in the questions, he took the opportunity to ask one of his own.

"What type of environmental mitigation have you planned," he queried, somewhat surprised that this issue hadn't been addressed yet.

"Environmental mitigation?" responded Branson, a faint scowl crossing his broad face.

"Yeah, environmental mitigation." Walt's heart was beating faster now. For some reason his question had raised Branson's hackles and he could sense conflict in the air. "From the map, it looks like we're working around a vernal pool area. This time of year, vernal pools are major reproductive sites for all sorts of amphibians and other creatures and they're very susceptible to changes in their environment. Headlights from a vehicle, for example, can disorient turtles and salamanders, which can really screw up their reproductive cycles. A nighttime training exercise like this one is going to have lights all over the place, as well as a bunch of plastic-coated bigfoots stomping around. Whatever's trying to breed in or near the pool is going to be negatively affected." Finishing his brief monologue, Walt could feel everyone's eyes focused on him. The hostility reminded him of seminars he'd held with scallopers and fishermen. No one liked being told how not to run his, or her, business, but Walt couldn't help himself. Wildlife protection was second nature to him, like it or not.

"Salamanders are going to be negatively affected?" Branson's eyes locked on Walt and the two men exchanged stares. "The training area's not a park, there are no known endangered species in the area and the property owner is glad to have us. We can't do anything anywhere without negatively affecting something and if we worried about every bug and bunny we might upset, we'd never get out of the office. Hell, we'd never have built this office in the first place 'cause of all the trees that used to be here."

Branson's closing comment got a snicker of approval from the rest of the SCOT but Walt refused to let it go.

"It's a vernal pool, Adam. It might not be on anyone's list of sensitive areas, but as an experienced wildlife biologist, I can tell you, just by looking at this map, that there are major wildlife issues here. You can't go forward with a training exercise like this without some sort of mitigation plan."

"I can't?" Branson's eyes bored into Walt's. "And who's going to stop me?"

"No one should have to stop you. What you're planning is wrong. But," Walt stared right back at the big man, "if someone needs to stop you, I will. The Federal Department of Fish and Wildlife isn't going to be happy when they find out you've trashed what is probably prime breeding grounds for half a dozen endangered species, whether or not someone's written it down on a list. You can't do it, and I won't let you."

"You arrogant son of a bitch." Branson took a step towards Walt. "You think you can come into my office, snoop around and then tell me what I can and can't do. I'll kick your Yankee ass right out of here if you try to stop me. I planned this exercise and it's going to happen."

Walt stood his ground as Branson approached. "I don't care if Jesus Christ himself planned this exercise, Adam. Without proper environmental mitigation, it's not going to happen. And I'm not going to let you bully me out of your way."

Branson's face turned beet red and his hands clenched and unclenched in violent spasms. "No one," he said in a voice full of fury, "but no one, tells me what to do here."

"I'm telling you. And you'd better listen." Walt could sense, rather than see, the members of the SCOT moving into some higher operational tempo as the tension in the room increased. He hadn't thought Branson would dare to threaten him in public, but perhaps he'd misjudged just how public the SCOT meetings were. "There are some things no one can do. Screwing with significant wildlife resources without proper mitigation is one of them."

Branson opened his mouth to speak, shut it and then, before Walt could move, he launched himself at the biologist. Grabbing Walt's right elbow in a numbingly painful pincher hold, he placed his foot behind Walt's knee and drove the smaller man to the ground. "You son of a bitch!" he muttered through clenched teeth, "no one tells me what to do."

Strong hands grabbed at the two men and someone said something rapidly in Spanish. As Walt's mind struggled to comprehend just how badly his elbow hurt, Branson released him and, with the encouragement of several of the SCOT members, he moved back towards the easel, still swearing under his breath. Other SCOT members hoisted Walt off of the ground and, his feet barely touching the ground, hustled him out of the office.

Several minutes later, Walt's elbow finally stopped throbbing and he began to think straight again. Branson had just assaulted him. If other members of the SCOT hadn't intervened, the redhead might very well have killed him. Though he had never seen it before, Walt was certain he'd seen murder in Branson's eyes back at the briefing room. "He's got a hot temper, huh?" he said in as calm a tone as he could manage.

Bill Pryor glanced quickly around the otherwise now-empty room and nodded his head. "A bit of one, yes."

"You'd think I'd killed his mother or something. All I did was try to save his ass from trouble later on." Walt doubted he'd get kicked off his temporary assignment for this altercation and, if he did stay on, it was important that at least some of the SCOT members not think he was a total idiot.

"I think it goes a bit deeper than that," Pryor said mildly.

"It does?"

"Yeah. Wildlife protection and Adam Branson don't have a very happy relationship, at least as rumor has it. You see, Adam grew up an Army brat and followed his old man into the service. Became a tanker, drove those big 60-ton beasts all over the place. Had some top secret assignments, too, ones that had nothing to do with tanks. As far as I know, he was a damned good soldier. Loved the Army. It was his life. Hooooah, and the whole nine yards.

"When he had twenty-two years in, two years after he could have retired, he arranged a tank training mission for his unit at some Army base in Georgia. He did most of the planning himself. Somehow there was a screw up and his tanks tore the shit out of part of the base that was off limits because of endangered species. Woodpeckers that live in dead trees or something. A bunch of local bird watchers got a hair up their collective asses and had their Congressman get the Fish and Wildlife people involved. The base commander needed to hang someone out to dry so he decided to hang Adam.

"At first they only tried to reprimand him, but Adam would have nothing of it. He argued that he'd done everything right, that the base environmental office had given him the wrong maps, but no one bought his arguments. So he asked for a court-martial. They gave him one and found him guilty of all sorts of stuff. In reality, he probably pissed everyone off with that temper of his and they decided to stick it to him. Whatever their reasons, they wound up kicking him out of the Army and taking away his retirement. From what I've been able to pick up, he took it pretty hard. I know I would."

"What did he do then?" Walt rubbed his elbow thoughtfully. Branson's current profession didn't seem to have much in common with being a tank officer in the Army.

"I'm not sure. He doesn't talk about himself much and, with a man like Adam, you don't want to poke around too much. My guess is that he worked for the CIA or the DEA or something. He's fluent in Spanish and had a top-secret clearance from the Army. Court-martial or not, the government doesn't let that sort of talent go to waste. Hell, for some work, a court-martial might even be considered a plus."

"Well, whatever happened to him years ago doesn't give him the right to beat the shit out of me," Walt said somewhat petulantly.

"No one's arguing that it does. But when you start talking wildlife protection to Adam, you'd better be prepared to see him get upset. Maybe you really were trying to do him a favor or maybe you were just trying to get under his skin," Pryor voice had hardened, "but regardless, don't expect any 'thank you's'. From him or from anyone else."

The tone in Pryor's voice told Walt that nobody would back up his story should he complain to Laste. They didn't want him here and they weren't going to narc on Branson just to make an outsider happy. Upon reflection, Walt couldn't say he blamed them. He was, after all, an interloper in their world. Branson's considerable abilities in conducting response actions was probably more important to the SCOT members than anything else. That made sense. With the wrong guidance during a real response operation, someone could easily get hurt or killed. The positions were clear. He was still with the Team, but he was on his own.

Two months later, Walt had still been unable to learn a single fact that shed any light on Katie's condition. To some extent, he knew, he was operating with a handicap. Although it was frustrating not to use all the knowledge he had, Walt had promised Harley he'd remain silent about the methyl ethyl chlorinate. As Harley had pointed out, Walt's knowledge of such an ultra-secret poison would probably result in more restrictions on his activities with the SCOT than would be worth any information he would be likely to gain. Accordingly, the two men had agreed to tell everyone, including Janice and Tillison, that a virus had killed the birds.

Disheartened by his lack of progress, every weekend Walt flew back up to Boston to spend Friday night, all day Saturday and most of Sunday with his little girl. He read to her, sang to her, talked to her, did anything he thought might get a response. But she never responded. She just lay there, immobile on her bed, her favorite stuffed animals, assembled by Walt when he'd help empty Julia's house shortly after her death, piled by her pillow in a vain attempt to make the room homey.

Late Sunday afternoon, Walt would lock the room's door and slowly, almost ritualistically, give his daughter a bath. He'd pull the sheets back and start with her toes, massaging as much as he was cleaning. He tried to squeeze life up through Katie's legs, torso and arms into her dull brown eyes, trying, unsuccessfully, to convince himself that her hair hadn't lost its luster and that her limbs were not becoming increasingly frail. No matter what he did, nothing worked. His daughter remained alive but lifeless, exercised daily by physical therapists and fed through a tube. By the time he finished the bath, rearranging the way Katie lay to avoid bedsores and repiling the stuffed animals in what he always hoped was a more stimulating display, Walt would be a wreck, his cheeks wet with tears and his breath coming fitfully between gigantic sobs.

Almost as if following a script, just as Walt put the last teddy bear on the pile, there would be a knock on the door. Walt would open it and Dr. Bocall would enter. Together they'd stand at the foot of Katie's bed, tears still streaming down Walt's cheeks. After five minutes, Walt would pick up his overnight bag from the table, put Katie's spoon in his pocket, and gently touch the doctor on the shoulder.

"Take good care of her, Doc, okay?"

"Okay." Their eyes never met. Both men knew there was little that could be done until an antidote was found and that the clock was constantly ticking on the little girl's chances for a complete recovery.

With one lingering backwards glance at his daughter, Walt would leave the room and head back to DC, his hopes of finding that elusive needle in the haystack dimming by the moment.

CHAPTER IX

19 JUNE
LOVETT ARSENAL, KANSAS

Ann Glen plucked nervously at her scarf. The director of the Federal Environmental Protection Agency, she had become something of a cover-girl for both single mothers–Ann was divorced and had sole custody of her two young sons–and professional women. Slim, attractive, and in her mid 40's, Ann ran a federal department in an administration dominated by older white males. Not only did she run it, but she ran it hard, never sacrificing scientific positions for political ones. Her integrity and thoroughness had brought her great respect among environmental professionals. Her enthusiasm and determination had brought her almost equal enmity from much of the nation's more conservative sectors.

In any case, whether acting as a Cosmo-era professional cover-girl, an environmental advocate or a regulatory scourge, Ann always felt she had to look the part of a woman who could do it all. Hence, the decorative scarf she was wearing despite the heat. It was the closest thing the director had in her wardrobe to a power tie.

"You never get used to it, do you Ann?" The slightly pudgy woman at Glen's elbow, almost as formally dressed, spoke in a lyrical, musical voice.

"No, Susan. Not really," replied Glen as she watched the TV crews set up near the podium. "Meetings I can do. One on ones with the President don't faze me. But put me in front of television cameras and I start to freak out that everyone's going to compare me to Michelle Pfeiffer, that they'll judge me based on how good an actress I am rather than on what policy I'm promoting." Amongst those few who followed environmental issues closely, Glen knew that this fear wasn't valid, but for the vast numbers of Americans who couldn't even spell EPA, how she looked on television was of paramount importance. Glen blamed it on the modern TV culture, but even she wasn't above using her good looks to help support a scientific discovery.

"Well, at least you compare more favorably than some of us." Susan Spock was the Assistant Secretary of Defense for the Environment. Long ago she'd accepted her poor appearance on camera, but she'd never learned to like it.

"You're a sweetheart, Susan," Glen laughed. "How long before you think we're ready to go live?" The EPA official was going to give a speech commending the Defense Department for its hazardous waste reduction success at the Arsenal. Spock was then going to give a separate speech announcing the start of a new EPA/DOD initiative destined to increase the Defense Department's cleaning solvent recovery rate to almost one hundred percent. For an organization with as many, and as varied, maintenance activities as the Pentagon, such an initiative was a major, and somewhat controversial, undertaking. While environmentalists loved the plan, a small but vocal number of professional soldiers and right-wing talk show hosts claimed that it was just one more example of feel-good environmental concerns interfering with the Pentagon's primary mission of force projection. Mission readiness would suffer, they argued, because soldiers would be more worried about meeting recycling and waste reduction goals than about making sure their equipment was properly maintained. As a direct result of the poorly maintained equipment, this argument ran, American servicemembers would be hurt the next time they went into harm's way.

Both women were aware of this resistance and they knew that the speeches they were going to make would not be received without, at best, considerable skepticism. But as harbingers of change in a shifting world, they were both used to it. This wasn't the military of the 1950's, they'd point out. It was a new world, with new norms. No longer was it appropriate to dump waste engine oil down the drain, throw half-full paint cans in the dumpster or empty battery acid containers behind the maintenance garage. The military, like the rest of America, was cleaning up its act and solvent recovery, where special machines in the maintenance facilities would collect and reuse spent solvents, was integral to DOD's future environmental efforts.

As the two women chatted, a motorcycle passed by a block away, just outside the secured riverside briefing area, its rumble cutting through the clutter of conversations in the small crowd gathered around the two women. Glen raised her eyebrows expressively as the cyclist shifted gears and the rumble changed into a full-throated roar that overwhelmed all conversation. The cyclist changed gears yet again and the rumble drifted away as the bike drove on.

"The guy must think he's flying an F-18," Glen joked. "If he comes back while we're speaking, no one will be able to hear a thing."

"Gee, do you think we could get him to do that?" asked Spock in mock seriousness. "If nothing else, it would shorten the question and answer session."

Both women chuckled and then went back to giving their speeches a final review as the press coordinator flashed them a five-minute warning signal.

Glen squinted at her papers and wiped at her right eye. Judging by the sting, a speck of dust must have gotten in behind her contact lens. She rubbed a little harder and felt the irritation spread to her left eye. This was a hell of a time for her allergies to start acting up. She turned to Spock. "My eyes just started bugging me. There must be pollen or something floating around."

"Yeah, my eyes are hurting too," Spock replied, pulling out a silk handkerchief and dabbing at the corners of her eyesockets where small tears were beginning to form.

Next to Spock, the press coordinator had removed his glasses and was rubbing his eyes with the back of his left hand. Behind him, the Assistant Director was doing the same thing. Glen looked down from the podium. The entire crowd of several dozen was dabbing at their eyes.

"Something's not right, Susan," she said in a shaky voice. "Everyone can't be suffering from pollen allergies." Tears were forming fairly quickly in her eyes now, making the Assistant Secretary appear slightly out of focus, and the insides of her nostrils were starting to sting.

Spock looked around. "Shit, Ann. You're right." As she spoke, the back of her throat began to sting. "Something's definitely wrong here." The burning sensation in her eyes had increased to the point of sharp pain and the stinging in her throat was moving down beyond her trachea. She instinctively grabbed at her throat and began rubbing it. "My throat's hurting now." Even as she said those words, a painful spasm racked her lungs and she wheezed for breath, grasping more forcefully at her throat.

On the edge of the small crowd, beyond the camera crews, Glen noticed people starting to fall to their knees. Panic spread as people ran blindly about, tripping over those who had already fallen. Shouts and shrill screams pierced the air.

"I can't see! Oh God, help me. I can't see!" It sounded like the press director's voice. Glen turned just in time to see his blurry figure totter and then fall off the edge of the makeshift stage on which they had been sitting. Her own hands now clawed at her throat, as the fire began to consume her. The pain in her eyes was unbearable, the world a blurred collection of light and dark images. She stumbled over something and fell, screaming for help but hearing the words come out as meaningless, animal-like grunts. On her knees now, Glen reached out with one hand, trying to feel her way through the cacophony of terrified people she could hear but not see. She felt the hem of a dress on a motionless figure sprawled across the stage. Susan Spock had been the only other woman by the podium.

"Susan?" she tried to ask. "Susan?" But even Glen couldn't understand her own voice. Her lungs were no longer functioning, no longer pumping life-giving air into her body. Instead they were exploding with pain, the agony dwarfing every physical sensation she had ever felt.

"Oh, God," the Director of the EPA, the divorced mother of two, the environmental professional, prayed without saying an intelligible word. "Oh, God. Please let it end. Please make the pain stop."

And, in one overwhelming flash, it did.

CHAPTER X

19 JUNE, 2000
WASHINGTON, DC

Walt had just returned to his temporary desk at the SCOT office with a fresh cup of coffee when Branson burst into the crowded room.

"Okay, folks, we've got a Code One. Briefing in the Sit Room in five minutes. We're flying out of National in forty minutes. Pryor!" Energy radiated from the big man–he was in his element.

"Yes." The lanky West Virginian swung his feet off of his desk. Like Branson, Pryor was a man who thrived on action. Smart, athletic, and always ready with a joke or a smile, he had been the only SCOT member who seemed at ease with Walt. And, as the person in charge of managing the SCOT's extensive supply requirements, he'd been able to teach the biologist some important logistical tricks to help better equip his own response team.

"Find out who's here and tell 'em to be in the Sit Room in five minutes. For everyone else, initiate a top priority recall with our rendezvous point at the Dulles gear locker."

To expedite long-distance response actions, the team kept full sets of response equipment ready to go at both Dulles and National airports. When a call came into the office, the duty officer, usually either Branson or Pryor, with a rotating schedule during non-business hours, would ask some basic questions. If the situation warranted, the officer would order a plane or helicopter readied at the appropriate airport. All available team members would receive a quick briefing at the SCOT office while a recall went out for members who were not present. Anyone not officially on leave was expected to be at the airport, sober, in forty minutes. If, for whatever reason, that were not possible, they had authorization to board any flight anywhere else that would get them to the response site as quickly as possible.

No more than three members of the team were ever on leave at the same time, and rarely was it more than one. This time, in the middle of a regular working day, all twelve men and women were still at their desks and they quickly gathered in the spartan Situation Room for Laste's initial briefing.

"This is big, people." Laste's voice was much quieter than Branson's and less overtly authoritative, but he spoke clearly and with confidence. "About twenty minutes ago, some chemical release appears to have occurred at the Lovett Arsenal just outside of Kansas City, Kansas. We're still getting confirmation, but it seems like both Susan Spock and Ann Glen are among the roughly sixty people believed dead." As one, the team took a collective gasp, both at the number of dead and at the identities of the two most prominent casualties. "Local emergency response teams have secured the site and are assessing the victims. If they can determine that there is no exposure threat, they'll probably start removing the bodies before we get there. At this point, all that's known is that the contaminant appears to be airborne and to impact the respiratory system, eyes, throat and other wet or moist body parts." The SCOT members didn't bother writing this fact down. A whole host of poisons fit this description, from irritants such as CS, known as crowd suppressant or tear gas, to the deadly chlorine gas of World War One. "Because the Armory has a history of explosive hazards, the Post Commander has asked for our assistance. Plus, some of the people who initially responded to the incident have reported some sort of blast crater in the area upwind from the site indicating that there may have been a chemical munitions explosion.

"We'll know more by the time we get to the airport," Laste concluded, "and still more when we get on site. But our mission will probably be to conduct a UXO sweep." Unexploded ordinance, UXO in day to day conversation, was the left-over bombs and rockets discarded or otherwise abandoned by the military at ranges, training sites and battlefields throughout the world. While some of these dumping grounds were known and well marked, others remained unknown until accidentally, and often tragically, discovered by soldiers on training missions or contractors sinking foundations. "The Arsenal borders the Kansas River and the water's been eating away at a known ordinance dump site for quite a while. The Corps of Engineers is running a clean-up operation there. The biggest problem they've run into are sodium canisters. If the canisters are cracked and water starts seeping in, they can explode. That becomes a real problem if there's other nasty stuff nearby. The Corps will have its project manager and some consultants available by phone once we're airborne to answer questions. It's too early to say for sure, but it's likely that whatever happened today is somehow connected with something that was dumped at the arsenal some time ago, whether or not it is in the area where the Corps is working.

"Now grab your gear and hustle out to the vans. We've already initiated the response calls, so no one will be expecting any of you home for dinner. When it is appropriate, you'll be able to make your own calls." Personal calls were forbidden from the start of an operation until either Laste or Branson decided the situation had progressed enough to lift the initial veil of security.

"Mr. Crawler?"

"Yes, Sir?" Like the bona fide members of the SCOT, Walt sometimes called Laste 'Sir.' He still hadn't figured out what to call Branson.

"You'll come with me. Pryor, you stay by me and Mr. Crawler, too."

Walt cringed internally. Even in the midst of a fatal response operation, one of the team's first priorities was to make sure he had a shadow. How much would he really learn from this response if they continued to treat him as a leper rather than one of their own?

When the team landed at Kansas City International Airport, a state police bus and three large vans were waiting on the tarmac. Walt was impressed with how little supervision was needed as, with the speed and efficiency of a highly choreographed dance routine, the team stored its equipment in the vans, boarded the bus and roared off.

Once on the bus, Laste turned to Walt. "What you're seeing, Mr. Crawler," he said in a voice that betrayed no emotions, "is the result of countless drills and never-ending vigilance. When it's time to go to work for real, there's no room for mistakes and no time for delays. As we say in the military, the more we sweat in peace, the less we bleed in war. And make no mistake about it, Mr. Crawler," Laste's voice had become solemn, "this is, in its own special way, a war." He looked out the window and seemed to loose his train of thought for a moment. "A war," he repeated as if speaking to himself.

Walt spent the 30 minute bus ride to the Lovett Arsenal lost in a maelstrom of emotions. He only vaguely followed the myriad of conversations and briefings going on around him as team members compared notes, reviewed information and issued instructions. This must have been what it'd been like two months earlier on their trip to Nantucket. The business-like clamor of the team getting ready, the tense looks as they adjusted their gear for the first site entry, and the horrible truth of the dead and mangled bodies waiting for them on the dunes. Horrible, but not personal. To some, Susan Spock, Ann Glen and the other dead were loved ones, friends, relatives. They were the Julias and Sarahs and Tracys and Katies of the Lovett Arsenal. For someone, for lots of someones, the world had ended as abruptly as Walt's had two months before. But for the Pentagon's Special Chemical Operations team, it was just one more response. Professionally, Walt knew that the detachment was necessary. He'd done it himself on operations. It wasn't that he hadn't cared, it was that he knew he'd crack if he let himself take it personally. But now, this mission-oriented detachment chilled him to the bone.

Maybe Branson and Laste had been right in keeping him off to the side in a strict observer status. The last thing the SCOT needed was for someone to snap during a response operation. It was almost too trite to be true, but one wrong move, something as simple as not using a non-sparking brass drum wrench to open up a rogue 55 gallon drum of unknown wastes, could result in a complete disaster.

Looking out the window, watching the countryside roll by, Walt realized he'd been gripping Katie's silver spoon tightly in his right hand. Over time, caressing the spoon had become a habit to soothe him when he felt alone or lost. Thinking of the bodies awaiting them just down the road, Walt felt completely and absolutely alone. Despite the dozen men and women sharing the bus with him, the only people who would be able to understand his misery were those who, like him, would never be able to forget how this day had changed their lives.

A sentry at the gate waved the small convoy through and Walt recognized the clean cut brick buildings so characteristic of an Army post. Strangely, once past the horde of reporters and photographers clustered by the gate, there was complete stillness. No cars moved on the streets, no children played in the yards, no soldiers marched or ran from building to building. With laundry drying on outdoor racks and bicycles randomly scattered on lawns and driveways, it looked like a neutron bomb had struck, removing the people and leaving only their inanimate belongings behind. The enormity of the disaster started swelling in Walt's brain. Somehow, in just a few hours, the Army had evacuated what appeared to be the entire Arsenal. Thousands of residents and workers ordered to move out, just like that.

He shuddered. No one made such heroic efforts unless the threat was both real and imminent.

Two miles down the road, the convoy pulled into an empty parking lot bordered on three sides by one story concrete barracks, now, as evidenced by the signs posted in front of them, used as office space. Through a gap in the buildings, Walt saw another parking lot, this one crowded with vehicles and people. Laste and Branson were doing it the right way, Walt thought, keeping the team away from the rest of the circus that was unfolding at the site. Other than specific coordination issues, the SCOT would probably operate entirely on its own, just as it had on Nantucket. When they were done, they'd turn the site over to local authorities, pack their gear and return to DC. The less interaction with the locals, the happier both Branson and Laste would be.

The team filed out of the buses and, with the help of two sergeants assigned to the Arsenal, began to unpack the vans and set up a response center. Handling logistics, Branson had decided, was the only acceptable place for the biologist to be during an operation so Walt was just as busy as anyone else. It made sense, he had to admit. It was the logistics, as Laste always said, that would make or break a response. Ensuring there was plenty of ice water and cooling packs to combat the heat fatigue the team would feel in the summer warmth, having plenty of good, easily consumed food ready when team members had time to eat, keeping track of information coming in from a variety of sources and making sure there was adequate and steady electricity were all simple, but vitally important, response considerations. To understand those elements was to understand the heart of any emergency response program.

While the team set up, Walt saw Laste and Branson walk over to the neighboring parking lot where the other vehicles and people were. Fifteen minutes later, as the team was finalizing its preparations, the two men returned.

"Okay, men, huddle up," bellowed Branson in a voice that needed no microphone. "You two," he pointed to the sergeants, "can go now. You know Captain Bulty?" Both men nodded. "Good. Go to him and stay with him until we don't need you anymore. If we need to contact either of you, we'll call the Captain's cellular phone. As of now, you're under our operational control. You don't leave Captain Bulty's side or get replaced by anyone else without my or Mr. Laste's written say so. Got it?" The men nodded again and ran across the parking lot, eager to get as far away as possible from whatever deadly work the SCOT was going to do.

"It's bad," Branson said bluntly as the SCOT members gathered around him. "We've got sixty-one people dead, including Ann Glen and Susan Spock, and another thirty-eight in the hospital. It appears that an airborne respiratory poison of some kind swept in suddenly, did its damage and, just as quickly, dissipated with the wind. The dead were all here." Branson displayed a large scale map of the Armory and pointed to a colored area representing the site of the day's press conference. "No one in this shaded area lived through the exposure. As far as we can tell, the people hospitalized all came from these areas." Branson tapped the colored dots representing hospitalized people with his fingers. "As you can see, the further you get from the site, the fewer casualties, hence, my thoughts about dissipation. But that isn't a certainty. We could have fewer casualties because there were fewer people exposed. Or maybe both.

"Now," he jabbed at the map again, "the wind's been blowing from the northeast at roughly six miles an hour all day. That indicates the blast occurred up here, somewhere, which coincides with word of a crater somewhere in this location." A sweeping motion of his ham-like hand covered the top half of the map. "The Corps of Engineers is running its remediation project here," another jab, "and there are several fill areas around here," more taps, "but what we're looking for may not be associated with any of that.

"At this point," Branson's back was to the map now, indicating that the rest of his instructions would not be terrain specific, "we basically don't know what the hell's going on. Readings at the press conference site are completely normal, both in air and soil samples. Whatever came through does not seem to have left anything behind. The fear, of course, is that what happened this morning could happen once more, so the Army has vacated the entire base." This wasn't news to anyone. "And we've asked all other response personnel to leave the area until we identify the threat.

"What we're going to do," Branson began passing out small versions of the board-mounted map, "is to move upwind from the podium in designated lanes until we find the cause of this mess. Then we'll evaluate the threat. If it's relatively safe, we'll let the locals remove the remaining bodies. If it's absolutely safe, we'll let the commander reopen the base. But it's our call.

"Look at the maps I just gave you." Walt had no map. He was still an outsider to Branson, a walking, talking security risk. "If you have a green map, raise your hand." Four members did so. "You men have the green lane. Yellow?" Another four were grouped by lane and then the same for blue. Branson regularly shuffled members around during all aspects of the SCOT's work. Cross-training, he emphasized, was a crucial factor for success.

"You'll operate independently, at your own speed. Two men in, two on backup. Charlie and I will be handling the radios. If we run into trouble, we'll redeploy as needed. If you see anything noteworthy, let us know. Keep a close eye on your air readings. If oxygen starts to drop, that means something else is taking its place so let us know immediately.

"Until we've identified the threat, we'll be in Level A full dressout. We'll dress down if the situation allows. If the wind direction shifts, our response site and decon area might be threatened by a blast and we'll cease operations. The post will turn the lights on at dark, so we can work through the night and we've got plenty of portable lanterns, if needed.

"Any questions?" Branson didn't look surprised when the team members remained silent. They were trained to understand situations like this without the need for much explanation and they'd been given detailed information on the Arsenal's history and physical layout on the plane. If something new popped up, they had radios.

"Crawler?"

Walt's head jerked up and he looked at Branson, trying to read behind his expressionless eyes. "Yes?"

"You'll stay right next to me. Understand?"

"Next to you. Got it." It wasn't worth getting upset about being treated like an errand boy at a time like this.

"One last thing." Branson had a flair for the theatrical, saving the biggest punch for last. "All of you look at this TV for a moment." He popped a tape in the VCR and the TV screen showed a full-face close-up of the EPA administrator adjusting her scarf and talking to someone. The camera slowly zoomed out, showing Susan Spock and several others on the stage. A babble of voices came out of the TV, occasionally drowned out by the cameraman or his assistant as they checked their equipment. A motorcycle roared over the voices and then the babble returned.

"Damn, I've got something in my eye," the cameraman's assistant said.

"That's too bad." The cameraman sounded unconcerned, focusing on a tight shot of Spock, Glen and the press chief. "Two minutes to go."

A muffled cough came over the TV's speakers.

"Knock it off," the cameraman said, "we're going live in 90 seconds and we don't want your coughing in the background."

"Jesus, my eyes are killing me," the assistant's voice was beginning to sound worried. On screen, Spock and Glen were dabbing at their own eyes. Another cough and the camera began to shake a bit.

"My eyes are starting to hurt, too." The cameraman's voice.

"Christ, I can't see shit," the assistant's voice was raspy, "and my throat hurts. What the fuck's going on?"

In the background, a clamor of voices was beginning to rise, punctuated with screams and shouts. The picture on the TV was getting shakier, but even so the team members could see Spock and Glen acting increasingly frantic on the screen. Spock's hand went to her throat and she fell down and out of the camera's shaky view. As the cries and screams increased to a deafening crescendo, the screen flashed the blue of the sky and then filled with a dull black object.

"That's a shoe," Branson narrated, his deep voice contrasting with the shrill noise from the TV.

The screams grew louder still, before with stunning swiftness, the TV went silent.

Branson flicked off the TV. "That, gentlemen, is what we're up against. So pay attention. Now move out."

The team was good, Walt thought. While no one could fail to be impressed by the short video, none of them seemed rattled. For them it was a risk that went with the job.

Walt reviewed his own feelings. Surprisingly, he was not as torn up as he would have expected. Julia and the twins hadn't died like that. For them, it has been one microsecond of explosive pain and then nothing. For Katie, it had been a much shorter and, fortunately, less lethal exposure. It was a horrible video, but it was someone else's pain, not his, Walt reflected as he sat in the response van watching the blank video monitors.

It took the green team just forty minutes to find the blast site.

"Adam, we've got a blast crater." It was Givens' voice.

"Where is it?"

"We're about thirty meters northeast of Point G-7." The maps Branson had handed out had alpha-numeric grid coordinates. "The crater's about two feet across. It's a round circle maybe two feet deep and then you hit water. Clods or dirt have been tossed up to fifty feet away. No buildings in the immediate area so I can't tell if any windows have been broken." The distance to broken windows was a field expedient method of measuring the power of an explosion.

"Any obvious threats?"

"None that I can see. But I can't see through the dirt or the water. No strange bumps in the ground, though."

"Any stressed vegetation or dead animals?" Toxins and poisons often left a tell-tale marker of dead or dying natural resources.

"Nothing that we've seen so far."

"Okay, I'll mark the spot and pass the information to the rest of the team. You guys snap some pictures of the crater but otherwise steer clear for the time being and continue the sweep. From the looks of it, with the wind direction and lack of buildings to block the airflow to the podium, this has got to be it. But we'll go another hour or two to make sure nothing else is obvious out there." Branson was in no hurry. Until they learned more about the poisons, he would take nothing for granted. An old chlorine gas grenade, for example, could have been tossed a hundred feet by the blast and then might have rolled two hundred more. Unlikely, but Branson had seen stranger things happen and to ignore the unlikely was to court disaster.

After an hour passed with none of the teams finding any new threats, Branson called them back to the response center. "We're going to break for two hours," he told the sweating responders, "that'll give the locals time to finish removing the bodies. In the meantime, you all look at these." He passed out pictures of the crater Givens had taken with a digital camera. "This is where the blast occurred. We need to learn why and determine if another release is likely before we can turn the site over to local authorities and allow the commander to open up the post again."

The team members looked at the photos silently. Once again, as expected, Walt hadn't received a handout. He wasn't one of them. While the others studied the photos, Walt studied their faces. This was, he knew, the most dangerous part of the operation. Determining exactly what had exploded that afternoon and if it were likely to happen again would require getting up close and personal with whatever was leftover in the crater. It could be nothing or, not as likely but still a distinct possibility, there could be something else lurking just under the soil or beneath the murky water. Something as unstable as whatever had exploded that afternoon. Something just waiting for a slight vibration or a magnetic anomaly to set it off.

This, of course, was what the SCOT was on site for, the potential combination of unstable explosives and deadly chemicals that required their unique skills. Whoever poked around the crater needed to instinctively know the difference between a rusty arming pin and an old nail, needed to be able to identify a hundred types of munitions from the tiny portions that might be exposed and needed the confidence to make decisions about probing in the dirt when a mistake could mean death. Few people had those skills. Walt looked around at the men and women he'd learned to respect, if not like, during the past several weeks and hoped they were up to the challenge.

He wondered what Branson would do next. Walt knew the team had a robot with cameras and radio-controlled sampling devices for remote entry and assessment, but he also knew those robots always performed better in the promotional videos than in real life. He peeked over Pryor's shoulder at the collection of pictures the West Virginian held. They showed a flat expanse of cut grass marked only by one small crater and a number of scattered clods of earth. While the crater looked entirely unremarkable, Walt knew Branson would want soil and water samples from its interior. They would also use metal detectors throughout the whole area by the crater to make sure no other bombs lurked under the ground.

Using the metal detectors on the grassy area around the crater would be safe enough. If mowing the lawn once a week didn't set anything off, hand-held detectors shouldn't pose much of a problem. It was the work immediately adjacent to the crater that would be dicey. Something, for some reason, had already gone wrong there. If he were in charge, Walt decided, he'd use the robot. If that didn't work, then he'd send in a man. Not a woman, he thought after reviewing the video in his mind. Enough of them had died already.

Walt looked at Branson, hulking over the rest of the team like a grizzly bear on steroids. He'd send in a man first, Walt knew. Unless the threat were far more obvious than it seemed here, the big man would want the feeling of commanding a person, not a machine.

"I've got some plans from the Post's Public Works." Branson passed out another sheaf of papers. "The buildings in this part of the Post are Vietnam era. Before that it was wetlands, with a stream running right where our crater is. That means this whole area is fill, and fill from an old arsenal can be just about anything. One possibility, and this is what the Corps has found at its site by the river, is that there was a container of sodium here. Somehow water came into contact with the sodium and, boom, we've got our explosion. Any poison in or near that container when it exploded would have been released by the blast, too.

"We're going to grid off the entire grassy area around the crater with strings and pegs four feet to a side, with the crater inside a central grid that acts as a guide. Then we'll use metal detectors to clear each grid square, working from the outside towards the crater. If you find anything suspect, flag it and move on. When we're done with the sweep, we'll probe the flags. When we've IDed all the flags, we'll work on the crater grid.

"Givens, you'll be the first one on that grid."

Givens straightened his back self-consciously. The youngest and least experienced team member, it was something of an honor to be chosen to go first. He nodded at the team leader. He could handle it.

Branson nodded back at Givens and finished his speech. "There's chow over by the bus. Make sure you drink lots of fluids and give your gear another check. We'll meet back here in two hours. In the meantime, Rodriquez, you give me a hand setting up some cameras by the field to feed the van's monitoring system. I want to be able to see everything that's going on." He didn't have to tell them not to leave the area. They were pros and had done this before. To a large extent, they operated on autopilot.

When the team gathered back together, Walt was surprised to see Branson single him out of the group. "Crawler, grab your gear. You can help with the grid sweep. You can work with Pryor and Givens."

There must be nothing to see, Walt figured, if Branson was sending him away from the response van. Regardless, he welcomed the chance to suit up and actually work with the team, even on something as mundane as a metal detector sweep. He could be an observer forever and still not get the operational insights he'd pick up from two hours in Level A with these people. "Sounds good to me," he replied. Walt shot a look at his two new partners and was pleased to see neither looked unhappy with their assignment.

Once they were dressed, the first team members began a slow, deliberate waltz through the grids. Still in their three sub-groups broken down into operating units of two, they moved ponderously around the field, working their way carefully towards the crater. Even at night, the summer heat was draining, and Branson made sure he rotated the teams often enough to maintain a high level of attention. The SCOT leader was calling all the right shots, Walt decided between sweeps as he slumped, suit half off and drinking a soda, by the decon line. Everything was slow, safe and by the book. Except Walt would have planned to use a robot for the initial crater work.

When it was his, Pryor's and Givens' turn with the detectors, Walt shrugged into the self-contained breathing apparatus and heavy plastic suit with practiced ease. Like almost any job that appeared exciting, hazardous incident response operations looked more glamorous the further away one got. On the spot, they were sweaty, boring, ball-busting activities that only got exciting when the shit hit the fan. It was, Walt reflected, remembering Laste's analogy, like war in more ways than one.

Walt was first on the detector. For ten minutes, as Givens and Pryor hovered nearby, he neatly swept grid after grid from corner to corner. Nothing. The sweat poured in small rivers down his body, stinging at his eyes and making small pools at his toes and fingertips. It was the eyes that bothered him the most. Unable to wipe the sweat away with his rubber suit encased hands, he just had to bear it. Psychologically, though, it was much worse. The irritation in his eyes, and the almost overwhelming urge to wipe at them, reminded him of the two women in the video, Spock and Glen. Their last moments had been spent trying to rub a deadly pain from their eyes and Walt's current discomfort was an unpleasant reminder of how close he could be to death himself.

Walt passed the detector to Givens who, ten minutes later, passed it to Pryor. None of the men found anything. Looking around the field, Walt was surprised at the lack of flags on the ground. Over the years, he would have thought all sorts of nuts, bolts, shell casings, coins and assorted metal bric-a-brac would have worked their way under the dirt as soldiers walked back and forth over the grass. If the fill were contaminated, there should be even more detections. But there were next to none, which Walt thought was odd.

The lack of hits made the sweep much easier, though. In relatively short order every grid but the center one with the crater had been swept and the small number of hits investigated and found harmless. Three quarters, five pennies, two wingnuts and an unfired .223 caliber bullet for an M-16 rifle was the extent of the field's treasures.

"Okay, gentlemen, we're doing the crater now, Branson told the SCOT as the team huddled by the response van during a break. "Crawler, you'll sit this one out again. Givens, you'll do a complete sweep of the grid, working up to the edge of the crater and then down. Pryor, you stay back and upwind. We all know this is the dangerous part. If Givens finds anything, he'll motion you to flag it. Move back when you're done. I want you at least twenty feet away. After fifteen minutes, you'll switch with Givens. If he's not done, finish the sweep. If he is done, sweep again. We're going to do everything twice here."

Branson was making the right moves, Walt thought. Safety in redundancy. While he could applaud most of Branson's professional methods, Walt was disappointed at being put back on the sidelines. For one brief period of time, suited up and sweating with the rest of them, he'd finally felt like he belonged with the SCOT, that he was, possibly, about to break the barrier between them. Walt would have welcomed a thaw in his relationship with his coworkers. But that was not to be. Branson had seen to that.

"When you guys have done 30 minutes, or the second sweep is done, we'll move Rodriquez and Taylor in to probe any hits you might have found and to start taking samples. Blue Team, you're at decon. Yellow, you're on backup. When Taylor and Rodriquez are done, we'll break again and review what we've found. We'll also run some field tests on our samples, which'll help us determine our next steps.

"If all goes well and we don't run into any problems, we could wrap this baby up in a couple of hours. If not, or we start acting tired, we'll be here longer.

"If there are no questions, saddle up."

Walt returned to the control van with Laste and Branson. On the van's monitor screens, now no longer blank, he saw Givens and Pryor, carrying a detector and a box of flags, walk slowly towards the crater. In the big oversuits, everything was done in slow motion. As the two men walked across the field, two more men, Taylor and Rodriquez appeared at the edge of the screen. Other screens showed the backup and decon teams staged at their respective positions. All systems go, thought Walt, wishing once more Branson would use a robot.

Paul Givens stopped at the string marking the center grid and turned to look at Pryor, standing patiently twenty feet away. He gave an awkward thumbs up signal, flipped the metal detector on and swung it over the line. Unless he had to, he'd stay off of his sound activated radio. Too much message traffic just confused things. Even though his heart was racing, his hands were steady and his eyes were focused on the detector's arrow. Like everyone on the team, he knew that, at this most dangerous part of the operation, any twitch by the arrow was cause for alarm. If there were other bombs around, they'd probably be in this grid.

He wondered briefly, as sweat stung at his eyes, why Branson had chosen him for this task. As the youngest, most inexperienced member of the team, he relished the chance to play such an important role, but, nonetheless, others probably would have been better choices. Rodriquez, for example, had a sixth sense about what was dangerous. Perhaps, Givens thought, if he spent enough time doing things like this, he'd develop a sixth sense also. Perhaps that was Branson's plan.

Five minutes into the sweep, he had finished the level part of the grid. "Finished the grass," he spoke into the microphone perched by his mouth, "Nothing there. I'm moving into the crater now."

"Okay," replied Pryor. "Be careful." Unless there were an emergency, no one else would transmit on that channel. "This is why you get paid the big bucks."

Givens knelt by the edge of the crater and studied it visually for a few minutes. Although the condensation in his clear plastic face shield blurred his view a bit, nothing looked out of place. There were no odd metallic protrusions, no shiny glints reflecting the beam of his headlamp, no unnatural and uniformly round clumps of earth. It looked, above the water at any rate, just like a bomb crater should look.

He swung the detector over the hole's edge and, keeping the detection plate just above the dark soil, began to run it over the crater's sides. His throat was dry and his hands were shaking a bit, but Givens attributed those sensations to the fast pace of the operation. Anybody in his shoes would have been a little nervous.

The needle pegged to the far right and Givens' heart leapt to his throat. There was something fairly big under the dirt by the water's edge! He ran the detector around in small circles, watching the needle fluctuate.

"I've got something, Bill," he said in a husky voice. "It's on my side of the crater, apparently right at the water level, maybe extending a bit below it. It seems to be longish and relatively narrow, like an 81 millimeter mortar shell, but a bit bigger."

"Okay, Paul. Good job," Pryor's voice was husky too. There was no use pretending he wasn't scared. "I'm coming up with the flags now. Just . . ."

Before Pryor could finish his sentence a powerful explosion ripped through the earth in front of where his partner was kneeling. Givens' body was picked up and hurled to the side by the explosion like a small child's, his thick protective suit ripped to shreds and his limbs twisted in obscene positions.

Pryor, protected by both Givens' body and the crater itself, was hit by a couple of dirt clods as he stood frozen, watching the dust settle with unbelieving eyes.

"Shit!" It was Branson's voice over the radio. "Full court press now! Pryor," Branson's voice was that of a born commander, strong and confident. "Return to the decon line."

"But, Paul . . ." Pryor was having trouble making his own voice work.

"Return to the decon line now." Branson's tone was insistent. From the video monitors it was clear that Givens was dead. Pryor, still on his feet, was not obviously hurt but he was probably in shock and had to be removed from the site immediately. Further, even if the man were physically okay, it was probable that his suit had been breached, exposing him to any poisons that may have been released. "To the decon now! Green Team will attend to Givens."

Reluctantly, his eyes fixed on his fallen friend, Pryor turned away and headed towards the decon line. Taylor and Rodriquez came up and covered him with an oversized plastic bag to help keep potential contaminants away from any punctures in his suit, then each man grabbed one of Pryor's elbows, and moved him swiftly towards safety. As the men approached the decon line, they passed members of the Green Team, monitors in hand, heading for Givens' body with a stretcher.

Sitting in the response van, Walt watched the rest of the operation in semi-stunned silence. That's what happened to Julia and the girls, he thought. One moment they were fine and then, boom! Even while deep in his morbid thoughts, Walt found himself marveling at how skillfully Branson wielded the SCOT's various abilities. Like a conductor guiding his orchestra, Branson barked orders, passed on information and gave encouragement to his troops as they cleared the site. Probing the crater again, this time with the robot, the SCOT found no new threats. Then using the robot to lay a hose, they pumped the crater dry and swept it again. Other than the explosive that had killed Givens, and which, fortunately for Pryor, had not released any toxins, the crater proved to be clear.

As the sun rose over the Arsenal, Laste declared the site clear. He'd already passed on the news about Givens, whose body had been taken to the post's morgue for the relevant investigations.

It was a bitter pill for them all, Walt could tell, but they swallowed it well. All of them, Walt was sure, would grieve for Givens when the time came. But until their gear was stored back in its mil-pack containers at Dulles, ready for the next response, the mission wasn't over. And for the professionals on the SCOT, the mission always came first no matter how many buddies they lost.

CHAPTER XI

Four days after the Arsenal response, Walt sat at his makeshift desk downloading information from an environmental news-user group onto his laptop. An empty desk fifteen feet from him bore mute testimony to Givens' death but the SCOT moved forward despite its loss. Branson and Laste had already conducted several interviews and soon they would find a replacement for Givens and the desk would be empty no more.

The four days since Givens' death had made Walt feel more like an outsider than ever. Although he'd had absolutely nothing to do with the accident, he received the cold shoulder treatment now more than ever. Only Pryor, who had been the closest to Givens, was halfway warm to the biologist. Possibly, Walt thought, because they had worked together as a team, if only briefly.

When his computer finished transferring a list of files, Walt disconnected from the internet and began sorting through the headlines of the stories he'd just downloaded. The list was long and Walt took his time, opening several that sounded interesting, including a few about the Arsenal response operation. Having had an inside view of the operation, Walt found it both interesting and informative to see how various media outlets reported it.

For the most part, however, his mind was on Katie and the flight up to Boston he'd take that afternoon to visit her for the weekend. The video of Spock and Glen dying, followed by actually seeing Paul Givens killed, had left an emotional void in him that only seeing his daughter could assuage. In fact, he'd wanted to visit her as soon as they'd returned from the Arsenal, but no one else asked to go anywhere so neither had Walt. He'd accepted the SCOT's hours when he joined it.

He scrolled through the stories, his mind four hundred miles away, and then sat up with violent jerk. Pryor, the only other person in the office, looked up from a stack of *Reader's Digest*s on his desk. "Something bite you?" he asked with a humorless smile. The young man had taken Givens' death hard. Walt had seen it before—survivor's guilt. In some ways, although Walt didn't tell Pryor, the West Virginian was going through some of the same pain he was.

"Just a cramp in my foot," Walt responded, hoping that a simple lie would divert Pryor's attention. Some instinct told him to keep the story he'd just found to himself.

Pryor seemed satisfied and Walt tried to act more relaxed as he opened the file. "Mysterious Illness Strikes Kansas River Bald Eagles." It was only one paragraph, a back page filler for anyone without a professional interest in wildlife, but the story had Walt's heart pounding with excitement.

"The deaths of a small colony of Bald Eagles on a rocky island in the middle of the Kansas River has stumped area wildlife management officials. The colony, consisting of about six adult birds, was suddenly found dead at their roost by a local bird watcher. 'Last night, they were fine,' he told officials, 'but this morning they were all dead.' Officials refused to speculate on the possible cause of the birds' deaths, although one environmental official did note that the proximity of the bird kill to the recent disastrous chemical explosion at the Lovett Arsenal might be more than coincidental. Pending further investigation, the official said, there would be no more comments."

Walt re-read the paragraph, every word blazing into his mind. Dead birds four days after the release. The timing was a bit different from the dead birds on Nantucket, but it was far too coincidental to be unrelated. "Hey, Bill," he said as casually as he could, "can you help me find some information on the Arsenal response?"

"Sure, what is it?" Pryor put down his *Reader's Digest* and walked over to Walt's desk.

"Can you get me an area map of the Arsenal and information on how the wind was blowing? I'm still trying to figure out airborne dispersion issues we might have to deal with on the Mass Military Reservation." It was, Walt thought, a plausible lie.

"Not a problem," Pryor seemed happy to have something to occupy him, to keep him from thinking about Givens.

Pryor returned in a few moments with a large map and a colored spreadsheet. "Here's the Arsenal," he said rolling the map open on Walt's desk and jabbing at it with a finger. "This spreadsheet says the wind was blowing at roughly six miles an hour, give or take, from the northeast. Of course, that information's from the county airport's log, but it's only four miles away so it should be fairly accurate. The blast was here," another jab at the map, "the wind then carried the chemicals in this direction and voila, you've got a disaster." Pryor was trying to treat the event lightly, but the tense look on his face betrayed his efforts.

"Can I write on this?" asked Walt.

"Sure. Do whatever you want to it. I just need to have it back unless Adam says you can keep it."

With Pryor looking over his shoulder, Walt made a bunch of meaningless marks on the paper, referring constantly to the wind data spreadsheet to make his work seem authentic as his eyes scanned the map for the island mentioned in the article. After a moment or two, he found what he was looking for, a small circle a hundred feet into the river. There was no name attached to the island, but its shading indicated an area of critical environmental concern. That would make sense for a Bald Eagle rookery. He made some more random marks on the map and looked again. There were no other such critical areas marked that weren't part of the Arsenal itself, which, like many military bases, was loaded with environmentally sensitive areas. Walt checked the distance from the blast to the island. It was just under a mile, directly downwind.

There had to be a connection!

Another thought blazed its way into Walt's mind and he carefully measured the distance from the blast crater to the actual podium. He wrote the distance down on a pad. "Thanks, Bill," he said as he rolled the map back up and handed it over. "That gave me a bit to chew on for a while. Now can you get me the video that camera man shot?" Branson had copied the footage of the doomed EPA director and her companions and had already used it twice to emphasize training points.

"I don't see why not." Pryor led Walt over to the TV/VCR setup and plugged in the video. "What are you looking for?" he asked as casually as he could.

"Nothing, really. I'm just wondering about crowd reaction issues during a release." So what if Pryor didn't buy his lie. There were a million reasons he might want to watch the video. Walt looked at his watch several times during the recording, making notations on his paper. When the footage ended he looked at his watch again. "Thanks a lot, Bill. It's getting late. I'm going to go grab a bite to eat. Can I pick you up something?"

"You going to the cafeteria?"

"No, I think I'll hit the food court across the street." Walt had never left the building for lunch before, but he now had several important calls to make in private before leaving for the weekend. "I'm kind of bored with the cafeteria food," he added in an attempt to explain this sudden break from his usual practice.

"Whatever." Pryor's appetite hadn't returned since Givens' death. "I'll just grab a sandwich here. Thanks anyway."

Walt put his laptop in his pack and hurried out. With any luck, his trip to Boston would include a detour to both Kansas City and Woods Hole. He'd finally found the clue he was looking for and he would follow it as far as he could. When he knew enough to make some sense of things, he could stop being so secretive, but not until then. Branson had him watched all the time at the office already. There was no telling how intense the surveillance would get if the redhead knew his unwanted observer was out chasing clues on his own.

CHAPTER XII

It was pouring rain when Walt pulled into the loading dock behind Harley's darkened lab. He took the cooler from the seat next to him and dashed up the stairs towards the door to his friend's office, his speed as much a factor of his excitement as his desire to stay dry.

The door swung open before Walt reached it. "Hello, Buddy," Harley's voice boomed above the drumming rain, "Glad you didn't get washed away."

Walt ducked into the door and stopped dead as he ran into a wall of cigar smoke. Through the haze, he saw a glowing cigar ember lighting up the hulking frame of the toxicologist. "Jesus, Harley," he wheezed, "you look like the Prince of Darkness here. Why are all the lights off?"

Harley's face broke into a maniacal grin as a flash of lightening lit up the room. "Thunderstorm, Buddy. I always turn off the lights in a thunderstorm. I like the effect." The grin widened as a peel of thunder echoed down the hall. "It helps set the mood. However, since I don't want you breaking your neck in here, let there be light." A massive hand shot out, flicked a switch and the laboratory was flooded with light from the halogen lamps overhead.

"That's better," Walt said with a smile of his own. It was comforting to see his big friend again, strange as the biker might be. He maneuvered around the cloud of smoke and found a relatively clear area in which to stand. "I've got the samples you said you'd need." Walt tapped on the cooler. "Bagged and packed in dry ice. You, me and an employee of the Kansas Department of Wildlife and Parks I conned a favor off, we're the only three people who know I have these samples, so keep it under your hat, okay?" The warning was unnecessary. Harley played everything close to the chest, but Walt still felt he had to emphasize the point.

"Jeff doesn't know?" Harley liked the idea of being one up on the Nantucket detective.

"No, Harley. Just the three of us." Walt's voice took on something of a conspiratorial tone. "I don't know what's going on here. The location of these dead birds is too much to be a coincidence, but until we know for sure, I'm not telling anybody anything.

"I need solid facts, Harley, and you are going to find them for me." He handed the toxicologist the cooler. "You think you'll know by Sunday night? I'd like to know as much as possible before I head back to DC. It's my last week and if I've got something to chase down, I want as much time as possible to find it."

"If God's willing and the creek don't rise." Both Harley and Walt winced as a flash of lightening and a deafening roar of thunder occurred simultaneously. "Or if a bolt of lightening doesn't knock me on my fat ass." Harley grinned again. "In payment for my past sins, you know."

"I just hope He lets me get away before He decides to fry your sinful ass," Walt punched his friend playfully on the shoulder. "I'll see you Sunday night."

"I'll be done." The grin disappeared from Harley's face. "You give Katie a big hug for me, okay?"

Walt felt the hard outline of the silver spoon he kept in his pocket. "A great big hug, Harley, a great big hug." He ducked back out the door and, despite a valiant dash, was soaked before he got to his car. He started the engine, turned on the wipers and cautiously drove out of the parking lot. It was going to be a long, damp trip to Boston.

CHAPTER XIII

25 JUNE
BOSTON, MASSACHUSETTS

Walt finished bathing Katie and looked at his watch. It was time to start heading to Woods Hole. He turned around and saw Doctor Bocall standing by the door. He wiped the tears from his cheeks and managed a brief smile. "At least she's not getting any worse, right?"

The doctor returned the smile but his eyes stayed flat. "For the time being, Walt. But I've got to be honest. I doubt she can stay like this forever. At some point, with a girl this young whose motor skills, mental abilities and so forth are developing at, or should be developing at, high rates, lengthy incapacitation can start to have irreversible consequences. Three months ago, Katie was toilet trained, she was speaking in complete sentences, she could recognize colors and count up to six. She was learning how her body worked and gaining spatial awareness. Now, she can't do any of that. At the least, she's lost valuable developmental time, growth that she'll have to make up later. Eventually, if she stays in a coma too long, her brain development won't be able to catch up with the rest of her. She'll have balance problems, verbalization problems, things like that, no matter what we do for her."

Walt swallowed and said nothing, his eyes focused on the motionless little girl in the bed. He'd brought two more stuffed animals this time, small ones that wouldn't topple the mound that already surrounded her, but he knew she hadn't seen them. Her eyes, while open, seemed incapable of registering anything besides light and dark. That Katie could do that much was, to Walt, a sign of hope, a signal that something in her brain was working, but he found it difficult to be thankful. His little girl was in an open-ended coma and bringing her useless stuffed animals was the best that he could do.

Or, it had been up to now. Walt checked his watch again. Harley would be waiting. With any luck, he would soon have something more helpful than a teddy bear.

Heavy thunderstorms had backed up the traffic out of Boston and when Walt pulled into the loading dock behind Harley's lab, the toxicologist was already perched in his battered chair, sheltered from the rain by a hastily rigged awning made from a discarded sail. Next to the biker, a tumbler full of an amber colored liquid sat on an upturned milk carton and between his teeth was the ever present cigar. From the look on the biker's face, Walt thought, he'd already been through a few glassfuls of whatever it was he was drinking. That was good news. If Harley was drinking, it meant he was in a celebratory mood, which, in turn, meant he'd found something definite. If he were still trying to figure things out, he'd have stuck with the cigars.

"You look happy," Walt commented as he got out of the car and dashed through the rain onto the dock. "You must have something good for me." He prayed Harley would say he had an antidote for Katie but was afraid to verbalize his hopes.

"I've got something good, Walt. Or at least interesting." Harley took the cigar out of his mouth. "But I'm sorry it's not an antidote for Katie."

Walt's heart sank and he huddled further under the awning, trying to stay dry and avoid the cigar smoke at the same time. "Well, what is it then?"

"Not to be a jerk, Walt," Harley leaned back, took a swig from the tumbler and placed the cigar back between his teeth, "but what we've got is a riddle wrapped in an enigma placed inside a puzzle."

"And that means?" Walt steeled himself to be patient. Harley liked acting coy when he was onto something.

"That means we need help figuring out what's going on." Harley finished the tumbler, then stood up and pointed towards the docks. "And, unless I'm mistaken, here comes our help now."

Walt looked in the direction Harley was pointing. "That's Jeff Tillison."

"Exactly. I thought we could use his detective powers right about now."

Walt felt frustration beginning to rise within him. "Harley, I told you. Only three people knew what we've got here, and Jeff wasn't one of them."

"He's not. If you want to send him home still ignorant of what we're doing, fine. But I'm stumped and he's sharp as a tack, even if he is a cop." Harley shot Walt a sobering glance. "Unless you're holding something back from me, buddy, we've just found more information but we've got no clue as to what it means. If you want to try and figure it out on your own, I can't stop you. But for Katie's sake, you probably want to let your friends help you out as much as possible."

The frustration disappeared. Walt knew Harley was right. "Okay, you win," he said as he huddled against the wall. "Now, you got any more of that rotgut left?"

Jeff Tillison walked up from the docks at a steady pace, not turning his head to look around him but obviously very aware of his surroundings. Walt had noticed this faculty many times before. Unlike some cops, his friend wasn't badge heavy in that he could frequently act like he wasn't a police officer, but he never let anything slip by unnoticed. That was one of the many attributes that made him such a good detective and Walt silently blessed Harley for asking Tillison to join them.

"Hi, Jeff," he called from the loading dock, "thanks for coming over." The twenty-five mile trip from Nantucket to Woods Hole was something of a hassle in the best of weather and during a thunderstorm it could be a real nightmare.

"Not a problem, Walt," replied his friend, water pouring off his slicker, "Harley said it would be important to you so I'm only too glad to help." If the detective was concerned about not having been told why his trip over would be so important to Walt, he made no mention of it as he joined the other two men.

Once the three of them had moved into Harley's office, drinks in hand, Walt began to speak. "I appreciate the help and support you two have given me," he said, thinking his words sounded schmaltzy even to himself. "It's meant a lot over the past few months." Walt choked back a sob as the truth in what he was saying struck him. In both their words and deeds, his two friends had gone beyond the call of duty. Jeff's recent trip to the mainland during a thunderstorm was just one example of how far they were willing to go for him. While he'd never been one to verbalize his emotions to anyone before, especially other men, he found himself unable to hold in his feelings anymore. "Since the blast, it seems like my world's gone crazy. If I'm not with Katie, I'm in DC thinking about her. When I'm with Katie, I'm kicking myself for not being able to help her. And, all the time, I'm hating myself for allowing this to have happened to my family. I wake up in the middle of the night and try to dig up old memories of happier times to keep from thinking of how shitty a father I wound up being to my girls. I'm not very successful at it. I know I'm a bear to be around, but you guys still treat me just like a friend, helping me when you can, making sure my head stays above water. You're my links to the real world and not a day goes by when I don't thank God for both of you."

Walt stopped speaking and rubbed his sleeve across his eyes as Jeff and Harley shifted self-consciously in their chairs. They weren't used to such monologues from Walt. Noticing his friends' discomfort, Walt changed gears and continued, "I'm not sure what's coming next, but Harley looks like he's swallowed a canary so, Harley, why don't you tell us what you've got, then I'll fill you guys in with what I know."

Harley sat his drink down and leaned back in his chair, his beefy frame challenging it to remain upright. "This'll be news to you, Jeff, but you know those birds you and Walt brought me?"

"Yes," replied the detective.

"Well, they appear to have been killed by some poison that included the chemical methyl ethyl chlorinate."

"I thought you said it was a virus." Tillison sounded annoyed.

"I did. Walt and I wanted to keep what we knew to ourselves until we got more data."

"Why in hell would you want to do that?"

"Detective," it was the first time that evening Harley had called Tillison by his title, "methyl ethyl chlorinate is secret. It's super secret. Hell, it's probably beyond that. If we'd told the truth about the bird kill, the entire Woods Hole complex would probably be shut down right now. And who knows where I'd be. Some secrets Uncle Sam wants you to take to the grave no matter what.

"Telling the truth would have gotten us nowhere. Even suggesting that the kill was related to the blast would have put us under a microscope and would have hurt our chances to learn more about what's going on. Have you ever seen the Feds take over something?" Harley rushed on without waiting for an answer, "I have. They push the locals aside and act as if they're the only show in town. Just like they did with the blast that killed Julia. We know there's something strange going on, but we get nothing out of telling anyone that.

"Further, it's not just any old top secret chemical we're talking about." Harley leaned forward for emphasis, "Methyl ethyl chlorinate wasn't even invented until 1989."

"That means . . .," began Tillison as his eyes widened in surprise.

"Yes," interjected Walt, "it means that it wasn't old cold war chemical bombs that killed Julia and the twins."

"But that's what they found," responded Tillison. "You saw the grenades yourself."

"I'm not arguing that's not what they found. What I'm saying, what Harley's tests prove, is that that's not what exploded. There was some other bomb, either mixed in with the cold war grenades or lying next to them somehow. A newer bomb with a top secret chemical coating or content that included this methyl ethyl chlorinate. It's this new bomb that went off. The Cold War grenades the SCOT found were only there for camouflage, to throw people off the trail. Just like they did."

"It gets more interesting," continued Harley, leaning back in his chair again and waving his battered remainder of a cigar for emphasis, "Walt took part in the response operation at the Lovett Arsenal, you know."

"Yeah . . ." The detective was watching Harley closely.

"Well, four days after that blast, he read about a rookery full of dead eagles a mile downwind of the blast site. The night before, someone had seen the birds and said they were fine. The next day, they were all dead. So Walt pulled a few of his wildlife biologist strings, went to Kansas City and got some samples of the dead birds. He gave them to me Friday night. I ran some tests over the weekend and at three o'clock this afternoon, you know what I found?"

"Methyl ethyl chlorinate," said Tillison softly.

"Exactly. A chemical so secret I doubt more than 100 people know it even exists. A chemical that wasn't even invented until 1989. A chemical that, according to a little ad hoc research I did in the last few weeks, seems designed to mimic regular chlorine gas but with much more intensity. And, finally, a chemical that breaks down relatively easily in water and other fluids.

"It's also, unfortunately for Katie, a chemical that can be specialty mixed with a variety of other compounds to create new poisons, which makes finding an antidote virtually impossible at this point.

"Finally, and I think I've dug up all I can about this stuff without being too obvious, it's a chemical whose total production was limited to six pounds."

"Six pounds?!" exclaimed Walt.

"Yes. Just six pounds, all of which were procured by the same unidentifiable part of the Pentagon. What happened to it after that, I don't know. Some went into the chemical bombs we've talked about, but not much. I ran some basic numbers, figuring on how far the stuff had traveled before hitting the birds, the wind dispersion factors and so forth and I estimate that these bombs had a total of a pound of methyl ethyl chlorinate. Maybe less, depending on what it was mixed with."

"So where's that leave us?" asked Walt.

"About where we used to be, except that now we can discount the possibility that these chemical bombs just happened to pop up by accident."

"Are you saying someone planted the bomb that killed Julia and the twins? That someone was trying to assassinate my family?" Walt's face had turned paler than Tillison's and his voice was unsteady. "You're saying someone meant to do that?"

"I'm not sure what I'm saying, Walt. That's why I asked Detective Tillison to join us. What I am sure of, though, as sure as I'm standing here, is that these blasts are not two unrelated events." He nodded at Tillison. "Detective, what do you think?"

Tillison hesitated before answering. "Walt, you said you'd fill us in on what you know when Harley was done. Do you have anything to add?"

"Well, nothing that would stand up in court." Walt thought back to the lack of marking flags in the field around the crater at the Lovett Arsenal. "But once we identified the blast site at Lovett we swept the whole area with metal detectors on a four by four grid. We went over the ground with a fine toothed comb and all we found were a few coins, some wingnuts and a bullet. Just normal stuff, and not much of it." He looked at his friends' blank faces. "Don't you see? It would make sense that the bombs and chemicals that killed all those people, and Paul Givens, too, were dumped in the field as part of a load of contaminated fill. Certainly that's the SCOT's position. But the odds of having a load of contaminated fill containing a couple of bombs and practically nothing else are pretty damned slim."

"Are you saying that field wasn't fill?" asked Tillison, starting to fidget with a pen in his hands.

"No. It was fill, all right. Back in the early sixties that whole area was a swamp. A stream even ran right through the spot where the bombs were. That's why the crater was full of water. The Army filled it around 1964 or so, but they used clean fill. The bombs came later. Considering what Harley just told us, I'd bet my life on that."

"But the EPA's working on some bomb disposal sites near there, right?" asked Harley.

"It's the Corps of Engineers, actually. They handle this type of remediation project at military sites. But what they're doing is not connected to the explosion. It's absolutely impossible that the stuff the Corps is dealing with is post 1989, which you say would have to be the case."

Harley nodded, his bald head bobbing up and down on his enormous shoulders. "Whatever blew at the Arsenal had to be post-eighty-nine."

Tillison finished his drink, reached across Harley's desk to grab the bottle and refilled his glass. "You know what we're talking about here, gentlemen, don't you?" He drained half the glass in one gulp, set the drink on Harley's desk and looked at his companions speculatively. "We're talking about some sort of conspiracy to kill Ann Glenn, Susan Spock and dozens of other people. Why, God only knows, but that's how I read it."

"It gets deeper," said Walt.

"How's that?" Harley and Tillison asked in unison.

"I reviewed the video Branson got, the one shot by the dead camera man. It shows Spock, Glen and everyone else getting exposed to the chemical agent."

"And?" Tillison was asking the questions by himself now.

"And a motorcycle roared by just a few moments before the video started showing people suffering from the chemical. It drowned out all the other noise on the tape."

"Like the noise from the explosion," said Tillison, comprehension flooding his face.

"Exactly. I measured the time between the motorcycle and the first symptoms, then figured in the wind speed and distance. It fits perfectly. The motorcycle came by at the exact time the bomb went off."

"It's a fucking cover-up for sure," breathed Harley.

"It gets even deeper, Harley," Walt felt Harley's excitement. Pieces were coming together. "Jeff, tell him about Nantucket."

Tillison cleared his throat and put down his glass. "When I looked at the Nantucket blast site through the eyes of a detective, it looked swept. Everything was too put back together, too perfect under the circumstances. Nothing I could prove, mind you, but I felt it in my gut nonetheless."

Harley took a deep breath. "Jesus Christ," he said slowly, "are you saying that the Pentagon's crack chemical response outfit is involved in a cover-up?"

"I'm not saying *anything*," replied the detective, "I'm just telling you what I felt. How much of this stuff we can take to the bank, I have no idea. Harley," he looked at the biker with eager eyes, "how much can you prove?"

"Nothing." Harley avoided the detective's eyes.

"Nothing?" Tillison voice was incredulous.

"C'mon, Jeff, you're a detective. You know the rules for getting bureaucrats to believe you. The chain of custody with Walt's samples is so full of holes you could drive a truck through it. We can't prove they came from the dead eagles out in Kansas. Besides the fact that there's no paperwork, which any self respecting bureaucrat is going to want, Walt lied to the guy he got the samples from about why he needed them. If we say we've found evidence that a top secret poison killed Glenn and Spock, the first thing anyone's going to ask is how can we prove it. Which, because we have no suitable chain of custody record, we can't."

"Harley, you can't be serious! We can't stay silent on this." Tillison was calm again, the talk of chain of custody lapses being readily understandable to the professional law enforcement officer.

"Jeff, we know something bad is going on. You're talking about cover-ups and conspiracies and assassinations yourself. I didn't bring that stuff up, you did. But we can't prove a damned thing. All we do by going public now is tell whoever put these bombs where they were that we're sniffing on their trail. Do you think we really want to do that?"

Walt thought of Paul Givens' body getting tossed back by the blast, of Julia and the twins lying dead in the Nantucket dunes, of Katie, helpless in her hospital bed. He rubbed the silver spoon in his pocket. "I can't speak for Jeff, Harley, but I'm with you. We've got no solid proof. No one's going to believe us right now." He lowered his voice and leaned forward. "What do you say, Jeff?"

"You're sure you can't prove anything, Harley?"

"Not now. Even if we could somehow examine the bodies from the Arsenal, I doubt we'd be able to find anything. Remember, this chemical was designed to break down in human bodies so as to be untraceable. The post-mortems on Julia and the twins showed nothing. If we could get some more eagle samples from Kansas, we might be able to find methyl ethyl chlorinate but even that's not certain. It would depend on what parts of the eagles are still available for toxicological work and how they've been stored. At this point, it's probably not worth the risk of going through formal channels to get new samples. That'd be too likely to send up a red flag that we've found something and not likely enough to get us the solid proof we need. Don't forget, everything we know so far indicates that there's some sort of connection to the SCOT here. We don't want to jeopardize whatever chances Walt might have to poke around down there some more."

"So," Tillison sounded unsure of himself, "where do you suggest we go from here?" he asked, tacitly agreeing with his companions that silence was the best course of action for the moment.

"I was kind of hoping you'd be able to guide us," said Harley. "Not to be obnoxious, but you're the detective."

"No offense, but I'm not sure you can help being obnoxious." Tillison smiled to remove whatever tension remained. "Still, you've done well. Are you sure you've found out everything you can on this methyl ethyl whatever the hell it is?"

"Chlorinate. Methyl ethyl chlorinate, and yes, I've pretty much tapped all my sources of information."

"Walt, you've got what, one more week down in DC?"

"Yes. I have a flight out of T.F. Green in two hours."

"Can you extend your assignment with the SCOT?"

Walt didn't hesitate. "Not a chance. Laste probably wouldn't care all that much, but Branson's a bear. He hated having me down there before Givens died. Now he's frothing at the mouth to get rid of me. The guy's a security nut anyway and he thinks I'm a major risk." Walt paused, then continued, "I guess he's right, in a strange way."

"What can you do in a week down there?"

"I'm not sure. I've checked everywhere I could for information on this stuff. Of course, I didn't have ready access to much in the way of files or databases. I doubt that'll change this week."

"The SCOT's the only link we've got right now," Tillison persisted. "Are you sure there's nothing you can do to expand your search?"

Walt chewed his upper lip thoughtfully. He remembered Pryor sitting at his desk, brooding over Givens' death, some part of the West Virginian blaming himself for his friend's demise. "The guy Branson set up to watch me, Bill Pryor, was good buddies with the fellow who was killed. That might be a crack. How much of one, I have no idea but it's worth a try. If I can get him to do any searches for us, how should I have him start?"

"First," said Tillison, "make sure he'll keep it close to his chest. We don't want him blabbing to Branson about this. Tell him only what you need to. Once he's on board, you can tell him more, but only enough to get what we need. If he won't help us, shut him off completely. Don't even talk about the weather to him. We don't want anything we let out coming back to haunt us." Tillison's mind was working rapidly, going over the situation with a detective's instinct. "If he's with us, have him do a file search for methyl ethyl chlorinate. Any articles, papers, whatever. The more we know about this stuff and what happened to it at the Pentagon, the better off we'll be. If you can get any insights into why the dune at Nantucket looked so odd, that would help, too. But be careful not to make him too suspicious. Let me know how it goes and we'll take it from there."

Taking the bottle off Harley's desk, Walt emptied it into their glasses. "Gentlemen," he said, rising to his feet, "a toast to success in wherever this search takes us."

"Hopefully our first stop is an antidote for Katie," Jeff intoned, for the first time in his life having more than two drinks in one evening.

"Amen, brother," Harley growled.

Fighting back the tears of gratitude he felt for his two friends, Walt tossed down his drink and felt the fire burn in his belly. "Amen," he concluded, "Amen."

CHAPTER XIV

Over lunch the next day, Walt found an opportunity to talk with Pryor. "What are you doing?" he asked the younger man, who was restlessly leafing through his stack of *Reader's Digests*.

"Playing the *Reader's Digest* game."

"The what?"

"The *Reader's Digest* game. You've never played it?"

"I've never even heard of it." Walt perched on the corner of Pryor's desk. "What is it?"

"It's pretty simple. What you do is you take a copy of *Reader's Digest* and try to guess which stories they'll offer as reprints just by looking at the titles."

"I don't get it." Although he had an ulterior motive for talking with Pryor, Walt's curiosity was piqued.

"See, *Reader's Digest* offers reprints of some stories in every issue. Given the nature of the magazine, once you get the hang of it you can generally figure out which ones they'll offer reprints of just by looking at the table of contents." Opening up a fresh issue, he ran his hand down the list of titles. "Here's a good one. 'How the Federal Government is Defrauding the Small Businessman.'" Pryor flipped the pages to the end of the story. "See, here it is," he said triumphantly, pointing his finger at a line offering reprints of the article in question. "If it's anti-government or an explanation on how to improve your sex life, they'll usually offer reprints. I don't know who runs *Reader's Digest*, but it seems like an odd combination to me."

Walt smiled. "I'm sure I can't explain it either." He looked around the room to ensure they were alone. "Say, Bill," he said in a hushed tone, "I'm actually looking for a favor."

"A favor? What type?" Pryor put the magazine back on his desk and looked at Walt skeptically.

"I need to know you can keep it a secret first."

"Secret from whom?"

"From everyone."

"Even Adam?"

Walt thought of Branson's security focused mind. "Especially Branson."

"I don't know, Walt. We're not much into keeping secrets from each other on the team." The skepticism had been replaced by something bordering hostility.

"Even if it might help explain Paul's death?" Walt watched Pryor's face closely. He hadn't planned on using the heavy artillery so early, but now it was out on the table.

Pryor's face went slack. "Excuse me?"

"You heard me, Bill. Givens' death wasn't your fault, but it's obviously been eating at you. You're looking for an explanation. I might be able to find one, with your help."

"What do you have?" Pryor sounded eager now.

"First I have to know that you can keep a secret." Inexplicably, Walt felt like he was playing some childish game.

Pryor hesitated.

"I'll tell you what," Walt didn't want Pryor to slip away from him, "you promise not to tell anyone for six weeks and I'll tell you what we're looking for and why." Tillison couldn't keep their search a secret for six weeks. At some point, when their private investigation stalled, the cop in him would take over and he'd formalize things. Getting six weeks of silence from Pryor was more than enough. "You don't have to promise to help me now, just that you won't tell anybody. You can decide later if you want to help. Okay?"

Pryor thought a few moments in silence. "All right, I won't say anything to anyone for six weeks, except if I think what you've told me needs immediate action for safety reasons. I don't want anyone getting hurt 'cause I kept my mouth shut."

Now it was Walt's turn to think. When it came down to it, he realized, he had no choice but to trust Pryor if he wanted to have any chance of moving forward. "I can accept that." He reached into his pocket and pulled out a small stack of folded papers Harley had given him. "Here. This is all I know about a chemical called methyl ethyl chlorinate. It's super deadly, it's top secret and only six pounds of it exist to the best of my knowledge." Walt was intentionally using the singular pronoun. He didn't want Pryor, or anyone else, learning of Harley's or Tillison's involvement unless absolutely necessary. "It wasn't invented until 1989 and may be mixed with other chemicals to increase its potency or to make it more difficult to trace. All six pounds of it were procured by an unknown Pentagon agency in 1989."

Pryor was half listening to Walt and half leafing through the papers when Walt dropped the bomb. "I have conclusive proof that this chemical killed birds downwind from both the Nantucket blast and the Lovett Arsenal explosion." He leaned over and whispered into the West Virginian's ear. "What I'm saying is that whatever destroyed my family was not the cold war gas grenades you guys found in the dunes. And not everything in that crater where Paul died was fill from the mix-sixties. Something, a bomb with methyl ethyl chlorinate in it, couldn't have been there until after 1989." Walt straightened up and watched as Pryor finished reading the papers.

When Pryor finally spoke, his voice was taut with excitement. "You're sure about this?"

"Absolutely."

"We've got to tell Adam and Charlie. This means Glen and Spock and all those others weren't the victims of a random accident."

Pryor half rose from his chair but Walt gently grabbed his arm and pulled him back down. "Wait a minute, Bill, you promised."

"I can't keep this to myself. It's huge!"

"Where's the danger factor, Bill? That's all you said you were concerned about."

"But, Walt, Jesus Christ, man. Don't you see what this means? We've got to let people know."

Walt's response was hushed but intense. "I know exactly what this means, Bill. It means that, after three months, I finally have half a shot at finding an antidote for my daughter, an antidote no one else is even looking for. Somewhere, somehow, something funny is going on and if we can figure out what it is, we might be able to help Katie.

"I also know something else," Walt spoke quickly. He had to get Pryor on board before people started filtering in from lunch. "I know that Adam Branson hates having me down here. Regardless of what Charlie says, if Branson gets wind that I'm looking for information on this stuff, he'll shut me out so quickly my head will spin. Think of it for a minute, Bill. He's obsessed with security and I'm not even supposed to know that this methyl ethyl chlorinate exists. If you were in my shoes, with the way Branson's treated me since day one, would you want your daughter relying on Adam for an antidote?"

The silence hung in the air between them. "Four weeks," said Pryor. "I'll be quiet for four weeks."

Walt thought of Tillison's reluctance to stay silent about their information. Four weeks would be more than enough. "You'll help, then?"

"I'll keep silent for four weeks. I'll have to think about actually helping, though. Besides, you haven't told me what you want."

"That's easy. I just want all the information you can get me on methyl ethyl chlorinate. Where it went in the Pentagon, who signed manifests or supply cards for it, how it was used. Whatever you can dig up." If Pryor dug up enough, Walt would tell him about Tillison's instincts regarding the dune and his own instincts about the Arsenal's fill material. First, though, he had to make sure there was a path to follow.

"Okay." Pryor handed Walt back the papers. "If I decide to help you, I won't need these."

"You'll let me know?" Walt wanted to close the deal.

"One way or another," Pryor was being noncommittal, "you'll know in at least four weeks."

"One last thing," concluded Walt as he stuck the papers back in his pocket, "you might want to look at the Arsenal release video footage again. There's a lot of motorcycle noise in the background at one point. Check out the relationship between the time of that noise, the time the cameramen started complaining about their eyes, the wind speed and the distance to the crater. When you're done with that, you might want to ask yourself why Branson never thought to make that connection. He's supposed to be the pro at this stuff."

Walt's final week with the SCOT was pure torture. Although he and Pryor continued to exchange pleasantries and Pryor gave him detailed instructions in some logistical support computer programs, Walt was unable to determine whether the West Virginian was going to help him or not. Now that his secret was at least partially in the open, the biologist felt especially self-conscious in the Team's offices, as if everyone knew he was some sort of double agent. This odd feeling of a guilty conscience, tinged with no small amount of physical fear, was magnified when he saw Branson. Walt shuddered to think of what the big man, capable of violence over minor questions about a training exercise, would do if he found Walt had tried to get one of his own lieutenants to rat on him. He prayed Pryor would, at the least, keep his promise about staying silent.

At the end of the week, with only the briefest of handshakes from the assembled Team members and nothing at all from either Branson or Laste, Walt left the SCOT for good, still unsure of what role Pryor was going to play in his search for an antidote.

CHAPTER XV

Adam Branson drummed his oversized fingers impatiently on the top of the counter. A busy man even when things were quiet, he took it personally when someone made him wait. Not that getting upset would help anything, but the information he'd just received was alarming, making his already short temper that much shorter.

The outside door swung open and another man, smaller than Branson but with an air of authority that was undiminished by Branson's size, came in and sat down opposite him. "Well, Adam," the man began with no hint of an apology, stroking his chin with well manicured finger, "what's going on that we need to talk about so badly?"

"It's that damned Yankee, Walt Crawler. He's up to something."

"So you said over the phone. Could you be more specific now that we're face to face?"

"I never liked having that guy so close to the Team. Right from the beginning, I thought he was a risk, so I decided to keep a pretty close watch on him. Nothing too severe, but I didn't want any surprises coming my way."

"That's understandable," murmured the man, crossing his legs and resting his chin on the steeple formed by his two forefingers.

"The second day he was here, I picked one of his credit card receipts out of the trash. I hacked into the credit card company and started getting reports on what our guest had been charging. That's the beautiful thing about a credit card society. We all leave evidence of everything we do." Branson chuckled menacingly. He left traces of next to nothing. "I also ran a credit check to make sure that this was his only card, which it is. So, starting just after he joined us, I began to review all of Crawler's credit card purchases. At first I did it every day, but when there was no cause for alarm I started waiting and looking them over several days at a time." That had been a dumb mistake, Branson acknowledged to himself. Complacency at any time was bound to bite you in the ass. It was Murphy's Law.

"To make a long story short, I didn't review Crawler's last bunch of purchases until this afternoon, shortly after he headed back up to Boston. It seems that when he flew home last week, he modified the ticket to fly into Kansas City first."

The head bobbed on the steepled fingers. "Which means?" The man's voice was neutral, giving no indication of what he thought Walt's altered trip might mean.

"I think Mr. Crawler found something related to the Lovett blast. Rather than telling anyone on the SCOT about it, he decided to go investigate on his own. Then, when he came back on Monday, he still didn't tell anyone. Either he didn't learn anything on his little side trip or he's keeping it to himself."

"Do you think he found something?"

"I don't know. He didn't act any different when he came back, but that doesn't necessarily mean anything. The worst case scenario is he's found some connection between Lovett and Nantucket. What exactly that would prove, I'm not sure." Branson looked across the counter and resumed his angry finger drumming. His first instinct when facing the unknown was to batter his way forward, relying on brawn and speed to pull himself through. In other circumstances, he would have snatched Walt off the street and conducted his own interrogation of the biologist, but he knew the situation was unique and he was forcing himself to slow down.

The smaller man pondered the situation for a moment and then spoke. "We need to know what Crawler knows and what sparked his curiosity. We very well may have overlooked something and we can't afford to have Crawler, or anyone else, digging it up. Have you tapped his phone and bugged his house and car?

"Of course," snapped Branson, annoyed at finding himself in this position. He was supposed to be the covert ops expert, and getting advice from an operational tinhorn was almost insulting.

"Good," responded the other man. "Before we let anything happen to Mr. Crawler, we need to make sure we understand what he knows, how he found out what he knows and who he's told. If he's dead or spooked, that information's disappears or becomes tainted. Plus, if he has told anyone anything, his disappearance would raise too many questions. I feel that thorough, but passive, observation is the best course of action right now. Unless the situation deteriorates completely, we should just watch him for the next several days. If we can determine he hasn't told anyone anything threatening, you can arrange for an accident to happen to him." The man shrugged eloquently. "Some sort of boating accident would be appropriate, perhaps even a suicide. After all, he's been through a lot recently."

"And if he has told someone something? We may not have enough time to come to a consensus on future actions." Branson snarled out the word "consensus." Asking for instructions in a situation like this was counter-intuitive and he had to fight the urge to throw the smaller man out of his office and do things his own way. When he'd agreed to join this environmental jihad, he'd also agreed, as always, to be the number two man, running the operational side of things while his counterpart worried about the big picture. Nonetheless, even though Branson knew he had no other options, he still chaffed at his lack of control.

"We snatch him immediately, rip what we need to know from him and start plugging up the leaks, no matter what the consequences." If he was offended by Branson's antagonism, the man didn't show it.

"Okay," Branson said reluctantly, "we'll play it calm for now." He obviously preferred the snatch and rip method.

"Remember, keep me informed. No cowboy bullshit." The steepled fingers separated and the man stood. "I mean it, Adam," he continued, pausing just inside the doorway, "We're almost there. Play it cool for a few days and then you can do whatever you want with Mr. Crawler."

Branson's fingers were still drumming long after his companion had left the room. He had his own reasons for being in this particular game, but he still hadn't figured out what drove the man who had just left the room. There were so many pieces, too many pieces, that just didn't fit together. Branson had researched his co-conspirator as thoroughly as he could but he had not found one shred of information on why the man would want to so savagely betray his own.

Sometimes he wondered who was using whom.

CHAPTER XVI

8 JULY
SIERRA NEVADA MOUNTAINS, CALIFORNIA

John Brocktor huddled deeper into his poncho and tried to smile as he trudged up a muddy mountain trail. Only twenty-six years old, he was one of the youngest people ever to head a major national environmental group. His age, combined with the 'back to nature' focus of Planet Earth, Brocktor's advocacy group, made him feel he had to put on a happy face even if he felt miserable. The rain seeped through the top of his poncho, running in cold rivulets down the back of his neck and making him wince despite his efforts to look serene. Damn it, he was miserable, but in the dog eat dog world of environmental advocacy, he couldn't let any other members of the group think that he, or his organization, was weak.

The group in this instance was a gathering of the presidents and executive directors of the United States' largest environmental groups. The heads of the Nature Conservancy, the Sierra Club, the National Parks and Conservation Association and a half dozen other environmental organizations gathered once every two years for team building group exercises. Trust falls, rope courses, river crossings and anything else designed to teach the groups' leaders how to better work together. What worked with river crossings, the logic went, would work on major environmental issues, where a divided public interest constituency was often its own worst enemy.

This was the first team building session Brocktor had attended and he'd hated almost every minute of it. The other attendees, while respected professionals, had snubbed him, he thought, because of his age and relative inexperience. The food had not been vegetarian, which rubbed Brocktor's eco-sensitivity the wrong way, and people seemed to spend half their time exchanging stock tips instead of environmental advocacy ideas. The rain, buckets and buckets of it, was the icing on the cake. He was, Brocktor decided, truly miserable. And it didn't look like it was going to get better, either.

Brocktor watched as the facilitator running the exercise pointed to a small clearing off the trail they were hiking. "You'll camp here," the facilitator hollered over the rain. "Put the fire over in that rock circle and the tents by those trees." He pointed to clarify which trees in the forest he meant, then flexed his right biceps and bent his head to give it a kiss. While Brocktor hadn't found much about the facilitator to like, he absolutely loathed this self-adoration aspect of the man's character. "All the equipment you need is in that trailer there." No need to point, there was only one trailer. "I'll be back in six hours with the next problem." Like a phantom, the facilitator floated into the woods and vanished from sight. Brocktor found the man's ability to seemingly conjure himself up out of thin air or disappear without a trace to be somewhat unnerving. He figured it was part of the whole teamwork idea, never quite being sure if you were really on your own. But all the same, this fellow gave him the creeps. It was like having a ninja as your Boy Scout leader. Brocktor wondered if the facilitator had worked in the area when it had been a military base. That could help explain his uncanny conjuring capabilities.

"Okay folks, listen up." The man from the Nature Conservancy was in charge for this exercise. Brocktor didn't envy him. They were all tired, cold and wet, with short tempers and shorter attention spans. Setting up camp under these conditions was going to be no picnic. "We've got two priorities," the Nature Conservancy man said. "The first is shelter. The second is warmth. You eight," he pointed, "start unpacking the trailer. Try to keep stuff as dry as possible. I'll mark out the tent sites and then we'll set 'em up. You three," he pointed to Brocktor and two others, "collect deadwood and see if you can get a fire started. Once we've got one going, we'll rig a tarp somehow over part of it so we can cook and get warm without getting soaked." That would be a hell of a trick, Brocktor thought, but it was worth a try. Even a wet fire would cheer things up a little bit.

As the other two fire makers collected wood, Brocktor set up a small teepee of tinder in the middle of the fire circle. It was a new location, he realized from the virgin grass growing inside the rocks. The facilitators probably rotated exercise areas to minimize the impact of their activities. Brocktor wasn't sure he'd do it that way. Things like fires and tents generally had the least impact if confined to specific areas, not shifted around from place to place. But this was their operation, he thought, shrugging his shoulders. They must have their reasons.

By the time Brocktor had the fire going, the rain had lessened and the tents were up. One by one, the other participants gathered around the fire, holding their hands, prunelike from all the rain, towards the flames to soak up the wonderful heat. The group grew until all dozen were by the fire and Brocktor added more wood so the blaze would be big enough for all of them. The flames rose higher and a sizeable collection of glowing red embers began to grow inside the rocks. The rain picked up a little, but the now roaring fire kept everyone together. People must be feeling more comfortable, Brocktor thought as he poked at the embers with a heavy stick, the conversation was turning back to the stock market again.

He jabbed at a particularly large coal, pushing it aside to allow more oxygen into the base of the fire. The flames responded by growing higher still and then, for one microsecond, the fire seemed to come alive. The flames shot to the sky, the glowing embers jumped into the air and the circle of rocks vanished as the earth erupted in a huge volcano of noise and fire.

Brocktor's pupils contracted as the fire exploded into dazzling light, but before his brain could register what was happening, something hard tore at his chest and the world went black.

CHAPTER XVII

Walt tossed restlessly in his bed, the pills he'd taken a few hours earlier making him painfully groggy but not bringing on the needed sleep. His nights, which had been rough enough while he was in DC, were getting even worse. Despite the prescribed sleeping pills, true sleep regularly eluded him, leaving him as worn and tired in the morning as he had been the previous night. He dreaded those dark, empty hours of a lonely night, when the ghosts of Julia and his twins floated through his head and asked him why he had failed them. Oddly enough, the only nights he could sleep halfway well were those he spent with Katie. Somehow the ordered world of the hospital calmed his ragged nerves.

Finally he thumped the pillow in frustration and gave up completely. Sleep was out of the question. On previous sleepless nights, he'd gone down to his basement and opened up some of the boxes he stored there. With a glass of scotch by his side, recklessly mixing his sleeping pills with alcohol, Walt flipped through old photo albums and fingered momentos he hadn't touched in years, reliving his youth and the early days of his marriage with an intensity that bordered on obsession. His doctor, who didn't know about the scotch, had told him not to worry, that deep remorse and introspection was normal with people who had suffered such a great tragedy. But the overpowering feeling of depression he experienced when he closed the boxes back up at dawn terrified Walt, making him wonder how self-destructive he could be. It was selfish and irresponsible, he knew, to be so careless with his own health. Katie had no one else to depend on, he had to make sure he was always there for her.

Fighting the desire to pour himself a scotch, Walt rose from his rumpled bed and padded over to his dresser. Despite the almost complete darkness, he managed to get dressed and leave his house without bumping into anything. Almost everything he owned, besides his bikes, had eventually found its way to the basement, leaving little to stumble over at night. Once outside, Walt unlocked his road bike, turned on his nightrider headlight and pedaled stiffly down the driveway. Hopefully a brisk ride to Sconset would do a better job of preparing him for sleep than the pills had done.

Lost in his reveries and still sluggish from the sleeping pills, he didn't notice the small car that pulled into the road behind him.

Halfway back from Sconset, Walt's head finally began to feel clear again. He'd taken it easy on the trip out, knowing that his bike handling skills would be impaired by the drugs he had taken, but now he thought he could let loose without fear. He switched into a lower gear and dug into the ride, feeling the bike come alive under his ministrations. Julia had often said he was more enthusiastic about touching his bicycles than he was about touching her. Perhaps she had been right, he thought as the dark Nantucket landscape flew by. He'd never felt entirely comfortable and in control when he was with her. Such intimate thoughts were progress, Walt knew. The doctor had encouraged him to examine his past and come to terms with his shortcomings. Only by resolving past issues, no matter how painful, could he expect to move forward.

A set of lights topped the hill behind him, one of a surprising number of cars to have passed him on his midnight ride, and Walt could see his shadow looming monstrously in front of him.

Shit, he mumbled half aloud, sadly acknowledging that Nantucket's rampant development was making it increasingly difficult to find solitude on the island, even in the middle of the night. Then flashing blue lights appeared on the car and Walt swore again, in a much louder voice. While he'd received a few tickets for breaking the island's conservative speed limits on his bicycle, no one had ever hassled him at night.

He slowed to a stop and remained motionless, feet still in the pedals, until the cruiser caught up to him.

"Christ, Walt, you're a tough man to find at times." Jeff Tillison sounded alert and full of life.

Walt's heart flipped as he realized who was talking to him. "Is it Katie?" he managed to choke out.

"No, I'm not here about Katie. As far as I know, she's fine." Jeff hurriedly explained. "I'm looking for you because of the explosions. There's been another one."

Walt felt as if a load had been removed from his chest. Katie wasn't dead. "Another explosion?! Where?"

"The Sierra Nevadas, in California."

Walt tilted his bicycle and rested one foot on the ground. "Are you sure it's connected."

"Pretty sure. Throw your bike in the trunk and I'll tell you about it while we head back to town."

An hour later, Walt and Tillison finally reached Harley. "Jesus," said Walt, into the speaker phone, "where've you been?"

"Hell, Walt," replied the toxicologist with a good natured laugh, "it's hardly even morning. The night's still young. The better question is, what are you doing up at this hour?" His voice grew sober. "Is it Katie?"

"No, thank God. Have you seen the news in the last few hours?"

"Uh-uh. Been busy, if you know what I mean."

Walt and Tillison exchanged glances–biker man meets willing woman. It was a scary thought.

"There's been another explosion." Tillison took over the conversation.

"Where?"

"In California's Sierra Nevadas. It happened about eight hours ago, way up in the mountains, so the facts are just coming out."

"Was it a chemical explosion?"

"We're not sure. I've talked to some friends out there and apparently no one died of any sort of poisoning. They're all blast and shrapnel victims."

"So how do you know there's a connection?"

"Each of the victims was the leader of a top ten environmental group. Sierra Club, NRDC, EDF. All the big ones. Seven are dead, two in critical condition and only one, John Brocktor from Planet Earth, is conscious."

"How do you know there's a connection?" Harley repeated himself, "explosions happen all the time."

"We can't prove anything yet, but I feel it in my bones. According to Brocktor, they were all off on a retreat of some sort. The facilitator had 'em set up a fire at a designated spot and, when they all gathered around the fire a while later, something blew up. The place used to be an old Air Force Base so the locals are saying they must have built the fire over some unexploded ordinance on an old range or something. They're saying that the heat of the fire eventually grew to the point where, bam, the round cooked off. Not too uncommon on old ranges or battlefields."

"But you feel differently?"

"It fits, Harley. Last month's Arsenal explosion killed two of the nation's most prominent environmental bureaucrats, plus a fair amount of support staff. The Nantucket dunes explosion raises a similar issue," Tillison looked away from Walt, focusing on an invisible spot on his office wall. "We haven't talked about this before, but I've been thinking about how close the blast site was to Senator Jackson's summer house. On a hunch, I talked to his chief of staff. It turns out that Jackson was planning a major environmental get-together there at the end of the summer. I did some calculations based on the prevailing wind at that time of year and you know what?"

"The dispersal pattern's right over Jackson's house." Harley's voice was almost respectful. "Jesus Christ. They were planning a massacre."

"Regardless of what they were planning, we've still got a big credibility problem. So far, we've kept everything we know a secret. No one will believe us if we say there's a connection between all of these explosions." Jeff didn't make any recriminations. They'd all agreed to stay silent.

"But if we can find methyl ethyl chlorinate in California, then we can start proving our case," said Harley.

"Exactly. But the problem, as I see it, is two-fold. First, no one, including the three bomb victims who are still alive, seems to have suffered from chemical poisoning and second, it's been raining cats and dogs out there all day."

The line was silent as Harley pondered these facts. "How much rain?" he asked.

"An estimated three inches since the blast."

"Shit! And, being out in the mountains, it took a while for the response people to get there. So all the bodies got good and wet, right?"

"Unfortunately."

"Jeff," Harley sounded deflated, "I can't claim to be an expert on this stuff, but I doubt methyl ethyl chlorinate'll show up. It's just too wet. We may get a small bird or mammal kill, but that's doubtful, too. Three inches is a lot of rain and this stuff is pretty soluble. Plus," the biker added, "I doubt they used it."

"Excuse me?" Walt and Tillison asked at the same time.

"Well, think of it. If it's what you guys are talking about, and I think it is, someone planted a bomb where those team builders were going to have a fire. They must have known something about the group's plans so that they could bury it deep enough for the cookoff to happen when everyone was likely to be around the fire. Or maybe the bomb was remotely detonated. We'll never know. But there would be no need for chemicals in either case. A group of people huddled around a bomb when it goes off are going to be chopped up pretty badly no matter what. Chemicals would be overkill. Plus, this way the connection with other incidents isn't as clear.

"Regardless, we can't make much of a case, not without a lot of back tracking and explaining why we lied and covered-up stuff ourselves. Then it becomes a Law of Significant Places issue."

"A what issue?" asked Walt.

"I forgot, you're a biologist, not a true scientist." Harley coughed smugly. In his book, the only true scientists were the ones who worked with microscopes, beakers and Bunsen burners. Being outside studying live animals didn't count. "There's a theory, mostly used by physicists, chemists and mathematician types, that nothing you do can ever be more accurate than your worst mistake. For example, if you wanted to make something simple, like water, all you'd need would be two hydrogen atoms and one oxygen atom. $H2O$. But if you add an extra oxygen atom, you've got $H2O2$. Just one extra oxygen atom, but the final result is hydrogen peroxide. That's an oxidizing and bleaching agent. Completely different from water."

Walt shot Tillison a blank stare. "So what?"

"Okay," said Harley, coughing again over the phone, "let me put it another way. You want to call someone, say a college girlfriend. There are ten numbers you'd use to call her, assuming she's out of the 508 area code, and you need to get all ten of the numbers dialed in the correct order or you can't call her. If you get nine right and one wrong, it's not like you're ninety percent talking with her. At best, you've got someone in her town, if it's one of the last four numbers. At worst, you've got someone in Alaska. In either case, just one number off and you can't communicate with her.

"It's the same way with us now. We've got information on the Pentagon's chemical programs, we've got information on response operations Branson ran involving chemical grenades, we've got bird samples with a top secret chemical, we've got a tape with a mysterious motorcycle, and we have a big pile of dead bodies." Harley's enthusiasm for his subject had overridden any tact he might otherwise have had and he continued on without thinking of Walt's reaction to his description of the bombs' effects. "Now, since the three of us all believe in each of these links, and some we can't quite put our fingers on, we have no trouble deciding Branson is an evil man and that he's connected to these explosions somehow. The problem is, we have to believe all of these links to come to that conclusion. If you two don't believe my story about the methyl ethyl chlorinate, for example, you stop suspecting foul play and I become just some kook with a crazy theory. The same thing goes for the bird samples you guys brought me from Shipwreck Rocks. If someone doesn't believe that you got the birds there, then the rest of our story doesn't hold any water. You've got to swallow everything, hook, line and sinker, for the story to make sense.

"Unfortunately, given the small amount of hard evidence we have right now, I don't think anyone else is going to swallow the whole thing. And if they don't take the whole banana, they won't get to our conclusion. They might reach a number someplace in our town, but it won't be ours. And anything that is not our number is not close enough."

"So what do we do now?" asked Walt, tired at the thought of being stymied when they knew so much. But what Harley said made sense. There were too many holes in their story for someone on the outside to believe it.

"The facilitator," responded Harley. "He's a connection."

"He's gone," said Tillison, frustration filling his voice. "The local cops and highway patrol are trying to track him down. But they've come up with squat. His apartment was hastily abandoned. His car's gone. They think he saw the explosion and panicked."

"They won't find him," Walt sounded sure of himself. "He was a plant."

"How do you know?" asked Harley, the speakerphone giving his disembodied voice an eerie echo.

"I don't, anymore than we really know anything. Except that these guys are pros. They don't miss much."

"Except the birds," said Harley.

"Yeah. Except the birds, which is all we've got. And we can't even share that with anyone. But this explosion was no accident. They'll never track the guy down."

"They're that sophisticated?" questioned Harley.

"Walt's right," said Tillison. "They must have planted one of their own men there. Probably gave him fake fingertips to leave untraceable prints, a random clump of hair in a comb to foil a genetics search and maybe some cheek implants and hair coloring to make pictures worthless. Or maybe they set someone else up as the facilitator, some innocent guy who looked enough like one of their own for a short term impersonation. When the time came, they knocked off the real facilitator and replaced him with their plant. Again, though, we won't be able to prove anything."

"So what's next?" asked Harley. "Can we question the guy who's conscious?"

"No way." Tillison frowned at Walt. "We have zero jurisdiction there. Hell, we don't even have an open case *here*. As far as anyone else is concerned, we'd just be another bunch of conspiracy nuts. We couldn't get near the guy."

The three were silent for a few moments, the hum of the speakerphone filling the room.

"Uh, Jeff. How did you find out what you found out?" Harley's tone was cautiously curious.

"I've got a few friends out in California. I heard about the explosion and something clicked in my mind, so I called them. Why?"

"If those guys are as sophisticated as we think they are, mightn't they find out you've been asking questions?"

Tillison thought for a moment. "It's possible, I guess. I asked my friends to keep my inquiries hush-hush, though. Besides, it'd be a tough connection to make. My name doesn't pop up anywhere."

"No, your name doesn't. But you're a Nantucket detective and the bad guys know there's a connection between this explosion and the one in Nantucket. Someone as eager for secrecy as these folks seem to be might be able to put that together."

Walt looked at his friend. "That means we might be keeping our secret from everyone except the killers."

"Shit!" Tillison snarled into the phone. "You're right. The odds are too strong that someone will inadvertently mention the word Nantucket. Harley, I'm going to let you go." The detective took control of the conversation, dispelling the cloud of fear that was starting to grow in Walt's head. "Put together everything you've got on what's happened so far. I don't care if it's so secret James Bond couldn't read it. We'll do the same. Tomorrow morning, we take the whole shebang to the Attorney General's office. We still won't be able to prove anything, but with our credentials maybe the AG should give us the benefit of the doubt. Of course, we'll look like total shits for not having brought all this up earlier, but at least we'll have gotten the ball rolling. The AG will have to take it from there. Then we won't know any more than anyone else and the bad guys won't care about us anymore."

"There's always revenge," pointed out Harley.

"Naah, these guys are pros. They'd get nothing from revenge except more risk of exposure. Trust me, we're safer this way."

"Jeff, have you ever been in a situation like this?" asked Harley.

"No. But I've watched lots of movies. We'll all be fine." Tillison's voice sounded breezily confident.

"I hope so," muttered the toxicologist, "but just in case you're wrong, why don't you make another dozen or so calls now. I don't want to be the only number these people find when they start dissecting what you've done in the past few hours."

Once Harley was off the phone, the detective began leafing through his address book. "Go try to catch some sleep," he told Walt. "I've got some calls to make."

By mid-morning, thanks to a few hours sleep on Tillison's couch and a river of strong coffee, Walt was at his desk and feeling human. Jeff had given each of the men a task to complete. Harley was to explain the tests he ran on the samples and how methyl ethyl chlorinate could have dispersed after the blasts and with what effects. Tillison was describing the blast site on Nantucket and what they'd surmised about the California explosion. Walt's task was to describe the response site at the Lovett Arsenal and discuss how the dead birds fit into their theory. That evening they would all meet on the mainland and put their products together into one comprehensive, if unbelievable, packet for the AG, with courtesy copies for the press.

After that, no one knew where the chips would fall. Walt rubbed Katie's spoon and tried to divine the future. Would this help her or hurt her? He had no clue. Perhaps he was betraying her, exposing himself to needless danger by advocating a conspiracy theory before they had enough facts to support their case. If the AG didn't believe them, Walt knew it would only be a matter of time before each of the three friends would have disappeared or suffered a fatal accident. Tillison's ideas about professional killers being above revenge held no water with him.

He shrugged his shoulders phlegmatically. Only time would tell.

The phone rang by his computer. "Crawler here."

"Walt, it's Bill. Bill Pryor from the SCOT."

Walt's heart stopped. "Hi, Bill, what's going on?" he asked as calmly as he could.

"Listen, Walt, when you told me that stuff about methyl ethyl chlorinate, I sort of tuned you out. I'm pretty torn up about Givens and I can only imagine how many times worse it must be for you with your family. I thought you were just making stuff up to keep hope alive. I'm sorry for that."

"That's okay, Bill. It's a pretty strange idea." Not half as strange as the packet we're giving to the AG tomorrow, Walt said to himself. "But what's up? You didn't just call to say you're sorry, did you?" Walt could tell by Pryor's tone that there was more to the call than that.

"Well, I found some, Walt. Some methyl ethyl chlorinate."

"You what?" Walt's voice betrayed his excitement.

"I found some supply chits with methyl ethyl chlorinate listed on them. After you went back to Boston, I reviewed the tape just like you suggested. I think you're right, the motorcycle was a cover-up. I don't know how Adam could have missed it. So I've been digging around a bit, just trying to prove you were wrong, to satisfy my conscience about Roy. And this morning I found four chits for a total of six pounds of methyl ethyl chlorinate."

"Do you guys actually have that stuff in your office?" asked Walt.

"Not that I know of. As you know, we don't keep much here besides computers, office supplies and some basic training equipment. I'd have to ask Adam where it all went. He's the one who signed the chits."

"Damn." Walt didn't want to ask Branson anything but he hadn't directly verbalized his fears to Pryor. "No disrespect to you guys, Bill, but I'd just as soon not ask Branson anything. Not until we get a better handle on the whole motorcycle issue. What else is on the chits?" Maybe there'd be information Harley could use, or even something that could help Dr. Bocall find an antidote for Katie.

"They have a whole laundry list of stuff. Acids, bases, neutralizers, reagents. You name it. A chemist's dream. But I never saw any of the stuff. It gets more complicated, though. When I saw the chits, I decided to do a file check on methyl ethyl chlorinate. I can hack around our system pretty well and I found several files that referenced the chemical."

"What'd they say?" Walt was on the edge of his seat.

"Not much, actually. Just that we'd gotten some. But I found two references in those files to some other files, and this new batch of files I can't open."

"So, where's that leave us?" asked Walt.

"I don't know. I was hoping you'd tell me."

Walt didn't have to think about his answer. "Why don't I come down and look at what you've found?"

"Christ, Walt, you can't do that." Pryor's voice was full of reluctance. "You don't have the proper security clearance anymore."

"Screw the security clearances, Bill," Walt retorted, "this is our one break to find out what really happened to my family and Givens, and to find out what's poisoning my Katie. You know Branson'll never clear me to come into the SCOT's office, especially if there's something rotten going on. I can look at what you've got, then I'll go over it with a friend of mine who knows all there is to know about chemicals. If anyone can make sense about this stuff, he's the one." Walt thought of the report he was putting together for the Attorney General. That would have to wait, this new lead was far more important. "I can probably scare up a plane and be down in a few hours," he pressured Pryor, "we can't wait on this."

"Okay, Walt," the reluctance was still there, but not quite as strong. "Adam'll kill me if he finds out, but I've gone this far...." Pryor let the sentence run out, seeking reassurance that he was doing the right thing.

"You can't stop now," Walt encouraged him, "you owe it to Roy to get some answers."

"I'll let you into the office after everyone's gone home," said Pryor, sounding more confident as he formulated a plan. "It's a really slow day here, everyone ought to be gone by four at the latest. I'll show you what I found and then we can figure out where to look next."

"You're sure you can get me in?" Walt would jump at any chance, however farfetched, to find some answers to what had happened on Nantucket, but he didn't want to find a locked door once he got down to DC.

"Oh, I can get you around security, if that's what you mean. But I'm serious, if Adam finds you in here there'll be all hell to pay."

Walt remembered the huge DOD operative attacking him after the vernal pool confrontation. That would be child's play compared to what would happen if he discovered Walt in his SCOT office. "Believe me, Bill, if I think it'll help Katie, I don't care what kind of hell we wind up paying." With Branson or with Tillison, for that matter. The detective wouldn't be pleased at having his report to the AG delayed, regardless of Walt's hopes for this new investigation. "I'll call you just before I'm airborne to let you know when to expect me."

"Okay. And I'll keep working on getting into those files. I'm sure I'll figure it out eventually."

Shortly after four PM, Walt huddled over a cup of coffee in a small café on the other side of the parking lot from the building that housed the SCOT. He pulled his cell phone out from its holster and dialed a number. "Harley?"

"Speaking," the toxicologist answered.

"I'm outside the SCOT building now. In ten minutes I'll talk to Pryor. If it's clear, he'll let me in and we'll start doing our research. I'll call you as soon as we're done."

"And Pryor knows about me? You're sure that this isn't some kind of setup?"

"Pryor knows I've got backup, if that's what you mean." Harley was raising the same concerns as Tillison had earlier. "He doesn't know about you specifically. If he's trying something funny, he knows someone will come looking for me. But I'm sure that's not a problem. He didn't dream the methyl ethyl chlorinate chits out of thin air."

"How do you know? You haven't seen them."

"Good point, but dreaming up the chits would have been too elaborate if all he wanted to do was to get me alone. Hell, he knows where I live. He could have just knocked on my door. I think he's being open with me."

"I'm glad you think so. But make damn sure he understands you've let people know where you are."

"I'm a big boy, Harley. I know how to take care of myself."

"Not in this crowd, you don't," Harley growled over the phone.

"And what's that supposed to mean?" Like Tillison, Harley hadn't been pleased with the idea of Walt going to DC alone, but now he sounded particularly anxious.

"I'm not trying to piss on your parade, Walt. I wasn't even going to tell you this, but you just asked. I've done some research on our buddy Branson. He's at the center of all this, and I figured the more we knew about him, the better. I didn't even have to look that hard. There aren't too many toxicologists with my security clearance and we can get involved in some pretty hairy stuff. Anyway, one of my peers, a guy I'm pretty friendly with, knows Branson. Had actually worked with him on some assignment a few years ago. Down in Central America someplace. He wouldn't say exactly where, what or when. But the mission crapped out on them and he and Branson had to get out on their own. The rest of the team didn't even make it out of the hotel.

"At one point they got captured by whoever it was they were screwing with. The local militia or security force or something. Whoever it was, they weren't amateurs. Six of them had the drop on Branson and this toxicologist. Now, my friend could kill you a million different ways with a junior high school chemistry set, but he couldn't beat his own grandmother in a fistfight and she's been dead for years. So it's really Branson and these six guys. Rambos is how my friend described them–big, fit, well-trained guys.

"Branson dropped his gun and put his hands in the air. The militia closed in on him, guns at the ready, and went to handcuff him. Before my friend could finish peeing in his pants from fear, Branson's got all six of them down. He couldn't believe how fast and powerful the man was, even after they got two slugs in him."

"Gee, Harley, I've heard people say the same thing about you after a brawl. Speed and power in a big man scares the shit out of a lot of people. And you've been known to take a slug or two yourself without slowing down." Walt's voice was falsely light-hearted. He knew from painful firsthand experience just how dangerous and unpredictable Branson was.

"Let me finish," responded the toxicologist testily. "In a fight like that, one against six, that single person isn't trying to kill. He just wants to incapacitate his opponents as quickly as possible. Blind them, maim them, scare them, do anything to keep them from getting the upper hand. And that's what Branson did. Dropped all of them with fast, painful strikes. Then, like someone picking weeds from his garden, he went to each man and snapped his neck.

"That's what really stuck in my friend's mind, the methodical way Branson broke those necks. Just as if he were husking corn, is how my friend described it. Grab ahold, pull and twist. I guess he still has nightmares where he hears six grinding cracks. Uncle Sam swears you to ninety-nine years of secrecy on this sort of stuff, so my friend never told a soul about it 'till I called. Then he spilled his guts. I think he'd been staying up nights just waiting for someone to ask him about Branson so he could tell his story, it was eating at him so bad."

"You think this is a setup?"

"I don't know. I'm just warning you to be extra careful. Branson is a first class homicidal nut."

"What about Laste? Did you check on him?" Walt prayed his friend didn't have another litany of horror stories.

"He was easy. I actually met the man once at a seminar. He's what Branson's not. A planner, a politician, a bureaucrat, albeit a unique one. I found some vague mention of family, but nothing I could clarify. Not too surprisingly, his bio'd been sanitized a bit. These top secret types don't want anyone tracking them or their families down if they can help it. Still, I don't think there are any scary secrets with Laste."

"Thanks, Harley, I'll be careful. Like being careful would help if Branson found him in the office. "I've got to hang up now, Bill's supposed to call to let me in. I'll buzz you as soon as I'm out of the office."

"Okay, and good luck."

Walt terminated the call and almost immediately the phone rang. "Crawler here," he answered.

"It's Bill. The coast is clear. You know where to go?"

"Yes."

"Okay. I'll open the door in two minutes exactly. If you're waiting I can get you in while the guard's roving. If you're not there, I'll call again."

"Don't worry. I'll be there."

Walt was waiting when the loading door opened. Without a backwards glance, he ducked through the door and disappeared into the building.

CHAPTER XVIII

9 JULY
WASHINGTON, DC

Adam Branson's fingers were drumming furiously on his desk as he looked across his tiny home office at the smaller, well dressed man sitting opposite him, his smooth face resting on neatly steepled fingers. Damnation, Branson thought, the man must have ice-water in his veins. No matter what happened, he never appeared ruffled, never lost his temper and never appeared nervous. It was like he didn't have any emotions. "That freaking detective, Tillison, is sniffing around our California operation," Branson said. "He's already focused on the facilitator. And last night he picked up Crawler from a bike ride and brought him back to the station. They're working on something, I know it. I just wish we had taken them out last night."

"And your solution?" The smaller man had no time to waste on should-have's.

"Tillison's got to go. And Crawler, too."

"How will you make it happen?" The man's face showed no expression. It was just another business decision.

"I'm not sure. Tillison's been in the police station all day and we can't touch him there. I pulled the surveillance off of Crawler to cover the detective until I can get more people on the island. The cop's going to be the more difficult target and I want to get him first. Then we can get Crawler. If we can make them both disappear, it'll be a lot easier. Plus, we'll need some time alone with them to find out what they know so we can respond. If we can't manage a clean snatch, we may just have to take 'em out in the open and let the chips fall where they will. There's no way either of those two can be walking free tomorrow morning. It's too risky."

"That makes sense." The man rose and glided to the door. "Just keep me posted. And make sure it's done by tomorrow morning."

"One way of the other it will be, don't worry." He waited until his visitor had left and then stood up and prepared to leave himself. While he had the capability of running operations from his home, he felt more comfortable working out of the SCOT's headquarters even when it came to illegal activities. For some reason, he felt more in control there. At this time of the evening, well after six, the place would be empty. And even if someone were there, he still had a completely private office there from which to run the show.

CHAPTER XIX

"I'm not sure where else we can look. Maybe we're just stuck with what we've got." Pryor's face, normally calm and boyish looking, was pinched and worried now. He'd catch holy hell if someone caught them in the office, seated around his computer like two sages consulting a crystal ball.

Walt tried to fight it, but the West Virginian's fear was catching. Although they'd gathered enough information to chew on for a week, things still weren't entirely clear and what he didn't get tonight, he'd never get. Methyl ethyl chlorinate had been listed on six other documents besides the supply chits. The other chemicals and equipment listed in those documents should give him an idea of what, if anything, Branson had done with the poison. But there had to be more. One didn't acquire six pounds of a top secret poison without a reason. With enough clues, Walt thought he could figure out that reason. But he knew he still had nowhere near enough clues.

"What about training and operational schedules?" he asked Pryor. "A lot of people use scheduling programs on their computers to keep track of things. If we use the California and Arsenal blasts as control dates, we may be able to find such a schedule here." It was a lame suggestion, Walt knew, but it was better than just random hacking.

Pryor's fingers stabbed at the keyboard as he typed in a series of queries.

"Wait a second," said Walt quietly, tapping Pryor's monitor with his pen, "here's a file extension with yesterday's date, the same as the California blast. Open it up."

"Give me a minute." The screen flickered and then filled with text. "Bingo!" Pryor said, "we've got something." He scanned the screen quickly. "It's a blurb on that team building program where the explosion was. Give me a second and I'll run a check for files created or saved at the same time. It's not foolproof, but often people save related documents at the same time." A file name blinked on the screen. "Looks like we've found one." He hit *enter* and a small table appeared. "It's an Excel spreadsheet. It's got those two dates and locations, along with another."

Walt peered at the screen. "Nantucket, 9-28-2000. 4:30 PM. That was the target date," his voice trembled as he realized he was looking at the clue that connected all the dots. "If my family hadn't gotten in the way, something would have happened on Nantucket on the twenty-eighth of September. I suppose it still could, but I doubt it. What Julia and my kids set off was supposed to blow six months later.

"Are you saying the SCOT's in on all this crap?" asked Pryor nervously.

"I don't know about the SCOT as a body, but Branson sure as hell is. It fits with what little I know about him. The guy's a homicidal nut. How else can you explain these dates in context with those supply chits you found?"

"But, that means Givens . . ." Pryor's voice trailed off and died.

"Was a sacrifice," finished Walt, seeing the whole picture all at once. "It fits perfectly. Givens was killed just to make sure no one ever suspected the SCOT of being involved in these blasts. How else to better prove to the world you didn't cause something than by offing one of your own in the line of duty? If someone had any suspicions, Paul's death would keep them from barking up that tree. That's why I got put on those sweeps with you, so Branson could finalize his plans in the trailer without me."

"And the grenades we found on Nantucket?"

"They were a cover-up, too." Walt's eyes flashed with excitement and he took out Katie's spoon and began tapping it against his palm. "The real bomb was supposed to go off, probably by some sort of remote command, and kill all the environmentalists attending Senator Jackson's party." Catching Pryor's blank look, he explained, "The Senator was planning a party on his property, which is adjacent to the blast sight, at the end of the summer. A release that powerful would have wiped out everyone at the party, if the wind was blowing in the right direction. Which it probably would have been, giving the prevailing winds at that time of year. Then, after the blast, the responders would have found the box of cold war chemical grenades and labeled the release as a freak accident. That would have been the end of the investigation. The explosion at the Arsenal fits, too. There's no reason anyone will look further than the Army's history of dumping dangerous stuff out there." He put the spoon back in his pocket and stood up.

"What do we do now?" Pryor's voice was still weak, "what's the purpose of all this?"

"I'm not quite sure. Right now, though, I've got to take a leak," said Walt, feeling a wave of weariness surge over him. It was all so outlandishly huge and evil, it made him feel utterly impotent.

"Go ahead." Pryor despondently pecked at his keyboard. "I'll see if I can dig up anything else while you're gone."

Alone in the bathroom, Walt splashed cold water vigorously on his face, trying to jolt some energy back into his psyche. The emotional rollercoaster he'd been riding was taking its toll. How exactly could he, a mere wildlife biologist, succeed in a battle against hardened killers? He splashed more water into his face and steeled himself to go back to Pryor with an upbeat attitude. He needed the West Virginian's help now more than ever and he couldn't afford to seem out of control.

Returning to the office, Walt knocked on the heavy door and waited patiently for Pryor to open it. It had always struck him as odd, having a hardened, top secret government facility stuck in the middle of a regular office building, but Branson claimed such siting actually improved the office's security by lending it an aura of normalcy. Of course, it wasn't normal. The suite's only obvious door was constructed of sturdy composite enamel and its lock was allegedly unbreakable. Hidden security cameras covered the hallway and all the floors, walls, ceilings and windows were of specially strengthened material. Short of using a tank, no one was going to enter the SCOT's office without an invitation.

Pryor opened the door and ushered Walt in. "Are you all right?" he asked, noticing the wet hair clinging to Walt's forehead.

"Yeah, I'm fine. I just splashed my face a bit. Did you find anything new?"

"Yes, I did. I don't know exactly what to make of it though," replied Pryor as he ushered his visitor back into the office.

The heavy door swung shut behind them and neither man heard the elevator open in the outside hallway.

"Check this out." Pryor pointed to a new display that flashed on his computer screen. "I dug out another schedule from the database. It looks like the one we found earlier, but it's got an extra location on it."

Walt peered at the computer screen. "Joshua Tree National Park, 7-15, eight AM. What the hell is that all about?"

"Joshua Tree's a park in Southern California," said Pryor, "and the time and date must mean something's planned then."

"Just like at Lovett," Walt breathed, wondering how many more staged disasters were planned. "He's rigged another release."

Sweat shone on Pryor's forehead. "I can't believe Adam would do this stuff," he said to no one in particular. "I knew he was hot-headed, but this is completely off the wall."

Walt walked away from the computer and picked up a phone on the other side of the room. "Bill, this is bigger than you and me. It's time to call for help."

As Walt picked up the phone, the office door opened and a hulking shape came into the room. Walt looked up in surprise, starting to stammer out an excuse for his presence in the SCOT's office but the words died in his throat when he recognized the man who had just entered the office.

It was Adam Branson.

With a speed that Walt couldn't comprehend, Pryor dove from his chair and launched himself at his boss. His long legs kicked and a pistol fell from Branson's hands, skidding across the floor towards Walt.

"Shit!" Branson roared as he exploded into action, driving Pryor before him with a series of punches and kicks.

Walt stood motionless for a split second, stunned by this sudden apparition, then he pulled a chair from the floor and charged at Branson, swinging the chair wildly.

Branson, a master at hand-to-hand combat, recognized the threat for what it was. An enthusiastic but unskilled attempt to drop him with a weapon designed for sitting. It looked good in the movies, but here, in real life, Branson stepped back from Pryor, ducked under the chair, grabbed Walt's arm and hurled him back across the room. Before Walt had even hit the floor, Branson was back pressing the assault on Pryor. He smiled wolfishly, the look of a predator surveying its prey.

"Found something you didn't like, did you?" Branson taunted, trying to break the younger man's concentration. Pryor was good at unarmed combat, very good in fact, but Branson knew he'd never been in a real fight, a fight where the winner walked away and the loser never walked again. A fight where the only rule was that there were no rules.

"What are you doing, Adam?" hissed Pryor, circling to his right, trying to get near the door. "You're crazy, killing people for what?"

The two men traded tentative blows, searching for the opponent's weakness, knocking furniture aside as they strove for an advantageous position. In the outer office a phone began to ring, its electronic buzzing sounding lonely and insignificant as it went on unanswered for a time and then stopped.

"I'm sorry it had to come down to this, Bill," said Branson evenly after a few minutes. He meant those words. All of his team members were like family to him, but sometimes there just was no choice. The mission always came first. "If you'd stayed out of stuff that didn't concern you, you could have gone far."

"If I'd stayed out of stuff that didn't concern me, I'd have helped you kill even more people. It's got to stop." Pryor tested Branson's reflexes with two quick kicks, low ones aimed at the knee. Branson deflected both of them and the two men squared off again, Branson still blocking the door. "You killed Paul, too, didn't you? The man thought you walked on water and you blew him to bits to help cover your sorry ass. How many more innocent people did you kill?" Pryor's voice was like a hissing snake.

"You know better than that, Bill. No one's innocent these days." Branson side-stepped to the left, maneuvering Pryor into the corner. Pryor was good, one of the best at sparring in a ring. Fighting among office furniture was different, however. If Branson could keep the fight close, his greater size and strength could overcome Pryor's speed and finesse. His left leg brushed up against the office's metal wastebasket. With the instincts of a natural street fighter, he kicked out, sending the basket rocketing towards Pryor's head. Pryor reflexively swatted it away, realizing only too late that Branson was charging in behind it. He dropped to a defensive stance and struck out viciously with both hands, catching Branson solidly on the chest and shoulders.

But it was too little, too late for Pryor. Branson's vast bulk absorbed the blows without slowing down. He slammed into Pryor with the force of a speeding train, hurling the smaller man backwards into a row of file cabinets.

Years of intense training had taught Pryor to function even when his body was screaming in pain. But as the metal handles of the file cabinet speared him in the back and the wind rushed out of his lungs like a balloon popping, he knew he was doomed.

He tried to raise his right arm for a block but it wouldn't respond. His knees buckled under him and, as he toppled forward onto the tiled floor, his blurred vision registered the towering figure of Adam Branson looming high over him. Then the world went black.

Branson sagged back against a desk, gasping for breath. At his feet, the crumpled body of William Pryor stared up at him with sightless eyes. Damn, that had been close! In his last flurry, Pryor had hit him several times, hard, and now his whole body ached. He looked down at Pryor's corpse. The fool! Why hadn't Pryor minded his own business, Branson asked himself rhetorically, uselessly. Now there was one more body to deal with, and he had killed someone he had come to like a great deal.

Branson touched his fingers to his face gingerly, exploring his wounds as he pondered his next move. His fingers touched something wet and they came away slick with blood. Pryor's last strike, a desperate stiff fingered eye gouge that would have crippled Branson had it succeeded, had, instead, left a long, deep groove on his left cheekbone that hurt like hell. He looked across the room where Walt had struggled back to his feet. He would find out what the biologist knew and what he had told to whom, and then he'd teach him what real pain felt like.

"You just couldn't stay away, could you?" he said menacingly, taking a step towards Walt like a tiger stalking a caged gazelle. "You fucking eco-freaks, always trying to save the world. Well, look who you saved tonight." Branson gestured roughly at Pryor's body. "I'll bet he appreciates the hell out of your efforts."

"You're an animal," Walt spat out, desperately thinking of what to do next. He wouldn't have a chance fighting Branson, his only choice was to run. He stepped backwards towards the exit as the bigger man approached. "It's bad enough you're letting my daughter rot away in a hospital bed, but you've still got to increase your body counts. You're nothing but a fucking animal."

"I won't argue the point, my friend," Branson's tone was pleasantly conversational, as if he and Walt were talking about baseball statistics, "but if I'm an animal, at least I'm a lion. And you, you're nothing more than a weasel." He took another step towards Walt. "And now you're going to tell me everything you think you know about what this lion's been up to."

With a burst of speed supercharged by fear, Walt spun on his heels and dashed for the door. It opened into the hallway and Walt knew he'd never get out of the building alive if he didn't squeeze through the door before Branson's huge hands locked on his throat. As his right hand clasped the knob, he heard the big man charging through the wreckage strewn about the office during his fight with Pryor. He flung the door open and threw himself down the hall, certain he could feel Branson's hot breath on the back of his neck. Despite the pain in his arm where Branson had grabbed him, Walt ran as he'd never run before, pounding down the hall, through the crashbar at the top of the stairwell, down the stairs and through the fire door into the empty parking lot beyond.

Behind him, hindered by the blows he had taken during his fight with Pryor, Branson's footsteps faltered, then died out completely.

Walt sprinted through the evening darkness, alone once more.

CHAPTER XX

Walt ran until he could run no more. When he finally stopped, gasping for breath and almost unable to stand because of the pain in his shins, he was sure he'd lost his pursuer. He leaned against the brick wall of a fast food restaurant and forced himself to think clearly. Pryor was dead and Branson, with whatever resources he could muster, was after him. The cops, Walt's brain flashed, go to the cops.

Could he go to the cops and tell them that Branson had just killed Pryor? Could it be that simple?

With a sinking heart, Walt realized that, assuming the police could get access to the secured facility, by the time they checked out his story, Branson would have sanitized the entire office. Walt had heard stories of how even a tall man like Pryor could fit into one of the large overpack drums kept in the office for training purposes. The thought of Pryor, the closest thing to a friend he'd had on the SCOT, being rolled in a barrel out to the team's secure loading dock made his stomach spasm. It was Walt's fault that the West Virginian had been there. It was his fault he was dead.

Walt forced himself to let go of that thought and to concentrate on his current predicament. He could shed tears for Pryor later. If he did go to the police, how could he explain what he'd been doing in a top secret government office without proper clearance? Branson might well get the cops to hold him for a day or two on some sort of trespassing charges. And anything could happen in a cellblock.

The safest course, Walt decided, was to remain free. He'd call Jeff Tillison and Harley and take the fight right back to

Branson. The AG would have one hell of a document in the morning. Still limping from the pain in his legs, Walt began walking down the street, searching for a dark, protected place from which he could make his calls.

Branson, cursing a blue stream under his laboring breath, returned to the office and began to put the furniture back together. His struggle with Pryor had been almost cataclysmic. While he'd gotten the upper hand at the end, it had not come easily and he was going to be very, very sore for a while. But he couldn't let that stop him. First, though he had to make the office look as if nothing out of the ordinary had happened. There'd be enough questions about Pryor's unexpected absence without having the place look like a war zone.

As he organized the furniture and folded Pryor's body into an overpack drum, Branson tried to decide what to do next. Crawler had escaped. The question now was where had he gone? Branson had no answer. The biologist probably had friends in the area. Everyone knew at least a few people who lived in DC, and Walt had just spent three months in town. That Branson had been unable to link him to any local inhabitants did not mean anything conclusive. He could still know people well enough to drop in unexpectedly if he wanted to get off the streets.

Or maybe Crawler would go further afield.

If he already had access to a car, there was no telling where Crawler might go. If, however, he didn't already have a car, Branson would make sure he couldn't get one. He picked up the phone. Moments later, Walt's credit card was invalid. All the biologist would accomplish by trying to charge something would be to let Branson know exactly where he was. The redhead hoped it would be that easy, but experience had shown him that it never was. Murphy made sure of that.

Would Crawler go to the cops, Branson wondered. Initially that scenario worried him, but then he realized that that would gain the biologist nothing. He had no documents to prove anything he might claim. He'd even left his backpack in the SCOT's office. Other than whatever he'd had in his pockets when Branson had thrown him across the room, Crawler had nothing. All he had going for him was a strange story of assassination plans, cover-ups and long-distance murders, if he even knew that much. That it was all true didn't bother Branson in the least, for the police wouldn't believe one word without stronger proof than just Walt's accusations. And Branson was going to make sure that such proof didn't exist.

No, for Walt, going to the cops was just going to compound his problems. He'd been dealt a solo hand. The question now was, how would the man play it.

The real issue was how much did Crawler know and what would he do with that information. Unfortunately, Pryor's computer had been disconnected during the fight, so there was no way to determine exactly what they'd gleaned from the SCOT's files. What had made Crawler so sure of himself, Branson mused, that taken such a huge risk in gaining unauthorized entry to the SCOT's office? How had he managed to convince Pryor to let him in?

A scowl creased Branson's broad face. Whether Crawler could prove anything or not, something had gone terribly wrong to have brought the biologist this far.

CHAPTER XXI

Walt stumbled down an overgrown trail and found himself in the midst of a small grassy field on the C&O Canal just outside of Georgetown. While the mosquitoes might, and in fact, were already starting to, eat him alive, he felt certain that Branson would never find him here. A mosquito buzzed by his ear and Walt swatted at it before settling down on a concrete abutment, his legs dangling over the stagnant canal water. He pulled his cell phone from its holster and punched in Tillison's number. He had agreed to call Harley when he left the SCOT office, but Pryor's death had changed things.

The phone rang and a woman picked it up almost instantly. "Hello?" She sounded anxious.

"Maria, it's Walt. Is Jeff there?" Walt was still reeling from the violence he'd just witnessed, his mind flashing unbidden to a picture of Pryor smashing into the filing cabinets, and he did not want to waste time on pleasantries.

"No, Jeff's not here. I was hoping it was him calling."

Walt thought he detected a slight tremble in her voice. "Do you know where he is?"

"No. He was supposed to be home for dinner an hour ago. I've tried him at the station and he's not there. His car's still out in the lot, but no one's seen him. I've got no idea where he went. He's never been this late for dinner without calling." Like any cop's spouse, Maria knew a hundred things, all of them bad, could happen to her husband at any time. What, for any other wife, would be something to get upset about was, for Maria, something to dread. At some point, a late husband never came home.

Walt looked at the phone dumbly. He knew what had happened to Jeff. Somehow, Branson had known that Walt had figured out his scheme before stumbling into him at the SCOT office. The detective wasn't late, he was dead. "Jeez, Maria," Walt stammered, not knowing what to say. As long as there was no body, she would still have hope. And they wouldn't find a body, he knew. If Branson had wanted them to, they'd have found it already, in Jeff's car or outside the police station. With no body, there'd be less of a chance of someone tracking anything back to the SCOT. Especially if Branson could bag Walt, too.

"Well, hopefully he'll show up in a bit," Walt offered, "he probably got sidetracked by someone at the whaling museum or something." He knew Maria wouldn't believe it, but he felt he had to say something. Besides, he didn't know for sure Jeff was dead. Certainly he couldn't prove it to anyone. "Just tell him I called, okay?" His hand was gripping the phone so hard his knuckles hurt. His best friend had just died and all he could tell Maria was 'tell him I called.' What was happening to him? How could he be so cold?

"Sure, Walt, I'll tell him you called." Maria's voice was leaden.

Walt clicked the phone off and sat motionless on the abutment, lost in vacant thought, unaware even of the hordes of mosquitoes that had descended on every bit of his flesh not covered by clothes. Only when the buzzing around his ears had reached almost thunderous proportions did Walt move. He slapped at the mosquitoes on his cheeks and then began slapping at his bare forearms, feeling dozens of the tiny insects get crushed under the blows. The stinging sensation of the slaps, repeated again and again, harder and harder, finally brought Walt back to earth, focused once again on the real, the immediate, the physical.

Tillison was gone, Pryor was definitely dead. The only other person he could turn to was Harley. Would he be in time, or had Branson gotten him too? The thought of the big toxicologist floating face down in Falmouth Harbor slammed into his psyche like a freight train and Walt's chest began to tighten, squeezing horribly in an anxiety attack that made it hard to breathe. What had he gotten into? What had he gotten his friends into? He rolled backwards, away from the yawning chasm of the canal, and curled into a fetal ball on the damp grass.

After a few minutes the attack, the first one Walt had ever suffered, was gone, leaving him a sweating, trembling mess. He staggered to his feet, found the phone and called Harley, praying that he wasn't too late.

After four rings the answering machine picked up. Harley wasn't home. What did that mean? Perhaps the biker had got tired of waiting for his call and had gone out to run an errand or have a beer. Branson couldn't have killed everybody already. Besides, there was no clear connection between Walt and Tillison and Harley. He had to be out for a few moments, that was all. Walt left his cell phone number and tried his friend's work number. There was no answer there, either, and, after leaving another message, Walt began to trudge slowly towards the lights of Georgetown, wondering just how far, and how quickly, Branson's arm could reach.

Walt turned into the first bar he passed and ordered a beer. He finished it in one long gulp and ordered another. The second went just as quickly and Walt settled down to nurse his third, chewing listlessly on the party nuts in front of him. His mind was racing at a thousand miles an hour. Would Harley call? If not, to whom could he turn? Not Charlie Laste, or anyone else on the SCOT. Even if Walt trusted them, which he didn't, he'd lost all his numbers when he left his backpack in the SCOT office and there was no way he could track them down through information. Janice, his boss? She was on a three week train trip in Europe, staying at Bed and Breakfasts and following no set itinerary. For Walt's purposes, with only a few days before Branson sprang his plan in Joshua Tree, she might as well have gone to the moon. The Attorney General? If Branson had Tillison, then there was no packet ready to go to the AG's office.

That was just one more closed door. Without Harley, he would be in it alone.

His phone rang and Walt almost knocked his beer over in his eagerness to answer it.

"Hello."

"Walt, Harley here. What's going on? One of my experiments started going haywire and I had to run down to the lab for a bit. I got your message when I returned."

"Branson found us in the office."

"Oh shit! What happened?"

"He killed Pryor. I barely got out. I tried calling Tillison, but he never made it home from work. Branson's got him, too. I'm afraid you might be next."

"Where are you?"

Harley sounded unfazed and Walt wondered what sort of top secret stuff his friend had done that kept the news of Tillison and Pryor's death from rattling him. "I'm at a bar in Georgetown right now. I can't go pick up my rental car because it's right next to the SCOT office. I'm stuck here for now. But it's worse. We found some files that indicate Branson's got something planned for Joshua Tree, California on the fifteenth of this month."

"Any idea what it is?"

"No. Branson jumped us just as we found the file."

"Can you find a place to stash yourself until I make it down?"

"How long will you be?"

"It'll take me a few minutes to get organized. If Branson's looking for me, I want to be out of here as soon as possible. Then another eight hours or so to ride down."

"You're going to ride? I've got a buddy in Chatham who has his own plane. You could be down here in a couple of hours."

"You know I can't fly. You put me on an airplane and I'll be a basket case when I get off. I'll be no good to anyone. You'll just have to wait a bit longer. I'll be down for breakfast. Now, where do you want to meet?"

Walt thought of a safe, unmistakable place. "Seven o'clock in front of National Cathedral."

"I'll be there. I'll call you if I'm going to be late."

Harley clicked off the line and Walt was left alone with his beer, thinking of his next move. Once Harley came down, he'd no longer be alone but he would still be unable to convince anyone that Branson was a chemical terrorist. His only choice, he realized, was to stop whatever Branson was planning in Joshua Tree. And that meant a trip West. He thought about Harley's fear of flying. He'd never get that man on a plane, so it meant a trip West on Harley's bike. That would make the timing tight, but it was doable. If they could get to Joshua Tree, figure out what Branson was planning, alert the authorities and stop the plot, the rest of their claims would gain instant credibility. At best it was a long shot, and how all that would help Katie was not immediately apparent, but there was no other road to travel.

He pulled out Katie's spoon and tapped it gently against his palm. Branson might be big and fast and well-connected. He might have murderous minions throughout the nation. He might be well-trained and capable, but he didn't have a three year old daughter slowly wasting away in a hospital bed. This vital personal interest in bringing Branson to justice evened the scales. If anyone knew what was poisoning Katie, if anyone knew what type of antidote to use on the girl, it was the redheaded SCOT team officer. The knowledge that, for months, Branson had looked him square in the eye, having destroyed his family and poisoned his little girl, even while he held the key to saving her, infuriated Walt beyond belief. He fought down the desire to guzzle the rest of the beer and rubbed the spoon instead.

By God, he would make that asshole pay!

Walt settled the bill and left the bar. The best thing he could do right now was buy a can of bug spray and find a bridge under which he could safely spend the night. Tomorrow was a whole new day and he wanted to be well rested.

CHAPTER XXII

10 JULY
WASHINGTON, DC

Walt awoke with the dawn, the sunlight filtering through a layer of raw looking clouds that had moved in overnight. He was surprised to find that he had no trouble immediately focusing on his situation. The anxiety of the night before was definitely vanquished. He had something real and immediate to focus on. Getting to Joshua Tree. He wondered what Julia would think of this new mission. There was no grieving for Bill or Jeff. Sometime during his sleep, he'd boxed them up, too. Yet there was a subtle change within him. For some reason, the boxes didn't seem as inaccessible as they generally were. Perhaps, he thought, when he needed courage, he could dig down into some of those boxes and find a pleasant memory. He rubbed the spoon in his pocket and thought of Katie at her second birthday party, waving a toy shovel he'd given her like a tomahawk, her hair full of ribbons and her face full of smiles. He prayed he would see the same smiles again one day.

Piercing hunger pains interrupted Walt's musings and reminded him that he'd forgotten to eat the night before. Three beers, no matter how badly needed, didn't count as dinner. His watch said just before six and he decided he had time to grab a bagel before meeting Harley. Knowing his friend, the first thing the biker would want to do once he got to DC was eat, anyway, so Walt didn't have to worry about stoking up for very long.

A half hour later, bagel and a large cup of coffee in hand, Walt settled down in front of the National Cathedral to wait for his friend. Around him the morning crowd was slowly thickening and Walt felt safely invisible amidst the gathering throng. That was where his strength now lay, in being invisible. As long as Branson couldn't see him, couldn't find him, Walt knew he had some hope. If Branson located him, however, he'd be forced to run and would lose the all-important initiative. If he even managed to live.

While he waited, Walt pondered his position. How many people could Branson have working for him? Certainly Givens and Pryor hadn't been. Were other members of the SCOT working with Branson? Or was he a lone wolf, working with underworld characters when he needed outside assistance? Walt had no idea so he decided to assume anyone on the SCOT was on the wrong side.

Did that mean Laste? That was a disquieting thought. While Walt had not had much interaction with the SCOT team leader, he'd found him to be a stable, dignified and resourceful man. More hands-off than Walt would have been in his position, but still competent and knowledgeable. A highly accomplished and respected federal bureaucrat, Laste should have no reason to join Branson on the redheaded man's murderous crusade. Remembering the leader's overruling Branson on Walt's original site visit on Nantucket, Walt decided Laste had to be clean. If he were rotten, he never would have let Walt near the SCOT.

Ten miles away, Branson was also up with the sun. He'd sanitized the office and removed everything from Pryor's desk that could possibly explain what Crawler had figured out. He'd even removed the hard drive from Pryor's computer and replaced it with a spare. When the rest of the SCOT came in, Branson would tell them that Pryor had asked for emergency leave the night before. There would eventually be questions about his permanent absence, but Branson could make things fuzzy enough so that no one would suspect the truth.

Dealing with Pryor hadn't been pleasant, but Branson knew that dealing with life's major challenges rarely were. He had decided on a course of action long ago and he'd carry out his duty, as he saw it, until he could do no more.

That was nothing new. Branson had done his duty all his life. He'd never shirked from an unpleasant task, never walked away from a dangerous situation. If the job had to be done, he'd do it. The mission came first. Always. A fat lot of good that attitude had done him in the Army, though, he thought sullenly. He'd been hung by his balls to protect some general's fitness report just because he'd carried out an agreed upon mission. But Branson couldn't change who he was. The mission would always come first. He'd just had to change the type of missions he believed in.

So he'd moved from the Army to another, more Machiavellian agency where the missions were clearer and there were no generals. But that hadn't lasted forever, either.

It had happened just six years earlier. He'd been on an operation to Central America to conduct a liquidation project. Posing as tourists, he, along with two of his best men and a chemist on contract, were to alter the water supply for a small town in the Costa Rican highlands a few days before several government officials showed up for a top secret conference. Less than a week later, the officials would be dead, along with all of the inhabitants of the town. Autopsies would show a freak bacteria had gone amuck in the local water delivery system. It would have been just one more example, albeit a very drastic one, of how tenuous potable water systems could be. It had been a classic plan.

But the environmentalists blew his cover. He still wasn't sure if it was a member of Rainforest Action or Earthfirst! or a birdwatcher from the Audubon Society, but someone on an eco-tour in the same hotel recognized the gear his chemist had brought along as being uniquely incompatible with a tourist's basic luggage load. He'd informed one of the tour guides, who, in turn, had alerted the local security forces. Branson had responded as best he could, but his men had been caught with their pants down. Only Branson and the chemist had escaped, and even then, just barely.

Those things happened, Branson knew. Murphy's law bit you in the ass every chance it got, usually at the very worst possible moment. But that didn't mean you sat around and took it without fighting back. Two of Branson's men, two of his closest friends, men who had entrusted him with their lives, had been butchered because some asshole from the States had come down to study the nesting habits of the red feathered fig pucker and couldn't keep his damn mouth shut. After four years, none of the seven members of the eco-tour remained alive. Branson wasn't sure which one had exposed his team, so they all paid the price.

But that hadn't been enough. Still bitter after being cashiered from the Army, he wanted to make the environmentalists pay a thousand times over for the misery they had caused him. When he was approached to create and run the SCOT, Branson had thought he could twist the position into one where he could deal out disasters, not just respond to them. He could not have dreamed how right he'd been, although it had taken a bit longer to actualize his revenge than he had hoped.

Branson shifted his thoughts to the distinguished man with the well-manicured hands. He'd been the real mastermind for the plan, supplying the dates, times and locations for Branson to hit. Anyone could blow up the meeting of a local bird watching club, the man had argued when they'd first met. That type of revenge would have been too shallow, too meaningless. Instead, with the information he would provide, the man had claimed Branson would be able to wipe out the environmental movement as it existed in the United States, if not the world.

Why his companion was doing what he was doing Branson did not know. All he knew was, shortly after having started working for the SCOT, he'd been approached in a mall by someone claiming to have an offer he couldn't refuse. The approach had been so pitifully amateurish that Branson had actually listened to the offer, his eyes widening in appreciation as the man outlined his plan. Branson had never learned how the man had figured out he might be a potential ally, but the choice had been a good one. After investigating his new contact and determining it wasn't a setup, Branson had begun to put things in motion. Using the SCOT to shield his movements and to obtain the necessary equipment, he had set a variety of traps that would destroy the cream of the world's environmental leaders in just a few short months.

Branson's position on the SCOT had also enabled him to pull in an assistant to help with the setups. He had known Manny Rodriquez in the Army. In fact, they'd met over an arm-wrestling match, with Rodriquez wrongly thinking he could best Branson's bulk. Despite having thoroughly trounced his opponent, Branson had been impressed with the Texan's spunk and had managed to get him assigned to his unit. Under the redhead's tutelage, Rodriquez prospered, eventually becoming a first sergeant. When Branson was cashiered from the Army, however, Rodriquez, had taken it personally and decided to get out as well. The two men moved together into the twilight world of covert ops and had been working side by side ever since, Branson always the leader, Rodriquez ever the ready subordinate. In fact, Rodriquez had been supposed to accompany Branson to Central America on the mission during which the redhead's team had been virtually wiped out. Only a last minute stomach virus had spared the Texan from being caught in that disaster. When he began to build the SCOT, Rodriquez had been the first person Branson brought on board, believing, correctly, that the wiry man would be willing to help carry out his secret agenda of revenge.

One of the most beautiful things about the plan was that, in all likelihood, the SCOT would be involved in any response actions, giving Branson the ability to further cover his tracks. He'd set it up that way, making sure there were always real bombs and chemicals to provide a safety margin even if the traps went off or were found by accident. Fatal accidents were bound to happen in a post-industrial society with such a long history of military and industrial manufacturing. A cold war chemical grenade explodes? A forgotten artillery shell cooks off under a camp fire? Too bad, but those things happened, and Joshua Tree was going to be the *piece de resistance*.

Stumbling across the methyl ethyl chlorinate during an excess locker inventory had been the clincher, allowing Branson to use an incredibly potent poison that anyone else would mistake for regular chlorine gas. No one would realize it was all part of a carefully orchestrated plan. If his luck held, he could keep laying traps forever, until environmentalists were as extinct as the animals they were so committed to saving.

But he hadn't counted on Crawler. It was Murphy again, with one hell of a bite this time. Of all the people to have had their family stumble across one of his traps, Walt Crawler had to be one of the worst. Somehow, Crawler had put all the pieces together. He knew what was going on. Or at least what had already happened.

It was all because of those fucking birds! Rodriquez had gotten that much out of Tillison before the detective died. Who could have known the chemical would have a different impact on birds? The initial tests had indicated it had a minimal, and relatively immediate, impact on wildlife. But the lengthy delay before the birds died had created a hole in the plan, one that the biologist had seized with vigor.

Did Crawler know about Joshua Tree? Pryor, already cremated and scattered in the Potomac, could not say what they'd known. Tillison hadn't seemed to know about it, at least. If the biologist didn't know about Joshua Tree, the rest of the operation would go as planned. Even if Crawler surfaced later, he would just be considered a nut. The problem would be if Crawler knew about the Joshua Tree operation and warned people. Not that anyone would believe him, but it would raise a lot of ugly questions after the fact.

Branson tapped a small packet of false IDs on his desk. If he hadn't caught Crawler by the time Joshua Tree went hot, he might even have to go into hiding. That might mean his war would have to stop for a while, but those were the whims of fortune.

He bit his lip and cursed Crawler for getting in the way. He should have taken him out right after the first blast, made it look like a suicide. That bit of preventive medicine would have nipped this problem in the bud. But he hadn't, and there was no use worrying about it now. Right now he had to focus on finding Crawler as soon as possible. The question was, where to start looking.

CHAPTER XXIII

Walt heard the rumble of Harley's bike long before the toxicologist arrived in front of the Cathedral. He stood up, tossed the empty coffee cup in a trash can and reached the street just as Harley finished parking his bike.

"Hi, Harley, it's good to see you," he said simply.

Harley turned around and a broad smile lit up his face. "It's good to see you, too, brother. I've been worried about you." He looked closely at Walt's face, grimy from sleeping outside and swollen with mosquito bites. "Are you all right?"

"As all right as possible, under the circumstances," Walt offered up a small smile to allay his friend's concerns. "Why don't we get something to eat and I can tell you what I think is going on and what we might be able to do about it."

"Sounds good to me. I could eat a horse."

Walt smiled again. Harley could always eat a horse.

Within a few minutes, the two men found a small café off of M street. They placed their orders and then found a table in the rear of the room where they could speak in relative seclusion. Walt explained what had happened in the SCOT office, going over in as much detail as he could what he and Pryor had discovered. Unfortunately, Harley agreed, they had only begun to scratch the surface on Branson's activities.

"Another twenty minutes and we would have been out of there," concluded Walt as the waitress brought their food. "I was just about to make a call to Jeff and ask him to contact the Attorney General immediately. It would have taken a little while, but my idea was to get someone to secure the building before anyone showed up for work this morning. Then we could have gotten a warrant to search the office. Everything else would have flowed from that. Or at least, that was my plan," he concluded sadly.

"You did what you could, Walt," comforted Harley. "Jeff and Pryor were both in on this because they wanted to be, because it was the right thing to do. It's too bad about them, but I'm sure they'd both do it all over again if they could choose. I know Jeff would. He always knew the difference between right and wrong and no one could ever force him to back down once he took up an issue. It was his character, who he was." Unlike Walt, Harley had no problem in immediately talking about Tillison and Pryor in the past tense. "Say, what are you eating?" Harley's voice took on a new, sharper tone.

Walt looked at his friend strangely. It was an odd time to be concerned about his dietary habits. "What am I eating?" he repeated, looking at the biscotti he was holding, "I'm eating biscotti, what'd you think?" He took a bite from one end to emphasize his point.

"No you're not."

"What do you mean? I ought to know, I ordered it." Walt was thoroughly confused. Now was no time for Harley to play the jester.

"How many times do I have to tell you?" Harley pinched the pastry out of Walt's fingers, "if you don't dunk your biscotti in your coffee, it's a freakin' cookie. You're eating a cookie now, just like you do when we hit the track in East Boston. And it pisses me off here just as much as it pisses me off there." He plunged the biscuit deep into Walt's cup and held it there for several seconds. "There," he said, handing Walt the soggy treat, "now you're going to eat biscotti. You can't let an asshole like Branson make you forget your values."

Walt sighed resignedly and sucked down a large chunk of the biscuit. There was no use getting upset. Harley was, after all, Harley.

By the time they'd finished breakfast, Walt and Harley had decided on a course of action. They would, as Walt had planned, ride Harley's bike to Joshua Tree. If they made decent time, they should get there a day or so before Branson's plot was to hatch, whatever it was. Hopefully that would be enough time to both identify the plot and to neutralize it.

As Harley paid the bill, Walt pulled the silver spoon from his pocket and tapped it lightly against his palm. Such a small spoon, so delicate he could probably bend it between his thumb and fingers, but durable enough to outlast him if it was treated right. Would he ever get the chance to give it to Katie? He could only pray he would as he joined Harley going out the door.

An hour later Walt and Harley were sitting on his bike, leafing through a California guidebook they'd picked up at a local bookstore. Walt flipped through the pages until he found the entry marked "Joshua Tree National Park" and they both read the entry to themselves. Originally a National Monument, Joshua Tree had only recently become a National Park, a change environmentalists characterized as a great victory, while local commercial businesses worried about big government taking over. Consisting of 1,238 square miles of rocky, mountainous desert, the Park had a colorful history of cattle ranching, rustling and gold mining. There was a detailed map of the Park and both men pored over it, trying to visualize its nooks and crannies, trying to see where Adam Branson could hide something terrible, trying to understand how they could waltz into the Park's security headquarters and explain that they were there to stop something they couldn't even describe.

Yeah, right pal, Walt told himself, that'll work just fine. They'll just freeze everything in its tracks, stop whatever it might be you're talking about, give you a medal for saving the world and send you back to the hospital with an antidote for Katie. Oh, right, they'll put Branson in jail too, end all of your worries.

Walt shut the book. "Let's get on the road," he said to Harley, "looking at this map isn't going to get us any place right now."

"Okay, man," replied Harley, handing Walt a helmet. "Where it's legal to ride without one, feel free to take this off, but otherwise you've got to have this brain bucket on your head whenever we're riding."

Walt thought of the crack in his bicycle helmet after his fall at Cockaponsett State Forest. "Don't worry, Harley. If you're moving, I'll be wearing this."

Harley stepped up on the starter pedal and, with a roar that made people jump with alarm, the big bike moved into the traffic and started heading west.

CHAPTER XXIV

Alone in the SCOT office, Adam Branson was ready to pound the walls in frustration. After reviewing a printout of phone calls to and from Walt's house since he'd set up the wire tap, Branson had decided to further investigate the three most frequently listed numbers. Two of the numbers, a teacher on Cape Cod and a doctor from the Mass General Hospital, had appeared innocuous, but the third, a marine toxicologist from Falmouth, had immediately seemed problematic. With a few phone calls, Branson soon learned almost all there was to know about Ross Mitchell and, without exception, everything he'd learned was bad news.

Unfortunately, the big man mused, Detective Tillison hadn't been the only dangerous friend Walt Crawler had brought into this game. It was too bad that Tillison hadn't lived long enough to explain all of that, and more, to Rodriquez, but once the detective had slipped his cuffs and pulled a backup derringer from an ankle holster, the Texan hadn't had any choice but to kill him. Branson allowed himself a mental shrug. Those were the breaks.

Still, Tillison's death and Mitchell's sudden appearance on the scene had left the SCOT operative with some major intelligence gaps. The only way to plug them, he'd decided, was to send Rodriquez, who was still on Nantucket in the hope that Crawler would return, across the Sound to Falmouth to investigate, and, if possible, to eliminate, the toxicologist. He'd given Rodriquez his orders hours earlier, and the subsequent wait was driving Branson crazy with frustration.

The phone rang and the redhead snatched it up. "Hello!" he barked.

"Boss, it's Manny," Rodriquez said unnecessarily. He was the only one who ever called Branson on this number. "It's not looking good up here."

"Oh shit," muttered Branson, wondering just how much else could go wrong, "what's up?"

"I've been by his house three times and each time there's been a cruiser out front. They're waiting for him. They probably want to ask him about Tillison."

That made sense, thought Branson. If Crawler, Tillison and Mitchell were working together, and Tillison and Crawler were both gone, the police would very likely be interested in talking to Mitchell. "Can you get in?" It was a pro forma question. Rodriquez could get in anywhere.

"Yeah, eventually. The cops aren't being subtle about being here. It's not like they're doing a stakeout, they just want to be here when Mitchell comes home. Once it's dark, I should be able to sneak through the back yard and go in through a cellar window. It's a one-story ranch so I won't have to worry about getting trapped upstairs if someone comes in while I'm there. I've got night goggles and he keeps his blinds drawn, so I should be able to do okay once I'm inside. But it's going to slow me down."

"By how much?"

"It won't be dark enough to move until after eight-thirty or so. And I'll have to make sure the cops aren't too alert, so it might be even later."

"So, you're talking about not getting out of the house until maybe as late as eleven or even midnight?"

"Yeah, probably. And that brings me to another problem. There's a band of thunderstorms moving down from New Hampshire that look like they're going to sock this area pretty good sometime tonight. If I'm not in the air before they get here, I may have to wait until they've moved through." Rodriquez had flown up to Hyannis in one of the planes, registered to dummy corporations, that Branson kept outside of DC. The speed and flexibility provided by the aircraft was impressive, but not perfect. "That means I might not get back to DC until mid-morning."

Branson gritted his teeth. "If that's how it plays out, that's how it plays out. Do what you can. But be careful," he cautioned, "Mitchell might have rigged up some sort of special home security system." As if having cops posted outside the door wasn't trouble enough.

"Not to worry, bossman, no one's made a security system yet that I can't beat."

"I hope not." Branson clicked the phone off and went back to waiting.

Rain had already started falling when Rodriquez began to work his way down the narrow strip of hedges that led into Ross Mitchell's back yard. While the rain might make his work a bit more uncomfortable, he was more than happy to trade that against the reduced likelihood that either of the two police officers stationed in front of Mitchell's house would venture out of their cruiser to check the back yard. With a bit of luck, he could pry the cellar window open, slip into the basement and, using his night vision goggles to get around, quickly determine what type of threat Ross Mitchell posed and how to best counteract it.

A short barreled .22 automatic dug into his back as he crawled under some bushes and Rodriquez rubbed it reassuringly. If anyone did stumble onto him during this surreptitious mission, it would be the last thing that person did. Rodriquez took his loyalty to Branson seriously. He would never give anyone the opportunity to interrogate him.

The cellar window popped easily and Rodriquez slipped softly into the basement. His goggles indicated no infrared light sensors for him to trip and a quick search of the window with a shielded penlight had not discerned any wires, magnets or electronic transmitters. There still could be weight sensors embedded in the floor or heat sensors installed overhead, but Rodriquez doubted it. Judging from the piles of bike parts and other cast-off junk that littered Mitchell's yard and porch, Rodriquez didn't believe that Mitchell had it in him to employ such high-tech systems. He would be careful, of course, but his instincts on such things had never let him down yet. And if they did, he still had his pistol.

The basement proved to be empty, other than some junked furniture and a combination furnace/boiler. By tracing the various lines coming out of the fuse box and studying the wires that snaked through the joists in the basement's ceiling, Rodriquez reassured himself that the house was not set up with pressure plates. If Mitchell had any security system at all, it was probably just a loop system around his first floor doors and windows. The type of system that would keep honest people honest but wouldn't keep people like Rodriquez out.

The upstairs was a replica of the basement, with the addition of a massive amount of motorcycle parts spread over every flat surface he could see. There was no computer, no filing cabinet, no bookshelf full of binders. If Branson hadn't told him about Mitchell's being a Ph.D., Rodriquez would have thought he was in the home of just another pseudo-unemployed biker. After thirty minutes of searching, he determined that the only thing of value was the answering machine, whose blinking light indicated it had seven messages. Taking the machine would be the easiest thing to do, but it would also alert Mitchell, whose phone and house had just been thoroughly bugged, that someone was investigating him so Rodriquez took out a small tape recorder and placed it next to the answering machine. If he couldn't get a tape of the messages, he'd write down each message and leave the machine where it was.

Jack Thorne had been a Falmouth police officer for only six months. Like any other rookie, he'd been assigned a partner for his first year, someone who could help fill in the educational gaps not covered by the Police Academy. Thorne's partner, Bill Grasso, was a heavyset, florid faced veteran of twenty-seven years with the Falmouth PD, an officer who knew better than to walk in the rain when it wasn't absolutely necessary. But if Thorne wanted to go get wet, that was his problem.

"Once you get soaked and get back in the car, I don't want you dripping all over my crap," Grasso grouched. "It's not like we have to patrol the place, we're only here to talk to Mitchell if he comes home."

"If he comes home through the front door, you mean," corrected Thorne in a youthful voice. "We can't see what going on in back."

"Like he's going to sneak in the back door of his own house, too," Grasso snorted. "He's not wanted for anything."

"Yet," said Thorne.

"Oh come on, Jack," exclaimed Grasso, "I've known Harley for almost a decade. All he's ever done is disturb the peace every now and then, and he hasn't even done that in years. Hell, he helped my son pick out a motorcycle. He's not going to be sneaking through the back door of his house in the middle of a thunderstorm. But if you insist on looking, be my guest." Grasso turned his head back towards the windshield and settled down lower in his seat. He'd been young and enthusiastic once too, he knew, but it still grated on him from time to time.

When Thorne hadn't returned after twenty minutes, Grasso tried raising him on the radio. When that failed, he struggled into his department issue raincoat and angrily got out of the car. After he was done with Thorne, the rookie would never, ever, leave his radio off again.

In the darkness of Harley's back yard, Grasso didn't see Thorne until he literally tripped over the young officer lying besides some bushes, a small hole just above his right eye.

Thunderstorms delayed Rodriquez' flight back to DC until after sunrise and it was almost ten before he walked into Branson's office. He put the small tape recorder on Branson's desk. "Here it is." He and Branson had already talked on the phone about the Texan's visit to Falmouth. "Any news from the Cape?"

"They found the dead cop. His name was Jack Thorne. Now they're actively looking for Mitchell, got an ABP out on him and everything." It wasn't Rodriquez' fault. Branson had known the risks when he sent the man into Mitchell's house. "No links back here, though, and, so far, no mention of anyone entering the house. All they've got is a bunch of loose ends."

"Unless they get Mitchell before we do."

"Which they'd better not." Branson pressed the on button and Rodriquez' tape player started to run. The quality was terrible and Branson had trouble separating the voices, but all of the messages seemed to be from different people. Most talked of motorcycles, but the sixth caller was cryptic. 'Harley, where are you. Call me at 393-1496.' Branson played back the message, and then played it again. "Does that voice sound familiar to you?" he asked.

"Not particularly, should it?"

Branson replayed the message two more times, frowning in concentration. "It's Crawler," he said finally, his hunter's instinct starting to tingle. "It's fucking Crawler!"

"Why would he leave his number on the machine? Mitchell called him all the time."

Realization shot through Branson's mind and he jumped up out of his chair in excitement. "It's a cell phone number. The asshole has a cell phone he never told us about." One of the requirements for Walt to have spent any time with the SCOT was that he had to provide all his personal information, including address and phone numbers, to the team as part of their recall roster. "He must have called from down here, after he got away from me. He called Mitchell but no one was home so he left this message. Mitchell called back, but never erased Crawler's message. Crawler told him what was happening and Mitchell took off."

"Off where?"

"I don't know for sure. But I'll bet you he came down here." Branson was pacing his office with long, aggressive strides. "And if Crawler's got his phone on, we'll be able to pinpoint his location with one call." He sat back down and began issuing detailed instructions to his subordinate. When they had located Crawler, he wanted to make sure they had the ability to act effectively and quickly. In a city as large as DC, that would take some planning.

CHAPTER XXV

Walt sat down opposite Harley at the battered picnic table and took a long slurp from his frappe. Milkshakes were what people called them at this roadside ice cream stand and the confusion resulting from his order had seemed an appropriate reflection of his current state of affairs. Nothing, not even ordering an ice cream drink, was as simple as it should be.

"Hey, man, don't look so down." Harley took a slug of his own frappe, his second of the morning, and managed a smile. "It's a beautiful day, the sun's shining, my bike's riding like a dream. We're on the move. It's not that bad."

"Thanks, Harley," Walt responded shortly, unconsciously picking at one of the many mosquito bites that dotted his face, "but I think you and I have different opinions on what's not that bad. I don't know what sort of stuff you've done in the past," Harley had never really explained his history in detail, relying on dropped hints of classified activities to make his stories more colorful, "but I don't seem as used to having people die as you do."

"Oh, come on, Walt," Harley replied, a bit of huff in his voice. "It's not that I'm used to having people die or that I don't care, it's that I know I can't do anything about it right now. Jeff would say the same thing, if he could, and I'd bet Pryor would too. We've got other things to focus on and moping over what's past just doesn't do anyone any good."

Walt put his frappe on the table and looked at his friend. "Three months ago, Harley, I would have agreed with you. I'd have said Jeff and Bill are dead but we've got a job to do so let's focus on that and, while we're at it, let's enjoy our ice cream too.

But I'm sorry, I can't say that anymore. I've spent the last three months trying to figure out why all of this is happening to me and I haven't come up with any answers. Katie is still sick, Julia and the twins are still dead. Now Jeff and Bill are dead, too. I know it's all Branson's doing, but if I had handled things differently, even going way back to when I was married, then maybe none of this would have happened."

"Walt you're wrong about this. The only thing that would be different, and it is a big thing, is that your family and Jeff, and maybe Pryor, would still be alive if it weren't for you. But everyone at the Arsenal would still be dead, and those people in Northern California, too. And whatever Branson's planning in Joshua Tree would be moving forward just like clockwork. I don't know if there's a reason for stuff happening like it does, and I wouldn't wish any of what's happened to you on anybody, but Branson's the bad guy here, not you. And we've got one chance to stop him. One chance to save whoever he's planning to kill in Joshua Tree, and maybe even to find an antidote for Katie.

"I can't tell you what I used to do or how I learned this stuff, but we have only one mission now. Stopping Branson. And I can assure you that enjoying your ice cream isn't as unimportant in succeeding in that mission as you might think." The burly biker took a long pull from his cup as if to prove his point. "It's just like the biscotti thing. If you start acting too rattled about the small stuff, the big stuff will fall all to pieces."

"Thanks for the pep talk, Harley," Walt eyed his frappe unenthusiastically. "I'll try to keep that in mind." He was still struggling for a more comprehensive response when his cell phone rang and ended the conversation.

"Mister Crawler?" the voice was shrill, with a strong southern twang.

"Speaking. Who's this?"

"This is the MCI Telnet Operator. We're having trouble with our relay station on Nantucket. It appears that some hacker's installed a computer bug in our main network which responds to specific phone frequencies from this relay. Until we isolate those specific frequencies we've had to turn the relay off to outside traffic."

"Okay," Walt's mind, dulled the events of the past few days, was having trouble following the talk of computer bugs and phone frequencies. "What's that have to do with me?"

"Well, we've narrowed the problem down to four specific series of numbers sent over the lines. That is, if one of the phones in question were to dial these numbers, it would initiate the bug. As you can imagine, if twenty-five, or fifty, or one hundred phones all dialed these numbers, we would have a regular black hole here. Now, can I ask you to do me a favor?"

"I guess."

"I'm going to read you the number series we've identified and ask you to enter them back into your phone. We'll be able to determine if your phone is one of the selected phone frequencies and clear the problem if it is. We've already found and cleared over fifty infected numbers, but a few have gotten through and they're starting to bog things down. We need to clear the rest of the numbers as soon as possible.

"Ready?"

"Uh-huh."

"Two-seven-six-five. Ready for the next one?"

"Uh-huh."

"Three-one-six-four. Next?"

"Go ahead."

"Five-three-two-eight. And this is the last one. Two-nine-seven-three."

"Got it. Anything else?"

"Not at this moment, thank you. Like I said, with a bit of luck, you won't have any problems using your phone later on. If you do, just call up the service number in your contract and they'll tell you what's going on. Thank you once more and I'm sorry we had to bother you."

"That's okay, good luck." Walt turned his phone off and slipped it back in its holster. "The phone company," he said bleakly. "It seems even they're having problems these days. Someone stuck a bug in their system and now they've got to clear all their phones."

"I've never understood the whole hacker thing," growled Harley. "Why some asshole thinks it's fun to mess with someone else's computer system is beyond me."

Walt finished his frappe. "Harley," he said as he stood up and motioned towards the bike, "there's a lot I'm finding I don't understand these days."

"Did you get it?" asked Branson impatiently. "I held him as long as I could." Voice altering equipment installed on his phone allowed him to talk to anybody without fear of recognition. The only question had been whether Walt would buy the story about hackers and computer bugs. Apparently he had.

"Give me a minute," said Rodriquez, sitting in front of a computer screen. "I'm almost there." Branson had pulled out all the stops to blanket the entire metropolitan area with people who could find and maintain contact with Crawler and Mitchell once they received a general idea of their whereabouts, but the slower they were in pinning down his location, the tougher it would be to make a successful tag.

Once these watchers, none of whom knew him personally, found the two men, Branson and Rodriquez would take over the action. Immense amounts of money would change hands and no one would ever remember a thing. Being able to pull together such large-scale operations with almost no notice was one of Branson's specialties, a benefit of having led such an active and varied career.

"Hey boss," muttered Rodriquez, "something's screwy. These points aren't adding up."

Branson pushed the other man aside and began tapping roughly at the computer keyboard. A small map of the world covered the screen and he tapped again, the map zooming in on a small red dot in the middle of the screen. Branson tapped for what seemed like an eternity, watching with increasing dread as the map grew more and more defined around the red dot. Finally he stopped his tapping and backed slowly away from the computer, his face drained of all color. "The numbers aren't matching up, Manny," he said in an unnaturally soft voice, "because you were trying to match his coordinates to a map of DC. The problem is, Crawler's not in DC anymore." Branson gestured towards the screen. "He's in fucking Memphis, Tennessee!"

"Memphis?!" exclaimed Rodriquez. "What the hell is he doing in Memphis?"

Without having to think about it, Branson understood everything. "He's going to Joshua Tree," he almost whispered, a hint of respect working its way into his voice. "The asshole's going to Joshua Tree. He's going to try to stop us there. Jesus Fucking Christ," he leaned back against his desk and started to chuckle, "he's actually going to try to stop us."

Rodriquez waited until Branson had finished laughing. "So where does that leave us?" He didn't see any humor in the situation.

"Well, we know where Crawler and Mitchell are." Branson was sounding much more upbeat now. "And we know where they're heading. And," he pulled a road atlas off a shelf, "we can figure out how they're going to get there." His muscular fingers began tracing lines across the atlas. "If they were in Memphis five minutes ago and they're going to Joshua Tree, California, I'll bet anything you want to bet that they're going to take Highway Forty west through Arkansas, Oklahoma, Texas, New Mexico, Arizona and on into California. They don't know that we know where they are so they're going to go straight on forty as fast as they can. We just need to figure out when they'll pass by a certain point and wait for them there.

"When we catch them, Mitchell goes hard down immediately. He's too dangerous to fuck with. Crawler we still want alive." Branson stabbed at the map. "We'll catch them here. Just east of Oklahoma City. We can make it in one hop on the number one plane. Crawler's car is still on Nantucket and Mitchell doesn't drive anything but bikes. Plus, he just won't fly. Unless they stole a car someplace, they've got to be riding Mitchell's motorcycle. We'll fly back and forth over Forty until we find them."

"There must be dozens of bikes with two people riding them." Rodriquez wasn't very impressed with Branson's fly-by plan.

"True, but if we get low enough we'll either recognize them or, more probably, pick up the license plate with a spyglass. Once we've found Mitchell's plate, we'll know we've found our men."

"And then what? Strafe them from the plane?" Rodriquez knew it could be done, but it sounded awfully messy.

"No. I want Crawler alive, if at all possible. And we need to make sure we check both men's clothing and anything else on the bike for documents. Then, if possible, we need to stash both the bike and the bodies somewhere. To do that, we need to be on the ground."

"And how are we going to catch them speeding down the highway on a motorcycle? Just ask them to pull over?"

"Exactly." Branson was formulating the plan as he spoke. "I've got contacts in Oklahoma City." He had contacts everywhere. "I'll have a police cruiser waiting for us when we've found them. Of course," he added, seeing the Texan's confused expression, "it won't be a real cruiser. But it'll have lights and look real enough to get Mitchell to pull over. We'll have a uniform for you. After we've found them, we'll land at a local airstrip, Oklahoma is full of them, and pick up the cruiser. We'll park at an overpass ahead of them, then, when they drive by, we'll pull in behind. When we've got a clear view ahead and behind, which shouldn't be hard on these country highways, you'll turn on the lights. Mitchell will pull over and you'll pull over right next to him. I'll be hiding in the back seat, and when you give the word, when we're right next to Mitchell, I'll sit up and pop him. Then I'll jump out and take out Crawler, toss him and Mitchell in the back of the cruiser and we'll take off. You in the cruiser, with the lights off, and me on the bike. We should be back on the road thirty seconds after they've pulled over."

Branson's eyes focused back on the map and his fingers lingered over the red line that was Highway Forty. "They won't know what hit them until it's too late," he gloated. "Then we'll find a nice vernal pool where Crawler can join those frogs and turtles he likes so much."

CHAPTER XXVI

Thirty miles east of Oklahoma City, Branson and Rodriquez sat in a late-model Ford Taurus and looked at the occasional car that passed beneath them on Highway Forty. Branson had been right about just how lonely stretches of this road could be, and both men felt comfortable that they wouldn't have to trail Mitchell long before finding the highway deserted enough to pull off their hit.

So far, everything else had gone according to plan. It had only taken them one pass on Forty, going east to west, to spot their quarry speeding along below them near Roland, just over the Oklahoma border. Rodriquez had pulled in low above them, too low for him to have felt entirely inconspicuous but just low enough for Branson to pick up the license plate. The tag having been made, Rodriquez had maintained the same altitude and speed for several minutes, slowly leaving the motorcycle in its wake, before maxing the throttle all the way to their selected landing strip. There, a look-alike cruiser and a uniform that seemed tailored for Rodriquez were waiting by an abandoned grain silo and, minutes later, Branson and Rodriquez were on their way to the ambush site.

Rodriquez checked his watch. Based on their calculations of Mitchell's speed, the bike should be passing within moments. "You ready, boss?" he asked in a husky voice. Although he had carried out dozens of similar operations over the years, they still got his adrenaline flowing.

"Absolutely." Branson waved his automatic pistol for emphasis. "Bring 'em on."

"Speak of the devil, here they come." Rodriquez pulled a small packet out of his shirt pocket and stuck two yellow plugs into his ears. The concussive effects of being inside the car when Branson started shooting would drive his eardrums through his skull if he wasn't protected. The Texan put the car into gear and pulled onto the highway's access ramp. "It's showtime."

Harley goosed his bike a bit and felt it buck underneath him. He grinned in sheer joy. Having that much pep even at seventy-five miles an hour was, to him, at any rate, a thing of beauty. Walt continued to be unimpressed, the thrill of riding bitch having worn off before they left Virginia, but, in Harley's mind, nothing beat a good, fast bike. The wind whipped over his bald skull and he hollered out to the skies, knowing that not even Walt could hear him over the motorcycle's rumble. Other than having the biologist behind him instead of a lithe young blond, a ride couldn't get much better.

Something flashed in his sideview mirror and Harley frowned. A light? He hadn't passed a cop since they left Arkansas, and that one was headed in the other direction. He eased up on the throttle and looked again. There was no doubt about it. There were flashing blue lights behind him. Oklahoma's finest wanted to have a talk.

From long habit, Harley reviewed what might have happened as he slowed down and pulled over to the shoulder of the highway. He didn't think Oklahoma had a speed limit on this stretch of road, but even if it did, seventy-five was fairly conservative for the open highway. It was legal to ride without a helmet and he hadn't been weaving between cars or pulling any crazy stunts. Maybe the cop just hadn't liked the bike's noise. That had happened before, and Harley had learned that few things are worse than a State Trooper whose nap had been terminated by a loud motorcycle.

Whatever it was, Harley would give the officer the typical routine. Yes, Officer. No, Officer. Three bags full, Officer. It'd slow them down a bit, but he and Walt should be back on the road in a half hour or so.

Unless . . . Something nagged at the back of his mind. He'd gone over eighteen months without getting pulled over. It was a helluva thing to have happen now.

"We've got company, huh?" Walt yelled through the helmet covering his face.

"Yeah," Harley brought the bike to a stop and balanced it on one foot, the engine still idling like a jet airplane on cruise control. "Just let me do the talking, okay. We'll be out of here in no time at all." He tried to put on his best 'I'm a good boy' face but knew, as he had known countless times before, he couldn't pull it off successfully. Something about being a large, bald man on a bike just didn't sit right with most law enforcement officials.

The police cruiser slowly approached them, a little to the left like most officers stop a speeding car. That way the cruiser itself provides some cover from oncoming motorists. But the car didn't stop the typical twenty feet behind the motorcycle. Instead it crept closer as if it were going to bump the bike over in retaliation for its having made a nuisance of itself. Harley's natural sense of wariness when dealing with agents of the law began to scream warnings and he studied the cruiser in his rearview mirror with sudden intensity. The cruiser wasn't going to bump him after all, it was pulling even with him. And there were funny yellow dots in the officer's ears. Dots that looked like earplugs....

With his senses on hyperalert, Harley didn't have to see movement in the cruiser's backseat before he recognized the danger. It was a setup! The cop was wearing earplugs. And you only wore earplugs inside a car when you were expecting a loud noise to occur. A loud noise like the firing of a gun.

In an instant, Harley threw his weight forward over the gas tank, counting on his bulk to keep the bike from popping up out of control, and threw the engine into gear before Branson's pistol had even cleared the cruiser's rear window. The big bike jolted and then, with a speed that would have been incomprehensible to anyone who didn't understand motorcycles as well as Harley did, it shot forward onto the pavement.

"Hold on!" Harley shouted an unnecessary warning to Walt, who had recognized both Rodriquez and Branson just as Harley had put the bike in gear. "We're in for a ride." He put some distance between him and the cruiser, then turned left and bounced the bike over the grassy median strip and roared back east, towards the overpass exit they'd just passed. Long dormant Army training told him that the best way out of an ambush was to turn right into it. If Branson had been waiting for him here, who knew what was waiting a mile or two down the road? But no one would expect him to go back the way he'd come. He'd hop off at the first exit and disappear down one of the many farming roads that criss-crossed this part of the country.

If Branson didn't have backup waiting at the bridge, and if he didn't have a good long rifle, they were in the clear.

"Fuck!" swore Rodriquez, punching the accelerator and sending the false cruiser rocketing down the highway after Harley, "he made us!" The Texan's knuckles were white as they grabbed the steering wheel. He loved car chases, but he knew his chances of catching Mitchell's big bike were slim in the borrowed, street legal car.

Several pops made their way through his earplugs and he saw Branson hanging out the rear window, futility emptying his automatic pistol at the rapidly disappearing bike.

Then the motorcycle made a left over the median strip, cutting its speed dramatically as it shifted course. Shit, Rodriquez swore to himself. He should have expected that. Mitchell couldn't know there wasn't more trouble waiting up ahead. Anyone with any training at all would have turned back into the ambush. He

tried to vector the car onto a collision course with his quarry, but
it was too late, he couldn't swing the turn tight enough. In the
back he could see Branson fumbling with something on the seat
and then the big man was screaming at him to pull over.

Before the car had even stopped, Branson was out the door,
a wicked looking rifle in his hand. Using the now steady Taurus'
roof as a firing bench, he threw the rifle to his shoulder and tried
to line up a decent shot.

Mitchell wasn't making it easy, however, and the bike swerved
erratically back and forth across the road, the driver realizing that
speed was no longer as important as unpredictability.

Crack. Crack. Crack. Branson was firing for center mass,
not caring if he hit a person or the motorcycle itself, just hoping
for something that would slow the machine down enough for
Rodriquez to be able to catch up. But his shots seemed to have
no impact and the bike bobbed and weaved down the highway
unhindered. Lead the target, Branson told himself, steady breath,
gently squeeze the trigger . . . Crack. Shit! the bike had dodged
again.

Almost as soon as it had started, it was over. Mitchell was
safely out of range, roaring down the highway, and the rifle was
out of ammunition. Branson tossed the rifle in the back seat and
jumped in besides Rodriquez. "Back to the plane," he ordered,
realizing that further pursuit was useless. Crawler had escaped.
Murphy had bitten him once more.

"So what now?" Walt was still nursing his first beer, feeling entirely out of place in the rural biker bar where Harley had decided to pull over for a break. Cigarette smoke hung so thick in
the air that Walt thought he could feel it seeping into his pores
and the heavy metal music made Harley's bike at full throttle
sound like a mild churchmouse. On top of that, Walt was not at

all convinced that Branson wouldn't come bursting through the door at any moment.

"We wait some more." Harley tossed back the last of his third beer and signaled the waitress for another. "We can't go back on the road until it's dark. That plane that passed us once we got into Oklahoma?"

"Yeah."

"That must have been Branson. Somehow they figured out where we were going and just flew down the highway until they found us. If they did it once, they'll do it again. We can't go anywhere until their eye in the sky is useless."

"How'd they find us in the first place, though," Walt asked.

"I've figured that one out, too. Hand me your cell phone."

Walt did as he was asked.

"When you got that call yesterday?"

"Yeah."

"There wasn't anything wrong with the relay switches or whatever it was they were talking about. They just wanted you to answer the phone. Once you picked up, they could locate you from the transmission. The story about the relay switches was just for show."

"But how'd they get my cell phone number. I never told anyone on the SCOT I had a cell phone and next to no one has the number."

"You left it on my machine."

"You mean . . ."

"Those assholes broke into my house and picked up my messages. I never erased your message with the number on it. That's how they got it." Harley opened the back of the phone and removed the battery. "They won't pull that trick again," he said, throwing the battery into a trashcan and handing the rest of the phone back to Walt.

"Jesus Christ," muttered Walt, his whole body deflating. "These guys can do anything."

"No," corrected Harley through a mouthful of beer, "not anything. So far, they can't catch you. And that's more important than anything they *can* do."

The two men fell silent again, Walt working his way through the warm backwash in the bottom of his bottle while Harley both started and finished his fourth beer.

"So, like I asked you before, Harley, what now?"

"We wait 'till it's dark and then we continue on our way."

"But they know we're here. They'll be waiting for us." Panic was starting to sound in Walt's voice. If he died, Katie would be left completely alone. And he'd come so close to dying already. How long would his luck hold?

"No, they don't know where we are." Harley was using his most confident tone of voice. He had to keep Walt from going to pieces under the stress he must be feeling. "They know where we were. That's completely different. Now we're forty miles away, at some no-name biker bar where my hog blends in with all the other bikes out there and won't attract any attention from anybody. If Branson's going to check out every biker bar in Oklahoma, then maybe we've got problems, but there ain't no way he's going to do that. Once it gets dark, we'll get back on the bike, but instead of heading west along Forty like we were doing before, we'll poke up north a bit." He reached into his pockets and pulled out a small highway map. "We'll stay on the backroads until we hit seventy, then we'll head west to Denver and then down through Las Vegas. From Vegas there must be a million backroads across the desert to get to Joshua Tree. Branson can't have the manpower to watch them all."

"How do you know?"

"Because if he had that sort of power, he'd have had a backup on the bridge just in case we got away. The guy's no fool, he's going to cover all the angles he can. I'm sure he's got connections out the ass, but he's short on actual manpower. I wouldn't be surprised at all if it were just him and that Rodriquez guy." He thought back to his Army days, to the classes he'd had on resource deployment. "They know where we're going, but they don't know how we're going to get there. For all they know, we could go West to LA and then come back East to Joshua Tree on the bus. Branson's going to settle in by the Park and wait for us to show up. He's got no other choice."

"And neither do we, I guess," acknowledged Walt, waving his arms for two more beers. "I just hope you're right."

CHAPTER XXVII

Adam Branson stuck another piece of gum in his mouth and chewed furiously. How the hell had Crawler gotten away again? The man was like a cat with nine lives, and he'd only used up two of them so far. How many more did he have up his sleeve?

Branson and Rodriquez were at a small airstrip in eastern New Mexico, watching the sun go down behind some distant unnamed mountains. Under other circumstances, the sunset might have been beautiful. To Branson, the sunset meant only one thing.

It would be dark soon. And Mitchell would be invisible in the dark. He knew the biker was probably laying low right now, waiting for darkness to cover his movements. Then he'd be off and running like a bat out of hell.

Would Mitchell stay on forty?

Maybe. But, instead, maybe he would drop south to highway 20 and then to highway ten and then maybe even further south to eight, heading north to Joshua Tree on route eighty-six. There were a million different ways he could go now, and Branson could not possibly cover them all.

He only had two choices. Find Crawler and Mitchell again. Or wait for them at Joshua Tree.

The first option was, by far, the more attractive. If he could find the two men before they got to the Park, he could negate their threat without anyone making a connection. If he wound up having to take them out at or near Joshua Tree, things were much more likely to get uncomfortably sticky.

The problem had once more become, how to find them.

Branson considered his options. Mitchell was easy. He couldn't be found, except the way one finds a winning lottery number. The man had no family, had called in sick to work and, essentially, seemed to have no ties to anyone or anything once he was on the open road. Hopefully, no one else would think of a better way to find Mitchell than just sheer chance, because Branson knew things could also get sticky should some highway patrol officer pull the biker in on an ABP. A dead police officer in his backyard would automatically get Mitchell some attention. If he had a toll receipt from his trip to DC that helped prove he was miles away from the murder, his and Crawler's conspiracy theory might sound attractive enough for some bureaucrat to clamp down on the Joshua Tree event. If nothing else, it would add credibility to their theory after the fact, which would almost certainly ruin Branson's own future.

But Crawler. He was a different story. Branson remembered the anger in the biologist's eyes when he'd snatched away the medallion, the numerous flights back to Boston while he was assigned to the SCOT, the way he'd constantly cradled that silver spoon he'd bought for his daughter. There was no way he'd go for long without checking up on her.

It was so obvious, Branson snapped at himself, he should have thought of it sooner.

He'd bug Doctor Bocall's line.

Actually, he could only bug the doctor's home line, but that might well do the trick. With the difference in time zones and the hours spent on Mitchell's bike, Crawler would probably have trouble catching the doctor at work. Branson unpacked his laptop and opened up an address file. There were several people who could get the tap placed within an hour or two, no questions asked. Once installed, he could monitor the tap himself via his laptop and a satellite uplink. With the voice recognition software available at the SCOT's office, anytime the tap fielded a call from someone whose voice met Crawler's parameters, Branson would get an automated phone call. He could then dial back into the SCOT's network and download the relevant message to his own computer. If it turned out the voice was Crawler's, the tracing system would tell him the exact location from where Crawler had called.

And if the doctor was, for some reason, suddenly ill, he wouldn't be at work should Crawler be looking for him. The biologist would have to call his house.

Branson made one quick phone call and smiled thinly at Rodriquez. "If Crawler calls his daughter's doctor's house anytime after ninety minutes from now, we'll know where he is almost before the conversation's over."

"And if he doesn't?" Rodriquez felt badly about losing Mitchell in Oklahoma, but Branson's newest plan didn't seem like much of a step forward.

"Don't worry. He will. I understand the man. He can't go long without checking on his girl. And I've just made sure that the good doctor, along with anyone else in the house, will be suffering from some severe nausea for the next few days. Crawler will have to call him at home."

"But what if he doesn't," Rodriquez persisted. "What if he just turtles it and goes to Joshua Tree without calling anyone?"

"Then we'll have to be waiting for him, won't we?" Branson pointed towards the plane. "We'll stay here tonight. Tomorrow we'll fly to Flagstaff. If Crawler calls and we get a location, we'll move on it. Otherwise, we'll rent a truck and drive towards Joshua Tree. I'd rather not fly anywhere closer than that. It's too likely someone will eventually check out planes taking off or landing from nearby airports after the event and I don't want to leave any traces." It would be very difficult, but by no means impossible, for someone to track the plane back to Branson. He wasn't willing to take that risk. "Besides, from Flagstaff we're only a six hour drive from the Park. If we get a location after that, we'll be able to vector into them over the ground. Plus, they've probably figured out our plane trick by now, we'll just alert them if we try any more overflights."

"You don't want to just fly over them and shoot them if we find them?" Rodriquez liked the mobility provided by the small plane.

"No, it's too uncertain. If they've got documents, or if we don't kill them, we just make our hole deeper. There aren't too many places to land out in the desert, so we'd never be sure if they were alive or dead or what. And if they were alive, we'd just have given their story that much more credibility." The cop Rodriquez had killed was becoming much more of a problem as the chase went on, magnifying the negative repercussions of any unsuccessful attack on Mitchell.

"Well, I guess it looks like we don't have much choice, then doesn't it." Rodriquez turned his attention to the darkening horizon. "I just hope we get it right this time," he said to no one in particular. "We're running out of chances to do it wrong."

CHAPTER XXVIII

13 JULY
NEVADA

As the barren Nevada desert began to give way to the ramshackle outskirts of Las Vegas, Walt couldn't help but be amazed at how, in the arid West, nothing could turn into something for no apparent reason. What was rocks and scrub brush on one hillside turned into an adobe hut on the next and then three cinderblock houses after that. With no discernible change in elevation, temperature, weather or even location, all of a sudden he found himself, still moving at seventy-five miles an hour on the back of Harley's bike, in the midst of Las Vegas. Not the Glitter Gulch or theme casino areas, but the long stripmalled, apartment buildinged and moteled stretches that lead into the heart of Vegas like the Appian Way led into Rome.

Christ he couldn't wait to get off the bike. They were travelling by day now and the blazing desert sun was baking Walt alive. Uncomfortably hot all by itself, the sun was also turning Walt's helmet into a small oven. He had sweated what must have been gallons of water through his pores and desperately wanted a drink and a shower, followed by another drink. How Harley remained so unflappable, driving the bike tirelessly along the desert highways was beyond him. Walt was having enough trouble just staying on the back.

He shifted his weight and felt the silver spoon in his pocket press against his thigh. Katie hadn't strayed far from his thoughts in the past few days, but he hadn't been able to talk to her doctor since leaving DC. He'd called the hospital once but Doctor Bocall had been out and Walt hadn't been able to leave a number at which he could be reached. To avoid being traced, he and Harley had stayed only at motels that accepted cash and didn't ask for identification. One trade-off was that these motels hadn't had in-room phones. Besides that, when they had finally pulled off the road for the night, Walt had had barely enough strength to shower and make it to bed. No matter how concerned he was about Katie's condition, he just hadn't found the strength to try to talk to her doctor at those moments.

But the questions still ate at him. How was she? Getting better? Getting worse?

He had to know.

Harley slowed the bike down and cruised up an exit ramp. "It's time for a break," he yelled back at Walt.

Walt flashed him a thumbs up, dreaming of something cold and wet sliding down the back of his parched throat.

It didn't take long to find a convenience store and both men went inside to get something to drink and escape the heat.

"About four or five hours to go," commented Harley, his chin stained red by the Cherry Slush that dribbled from his cracked lips.

"That'll put us at the Park by about eight or so, then," said Walt, his mouth full of crushed ice.

"It should. If we keep going."

"What do you mean, if we keep going?" Walt just about spit out his ice. Harley couldn't be thinking about quitting now.

"Calm down, Walt, calm down. We'll keep going. I just meant, if we keep going today. I've got to admit, I'm beat. This heat is kicking my ass and, as much as I like riding it, my hog ain't meant for major long distance driving. I've done three thousand miles in the past few days, which is a lot all by itself. Add you on the back and it's starting to wear me out."

"So what are you suggesting?"

"That we spend the night here. We can get a motel just out of town, grab a bite to eat, shower and hit the casinos for a bit, then crash and start out again tomorrow morning. If we're on the road by six, we should be at the Park before eleven. If we keep going today," Harley had obviously been planning this for a while, "we'll wind up having to get a hotel when we get to Joshua Tree and we won't get anything done before nine tomorrow morning anyway. At most, we're losing a couple of hours."

Walt shot his friend a sidelong glance. "Are you sure that's all, Harley?"

Harley looked towards the doorway. "No, I'll admit it, that's not all. But it's true. I don't know how many more miles I have in me today before I start losing my edge. And remember, Branson and Rodriquez are going to be waiting for us someplace around Joshua Tree. If they lock onto us when we're dead tired, we're just going to wind up being just plain dead.

"But the fact that we're in Vegas doesn't hurt. If we've got to stop someplace and rest up, this is the place. This is the gambling Mecca of America. It might even be the gambling Mecca of the whole world. The next couple of days are going to be crazy," Harley seemed unfazed by the dangers they were facing. *Crazy* was as strong as he'd put it. "And if we don't take advantage of this opportunity, we might never get another one. Or, at least, I might not. I don't think I want to make that ride again, and I'm damn sure not getting on a plane to come out here. So I very well may never see Vegas again."

Walt looked at his friend. A trail of dead bodies and assassination attempts drifted all the way back to Washington DC and Nantucket, yet Harley was interested in going on a gambling spree. Still, there was sense in what the biker said. Walt was beyond running on empty. He had nothing left. He'd worried himself sick over Katie and had said his prayers again and again for Jeff and Bill. He'd worn himself out thinking that every passing car carried Branson and now he needed a boost, a shot of enthusiasm for life that maybe he could find by locating a good set of horse races. Under other conditions, spending some time at the races with Harley rarely failed to restore his spirits. Maybe it could prove as rejuvinative this time.

Besides, as Harley pointed out, they weren't losing much in the way of time. And he so desperately wanted a shower.

"Okay, Harley. We can spend the night here. But we're on the road no later than four AM."

"Okay. But that brings us to another problem."

"It does?"

"Yeah, it does. We want new wheels?"

"We do?"

"Absolutely. If Branson and whoever he's got working for him are waiting for us around Joshua Tree, they'll be looking for a bike with two riders. Just like they did on highway forty. We need to pick up a jeep or something tomorrow morning before we leave. That way we'll be less conspicuous. Plus, if we pick up a detailed map, we might be able to get to Joshua Tree without travelling on the main roads at all."

"Come on, Harley, we know Branson's got my credit card tagged by now. If I rent a jeep tomorrow morning, he's going to know the model, color, mileage, even the type of radio it's got, before we get out of the rental lot."

"So?"

"Whatdya mean 'so'? He'll know exactly what we're driving. He'll know just what to look for."

"So what? He already does. And I'll bet a Jeep Cherokee or Ford Explorer with tinted windows would be a lot better at hiding us out here than a motorcycle like mine."

Walt thought about it. "I see your point," he conceded. "Let's just make sure we rent something with a good air conditioner."

After showering at a small motel that accepted cash and didn't ask for a name, Walt and Harley loaded themselves back on the bike and headed for the heart of Vegas. They left the bike at a small lot and, despite the heat, decided to walk down the strip.

Walt marveled at the sights, sounds, smells and physical sensations assaulting him from every side. The sun turned the building-lined street into a canyon of heat, where tar patches on the road turned into semi-aqueous puddles. Every other doorway seemed to pour a river of cold air onto the sidewalk in an effort to entice passers-by into the air-conditioned interiors of a myriad of second-rate casinos. The jangle of coins spilling out of slot machines, the occasional blare of a car radio on the street and the shouts of casino barkers bullying people to their tables added to the circus-like atmosphere created by the garish signs and neon lights lining the street. People scurried from door to door, like oversized penguins looking for any respite from the terrible heat.

Despite the fascinating surroundings, the heat quickly wore the edge off of Harley's curiosity. "What do you think about getting in from this heat before we melt?" he asked in a tone that didn't sound like a question.

Walt looked to the right. Set back a hundred yards or so from the road, a large casino beckoned enticingly. "Sounds good to me," he agreed, turning his steps towards the casino. He looked forward to air-conditioning and simulcast racing. And a cold beer or two wouldn't be hard to take either.

After the scalding temperatures of the sun-baked asphalt strip, the air-conditioned climate of the casino made Walt feel as if he'd just walked into the world's largest freezer. The garishly colored carpeting and the din of hundreds of slot machines, combined with the swirling crowds of desperate looking gamblers and scantily clad cocktail waitresses that sashayed up and down the aisles, made him think of a larger, indoor version of the carnivals that used to visit his hometown every summer when he was a kid. Flashy looking and exciting, but the beauty never even ran skin deep.

Although he wasn't a seasoned gambler, Walt's racing jaunts with Harley had given him enough experience to recognize the look on the faces of most of the people around him. They were scared and tense, learning the hard way that losing money wasn't as much fun in real life as it appeared in the promotional packages. And, these people were also learning, losing money was a hell of a lot easier than winning it.

But this was slots, Walt reminded himself. Man against machine, hoping for a piece of dumb luck, just like the lottery. It wasn't like playing the horses where the flare of equine nostrils, or the jaunty swagger of a jockey, or, much more likely with Walt, the poignancy of a name, added a human touch and gave your gut something to go on. Sure, you could lose money playing the horses. He'd done so for years with Harley. But even when he lost, it was a living, breathing, emotional experience, cheering on his pick, feeling the hooves cut into the track and watching the peak of generations of breeding put every ounce of heart, sinew and soul into eking out a victory. It was alive, unlike the impersonal flashing lights and metallic feel of the one-armed bandits. And, somehow, that life made losing easier to take.

Walt followed Harley through the depressing mob, conscious now of a somewhat noxious odor permeating the air. A combination of sweat, dirty clothes, bad breath and cigarettes. He recognized it immediately. It was the smell of fear, the smell of next month's rent check disappearing inside the belly of a squat metal machine, the smell of the double or nothing, please-Lord-just-let-me-win-this-one-and-I'll-stop-betting prayer. It was the smell of losers and Walt knew it was as much a part of this room as the slot machines and the middle aged, over-weight conventioneers camped out at their favorite machines. The smell was Las Vegas and the casino owners would never get rid of it.

Exiting the maze of slots, Walt and Harley found themselves in a large atrium. To their left a line was beginning to form for the afternoon's lounge show while directly ahead dozens of tables offering roulette, craps and blackjack occupied an area the size of a small ballroom. Despite the large numbers of people flocking around the tables, the sheer enormity of the hall made it seem half-empty. Compared to a simple horse track, the size and complexity of this gambling operation was staggering and even the unshakeable Harley seemed taken aback.

"Jesus Christ Almighty," he whispered to himself, "they don't fuck around with this stuff do they? Hey, look over there!" He pointed to the right, through a small foyer where a series of what looked to be overhead TV screens showed horse races from around the world. "Simulcast Heaven." Leaving Walt bobbing in his wake, the biker shouldered his way through the crowd, eager to get his first taste of what Las Vegas had to offer.

Walt chased after his friend, his nose rapidly becoming immune to the casino's noxious smell that he'd noticed earlier. As they approached the simulcast area, however, he noticed a row of phones in an alcove. "Hey Harley," he called above the muted roar of the game room, "You go ahead. I'll catch up with you in a few minutes." Without waiting to see if his message had gotten through, he ducked between two crap tables and headed to the phones. Harley could recharge his batteries at the races. He would try to do the same by talking to Doctor Bocall.

Not surprisingly given the time, the doctor wasn't at the hospital. Walt rummaged through his wallet until he found the card on which Doctor Bocall had written his home number and gave that a try. If he couldn't get through to the doctor today, God only knew when he'd have another chance.

"Hello?" It was Doctor Bocall, but his voice sounded feeble and hoarse.

"Doctor Bocall, it's Walt Crawler here."

"Walt! How are you? Where've you been?"

"I can't really tell you that." Walt had decided to keep his trip to himself. He'd brought disaster to enough people already without roping Katie's doctor into it, too. "I'm just checking up on Katie. How is she doing?" He tried to stop himself from asking the loaded question, but couldn't. "Is she any better?"

"I'm sorry, Walt, but no. She's not." There was a spasm of heavy coughing over the phone and then the doctor spoke again. "Sorry about that. I caught some kind of bug. It's just about knocked my socks off. Don't worry, though," he added reassuringly, "I'm still looking after Katie, it's just that I have to do it over the phone for a day or two. I'm afraid I'm in no shape to go into the hospital. I can hardly make it to the bathroom." There was another long spell of coughing and then the doctor was back. "There's no easy way to put it, Walt, and I've always tried to be honest with you. I'm sorry if this sounds gruff, but Katie's vitals have started to drop dramatically and reflex response time is way down. It's almost to the point where we're willing to start experimenting with antidotes, even though that's not much better than medical Russian Roulette."

Walt's stomach spasmed at the analogy. "How long before you think you'll have to do something?" he asked, his mouth suddenly dry.

"We'll keep her as is for another forty-eight hours or so unless the slide speeds up even more. But if she doesn't plateau by then, we'll have to start taking chances. Will you be coming back soon?"

"I don't know, Doctor," Walt's gut churned at the thought of someone doing experimental medical procedures on his girl without his being there. "Would it help if you knew what the chemicals might be within forty-eight hours?" He knew he was grasping at straws. Even if, somehow, he foiled Branson's assassination plans, that would not necessarily lead to learning what chemicals were poisoning Katie. In time, with Branson's crew broken, they could probably figure it out. But in forty-eight hours? Doubtful.

"At the outside, Walt. Once we know exactly what the chemicals are, we'll still have some work to do to develop a proper antidote for her. Why? Do you think you might have something?" Hope had crept into the Doctor's voice.

"I don't know, Doctor," responded Walt, still unwilling to tell Doctor Bocall anything else. He didn't want another body on his conscience. "I'll let you know as soon as I find out for sure." Without waiting for a reply, Walt slipped the handset back into its cradle and, head down, trudged slowly back through the crap tables to the simulcast room.

The phone buzzed silently against his hip and Branson picked it from its holster with a jerk. He checked the message display and smiled. "I told you he couldn't stay away," he said to Rodriquez.

"Are you sure it's him?" As usual, Rodriquez was driving, the four wheel drive Bronco eating steadily at the miles between them and Joshua Tree National Park.

"Give me a moment and I'll check the message itself, but no one calling Doctor Bocall's home number is going to meet Crawler's voice parameters except Crawler. I'm certain it's him." Branson twisted his body so he could access the laptop setup in the back seat. A minute later Walt's voice came through the laptop's speakers. "Told you," he gloated when the brief message was over, "he's got to stay in touch with his daughter. Now we just need to figure out where he's calling from." He punched at some keys. "Caesar's Palace, Las Vegas. Sonuvabitch. He went up North to get by us. He's making a great big loop."

"They must be just about dead by now, all that time on a bike in this weather. Even at night it's got to be tough," commented Rodriquez, impressed at how quickly their foes were moving.

"Just about dead isn't close enough. We're going to find them and finish the job."

"Do you want to take 'em out at the Palace."

"No. They won't spend the night there. They haven't used Crawler's credit card since they started this trip and they're not going to now. They'll find some fleabag place that doesn't require a credit card security and spend the night there instead."

"How do you know they'll spend the night?" Rodriquez wasn't questioning the veracity of his boss' statement, Branson was rarely wrong, but he didn't understand the logic.

"Couple of reasons. One is, they've got four or five hours to go across the desert. Even at night, it's going to be brutally hot. Crawler doesn't have a motorcycle license, so I figure Mitchell's been doing all the driving. And it's been a lot of driving just to get them this far. He's going to need a break. There's less than nothing between Vegas and Joshua Tree, so he's going to have to take that break in Vegas. Add to that the fact that Mitchell likes horse racing," despite some data gaps, his intelligence had given him a pretty good profile of the biker, "and you've got all the reasons for stopping now. Remember, Crawler called from Caesar's Palace, not from some fast food joint. You don't drop into a place like Caesar's just to make a quick call and get back on the road.

"If they try to get to Joshua Tree tonight," continued the redhead, "they're not going to get there before ten or eleven, at the earliest. At that time of night, in a place as small as the Morongo Basin around the Park, a guy like Mitchell will stick out like sore thumb. They've got to know we'll be looking for them, so they're going to want to be as inconspicuous as possible."

"They won't be any less inconspicuous tomorrow," countered the Texan.

"Ah, there you're wrong. Or at least, they'd like you to be wrong. Crawler hasn't tried using his credit card yet. He doesn't know I've cancelled it. I'll bet you a million bucks that the first thing they do in the morning is try to rent a car. All they want to do is get to the Park, and, even if we were looking for it, a car would be tougher to find than Mitchell's bike."

Branson smacked his lips enthusiastically. He knew he was right. "Besides, it doesn't really matter when they leave Las Vegas. We'll still be able to head 'em off." Branson poked at the map he'd opened on the dashboard. "They'll take Fifteen south to Mountain Pass and then get off on one of these upgraded dirt roads. We can be south of Kelso-I've never been there but I doubt it's more than two trees and a house-in three hours, long before they make it there even if they left now. We'll keep a watch all night for the bike, one on, one off, so if they do take off tonight we've lost nothing. But I'll bet we won't see them until tomorrow morning. In either case, when we see them in that back county desert, there won't be anyone else watching." He patted the rifle, complete with a night vision scope and a newly filled magazine. "We won't miss this time."

"And if we do?" Rodriquez was playing devil's advocate again.

"Christ, you're a tough sell, Manny," sighed Branson, "but if we haven't seen them by nine in the morning, we'll have to drop back to the Park itself. It is possible, although doubtful, that they'll go another way from Vegas to Joshua Tree. Remember, they went up to Vegas to lose us. They think they've done that and they're not going to be worried about running into us again until they get right outside the Park itself. They're fat, dumb and happy now. Otherwise they wouldn't be passing their time in Caesar's Palace.

"It's got to be that way," concluded Branson, almost as if he were trying to convince himself. "It's got to be."

CHAPTER XIX

14 JULY
LAS VEGAS, NEVADA

Walt awoke the next morning with a sullen pounding in his head. He lay still for a few moments, trying to figure out how much of the noise he was hearing came from the buzzing alarm clock and how came from what promised to be a massive hangover. It seemed, he had decided, to be about a fifty-fifty split when a massive hand smashed onto the top of the clock, silencing it for good. The noise in Walt's head continued unabated.

"Cheap ass motel," growled Harley from the other bed, "doesn't even give you a clock radio, gotta wake up to this buzzing crap." The biker rolled out from beneath the covers, mountains of them necessitated by the motel's aggressive air conditioning system, and padded towards the bathroom. "I'll shower first," he said over his shoulder, "you could probably use a few more minutes of shuteye."

That was a true statement, Walt conceded, closing his eyes and trying to remember just what the hell he'd done the night before. He'd stayed by Harley's side, matching him drink for drink, courtesy of the attractive young waitresses who ceaselessly patrolled the gaming floors. Unfortunately, while the river of liquor he'd imbibed seemed not to have affected Harley in the slightest, it had knocked Walt's socks off. He blearily remembered winning a fair amount of money at the simulcast races, followed by an impressive winning spree at the roulette tables. And then an equally impressive losing spree at the crap tables. He frowned into his pillows. Maybe it had been the other way around.

Had he told Harley about calling Doctor Bocall? He didn't think so. It had been a depressing conversation and Walt had seen no need to pass the bad news on to Harley. Actually, Walt admitted to himself through the clouds of nausea that were rolling through his body, he just didn't want to see the biker take the news as casually as he seemed to have taken Tillison and Pryor's deaths. They were talking of playing medical Russian Roulette with his daughter and, while Harley certainly cared about what happened to Katie, he was showing a disturbingly consistent ability to shrug off bad news without much of a comment.

The irony of his situation was not lost on Walt despite his hangover. Here he was, in a cut-rate motel just off the Vegas strip, on the run both to and from the ruthless killer who had decimated his family and killed his friends, and he was worried that his biker companion wasn't being emotional enough! If only Julia could see this now. He was the one upset at someone else's compartmentalizing things!

His thoughts of Julia and Branson and Jeff and the rest of the mess he was in just made his head hurt worse. What had he been thinking, Walt groaned inwardly, to have tried matching drinks with Harley? The guy was a human partying machine. He owed it to Katie and the memories of all those Branson had killed to stay focused on the job at hand, to concentrate on getting to Joshua Tree and on somehow stopping Branson and not to drown his sorrows, regardless of how pretty the waitresses might have been.

The bathroom door swung open and Harley's cheerful voice boomed across the room. "Moving slowly this morning, huh buddy?"

"Shit, Harley, why the hell'd you let me drink so much last night?"

"I didn't *let* you. You did it all by yourself. It was all I could do to get you back here in one piece. It's been a while since I've seen anyone that drunk. I literally had to sit you in front of me and hold you there what I drove back. Damn good things the cops didn't see me, we'd both be in the pokey right now."

Shit, Walt said again, this time to himself, he'd been beyond irresponsible. To have gotten this far, at such expense, and then to have risked loosing it all because he was too drunk to sit up straight. "I'm sorry, Harley, I guess I just sort of snapped. I didn't mean to get so carried away. I'm paying for it now, too, let me tell you." He sat up and swung his feet over the edge of the bed, trying to ignore the way the room swam in front of him. Forgetting that they were going to rent a car, Walt thought of the hot desert sun, the throb of Harley's bike and the sauna-like interior of the helmet he insisted on wearing. This morning was going to be pure hell. The room swam faster and Walt rose to his feet, lurching as quickly as he could towards the now vacant bathroom.

By the time he was through retching into the toilet, Walt had remembered the rental car. "Tell me," he said as Harley cracked open the door and peered in, "tell me it's going to get better. We'll have a comfy car with air conditioning and good springs and I'll be able to sleep in the passenger's seat. Tell me that's the way it's going to be this morning."

"I can't promise you that, buddy" said Harley putting one of the motel's small plastic cups on the counter next to Walt's head, "but toss this back before you get into the shower and by the time you finish drying off, you'll feel as good as new."

Walt wiped some vomit from his lips and raised his head cautiously, trying to avoid any sudden moments that might overwhelm his equilibrium. "As good as new," he repeated, eyeing the cloudy liquid in the cup suspiciously.

"As good as new," reinforced Harley with a smile. "Trust me, I'm a toxicologist."

Harley's mixture was as good as his word, and by the time they left the motel room Walt was feeling as if he'd had a full night's sleep and had never touched a drink in his life. "What's the secret?" he asked his friend.

"Can't tell you that," replied Harley. "If I did, I'd have to kill you, cut your head off and stick your brain in a safe. Remember what I told you. Some secrets Uncle Sam wants you to keep forever."

"Or for ninety-nine years," corrected Walt.

"Whatever. In either case, that means longer than one morning. Just be happy it worked."

"Believe me," responded Walt earnestly, "I am very happy it worked."

The two men rode to the nearest rental agency without speaking, Harley trying to keep the bike's engine to a low roar in the quiet pre-dawn hours. Even at this, the coolest time of the day, when the sun hadn't started to rise, the heat was still a living creature, laying over everything with an intensity that dulled the senses. It was, Walt decided with absolute conviction, one hell of a place to build a gambling mecca.

Harley turned into the first rental lot they passed, bringing the bike to a halt in front of the mirrored glass hut where the rental agents worked. "We're going to make this guy's night," he said with a nasty chuckle, "he's probably been sleeping for hours and he's going to wake up to see us come through his door." Harley knew his bulky frame and clean shaven skull intimidated a lot of people, but he also knew that Walt's red eyes and haggard, unshaven face were going to be even more unsettling to someone at four in the morning. Harley always figured that he looked like what he was, a big biker, but he could see that things were starting to take a toll on Walt, who was beginning to resemble a Manson follower. A gaunt and disturbed looking Walt wasn't going to make it any easier to sell their story at Joshua Tree, although Harley was wise enough not to say anything. It wasn't Walt's fault he was looking peaked, it was the series of awful curve balls life had recently thrown his way that had created that effect. Harping on it would change nothing.

CHAPTER XXX

13 JULY
NEW YORK CITY

Brian Flannigan pulled back the drapes of his livingroom's floor-to-ceiling windows and peered through the grimy pane of glass that overlooked Central Park. He smiled without humor. The windows had been cleaned earlier that week and already the city's toxic air had made them filthy again. To think people actually had to breathe that shit. And it was much worse at street level. The smile disappeared, replaced by a frown. This dirty window was just one more sign that the world was becoming increasingly putrid, increasingly in need of his help.

Although he wasn't scheduled to leave for another five minutes, the limousine was already waiting in front of the canopied entrance to his luxury co-op. That, at least, was a good omen. Everything had to go according to plan on this trip. The outcome was far too important to get fouled up by transportation failures.

The Director of the United Nations Environment Programme, Flannigan, a thickly built forty-nine year old with male pattern baldness, was about to get a ride to Kennedy airport, from which he would catch a flight to Palm Springs, California. From there, he'd take another limousine to Joshua Tree National Park, where he would join with a variety of regional, national and international environmental leaders to declare the National Park an International Biosphere, marking the desert Park as a region of international environmental significance.

He would also, should the opportunity present itself, take a moment to memorialize his comrades in the environmental movement who had been so tragically killed or maimed in the explosion in Northern California. Somewhere in that disaster, he thought, there was an analogy to the complex dangers facing the environment, but now wasn't the time to make it. Instead, he'd just say something relatively bland. He did have a gas mask packed in his bag to use as a prop illustrating the everyday industrial dangers facing regular people, but the real analogy would come later in some sort of an essay, when the dust from the explosion, so to speak, had settled. Maybe he'd send it to the New York Times or the Washington Post. They tended to like that sort of thing.

Flannigan wasn't sure exactly what he was going to say about the Biosphere designation itself during the ceremony. It had been a fairly controversial nomination, with mountains of calls, emails and letters opposing the designation, mostly from western conservatives fearing a New World Order takeover of their land. Flannigan wished it could be that clear-cut, that the UN could just move in and take control of things, but the designation carried no legal teeth. It wasn't as if the UN was going to send in troops to keep miners or campers out of the Park. Of course, there was no explaining that to some of these people. The UN, they'd argue, had soldiers, including US troops under its command, all over the world. Joshua Tree was just one more place where it would keep its black helicopters.

In reality, given the lack of enforcement power provided by the designation, the whole ceremony would probably have a negative effect on the environment, Flannigan thought angrily. Flying him, and dozens of other people, to California, routing them around in limos, throwing lavish parties and the rest of the gig would consume enormous amounts of resources, both financial and environmental. And for what? It was ironic, Flannigan decided, that he was in charge of the program and yet had so little faith in its ultimate value. Population control was where the real action was, he mused. Without that, no amount of biosphere designation would make much difference in the long run.

And that, of course, was where the environmental movement had gone wrong. It lacked leaders with the vision to see what the future held without serious population control. Instead, it had people who used vast amounts of paper in mass mailings opposing logging on federal lands, who organized campaigns to ban drift nets while barbecuing salmon, who drove their SUVs to participate in protests against offshore oil exploration on George's Bank. In short, it was full of self-righteous hypocrites who thought declaring Joshua Tree National Park an International Biosphere was going to save the world.

Flannigan knew better.

He was going to save the world. It was just going to take some time.

The buzzer sounded and a muffled voice came over the livingroom's intercom. "Mr. Flannigan?"

"Yes, Dennis." Flannigan recognized the voice. He usually had the same driver/bodyguard on his trips to the airport.

"I'm ready to go whenever you are."

"I'll be right down, Dennis." He walked over to his bed and picked up his travel bag. In one motion he slung the bag over his shoulder while at the same time pulling a .32 automatic pistol from its outer pocket and tucking it into a waistband holster. Licensed to carry the pistol even aboard airplanes, Flannigan viewed the small automatic, with a built-in silencer and a ten round magazine, as insurance for those times when Dennis wasn't around. He'd never actually used it outside of a firing range, but it always paid to be prepared.

After all, it was a dangerous, uncertain world even when you left New York.

CHAPTER XXXI

"You've got to be shitting me," groaned Walt over the chest high plywood counter that separated a groggy-looking rental agent from the unwashed masses that flowed in and out of the office. "How the hell can my card be void? I've never even paid a bill late!" Warning bells were going off in the back of his mind, but he was too hyped up to pay attention to them.

"C'mon, Walt, let's go," said Harley, tugging at his friend's elbow.

"Wait a minute, would you, please?" snapped Walt, shrugging off Harley's big hand, "I want to know why this asshole can't get my card to work."

The clerk, a veteran of dozens of confrontations with down-on-their luck gamblers who insisted that their credit cards were still good, looked uncomfortably at Walt and then flashed a warning look towards Harley. "I'm sorry, sir," he said in a voice that wasn't at all apologetic, "I have nothing to do with what your credit card company does. Why your card is now void is an issue you should discuss with them, not me." His hands were invisible below the countertop and the groggy look was rapidly disappearing.

"C'mon, Walt, drop it would you? It's not this guy's fault. Now let's get out of here." Harley's hand closed Walt's elbow again, with a much firmer grasp this time.

"Let go of me, would you?" Walt jerked his arm with a violent motion, but Harley's hand stayed put.

"I'm sorry about this," Harley said to the clerk, a fake smile plastered across his face, "it was a bad night for him.

You know how it is." Then, before Walt could respond, he'd twisted his friend's wrist behind his back and was half-lifting, half-pushing him out of the office.

Behind the counter, his hands still invisible, the rental agent relaxed. He did, in fact, know how it was.

"Fuck, Harley," screamed Walt as he was bounced painfully through the door, "let go of me, would you."

"Not until you promise to shut up and get on the bike." Harley twisted Walt's wrist a bit more. "This guy didn't void your card," he muttered into Walt's ear, "Branson did. And getting in a fight with some poor soul on the graveyard shift in a car rental agency doesn't help us at all. In twenty seconds Branson's going to know where we are, and he knows we can't rent a car. He'll fly around in that plane looking for my bike and then we're toast. We've got to get the fuck on the road now, while it's still dark, if we want to get to Joshua Tree in one piece."

Walt relaxed in Harley's grasp. "Oh shit," he breathed softly.

When Harley kicked the bike into gear, the windows of the rental agency rattled from the thunderous roar. Speed was the only thing that mattered now.

The phone buzzing against his hip woke Branson from his sleep. With the uncanny ability of a man who hunted other men for a living, he knew immediately where he was. On the backside of a ridge overlooking an unnamed road just south of the desert village of Kelso, California. It was Rodriquez' turn to stand watch over the road below, but the buzzing phone told Branson they could afford to relax for the next couple of hours. Even before he confirmed it, the redhead knew that Walt Crawler had just learned that he could no longer use his credit card.

Denise Wallace heard the drone of the engines at the same time the vehicles topped the hill behind her. Silhouetted against the rising sun, two pickup trucks sloughed around the corner and dropped down into the valley towards Denise. She swore without enthusiasm. Visitors. Why not, everything else had gone wrong. First her radio had gone on the fritz, then she'd gotten a flat tire and then her jack had snapped. What more could happen? She slid out from beneath her jeep, pieces of the broken jack in her hands, as the trucks pulled up behind her crippled vehicle.

"Having trouble, lady?" a short fat man asked as he dismounted from the first truck. Despite the words, there was nothing helpful in his tone.

"Nothing I can't handle, thanks," replied Denise, counting the newcomers as the rest of them got out of the trucks. Four other men, more or less replicas of the first. Grimy, unshaven, tattered clothing and skin so sun-beaten it resembled leather more than anything else. One man was shorter, three were taller and all were somewhat thinner, although all of them had plenty of meat on their bones. One was bald, one wore a ponytail and one, the man who had first spoken, had the gap-toothed smile of a hockey player. All in all, Denise decided, it wasn't an unlikely collection of drivers for this time and place.

Of course, that it wasn't unlikely didn't make her new group of companions any more welcome. At this hour of the day, Denise had a pretty good idea of what these men had been up to even before she smelled the beer on their breath. They'd been out drinking and driving, tearing up the desert in their four-wheel drive trucks and probably, she added, looking at the light bar mounted on the cab of the first truck, jacking anything that moved. She shot a quick glance into the cab of the jeep where her Baretta lay tucked behind the driver's seat. Could she reach it in time? Should she even try or was she overreacting?

The men fanned out around her, not overtly threatening but forcing Denise back against the jeep's tailgate all the same. All of her senses were on full alert, now. Going for the Baretta wouldn't be overreacting in the least.

"Helluvplace for a woman to break down in, huh ma'am?" commented gap-tooth with mock politeness.

She couldn't make it to the pistol, Denise decided, but none of the men appeared to be carrying a weapon and the jack handle in her right hand might even the odds. Unfortunately, *might* was the operative word. None of the newcomers looked like a soft-bellied choirboy. "That's okay," she said confidently, slowly edging around the side of the jeep. If she could just get a few steps closer to her seat, she might be able to grab the Baretta before they could stop her. That would probably end the discussion right there. "If you've got to break down someplace, it might as well be here. It's nothing I can't handle." She tossed her head a little, allowing her jet black hair to swirl rebelliously around her shoulders. So what if she was alone. No wild bunch of desert rats was going to crowd her.

"Actually," the man with the ponytail spoke, "it's really a helluva place for a *black woman* to break down in, I'd say. Especially an *attractive black woman*." The semi-circle of men drifted closer.

That settled it. In her ten-plus years as a Ranger for the National Park Service, no one mentioned "black woman" to Denise's face unless they were getting ready to try and smash it. And, in all her years as a Ranger, no one had ever succeeded in smashing it, but then she'd never faced five tough-looking men alone on a desert road before.

She made a quick feint towards the gun, knowing that the men would react accordingly by rushing her. No matter how desperate the situation, the cop in her couldn't bring herself to let loose with the jack handle until they made the first move.

The ponytailed man was the closest, and when he came at her Denise was ready. Spinning back to face her attackers, she grabbed the jack handle in both hands and aimed a vicious chop at the man's knees. The blow was completely unexpected and the man went down as if someone had cut off his legs. Another man stumbled over his friend and Denise swung at his ear, managing only a glancing blow off his head as she dodged away from the rest of the men.

Her respite lasted only a moment, however, as the men still standing began to swarm at her. She swung the handle again, felt a bone crunch under the blow and another man went down, but then strong arms grabbed her legs and she toppled sideways. A face appeared in front of her, the beer breath from the gap-toothed mouth flooding her nostrils, and she rammed the end of the jack handle into the gaping maw, noting with satisfaction that two more teeth disappeared.

But now she was on the ground and even her considerable strength couldn't shake the mass of bodies off of her. Her side ached where someone had kneed her and she was forced to let go of the jack handle as a pair of sinewy hands forced her fingers back to the breaking point. A sweaty, smelly body covered her face, someone got a chokehold on her throat and she began to struggle for breath even as she tried to sink her teeth into the flesh above her. Another hand forced her jaw shut before she succeeded and, still thrashing wildly, Denise's body began to shut down for lack of oxygen.

Harley drove the bike through the gathering light like a demon riding the wind. Every mile they covered before true light came made it more likely they'd get to Joshua Tree in one piece. If they were still out in this deserted patch of desert when the sun rose and Branson could search from the sky, he and Walt were as good as dead. The big bike wasn't made for off-road riding, and the improved dirt and gravel road hadn't been made with bikes like Harley's in mind, but he pushed his machine to its limits and beyond. No matter how dangerous the ride, speed was safety.

He topped a low hill, the bike's shadow spilling far in front of him as the sun cleared the eastern horizon, and saw a cluster of vehicles below. Harley's first thought was that they'd blundered into another ambush, but there was nothing he could do about it now except try to crash through, trusting to his speed to foil the would-be assassins. As he roared down the hill, though, the echo of his bike almost deafening as it bounced back and forth between the narrow canyon walls, he noticed something was clearly wrong.

Rather than a group of riflemen ranged out behind the vehicles, waiting to drop the riders as soon as they had a clear shot, Harley saw a sprawling mass of bodies almost completely blocking the road. He knew one of the first principles of an ambush was to throw out obstacles to slow down the ambushee, but this was absurd. Nonetheless, nothing was beyond Branson, and Harley threaded his way through the writhing figures without slowing down.

He could feel the men looking at him in shocked surprise, noting their ratty clothes and dirty white bodies as he blasted by them. This was definitely not Branson's crowd. A flash of dark skin and black hair momentarily showed from the bottom of the pile and Harley realized what was going on.

It was a lynching.

Every second they rode toward Joshua Tree made them safer, Harley knew, and this wasn't his fight, but he didn't hesitate. He hit the brakes on the bike and skidded to an abrupt stop, throwing up a cloud of dust and dirt that momentarily obscured the struggle in the road behind him. Without waiting to see if Walt was following him, Harley leapt from the bike and charged back to the pile of men he'd just passed. He might be outnumbered, but he still had the element of surprise on his side and surprise, in any sort of combat, was the ultimate force multiplier.

Without warning, the chokehold on her throat disappeared and oxygen flooded Denise's lungs. The pile of bodies holding her down shifted violently and all of a sudden she was unexpectedly free. She rolled to her knees, still gasping for breath, in time to see a mountain of a man with a bald head wade into the men who attacked her. Behind him, a smaller, wilder looking man, was running to join the fray. The big man tossed one of the desert rats to the ground and launched another face first into the jeep while his companion wrestled with the now-risen ponytailed man. For a brief moment Denise thought the fight had ended, then the gap-toothed man moved forward, swinging the jack handle like a baseball bat into the side of the big man's head. The man dropped like a stone and lay motionless on the ground and the jack handle rose up to the sky to administer the coup de grace.

With no time to think, Denise just reacted. Despite the pain that still engulfed her body, she rose to her feet and dove for the arms holding the handle. She drove her knee into his gut, aiming for, but missing, the man's groin, and then forced the handle down and sideways until she had ripped it from the man's grasp and held it once more in her own capable hands.

The gap-toothed man, blood streaming from his recently shattered mouth, backed from the Ranger and surveyed the scene. The ponytailed man, his nose a red faucet, had broken away from one of the newcomers and the other three men had stumbled back to their feet. Even though numbers were still on their side, the assailants realized that they'd lost their momentum. The woman had hurt them before with the jack handle and she looked more than willing to do so again. And while the big man on the ground still wasn't moving, his wild-eyed companion seemed ready for action. All in all, it had become more than they had bargained for and, as one, they broke before their antagonists and ran for the trucks.

Seeing an opening, Denise dashed for her own vehicle, scrambling to get her pistol out before the desert rats could pull out whatever guns they might have in their trucks.

Further fighting appeared to be the last thing on their minds, however, and the two trucks were moving even before the last of the men climbed on board. Denise had her pistol up, ready to fire, but was forced to jump aside as the first truck nearly ran her down. The second truck followed directly behind the leader, swerving only slightly as it passed Harley's motorcycle. It wasn't much more than a bump to the truck's driver, but, in one brief instant, the vehicle's reinforced aluminum brush guard removed the motorcycle's front wheel and, with it, Walt and Harley's hopes to get to Joshua Tree National Park before the sun was high in the sky.

Denise, pistol still at the ready, watched the trucks until they were out of sight. Then she turned to Walt. "Thank you," she said quietly. Before Walt could respond, she had turned her attention to Harley, who had struggled to a sitting position and was holding his left hand to his bloody head. "Are you okay," she asked as she knelt by him.

"Yeah," responded the biker in a thick voice, "I'm alright. If he'd hit me another inch or so higher, I'd be dead, but as it is, I'm just going to have a headache and a sore neck." He looked at Denise appreciatively. "Unless I miss my guess, you kept him from taking another whack at me."

"I did."

"Thank you. I think you saved my life."

"No more than you did mine. Now let me get something for that cut." Denise went over to the jeep and fished out a first aid kit. She bandaged Harley's wound and then dug through the kit until she found some aspirin. "These might help a bit," she said, holding out the pills, "I've even got water to wash 'em down with if you want."

"No thanks. I can do better than that." Harley lumbered to his feet and turned towards his bike. "Oh shit," he swore, noticing its condition for the first time. "Those fuckers ran over my bike." He kicked at a crumpled plastic shell and looked at Walt. "They ran over your helmet, too."

"Uh-huh," said Walt laconically, leaning against the jeep's bumper and surveying the wreckage in front of him. "Now what the hell do we do?" He looked at Denise hopefully. "Do you think you could give us a ride to Twenty-nine Palms or Joshua Tree? We're kind of in a hurry, but Harley's bike ain't going to get us there."

Denise put the first aid kit back in the car. "I'd love to," she replied, "but my jeep's not going anywhere either. I've got a flat and the jack's broken." She kicked at the disabled tire as if to prove her point. "I'd call for help but my radio's broken as well. Until someone else comes along, I'm afraid we're basically stuck."

Harley picked a small packet from the ruined motorcycle and then walked over to the jeep. "Have you loosened up the nuts?" he asked.

"Yeah. Took 'em all the way off and stuck 'em on the back seat, but I don't see what good it'll do us with a broken jack."

"Where's your spare?"

"I already took it out. It's on the other side of the jeep. Why?"

Harley didn't say anything, but went around the vehicle and rolled the spare tire back next to the flat one. "I'm going to pick up the back of your jeep," he said simply, like it was nothing more than lifting a sack of groceries to the kitchen counter. "Walt, you pull the flat tire off and you," he gestured at Denise, "put the new one on."

He moved to the jeep's bumper. "Don't get under the jeep," he warned, "just in case something brakes. Now, on the count of three." While his companions looked on in amazement, Harley counted to three and heaved the back of the jeep high in the air. "C'mon, move," he grunted, the veins in his neck and arms sticking out like small snakes, "replace the damn tire!"

Galvanized by his words, Walt pulled the flat tire from its lugs and, almost before he had put it on the ground, Denise had replaced it with the spare. A few seconds later, the lugnuts were in place and Harley gently let the vehicle slip back to the ground.

"That's one hell of a trick," murmured Denise in awe. "Now, who are you guys?"

"Why don't we tell you that once we're on the road," said Walt. "I'd hate to be here when those fellows come back with a bunch of automatic weapons." That should be reason enough to get their new friend moving quickly. He saw no need to tell her his more pressing concerns about Branson and the searching airplane.

Walt vaulted into the cubbyhole that served as the jeep's back seat and Harley, much less gracefully, clambered through the cutout that served as a door to the vehicle's open cab, settling his mass as comfortably as possible in the front seat. While Denise stuck her pistol back behind her seat and got the jeep running, he fumbled through the packet he'd retrieved from his bike and dug out a small vial of pills. "Perfectly legal," he grinned at Denise, "but a whole hell of a more effective."

"So, who are you?" Denise seemed unconcerned with the vial. "It's not every day two total strangers save my ass from a bunch of rednecks. It'd be nice to know your names." She shot a glance at Walt in the rearview mirror. Several days' growth of beard and blood-shot eyes, matched by clothes he'd worn for days, gave him a somewhat menacing atmosphere and she wondered if she should have stuck her pistol in her lap instead of tucking it back in its holster. Sometimes, she knew, the folks who rescued you merely took you at of the frying pan and tossed you in the fire.

Harley noticed his driver's suddenly wary attitude and grinned again. "Don't worry about us, ma'am. We're just in a hurry, that's all. As we say in the world of the iron horse, we've been ridden hard and put away wet." He dug a cigar from the packet, clipped the end with a small penknife and stuck it in his mouth. "Do you mind if I smoke?" he asked.

Denise eyed the cigar. "I suppose you've earned it," she said reluctantly. "Now, who, exactly do you mean by 'we?'"

"I'm Ross Mitchell," the biker stuck out a huge hand and Denise took one hand off the wheel to shake. "My friends call me Harley, though." He studied Denise's high cheekbones and aquiline nose, framing clear brown eyes that seemed aware of all that was going on around her while still staying focused on the rough road she was navigating. There was no doubt about it, she was an attractive woman. And she could fight, too. "I hope you'll call me Harley.' He pulled a pack of matches from the packet and lit his cigar, puffing fiercely until the tip glowed bright red.

"And the young man behind you is Walt Crawler," Harley continued. "I know he's looking a bit on the scruffy side, but like I said, we've been ridden hard and put away wet."

"Ridden hard from where?"

"Believe it or not, just a few days ago I was in Falmouth, Massachusetts where I am a senior marine toxicologist at the Woods Hole Oceanographic Institute. And Walt was on the island of Nantucket where he is a respected wildlife biologist for the Massachusetts Department of Fisheries, Wildlife and Environmental Law Enforcement. We spent last night in Las Vegas and we were on our way to Joshua Tree National Park before we ran into you, fair maiden, a damsel in distress."

Sitting in the back, Walt wished he could kick Harley through the seat. No matter how pretty this lady was, there was no need for Harley yap on like a smitten teenager.

"Well, my name is Denise Wallace." She smiled at Harley and twisted her head to flash her teeth at Walt.

"Not to pry into your personal life, Denise" said Harley, "but what exactly was going on back there?"

"It's not prying. Besides you lost your bike out of it, not to mention damn near your head. You have a right to know. I was out camping in the desert last night and was heading back to town this morning when I got a flat. The jack was bust and I was just trying to figure out what to do when these morons decided to try to rape me. Or whatever it was they were trying.

I used the jack handle to give as good as I got, at first, but once I went down that was the end." She massaged her side where she had been kneed. "Or it would have been if you two hadn't come along. I'm going to be one sore lady once the adrenaline wears off." She reached over to the vial Harley had put on the dashboard. "You're sure it's legal?"

"Absolutely. Trust me. I'm a toxicologist, remember? Just one will do you wonders."

Denise popped a pill into her mouth, swallowing it without water. "Sorry about your bike," she said meekly. Bikers were notoriously fickle about what happened to their wheels, although her passengers appeared to be surprisingly nonplussed.

"Hey, don't worry," Harley welcomed the opportunity to grin again. "That's why I have insurance. As long as we're not walking, I'm happy."

Alone in the back seat, Walt looked into the rearview mirror and stared at Denise's smooth face. Who was this lady? Loose fitting slacks and a light colored t-shirt accentuated, rather than disguised, the strength of her trim frame and, even while driving, she gave the impression of being a coiled spring. Despite the fresh blood that stained her clothes, she seemed to have shrugged off the earlier fight as nothing more than a schoolyard scuffle. She caught his eyes in the mirror and held his gaze with an unblinking stare of her own and Walt knew, beyond a doubt, that the woman in front of driving the jeep was a cop of some sort.

The three of them bounced along in awkward silence, the rising sun starting to beat at them as they tried to figure out where the conversation should go.

Harley was the first to break the silence, eager to learn more about the attractive woman next to him while directing attention away from him and Walt. "So, Denise," he asked, "still not meaning to pry, but where'd you learn to handle yourself in a fight like that?" Yet another grin.

"I've got three older brothers and two younger ones," she grinned back, "I had to learn how to take care of myself before I could even walk."

"There's more to it than that, I'll bet," said Harley. "No one learns to swing a jack handle like that just by fighting her brothers over who rides by the window."

"For a biker, Harley, you're pretty astute." She smiled to make sure the comment carried no edge. "I've had a bit of experience fighting, although never with an jack handle."

"Well, fair maiden, do tell. Since I no longer have to concentrate on my driving, I'm going to expect you to keep me entertained."

"Fair enough," said Denise pleasantly, "it's not exactly a fairy tale but I'll start it with 'once upon a time.' So, once upon a time, there was this little black girl who lived in a small town on the Mississippi Delta. Her daddy worked the river on a tugboat, her momma spent most of her time taking care of their brood of kids. The little girl decided she want a bit more out of life than the Delta offered, so she got a scholarship to Ole Miss and majored in environmental studies. When she got graduated, *cum laude* by the way, she got a job as a National Park Service interpreter at Vicksburg National Park, explaining Union Army positions to northern tourists. After three years of describing how the Union artillery had bombarded the hell out of Vicksburg and how everyone in town had been forced to live in caves, she decided that wasn't a hell of a lot better than working the river. I don't know if you've ever experienced one, but Vicksburg summers aren't meant for wearing a uniform and standing outside explaining things to people.

"So the little girl in question decided she really wanted to become a Ranger. In the National Park Service, that means you're part cop and part game warden. It's not a bad job, if you can get it, and this little girl eventually got it. So the Park Service sent her off to all sorts of training and she finally became an honest to God National Park Service Ranger. Gun, hat and all." Denise smiled proudly. "Not bad for a girl whose Daddy never graduated from high school."

"Where's the happily ever after part?" asked Harley, purposefully preempting any comment Walt might make about her being a Park Ranger. He didn't want to appear overly anxious about the Park quite yet.

A frown crossed Denise's face. "The little girl has often wondered that. Being a Ranger, it turned out, wasn't all happily ever after." She slowed the jeep to a crawl and pointed to a group of buildings. "See that?" she asked.

"See what?" asked Harley.

"Those houses."

"Yeah, what about them?"

"That's Kelso."

"So?"

"On the other side of that little town, this road goes through a pretty steep canyon. Those good ol' boys you helped me chase off may very well be waiting in that canyon for us. From the dust hanging in the air, they've obviously passed through here not that long ago. If they're looking to even the score, that's where they'll do it." The jeep ground to a stop and Denise reached under her seat for a pair of binoculars. Walt and Harley stayed quiet as she surveyed the land in front of them. "I don't see anything, but that doesn't mean much out here. It probably looks wide open to you easterners, but once you get up to the hills, there's a million places you could hide an army."

Walt and Harley exchanged glances. If one could hide an army out here from a Ranger, whatever Branson was planning would be that much tougher to detect.

"You think they're waiting for us?" asked Walt. As if Branson weren't enough. Although he hadn't had a chance to speak to Harley, he'd decided Branson had given up on the plane idea. If he'd been flying, they'd have seen his plane already. That meant, thought Walt, that Branson was also lying in wait someplace up ahead. Hopefully he was just looking for two men on a motorcycle, but even a blind man would have trouble not noticing Harley in the open jeep.

"I don't know. It could happen."

"Would they shoot us?"

"Maybe, but I doubt it. They don't usually."

"Usually?" asked Harley and Walt in unison.

"Yeah, usually. Most of the time, they just throw empty beer bottles. Good thing, too, 'cause the full ones hurt a lot more. Over on Lake Meade, a buddy of mine was trying to stop some drunken jet skiers in a cove when a bunch of campers on the cliffs overhead started throwing things at him. He got hit with a full sixteen ounce Budweiser bottle. Funny thing, actually. The bottle was fine, he's got it up on his mantelpiece, but it broke his arm in two places."

"Excuse me for prying even more," Harley wasn't grinning now, "but how often does shit like this happen out here?"

"On a personal level, not often at all. On a professional level, it's a big problem."

"What the hell's that mean?" Harley was feeling comfortable enough with Denise to swear casually in front of her.

"It means, when I'm by myself, just being me, like I was last night, I don't usually run into trouble. There's lots of nothing out here, of course, so it's smart to be prepared for trouble, but this morning's run-in was the first one I've ever had. Most folks around here will go out of their way to pull you from a ditch or give you some gas if you run out. Those jerks this morning were an abnormality."

"In more ways than one," muttered Walt under his breath.

"But professionally," continued Denise, ignoring Walt's comment, "running into trouble happens a lot more often. It's rarely violent trouble, but there's always that possibility. And it's not just when we're responding to a call, either. Sometimes it's just because we're who we are."

"And who's that?" The conversation was really between Harley and Denise. Walt fidgeted in the back seat and wondered how the hell they could figure out what Branson was up to, much less stop it, in a land as surprisingly wild as the California high desert.

"We're Park Rangers, Harley. That's the 'we' I'm talking about."

"So?"

"Harley, what do you see on either side of us?"

"Desert. Rocks. Hills. A fence. That's about it."

"No, Harley," Denise's tone was short. "That's not 'about it.' What you're looking at is government land, Department of Agriculture property. Sometimes it's DOI, Interior, or it's the Defense Department, but for the most part it's all the same. Property of the federal government. As far as you can see, it's Uncle Sam, for miles and miles and miles. How much land do the Feds own back where you come from?" Denise's questioning reminded Harley of a District Attorney friend in Boston.

"There's the Cape Cod National Seashore, some Coast Guard stations," the biker answered hesitatingly, feeling he was failing some sort of test. "And the National Park Service runs stuff all over Boston and in Concord and Lexington. Mostly Revolutionary War sites."

"Okay, and how much land is that, fifty thousand acres, a hundred thousand acres? How much?"

"God no, not that much," Harley tried to anticipate Denise's next question. "A couple acres here and there. A few dozen square miles, maybe."

"Harley, out here the Feds own enough land to swallow all of that whole. You'd never even find it. You'd lose your whole state here if someone plopped it down in the middle of this territory. It's not possible for the federal government to own that much land and not raise some suspicions with the folks who live nearby. And DC is so far away, it's almost another world." Denise's voice was starting to get heated. "You can drive down to DC in what, eight, ten hours if you want to pigeon-hole your Senator or some federal bureaucrat? Or fly down in the morning and be there by lunch. Compared to these folks, you're practically next door to DC. For them, it's a huge trip. Two, three days driving or maybe a full day on the plane.

"Even for me, a federal employee, it sometimes seems like DC is as far away as the moon. And DC is where the people in charge of all this property we're driving through make decisions concerning this land. How much to mine, what species are endangered, how much grazing fees should be. Whatever.

"Now, I'm not arguing that they're making the wrong decisions. If anything, they should be tougher. Without federal protection a lot of this land would be so over-grazed or strip mined you wouldn't even recognize it. But to some of the people who live out here, to a lot of them, actually, this is their land. They look at the federal government as a bunch of unwanted, ignorant busybodies who should butt out.

"Which brings us to me, the "we" I mentioned. I'm the federal government's representative out here. The man on the spot, so to speak. Worse than that, to some folks, I'm a Park Service Ranger. They honestly think I'm going to pull into their driveway, take away their guns, turn their home into a National Park and kick them onto the street. They believe that so strongly, some of them, that they'd shoot me before I'd have the chance to explain that I was just looking for directions.

"Of course, being black doesn't help either. I don't get much grief about my skin color, but I stick out like a chocolate chip at a marshmallow roast all the same. It makes me that much easier to identify, which, in turn, makes me a bit more nervous.

"You see, Harley, there's something of a war going on out here. It's what some folks might call a low intensity war, and others call a bunch of terrorist acts and still others call a property rights movement. To the soldier on the ground, like me, it's just a war. A lot of so-called states' rights people want the Feds out of here. They want their counties or states to own all of this land, to regulate it or to sell it off or to give it to private parties and they're willing to fight to make that happen.

"Unfortunately, their idea of fighting doesn't necessarily mean going to the op-ed pages of the *Washington Times*. For too many of them, it means bombing Ranger Stations, shooting at Forest Service workers or bulldozing roads through federal property while nearby federal agents worry about getting lynched by onlookers. And it means blowing up federal buildings. Whatever they can think of, some of these guys will do.

"Out here, in the West, there's miles and miles of nothing. We're not supposed to patrol alone and we're supposed to call in our locations when we do go out. We don't wear our uniforms out in town or basically do anything to let folks know we're Park Rangers. Folks think I'm crazy for going camping on my own. There's always the risk of hoodlums like this morning's thugs, but there's also the problem with maybe someone realizing you're a Ranger. Or following you because you're one. It happens.

"So I'm not one to take chances. Rather than going through that canyon and hoping we don't get our ears chopped off by falling beer bottles, we're going to swing up this ridge here," Denise pointed, "and swing west of Kelso. It's a little bit longer, but we won't have to worry about getting to town in one piece."

Denise put the binoculars between the seats and Walt grabbed them. If five drunken punks could force a Park Ranger to change her route, what could a hardened terrorist like Branson do? He scoured the surrounding hillsides, trying unsuccessfully to envision where Branson was or what he could be doing. This world, with its jagged, barren slopes, its sharp edged cacti and its almost complete silence was as foreign to Walt as the face of the moon. He couldn't imagine anything. Once again, it all seemed so hopeless. He put the binoculars down and pulled the silver spoon from his pocket, rubbing it feverishly to rebuild his confidence. Forty-eight hours, the doctor had said. He couldn't loose focus now, he had to believe they would succeed. Otherwise it really would be hopeless.

As the jeep began churning up the trail around Kelso, Walt couldn't contain himself any longer. Harley might be happy to exchange grins and life stories, but he couldn't drag his mind away from Branson and Joshua Tree for more than a few seconds. "So," he asked as blandly as he could, "are you a Park Ranger at Joshua Tree?"

"Yes. Not much else to be a Park Ranger of out here," Denise laughed. "Why, is that where you were headed in such a hurry?" It had taken her a while to work the question in, but the strange circumstances of running into Walt and Harley had piqued her curiosity, both personal and professional.

"As a matter of fact," interjected Harley before Walt could say otherwise, "it's not exactly where we were headed, but close. We've got a biker's rally at Palm Springs we're supposed to join at noon. We'd have been there no problem but I couldn't come all this way without swinging by Las Vegas to play the horses. That's my hobby, you know," he clarified in a confidential tone. "I did okay at the simulcast, but we wound up staying the night and we're way behind, timewise. Of course," he added sadly, taking the lie as far as he could, "now that we don't have a bike, making the rally doesn't really much matter."

"You rode all the way here from Massachusetts to go to a bike rally?" Denise was amazed.

"Yeah, basically. You're not a biker, are you?"

"No, can't say that I am. Life's dangerous enough for me anyway without inviting trouble."

"Well, bikers do weird things. And the club I belong to," Denise couldn't know Harley didn't belong to any clubs, "has three races a year. One's north to a rally in Quebec. That's a short ride, so everyone does it. One's south to the Bike Week at Daytona Beach in March. A great time of year to be in Florida, so just about everyone does that, too. And the third is the Palm Springs rally. It's a lousy time to ride in the desert and it's a zillion miles away so, this year, no one's doing it. Or, no one besides us and, with no bike, we're not doing it either, anymore."

"What's the prize? If you'd made it?"

"Oh, not much. A silly goat's head trophy with your name on it. Mostly it's just a chance to prove how crazy you are. Running into you will make a better story, and, like I said, I've got insurance on the bike."

"Don't you have to go get it?" Denise had been puzzled for a while. Why was Harley so willing to leave his bike, damaged though it was, in the middle of the desert?

"For what? You don't know bikes, but I could tell by just looking at it that the bike was totaled. The front wheel was just about all the way off, the frame was bent, it looked like the rear axle was bust and the engine looked pretty chopped up, too. I don't know what happened to it," Harley knew he had to be careful here, he'd been unconscious when his bike had been run over, "but it's history now. I'll file a claim and say it got stolen." He looked at Denise. "You'll have to file a report on what happened, right?"

"Of course."

"Well, I'll show that to my claims adjuster and they won't question a thing. No one's going to expect me to salvage a busted up bike in the desert miles from nowhere with a bunch of homicidal maniacs running around. If we were to go out to get it later on, it would probably be gone anyway. So stolen sounds fair to me. We'll catch a flight home tomorrow-insurance ought to pay for that, too-and in a couple of days I'll have me a brand new bike." He grinned happily, almost buying the story himself.

"And Walt rode all the way behind you, or is he part of the motorcycle club too?" Not that she cared about anyone's sexual orientation, but Denise didn't think Harley was into men. In fact, judging from the way his eyes moved over her body, she was fairly certain he felt at least some attraction to her, but it was always a good idea to get these things sorted out first.

"No, not exactly. Walt's taking a break from life." He glanced behind him, but his friend was looking through the binoculars again, completely oblivious to the conversation up front. Harley dropped his voice. "I don't know if you read about it, but there was an explosion on Nantucket a few months ago. Killed a woman and her twins."

"Yeah, I remember. It sounded terrible."

"The woman was Walt's ex-wife and the twins were his daughters."

"Oh my God!" Denise's hand involuntarily flew to her mouth. "That's awful."

"It gets worse. His third daughter, Katie, was hurt, too. She got a dose of some sort of poison and she's still in the hospital in a coma."

"So what's he doing out here? Why isn't he at the hospital with his daughter?" Denise's voice was low now, too, and she'd tilted her head closer to Harley's.

"He just about lived at the hospital for the first few months," said Harley, thinking quickly, "but he started getting jumpy and the docs told him he needed a break. I guess parents can really flip out if they see their kid lying helpless for so long. They go a little crazy, start pulling wires and tubes. It can get bad. So they told Walt to take off and I decided to take off with him. I remembered this stupid Palm Springs thing and here we are. We call twice a day and if Katie's condition changes, Walt can be home on the next airplane."

"God, it sounds just terrible."

"It's worse than terrible. It's eating him alive." Harley raised his voice. "So," he asked, changing the subject, "is there anything interesting going on at Joshua Tree these days? Since we won't be going to Palm Springs, we might as well do something constructive with our time." He'd been dying to ask Denise this question ever since she said she was a Park Ranger. If something big were scheduled, it might give him an idea of what Branson was planning. Later on, if the opportunity presented itself, maybe they could fill Denise in on what was really happening, but Harley didn't want to dump all that on her at once. He was sure that she dealt with a fair share of nuts already, he didn't want her to lump them in the same pile.

"As a matter of fact, there is. Tomorrow morning there's going to be a big celebration at Barker Dam because the UN's designated the Park an International Biosphere. Some bigwig from the UN named Flannigan's going to be there, along with the Vice-President. It ought to be something to see." She snorted and fell silent again, the look on her face telling Harley what she thought of the whole affair.

Harley looked back at Walt again and saw his friend had put the binoculars back down and was paying attention to the conversation. The two men exchanged meaningful glances. That's what Branson was planning! He was going to take out Flannigan, the Vice-President and anyone else who happened to be there at the celebration. The two previous explosions had just been warmups.

But how, exactly, was Branson going to do it?

CHAPTER XXXII

Branson squinted through the morning sun and cursed softly. The road below remained empty for as far as he could see. He checked his watch, knowing it was no more than a minute or two since he'd checked it last, and then stuck another piece of gum in his mouth. It was almost nine and he was getting very fidgety. If Crawler and Mitchell didn't come through soon, he'd have to pull back to Joshua Tree and the thought of making a hit there, as opposed to on this barren stretch of backcountry road, was not very pleasant.

How could they have missed them? He and Rodriquez had been in this overwatch position for hours, one on, one off, and the only vehicles that had passed had been the two beat-up pickup trucks that had sped by just a few minutes earlier. Rodriquez had scoped them out as they approached and he had been certain that none of the men in the trucks had been either Crawler or Mitchell.

That meant the two men still had to be somewhere further out on this road.

They had to be.

Unless, which Branson thought was very unlikely, Harley had decided the desert backroads were too much for his bike. Branson knew that not to be the case, so a bike nut like Mitchell would have to know that too. The roads would present something of a challenge, of course, but by no means an unmanageable one.

Perhaps they had gone a different route, afraid that they'd been tracked down when Walt tried to use his credit card?

That was possible, too, but Branson doubted it. They'd already made a great big loop through Colorado and Nevada, they'd want to get this part of the ride over with as quickly as possible. Plus, from their perspective, coming over the backroads on a motorcycle could have been a calculated gamble. Most people wouldn't expect that, and Mitchell and Crawler very well might have decided that this was the safest, most likely not to be watched, route.

Where his logic had gaps, Branson's hunter's instincts provided bridges. He knew the men he was chasing would take this road.

A glint of metal on the far side of the valley, just short of the village of Kelso, caught his eye. He nudged Rodriquez and the Texan handed him the powerful telescope they were using to survey the road.

"Hey, Manny," Branson said, "there's something that looks like a jeep stopped on the other side of town."

"Okay." Manny sounded unimpressed. They were looking for a motorcycle.

"It's starting to head up that ridge to the west."

"Yeah," said Manny, looking through a less powerful pair of binoculars, "I can see the dust."

"Why would they be doing that?"

"I don't know. Maybe they're just out four-wheeling, having a good time going up and down the ridges. Maybe they don't like Kelso. I don't know. Why?" He put the binoculars down and took a sip of water from a canteen at his side.

"I don't know why, I'm just wondering. For one thing, the timing's mighty peculiar. I mean, right about now is when we're expecting Mitchell and Crawler to come by."

"True, but they didn't have a jeep last we knew."

"But they might now."

"And they might have a limo, too, and they might be getting a chauffeured trip on hardtop roads door to door." Rodriquez knew he was being unusually short with Branson. The stress of the chase was wearing him down, he thought, just as it must be wearing down the men they were chasing. And if the chase was a failure, Rodriquez would be in the hotseat every bit as much as his boss. Not for the first time, he wished they'd just shot Crawler and Mitchell from the airplane way back in Oklahoma. "We could *might have* ourselves to death if we're not careful. You said if they're not here by nine, we fall back to the Park. That sounds like a good plan to me, and we can't go chasing every truck, jeep and station wagon we see in the meantime."

"Okay, Manny, calm down." Branson had to keep himself from barking at his companion, they'd gain nothing by bickering. The Texan was right. That's what they had planned. But there was still a bit of time before nine o'clock rolled around. Branson put the spyglass to his eye again and followed the jeep as it bumped up the ridge.

At the top of the ridge, Denise pulled over to the side of the trail onto a small gravel ledge and gestured towards the east. "You can see what I mean from up here. There are a few houses below us, surrounded by a huge ocean of nothingness. Try telling someone who lives in one of those houses that anyone writing regulations in Washington understands how he lives or what's important to his family. A lot of the people who live out here are convinced that these federal bureaucrats don't have a clue as to what life's like out here." She stared across the vast landscape. "And it's probably true, too. I doubt anyone understands those people in Kelso other than the folks in Kelso. Or maybe the inhabitants of Perth or Amboy or some of these other dry-as-dust places."

Unlike Denise, Harley had to shield his eyes from the sun to admire the view. "You make a pretty good argument, Ms. Ranger," he said, "it's almost as if you thought people around here are right in wanting the Feds out."

"No, that's not true. Like I said before, if the Feds took off, the folks who lived here, or enough of them, would plunder and abuse this land so much that in a generation it would be a complete wasteland. I really think the federal government has an important role to play out here. Maybe it's because those bureaucrats *are* so far away that the land has held on as long as it has. But if you look at it from a local's view, not through the eyes of a transplant from the Mississippi Delta, you've got to admit that Uncle Sam can be an overbearing neighbor, to put it mildly."

"Is that what you meant by saying that the little girl's Ranger story didn't end 'happily ever after?'" Despite his size and tough guy demeanor, Harley could sound surprisingly tender when he wanted to.

Denise looked out over the empty desert and smiled through tight lips. "No, it wasn't. But it's not the most pleasant story. Are you sure you want to hear it?"

"If you don't mind telling us."

The Ranger took a deep breath as if marshaling her thoughts and then started to speak. "After I became I Ranger I was stationed at the San Padre National Seashore in Texas for a few years. It was a lot of fun, but it's more like being a cop than anything else. People getting drunk and abusive at campgrounds, dealing drugs in the parking lots, trying to steal endangered plants and animals from the woods. There's a huge market in endangered species, believe it or not."

Walt grunted from the back seat. He'd seen it himself on Nantucket.

"And then one day my partner and I made a routine traffic stop. Some guy had failed to stop for a red light. It's the sort of thing that happens all the time. We ran the plate and it came back clean, so we both got out of the car without worrying too much. There's always a pit in your stomach when you first approach a car 'cause you're never quite sure what you might have uncovered, but this one seemed pretty normal. A red, two-door hatchback with two guys up front, a third in the back. No big deal.

"My partner had been driving, so he went up to the driver's side. I was further behind on the passenger's side. As my partner, his name was Fred, Fred Jaskow, got up to the driver's window to collect the license and registration, I saw the guy in the back of the car move suddenly. Don't ask me how I knew, because all I saw move were his shoulders, but I knew he was grabbing a gun.

"I screamed 'gun!' at the top of my lungs and started to pull my pistol out of its holster. And then everything went to shit all at once. The passenger's side door opens up and an absolute moose of a man jumps out with a sawed-off shotgun. I can remember thinking 'he's too big for center mass, it's got to be a head shot.' You'd be amazed at how many shots a body can take and still keep functioning, especially if you're just using standard nine mil ammo. And that's independent of any body armor he might be using. That armor stuff can be pretty effective, you know. If I didn't drop him with my first shot, I knew I'd never get a second chance. He'd have cut me in half with a shotgun at that range.

"At the same time, I'm hearing pops from inside the car and Fred drops out of sight. As near as we could figure it out later, he hit the ground when I screamed and those first shots missed him.

"I don't even remember drawing my gun, much less aiming it but the next thing I knew is that monster with the shotgun drops the gun and gets knocked back into the car. Turns out I hit him smack between the eyes, literally. Any place else and you'd have made your rally. He was wearing armor." Denise tried a soft smile to take the edge off of her story. "I tapped him twice more, just to make sure, center mass this time, not that it would have done any good had he been alive, and then I dropped and rolled to my left. You don't want to stay in one place very long in a firefight if you can help it. I came up just behind the car's left rear bumper. If I'd rolled a bit quicker I might have saved Fred.

"By this time Fred had his own gun out. I heard him holler 'drop it' and then I heard two big bangs. Made my nine mil sound like a pop gun.

"When I cleared the bumper, I saw the driver getting out. He was a moose, too, just like the other guy. Turns out they were brothers. He's got a .44 magnum in his hand and, believe me, when you're that close to the bad guys, a pistol like that looks like a cannon.

"I saw Fred rolling across the road and knew what had happened before I even finished seeing it. Fred had given the guy a chance to drop his gun, and instead of dropping it, the asshole plugged him.

"Now, my Daddy, bless his soul, may never have graduated from high school, but he's a long way from being anybody's fool. When he found out what a Park Ranger did for a living, he said to me, 'Denise, you know I try not to tell you what to do, but promise me you'll remember just one thing. It's better to be judged by twelve than carried by six.' I promised him I would, and I remembered that promise that day.

"I had the driver dead to rights. He was off balance, getting out of the car, and there was no way he could swing his gun to his left to get a shot at me if he'd tried.

"It's funny. I remember this part well. I was looking down the barrel of my pistol and at the far end, perfectly balanced on the yellow dot at the tip of my sights, I could see a big head with curly hair. I was so close there was no way to miss. I suppose I could have dropped my aim a few inches for his shoulder or leg and tried to take him alive, but instead I just pulled the trigger. Didn't even think about it.

"Then I got up and looked inside the car, still from the back corner. They teach you that at cop school. It's tougher for someone inside a car to shoot you if you're behind them since they can only turn their torsos, not their whole bodies, to get a bead on you. It's like shooting over your shoulder.

"So I looked inside the car and the third scumbag, the guy in the back who I'd seen move in the first place, is scrambling to get out of the passenger's side door. You know how hard it is to get out of the back of a hatchback under the best of circumstances. Well, the guy I'd shot before was hanging half in the car and was pretty much blocking the door. So that third guy was having trouble getting over the body and out of the car.

"I guess I could have winged him then, or jumped around the car and pepper sprayed him or got the drop on him or something. At least that's what they said afterwards. But my partner was dead or dying to my side, I'd just shot this jerk's two buddies and this guy had a nasty looking pistol in his hand. That one turned out to be a tech nine. These guys weren't kidding around.

"So instead of trying to take him alive, I popped him three times through the rear window. Center mass again, right in the back. He wasn't wearing any type of body armor, so that did the trick.

"He wasn't around to testify at the hearing, either, for whatever that was worth." Her smile was grim this time.

"The investigation took three months. Fred lasted through two of them, although he never opened his eyes or spoke again. Fred's wife visited him every day for the first month and a half. You'd never have had a clue that he knew she was there, though. He never responded at all. After seven weeks, she needed a break. I can't say I blame her. She was wearing herself down to nothing. A friend got her a good deal on a Caribbean cruise so she took off for a few days. Fred died while she was on an emergency flight back from St. Thomas. Somehow he knew she'd gone and he decided that it was time for him to go, too. In all honesty, it probably was time for him to go. The prognosis was completely hopeless. But his wife hasn't gone a day in her life since then without blaming herself for his death. I'd hate to see that happen to anyone else." She looked into the rearview mirror at Walt. "Harley told me about your daughter, Katie. I'm sorry."

Walt cleared the lump in his throat. "Thanks. I don't want to see that either."

"Anyway," Denise continued, "the Service didn't know what to do with me. The three guys in the car had just stolen it, which is why the plate ran clean. It was full of crack they were running down the coast. They were full of crack, too. It was pretty messy for everyone.

"A few people tried to make a racial thing out of it. They said I'd unnecessarily shot the three guys because they were white, but that argument didn't go far. All three of them had rap sheets as long as your arm and they had enough firepower in their car to send an armored division running for cover. Just owning a gun was illegal for these guys, given their criminal records. Plus, there was Fred.

"Eventually the paper pushers decided that they couldn't blame me for acting as I did. In fact, they commended me for my quick response to a dangerous situation and gave me a medal." Denise paused, dabbing at her eyes as if some dust was bothering her.

"By the end of the investigation, I was ready to explode. I kept reliving the incident every day as I told my story again and again. Now it's not too bad. It's almost a requiem for Fred, but back then it was driving me crazy. So I asked for a transfer, anywhere—Cape Cod National Sea Shore, the Statue of Liberty, I didn't care. The Service looked around to find a good fit and wound up sending me to Joshua Tree National Monument. That was right before it became a Park.

"I've been there now about four years. Believe it or not, I love it! I went back to school and got my Masters Degree in Wildlife Management. My specialty is bats." Without looking at him, she knew Harley had a look of disbelief on his face. Marine toxicologists didn't have to know much about desert ecosystems. She checked the rearview mirror again. Walt was looking through the binoculars, apparently uninterested in her bat story. "It turns out that the desert's full of bats. They love all the old gold and silver mines. They're about the only cool places the bats can roost in anymore now that the area's become so developed.

"Bat habitat, or the lack thereof, is actually a big problem in the desert," Denise continued, warming to her subject. "The bats provide a huge ecological benefit as far as pest control and filling a niche in the food chain is concerned. But the mines can be dangerous. People go exploring in them. The mines are all pretty old and every once in a while a shaft collapses and kills or hurts someone. Or maybe folks get stuck inside the mine. In some of the larger mines people have even gotten lost.

"So there's a big public safety and legal liability issue. No one wants to own the mine that crushes a group of high school kids. The easy way out is just to dynamite the entrance shut. Generally they blow 'em up during the day and trap all the bats inside. Boom, no more bat colony. Even if they blast at night the bats get screwed, especially in the summer, when they can't get back home. One hundred fourteen degrees will bake a bat stuck out in the rocks. It'll bake just about anything stuck outside. You too, if you were dumb enough, or unlucky enough, not to get indoors.

"So now I do a lot of bat related stuff for the park—protection plans, population surveys and so forth.

"I guess that's probably more than you really wanted to know about the 'ever after part,' Denise laughed shyly. "I guess I'm happy now, and I know the bats are better off. But sometimes I think about Fred or jerks like the ones we saw this morning or my buddy from Lake Meade and it doesn't seem quite as much like a fairy tale as it did when I was in Mississippi."

"That's quite a story, Denise," Harley said sincerely. "If nothing else, it sure explains the jack handle business." He looked back at Walt, "Say, I've got to go find a bush before we go much further. What about you?"

Walt picked up Harley's unspoken message. "You don't mind?" he asked Denise.

"Hell, no. If you've got to go, you've got to go. Lots of bushes to choose from around here, but watch out for the snakes and cacti."

"Oh joy," growled Harley as he squeezed out of the jeep, "just when I was starting to feel at home in this part of the country you've got to remind me of snakes and cacti."

Denise snickered to herself as the men walked to the edge of the clearing. Like they had something to complain about. At least men could pee standing up.

CHAPTER XXXIII

The spyglass jiggled in his hand and Branson shifted his position to steady it on the small pile of rocks he'd set up as a brace. At this distance, even minor trembling movements could really blur the glasses' exceptionally narrow field of view. Like everything else in life, optical gear came with tradeoffs. While Rodriquez' binoculars could stay clearly focused on the jeep as it moved up the ridge, they were too weak to decipher much more than the fact that it was a jeep with three people in it. Branson's spyglass, on the other hand, would give him a good look at everyone in the vehicle, as long as it, and his hands, stopped moving.

The jeep turned off at the top of the ridge and was lost behind a small clump of scrub brush in front of Branson. He swatted at an ant that had started crawling up his forearm and waited for the vehicle to reappear. When it hadn't become visible a few seconds later, he nudged Rodriquez again. "Hey, Manny."

"Yeah, boss?"

"That jeep?"

"Yeah?"

"I lost it at the top of the ridge. Scope it out with the binos for me, would you? I think it's parked where I can't see it, I'm not sure."

Manny peered through his binoculars, sweeping the opposite ridgetop and the vast empty spaces behind it. "It's not out there, boss. I think I see a piece of it sticking out from those bushes in front of us. When they move on, they'll come back into our view. Whoops, there they are now. Two figures, can't tell if they're men or woman, walking at the nine o'clock position on that bush." Like any good spotter, Rodriquez used the points on a clock face in reference to a known point to guide Branson to the figures in question.

"Okay, I got 'em. It's two men . . . Holy Shit!" Branson exclaimed. "It's Mitchell and Crawler." He shut up and peered through the spyglass. Jesus Christ, they're taking a leak. They're taking a goddamned leak!"

"Do you think you could tag them from here?" Rodriquez knew it was hopeless, but he asked anyway. Even the best sniper, with a .50 caliber weapon and a stable rest, would have found it a tough shot. With a simple 7.62 rifle, an automatic at that, and a folding bipod for a brace, getting close enough to the two men to scare them would be a minor miracle.

"No, not a chance." Branson put the spyglass down. "They're taking their time about it, though. It's clear that they don't know we're here."

"Then why'd they go up that trail instead of coming down the road?"

"I don't know. Maybe whoever's driving them," Branson made the assumption that his quarry were passengers in the jeep, "wanted to show them something. Maybe the driver doesn't like Kelso. I've got no clue. But if they knew we were here waiting for them, they wouldn't be standing out in the open over there, waving their dicks around like they don't have a care in the world."

"So what do we do now?" Part of Rodriquez was thrilled to have found their prey, but another part wondered at how they had escaped the trap yet again.

"We chase them." Branson tucked the spyglass into its case, grabbed his rifle in the crook of his arm and began to crawl back to the Ford Bronco they'd left parked out of sight in a steeply sided gully thirty yards away. When he reached the truck, Branson took the binoculars from Rodriquez and surveyed the spot where he'd last seen Mitchell and Crawler. A faint trail of dust led away from the hilltop, headed southwest towards Joshua Tree.

Branson opened the driver's door and pulled out a small guidebook to the high desert he and Rodriquez had bought at a camping supply shop in Flagstaff. The map hadn't been the only thing they'd picked up for this trip, either. The rented Bronco was loaded with a bewildering variety of bomb making materials they'd bought at a couple of hardware stores and supermarkets, along with a small collection of wipes, chemicals and powders would allow them to erase any traces of their presence. Like the good Boy Scout he'd once been, Branson believed in being prepared.

He opened the book to the section of the Kelso area and studied the enclosed map. "They're taking this route," he said to Manny, tracing some faint red lines on the map. "It'll take them out to 62 a bit further west than this road would, but, unless they cut through the Marine Corps base," the high desert basin was home to both Joshua Tree National Park and the sprawling Marine Corps Air Ground Combat Center, "they won't gain any ground on us. We'll take this road back to 62, then bang west and catch up to 'em before they get to 29 Palms." If the jeep made it to the small town of 29 Palms, adjacent to the Park, a surreptitious hit would become much harder, and the consequences of failure that much greater.

For the first time since leaving DC, Branson began to worry that he'd completely lost control over the situation. While the chase had spread across Oklahoma and Arizona and Nevada and the California desert, he had still felt he had a comfortable safety margin. If he didn't stop them in one place, he could always stop them someplace else. But now his back was up against the wall. The cat had used up another one of its lives and the closer Crawler and Mitchell, and whoever was driving them, got to civilization, the bleaker Branson's prospects were.

Could they stop his plan?

No, probably not. But they could force him underground forever once he'd carried out the operation.

Actually, there was no carrying out of the operation to be done. Like any good ambush, things were on autopilot now. No one could stop it.

Not even the man with the manicured hands and steepled fingers. Branson hadn't talked with him since the meeting at his home. His counterpart probably had no clue that things were unraveling so fast. He'd never really paid attention to the operational details. He'd provided the dates and places and times, it had been up to Branson to do the rest. Branson had said Crawler and Tillison would be dead, and there was no reason for the man to think anything other than that had happened.

Branson's hands drifted to his cell phone. Should he try to reach him now, let him know there was a potential problem? His lips turned up in a bitter snarl. No, he'd handle it himself. He was the man on the ground, not that two-bit bureaucratic tinhorn. If he screwed it up, ol' steeple fingers would find out soon enough.

With a screen of boulders and scrub brush between them and Denise, Walt and Harley finally had a chance to review their situation.

"Jesus, Walt, what do you know, we've befriended a Ranger."

"Yeah." Walt sat on a boulder and kicked at the sand by his feet. "Now what do we do with it."

"What do you mean?"

"Well, we can't just tell her to call the Secret Service and tell them to cancel tomorrow's event. Even if she believed us, which is a stretch, no one is going to believe her. We need a better plug than just a say-so on our part."

"Like what?"

"I don't know, Harley. I guess we need to learn more about what's going on tomorrow. If we see something obvious, we'll try to get her on board. At the least, we can ask her to take us to the place where they're having the ceremony. Knowing what we know, maybe we'll see something out of whack that'll give Park security enough reason to close things down. Hell, she owes us something, after all. Even if she doesn't believe us, she ought to listen to us."

"We can't afford to come off as too kooky, though," said Harley "or she'll toss us out on our ears. I suspect the desert's full of more crackpots than you could shake a stick at. If we haven't got her to let her defenses down at least a little bit before we dump our load on her, she'll thank us for saving her life and then drop us off on the side of the street."

"You're right, Harley. Why don't you do that?"

"Do what?"

"Get her defenses down. Ask her about tomorrow. Just talk to her like you've been doing. You can get her to trust us," Walt managed an exaggerated wink, "she likes you."

Harley smiled and turned back to the jeep. "I just about got my head knocked into next week because of her and I *did* lose my bike on her account. She damned well better like me."

"Everything come out okay?" Denise asked playfully as the two men approached the jeep. She still wasn't sure about her riders and the few minutes the men had been gone had made her worry even more. They could have been planning something truly awful on the other side of the line of boulders. Even though they had, no doubt, kept her from being raped, or worse, they might not be white knights. Harley's rally story seemed solid, and Walt played the part of a withdrawn, grieving parent well enough, but over the years she'd seen plenty of psychopaths who could get you to believe anything at the drop of a hat.

All the same, she wanted to believe them. Truth be told, she sort of liked Harley. A wild man, but a smart one. And, she'd noticed, a tender one at times, too. Once they got to Twenty-nine Palms, she'd let her guard down. In the interim, she'd taken the precaution of putting an empty magazine in her pistol and placing the mace she kept in her glove compartment in her left pocket. If they were who they said they were, they'd never catch on to her suspicions.

And, if not . . . She'd wargamed out the most likely scenario. Walt would probably grab the pistol from behind her seat and try to force her to stop the jeep. Harley, with his vast strength, might grab her right arm. However, without bullets, the gun would be useless and Harley could squeeze her arm as hard as he wanted but, as long as her left hand was free for two seconds, anyone who messed with her would get a blast of pepper spray that would turn him into a quivering mass of jelly for at least five minutes. She'd seen it happen to bigger men than Harley, and ones who were strung out on drugs as well. The Park Service didn't mess around when it came to giving its Rangers non-lethal weapons.

"Yeah, everything came out just ducky." Harley's cheerful voice boomed across the desert. "I think I can ride the rest of the way in comfort."

Harley and Walt climbed into the jeep and Denise started driving down the trail, trying to conceal the fact that her senses were on red alert.

"So tomorrow promises to be a busy day, huh?" Harley said conversationally.

"That's putting it mildly," Denise responded, trying to figure out if there were a hidden message in the question.

"With the Vice-President and everyone coming out tomorrow, how do you make sure they stay safe?"

"It's not something I've been working on. The Secret Service has been on site for a while, checking out the area, working with us on security. They're the ones who are responsible for the Vice-President's safety. They protect the other bigwigs like Flannigan, too, on an occasion like this."

"So how exactly are all these people going to be protected tomorrow? I mean, you seem pretty low key about it."

"Hell, I probably won't even get close to the them," Denise said with a shrug. Why would Harley care so much about this? "We're mostly doing crowd control. They're expecting something like ten thousand spectators. The valley's gonna be packed. The

Sierra Club, Friends of the Desert, Earthfirst! are all bussing people here from as far away as San Francisco and Seattle. And they're not the only ones who'll be here. The NRA's got busses, the All-Terrain Pleasure Riding Association's got busses. It's going to be a madhouse. I'll take you out there afterwards, if you want. You'll see how tight it is. It's crazy. With a crowd that size, if a disturbance spreads and people start trying to get out, folks will get trampled. And once that starts and other people hear the screaming, it would become a full fledged disaster. It'd be like those pictures of Chinese bomb shelters in World War II, where mountains of people were crushed trying to get away from the Japanese planes.

"Of course, if things start going south, the Secret Service will whisk the VIPs away so quickly you'll think they were Santa's elves. They'll have a couple of choppers overhead for surveillance, so if the road's blocked they'll just get folks out in the birds. They'll spy rig 'em out if the choppers can't land."

"Spy who them?" asked Walt from the back seat.

"Spy rig them. Hook them up to rope ladders hanging from the choppers and fly away. You look like a bird swinging in the air."

"How long's that take?"

"They'd be gone before you could say 'boo.' But I've never heard of that happening. It's just part of the contingency plan. Or, at least I think it is," Denise clarified herself. "Like I said, I'm only doing crowd control. Or, more accurately, helping with it. The real crowd control's going to be done by the Park Police units brought in from San Francisco and DC. They've got a lot more training and experience along those lines than us Rangers do. Other than crowd control, everything else is Secret Service, with a little help from UN security and some Marines from the Combat Center."

"If it's going to be so crazy, why are they doing it?" Harley asked the obvious question.

"Why do you think? Politics. California has fifty-four votes in the Electoral College. The environmentalists want those votes on their side so they can be out pushing eco-issues every chance they get. In reality, this biosphere designation won't do squat, but politically it could be a big boost for anyone looking for the environmental vote. Like the Vice-President. The more time he spends at events like this in California, the less trouble he'll have taking this state when he runs for President.

"You see, in California, a lot of people put themselves on the environmental advocate side of the fence.

"But here, in the desert, environmental stuff cuts both ways. That's why tomorrow's going to be so crazy. For some people, it's as simple as the New World Order thing, with the UN just looking for another place to land their black helicopters. But for an awful lot of people out here, people who came out here to get away from it all, adding more layers of regulation, no matter how meaningless, to a chunk of land this big is a major threat to what they believe in.

"It's a little subtle for you, I guess," Denise added after taking a look at Harley's blank face. "It boils down to this. There are two types of environmental issues. The 'L' issue, that's land. And the "P" issue, that's pollution. Back east, where people have owned the land for centuries, environmental stuff is a "P" issue. Folks are worried about pollution.

Walt, listening intently in the back, nodded in agreement, thinking of all the response operations he'd been on.

"But, out here, where the Feds own zillions of acres all over the place and rivers aren't catching on fire and so much of the local economy depends on land uses like ranching and logging, environmental stuff is an 'L' issue, a land matter. And anything that smacks of keeping locals from using whatever land they want, however they want, is sure to get a lot of people very upset.

"So tomorrow's going to be crowded and crazy and something of a powder keg, with all the different people there. If something goes wrong, it's going to go very, very wrong.

You don't know the half of it, thought Walt, not the half of it.

When they reached highway 62, Denise turned right and picked up speed as she headed towards Twenty-nine Palms. Walt held the binoculars tightly in his hands, using them to look all around them every minute or so. Other than a few birds far away, soaring in the thermals by the mountains, the entire desert seemed empty. Not even an oncoming car broke the almost hypnotic spell of the Jeep's tire's humming over the pavement. Branson was out there somewhere, Walt told himself, sweeping the surrounding terrain with the field glasses. The question was where. And doing what? Was he up ahead, waiting behind some big boulders to shoot them as they drove by? Was he near the Park headquarters, figuring they'd go there first? Did he have anyone else working for him besides Rodriquez? These were all answers Walt was afraid he wouldn't be able to answer until it was too late.

The sun was fairly high in the sky by now and Walt was able to look east without any trouble. The far away glitter of metal and glass told him that another vehicle had come out of the desert and turned onto the highway. He focused the binoculars on the vehicle and determined it was a big four wheel drive truck, like a Bronco or an Explorer. Even at this distance, he could tell the truck was moving fast and would catch up to them within a few minutes. As inconspicuously as he could, he caught Harley's eye and motioned behind him.

"How quickly will we be in town?" asked Harley.

"About ten minutes or so. Why?"

"Just curious. It still seems so empty out here." He turned his head as casually as possible and looked down the road behind the jeep. Even without binoculars, he could tell the truck was closing quickly.

Walt's body was slowly stiffening as he followed the truck with the glasses. The indefinite shapes in the cab slowly became more substantive and soon, although he still hadn't recognized the people behind him, Walt knew beyond a shadow of a doubt that Branson had found them again.

"He's found us," he said in a deadpan voice.

"Oh shit," said Harley.

"Who's found you?" asked Denise, wondering what they could be talking about. They were strangers in this area, how could anyone find them? She took her left hand off the wheel and let it drift down to her pocket.

"Denise, we don't have much time." Walt was leaning over the driver's seat, his mouth by Denise's ear. "We haven't been entirely honest with you so far, and you're going to have to trust us on this."

"On what?" Her hand entered her pocket.

"See that truck behind us, going like a bat out of hell?"

"Yes."

"Inside it are Adam Branson and Manny Rodriquez and maybe some other people." Walt was trying very hard to sound rational. If Denise didn't but his story the first time and do something, exactly what, Walt wasn't sure, Branson would have caught up with them. "You don't know them, and they don't know you, but if they catch us," he said as calmly as he could, "they will kill both Harley and me. They've killed a lot of people recently, so I doubt they'll hesitate before killing you, too."

"What the fuck are you talking about?" Denise used her best tough cop voice. If these two screwballs thought they could pull her chain that easily, they were in for a rude awakening.

"Denise," interjected Harley, "you know that explosion I told you about? The one that killed Walt's ex-wife and kids?"

"Yeah?"

"Branson was responsible for the explosion. He was also responsible for the Lovett Arsenal explosion and that explosion in the Sierra Nevadas. And he's got something planned for tomorrow's UN function. We're the only ones who can stop him. You can't let him catch us," Harley spoke rapidly, his face tense. "If he catches us, we're all dead."

"Come on guys, give me a break." Her hand was holding the pepper spray now. "I appreciate your saving my ass back there and all, but let's not take it too far, okay."

"Jesus Christ, Denise, he's catching us." Walt couldn't keep the panic out of his voice. If Denise didn't do something fast, Katie's last hope would be gone. He looked over the highway at the empty desert around them. Staying with the jeep was his only chance. If he jumped from the moving vehicle, assuming the fall didn't kill him, he'd be an easy target for the gunmen in the Bronco. His knee brushed the pistol hanging behind Denise's seat, and, in a fit of desperation, he pulled it out of the holster. He would have one final surprise for Branson, he thought, tucking the pistol into his lap and twisting his body sideways to allow for a more comfortable firing position when the time came.

Denise felt Walt fumble behind her seat and knew he'd removed the gun. Her hand lingered on the pepper spray, waiting for Walt to do something. As with the men who'd attacked her earlier, the cop in her needed the other side to make the first move. Macing someone who was holding an empty gun and hadn't yet threatened her would be tough to explain down the line. "Put the gun back, Walt," she ordered, trying to take charge of the situation.

"They'll kill us, Denise," Walt replied. "If you don't drive faster, we're as good as dead. The only thing I can do is shoot first."

"Not with that gun, you can't." Deep inside Denise, a small bubble of anxiety began to surface. Perhaps she shouldn't have unloaded her pistol. The truck behind them *was* driving awfully fast.

"Whadya mean?" Under his darkly tanned skin, Walt's face had gone pale.

"It's empty. I took the bullets out." The situation was beyond Denise's comprehension. Walt obviously intended her no harm, but he was willing to open fire on a random truck because he thought they were being chased by assassins. No one talked about shit like this at Ranger school.

"Oh fuck!" Walt turned his body forward again and looked at Harley, ignoring Denise. "He's going to have enough firepower in that truck to blow us to high heaven, Harley. You got any last minute ideas?"

"Just one." Moving with blinding speed, Harley slid off his seat and wrapped his left arm around Denise's shoulders, effectively pinioning her left arm to her side. With his right arm, he seized the wheel and turned it hard to the left, while at the same time knocking Denise's right foot off the gas and replacing it with his own.

The jeep's tires screeched over the blacktop as it turned, leaving thick black skid marks on the road, and Harley prayed they wouldn't flip. Either of the two pickup trucks they'd seen that morning, with their jacked up bodies and big tires, would have rolled like a ball, but Denise' jeep was made for this sort of treatment. It kept its grip on the road and, in the blink of an eye, had darted off into the desert alongside the road like a startled jackrabbit. There was one brief moment of hesitation, then Harley's big foot punched down on the gas and the jeep took off.

Next to Harley, Denise's heart leapt to her throat. They were nuts! She struggled to pull her left arm free so she could use the pepper spray. One blast in Harley's face and she'd be in control of the jeep again. She could bring it to a stop and then take care of Walt. With an unloaded pistol, she didn't think she'd need the mace for him.

Harley's grip shifted as he tugged on the wheel and Denise worked her arm free. Her hand streaked from her pocket and she shoved the mace canister into Harley's face. "Back off, Jack!" she snarled, giving him a blast of the spray.

Instantaneously, Denise was free. The shock of the spray had knocked Harley back in his seat, his hands clawing at his eyes and his mouth opening and shutting with howls of rage and pain.

Denise punched the clutch and hit the brakes simultaneously, trying to bring the jeep to as quick a stop as possible so she could deal with Walt.

Then she noticed the hole in the windshield.

As she stared, another hole appeared, and then the rearview mirror disintegrated. Next to her, Harley's body jerked and a shower of red sprayed the inside of the windshield.

With the instincts of a professional, Denise popped the clutch back out and put the jeep into gear. Almost immediately, the jeep was moving at twenty miles an hour over the boulder strewn ground. She swerved left and then right, knowing that the men behind her would have more trouble hitting her if she didn't drive straight, and then stole a look in the sideview mirror. The Bronco was bouncing across the desert after them, a big-looking man hanging out of the passenger's side window. Some pops sounded above the roar of the jeep's engine, but Denise wasn't concerned. With two moving vehicles and the rough terrain, it'd be dumb luck if the shots came anywhere close to the jeep. Now it was a race. The Bronco probably had more power, but she'd been driving in the desert for years and knew that few people could match her off-roading skill. If she could just stay in one piece long enough to reach the Park's boundaries, she'd take the Bronco on a ride they'd never forget.

A clear patch of desert opened up in front of her and Denise took the opportunity to look at Harley. He wasn't moving. What that meant, she wasn't sure. Sometimes people passed out after getting maced. Or the bullet may have knocked him unconscious. Or he might be dead. His body jerked with the movements of the jeep and she forced herself to concentrate on the driving. Harley was either dead or he wasn't. If she screwed up the chase, there wouldn't be an 'either' for any of them. They'd all be dead.

"Give me the bullets," Walt screamed into her ear. "At least we can shoot back."

Denise dug a loaded magazine out of the same pocket where she'd stuck the mace and passed it back to Walt. "If we can stay ahead of them for another mile or so, we'll be okay," she yelled, hearing a few more pops from the Bronco. "Don't bother shooting unless they're a lot closer. You'll just waste the bullets."

Walt switched magazines and tucked the loaded pistol into his waistband. Then, trying not to get jarred clear of the bouncing jeep, he leaned forward and checked Harley's pulse. "He's alive," he hollered, checking the wound. "The bullet went all the way through, but the bleeding's not too bad." He pulled out Denise's first aid kit and, bracing himself against the jeep's rollbar, began to patch the wound. "What'd you hit him with?" he shouted. Harley's eyes were a red, teary mess, but there was no use in blaming Denise for thinking Harley was attacking her. They should have been upfront with her at the start. At least his friend was breathing. That was the important part.

"Park Service issue mace," Denise shouted back. "It's just about the strongest stuff on the market. It shouldn't have knocked him out though. The shot to his arm probably did it. Shock. If he's got a pulse and you've stopped the bleeding, then he'll be okay. It's a through and through wound to his arm, the slug didn't bounce around his chest cavity or anything so there should be no internal bleeding. Give me a few minutes and we'll loose these creeps." Denise was driving as if it were second nature to her, looking over at Harley and back at Walt periodically as she dodged rocks and shrubs.

Branson had fallen further behind as the jeep bounded towards the distant mountains marking the edge of the park. Occasionally, Denise could see a flash of metal as the Bronco topped a gully or turned a corner, but the distance between the two vehicles had grown to the point where even luck wouldn't be enough to allow a hit. At least here. When she hit the base of the mountains, she'd have almost two miles on an improved gravel road. The danger would increase, there. Before she had an opportunity to turn off into the maze of mining trails leading into the mountains,

Branson would have at least a few straight shots. If all he had were pistols, they were in the clear.

If he had a long rifle, however, all bets were off. Both vehicles were moving and the road was still going to be quite bumpy, but if he could get enough rounds off in the general direction, one or two were bound to hit something. Or someone, she added, looking at the sheen of Harley's blood that covered the windshield.

They reached the road and Denise downshifted to third gear. Initially gentle, the road got steeper just ahead, but with enough momentum she could keep the jeep moving in third through the steeper spots and wouldn't loose speed to further downshifting. It would only save them a few seconds, but this was a race where seconds counted for as much as they ever had in her life.

The Bronco crested the road's shoulder and Denise saw the big passenger drop back into the vehicle's cab. A moment later he reappeared with something long in his arms.

He had a rifle.

Before her pursuers had a chance to shoot, Denise swung a corner and the truck vanished, but only for a moment. The road was a relatively easy drive, and Denise's superior skill in off-roading would no longer make a difference. In fact, the Bronco, with what was probably a more powerful engine, might very well close some ground. They wouldn't catch up, she knew, but they'd get a few shots with the rifle.

And a few were all it might take.

"He's got a rifle, Walt," she screamed over the whine of the jeep's engine. "We'll probably take some lead in a minute, there's a straight stretch coming up and he'll have a decent shot. If we can hold out for another two or three minutes, we're safe. If not . . ."

Before Denise could finish her sentence, the Bronco sprang into view and, almost immediately, another hole appeared in the windshield. Then another and then the truck lurched like a drunk stepping into a curb.

"Shit!" she swore violently, fighting to keep control of the jeep, "we've lost a tire." She turned another corner and the shooting stopped. The jeep's speed was decreasing significantly as the now flat tire flopped against the ground. Denise did some quick math. "Walt," she yelled, unsuccessfully fighting to keep the panic from her voice, "we're losing speed. They'll catch us in a minute or so. We've got to get out of the jeep. Can you carry Harley?"

Walt looked at the motionless hulk of his friend. "How far?"

"There's a turnout for a mine just up ahead. I'm going to pull up in front of it. You haul Harley into the mine. Give me the pistol and I'll try to hold these guys off." She stuck her hand back and Walt passed her the pistol. "You'll only have about ten seconds to get Harley from the jeep and into the mine. Once we're in, we should be able to hold them off for awhile."

The road opened up and Denise swung to the left, braking the jeep sharply. "Go!" she screamed, dropping out of the jeep herself and taking cover behind the front bumper. The engine threw off an immense amount of heat and Denise winced as she braced herself against the jeep and steadied her hands to shoot. She might squeeze off a couple of shots, but she was sure that Branson would be ready to respond in kind. If she wasn't in the mine herself within seconds, or if the men chasing her weren't incapacitated, she'd be as good as dead stuck out by the jeep.

The jeep rocked as Walt pulled Harley from the cab. The big biker was a heavy load, Denise knew, wondering how long would it take the smaller, though muscular, Walt to carry him into the mine. If he wasn't fast enough, he would be dead. It was that simple.

Moving at a rate of speed far greater than she'd anticipated, the Bronco swung the corner and came into the clearing. Denise had decided to try for the driver, figuring that if she could send the vehicle out of control, the passenger would be unable to shoot.

She lined up her sights, her heart racing in her chest, and pulled the trigger, the bang of her pistol beating at her eardrums.

The jeep shuddered violently again and again and Denise knew that the passenger had focused his rifle on her. Judging from the shakes of the vehicle, it was an absolute cannon. Or maybe he was using special ammunition. In either case, it was bad news. Out of the corner of her eye she saw Walt hauling Harley over the rubble strewn about the front of the mine. She needed to hold out for another few seconds. If she broke and ran now, Branson would concentrate on Walt and Harley, and they had no cover. She had to stay put a bit longer. She snapped the trigger again and again, trying to force the driver to react. If she got lucky, she'd hit him. No matter how much he crouched down behind the wheel, enough of him would stick out over the hood to make something of a target. Stranger things had happened.

She'd lost count of her bullets, something a cop should never do, but she kept squeezing. When she had no shots left, then she'd run.

The Bronco seemed to jump suddenly and Denise knew she'd scored a hit. The big man hanging from the window lost his balance as the truck swerved and his rifle swung to the side, pointing harmlessly into the air for a brief second.

A brief second was all Denise needed and she rose to her feet and dashed for the mine. Time froze as she sprinted across the open ground to the dark, gaping hole, and the three count seemed to drag forever. Three was the magic number when moving under fire. A typical marksman needed enough time to line up the target, one, steady his breathing, two and squeeze the trigger, three. But Denise was certain the man with the rifle was no typical marksman. She could only hope that the Bronco's sudden movement would slow him down.

Denise dove into the mineshaft just as the first shot rang out, the bullet ricocheting harmlessly into the shaft's murky interior. Landing on her side, she rolled to the right and came up behind a small mound of rocks inside the mine, pistol at the ready, involuntarily ducking as three more shots rang out. She could hear Walt breathing to her left. "You okay?" she asked, her breath only slightly winded by the short sprint.

"Yeah. What about you?"

"I'm fine. How's Harley?" Her voice took on a softer tone of concern.

"I bumped him up pretty good getting him in here, but he's still breathing. When my eyes get used to the light, I'll redo the bandage. His arm's started to bleed again. How long do you think he'll be unconscious?"

"I don't know. Like I said, the mace alone shouldn't have done that. It was either the shock of the bullet or the combination of the bullet and the mace. Shock can knock folks unconscious for a long time." It could also kill them, Denise knew, but there was no point in discussing that. She stuck her head cautiously over the rocks. The Bronco was parked nose first in a small ravine on the far side of the clearing. "It looks like they're stalled out over there." She looked closer. "I can still see the driver. He's not moving, but I've got no idea where that big guy is."

"His name's Branson. The driver was Manny Rodriquez," Walt said. "They're rogue government agents who are out to kill environmentalists."

"Come again?" At this point, Walt's simple explanation seemed anti-climatic.

Walt began to work on Harley's bandage, his fingers becoming slippery with Harley's blood. "It's a long story, Denise," he said, thinking back to the bicycle race at Cockaponsett State Forest and the response action on Nantucket.

"Well, it looks like we're stuck here for a while. Why don't you tell it to me."

CHAPTER XXXIV

Brian Flannigan eased into the rear of the waiting limousine, noting with disdain the lengthy line of waiting luxury vehicles at the Palm Springs airport. An oasis in the desert, the brochures all said. From the air, that statement seemed true enough. Miles and miles of brown parched earth ended at the foot of San Jacinto Mountain, where green golf courses sprouted like huge algae blooms from the barren desert landscape. It was truly amazing, Flannigan reflected, what one could do with enough water.

And all of it was unsustainable. The showers, restaurants, pools, golf courses and God only knew what else in Palm Springs and the surrounding towns were draining the aquifer like a huge sponge getting squeezed by a giant. Like all of the great cities of the west-Las Vegas, Phoenix, Santa Fe-Palm Springs was built on the borrowed time of not enough water. When the water ran out, as it surely would, these cities would dry up and blow away with the tumbleweeds that bounced along the dry desert floor.

How quickly would the water run out? No one was sure. Flannigan knew that the Colorado River rarely reached the Gulf of California anymore, its waters diverted throughout the arid southwest via aqueducts such as the nearby All-American Canal. Development was booming and there seemed to be no end to the region's population growth. Environmentally, it was an ongoing, and ever increasing, problem.

And water wasn't the only problem. He looked up at the bulk of San Gorgonio, its towering peak lost in the smog. Even the air was changing for the worse out here. The air that had once been a tonic for people suffering from respiratory ailments was now choked with the emissions of tens of thousands of vehicles and planes. Day after day, these pollutants-ground level ozone, PAHs, TPHs and a host of acronyms he didn't even know-banked up against Gorgonio's foothills and turned the Palms Springs air into a toxic, hazy stew.

But he was going to fix all that, Flannigan thought as he watched the oasis of Palm Springs roll by the limo's tinted windows and turn, like the flick of a page, into barren desert. It would all be different very soon.

CHAPTER XXXV

Walt finished his story and risked a peek out the mine's entrance. Other than the Bronco with its still motionless driver, there was nothing to be seen. Periodically, Branson fired a few shots into the mine. He wasn't really hoping to hurt anyone, Denise had explained, he was just messing with their minds. From Walt's perspective, Branson's plan was certainly working.

"That's a hell of a story, Walt," said Denise, "I'm sorry for not believing you when you first told me about Branson." She reached over and gently stroked Harley's head, the stubble of his hair rough against her fingers. "If I'd listened, maybe Harley'd be okay."

"Don't kick yourself too hard, Denise," Walt reassured her, "we put you in an awkward position. We're just lucky you caught on as quickly as you did."

"Not lucky enough," Denise muttered half to herself, still stroking the biker's head.

They sat quietly, the silence of the desert outside magnified by the mine's own noiseless void. Other than their own breathing, silence reigned supreme.

"What do we do now?" Walt finally asked. They were still alive, but Harley was hurt and Branson was outside the mine with a rifle. From his perspective things didn't look much less hopeless than they had before. "We can't go forward until nightfall. And even then, Branson's probably got some fancy night scope that'll let him pick us off like sitting ducks. Is there anyway we can call for help?"

"No, we can't call anyone. Even if I could get to the jeep, my radio's just as broken now as it was earlier this morning. Our best hope is to wait here until someone comes up the road. Hopefully that'll create enough of a diversion that we'll be able to sneak out." Although she suggested it, Denise knew it was a shallow hope. If someone did, in fact, come by, Branson would most likely kill them, too, without letting his attention be distracted for more than a few seconds. And a few seconds was hardly enough time for three people, one of whom was unconscious, to sneak off into the desert.

"Do you really think that'll work?"

"Honestly? No, not a chance. But what else can we do? I've done some bat tracking through this mine as part of our resource counts, and I know there's a second entrance someplace, but I've got no idea where it is or if it's even big enough for humans. Plus, as soon as we back away from the mine's entrance, Branson's going to come in here. Like you said, he's probably got night vision goggles, as well as anything else you can think of, in that truck. If we don't stop him at the entrance, where he'd be highlighted against the outside daylight and we're behind cover, we're history. I got lucky plugging Rodriquez, I wouldn't count on getting lucky again. Not against a guy with night vision goggles and an automatic rifle.

"And don't forget, we'd have to move Harley, too. Carrying someone that heavy in one of these shafts would slow us down a lot. Branson would have plenty of time to catch us. I don't see any option but to stay here."

"We can't stay here," Walt said. Denise's comment about the Bronco's being loaded with equipment had fired something in his mind.

"Why not? I'm telling you, we're dead if we move more than ten feet back."

"We're dead if we stay here."

"What do you mean?" Denise sounded agitated.

"You said it yourself. Branson's going to have all sorts of stuff in that Bronco. I spent three months with him and the rest of the team. That man knows explosives. Whatever he's got in his truck, I can guarantee you that he can mix something together that'll blow this mine sky high. He's hoping we'll stay by the entrance, just like you said, and then he'll be able to throw a bomb right on top of us. Once he's done that, he hops in the Bronco and he's hundreds of miles away by tomorrow morning. Even if someone does drive by after he's blown the mine, they'll have no clue about what Branson's planning."

Walt rose into a partial crouch. "We've got to move as far back as we can immediately." The tone of his voice allowed for no discussion. "Grab Harley's left arm and we'll hoist him up. Then we start heading back. Okay?"

Denise was uncomfortable with the idea of giving up their defensive positions at the front of the mine, but what Walt had said made sense. Besides, Branson had been quiet for a while, as if he were mixing some explosives and getting ready to throw them in the mine. "Okay. But take short little shuffle steps. These old mines are loaded with craters and debris that can twist a knee or an ankle before you know it. Especially if you're carrying someone like Harley."

They pulled Harley to his feet and, his huge arms draped over their necks, Walt and Denise began to half carry, half drag him further into the mine shaft. After thirty seconds, Denise looked back at the receding pool of light at the front of the mine, fearing that she'd see Branson's hulking shape looming against the far away sky. But there was nothing. She couldn't decide if that made her feel safer or not.

On the steep slope overlooking the mine shaft, Adam Branson tightened the caps on a pair of gallon water jugs. The jugs, opaque plastic ones with blue, screw-on tops, were each attached to the same piece of rope and neither contained water. He checked his watch. In exactly three minutes the chemicals he had mixed inside the jugs would start to react very violently with each other.

The resulting explosion, called an extreme exothermic reaction by high school chemistry teachers, should be strong enough to collapse the beams inside the mine and the stones in and around its entrance.

Everyone not immediately crushed to death, and that should be anyone in the first fifty feet or so of the shaft if the mine was constructed like most of the gold holes in the High Desert, would have their lungs seared by the chlorine gas that would float down the pit. Not a pleasant way to die, but Branson knew he didn't have many options. Even if he sprayed the mine with bullets, he'd be a dead man as soon as he entered the mine, silhouetted against the opening as he went in. Whoever managed to shoot Rodriquez knew how to handle a gun far too well to tempt fate like that.

But they hadn't gotten away scot-free, either. Crawler had been carrying Mitchell into the mine, so at least one of Branson's shots had hit flesh. What was even better was that, as long as they had to worry about Mitchell, Crawler and his new companion would have to stay by the mine's entrance. They'd be crazy to move back away from the entrance, slowed by Mitchell's body while also losing the ability to stop an assault with ease. They'd stay up front, behind those piles of rocks, until Branson dropped his jugs on them. And then it wouldn't matter how far or fast they ran, it would be too late.

In the passenger's seat of the Bronco, Branson could see the crumpled figure of Manny Rodriquez. He was sorry about losing the Texan but, more importantly, it posed strategic and logistical difficulties. Without Rodriquez to keep Crawler and his friends pinned down, Branson was taking a risk working with the jugs. Either Crawler or the woman, at least he thought it was a woman based on the hair, could choose just the wrong moment to rush out of the mine. With only the jugs in his hands, Branson would be defenseless up on the hillside. But he doubted that would happen and he didn't have time for subtleties. Even in the dead of summer, this was probably a fairly popular road and he couldn't let anyone else stumble onto this fiasco. Time was of the essence. In ten minutes he'd be driving away, leaving behind a crumbled hole in the ground. In thirty minutes, once the dust had settled, no one driving by would be any the wiser about the day's events.

Of course he still had to dispose of Rodriquez' body and clean some of the gore from the Bronco's interior. He didn't need some truck driver noticing the bloody dashboard and calling the police. Those were relatively minor details, however. What to do with the jeep would be his main concern, but he'd worry about that once the mine was blown.

Bowed under his share of Harley's weight, Walt hurried through the inky black well of the mine, trying to imagine just how it was set up. He'd never been in a mine, but Denise's warnings about fallen timbers, cave-ins or open pits seemed appropriate from what he had seen. It would only take one unseen timber to twist a knee, an incapacitating injury this deep inside the bowels of the earth. If that happened to him, Walt knew he'd wish the explosion he was expecting had killed him directly. The gas created by whatever explosive device Branson was likely to put together would almost certainly contain large amounts of chlorine as a byproduct of the chemical reaction. A knee injury at this point would leave him, and the still-unconscious Harley, helpless to escape the poisonous gas that would fry his lungs with every breath he took.

At least Harley wouldn't feel anything.

Overhead he heard a rustling and creaking sound. Then something brushed by his face. Bats. Denise's bats. The place was full of them.

"Denise?" Walt's voice, livingroom calm, was like a physical presence in the dark, silent mine.

"Yeah?"

"You got a flashlight?" He should have asked before, but he hadn't really been thinking of how dark it would get further in. Plus, of course, they wouldn't have wanted to shine a light too near the entrance for fear of letting Branson figure out what they were doing.

"Yeah. I've got a mini-mag in my pocket." Good thing, too, thought Denise. Like Walt, she, too, hadn't thought about how they would travel through the mine's blackness.

"Turn it on, would you?"

Denise fumbled momentarily in the dark, then a beam of light pierced the gloom.

"Holy Christ!" murmured Walt, temporarily forgetting where he was, "this place is crawling with bats."

"Something like two million of them," responded Denise.

"It's something else," said Walt, before focusing on the immediate situation again, "now let's get moving or we'll be toast."

The two moved as quickly as they could through the shaft, trying not to handle the increasingly heavy Harley too roughly. Fifty yards into the tunnel they came to a V in the tunnel, where the real work had started a century earlier. The desert's pioneers would tunnel into the hills, shoring up their caves with timbers hauled by mule train from the surrounding mountains, until they either found a likely looking vein or gave up and dug a new pit someplace else. If the vein was good enough, they'd follow it until it played out, running the extracted rock out on handcart trains that sometimes ran for miles under the surface.

Walt stopped for a second. "Which way?" he asked.

"I'm not sure. Things aren't simple in these big pits. I know one of these shafts runs outside eventually. Like I said, we've tracked bats through it using small radio transmitters strapped to their legs. But I don't know which one." She stopped speaking and her voice died immediately, the air hanging over their shoulders like a dark, oppressive beast.

"Okay, we'll take this one," Walt said with finality, taking the branch that led upwards, to the right. Any gas Branson's explosion produced would probably be heavier than air and, if it made it this far, would flow on down the lower shaft. They had just begun to shuffle up the tunnel when a brilliant flash of light briefly illuminated the tunnel's interior. Something hit Walt in the side of his head, and he stumbled, falling to his knees as the force of the explosion filled the air with tumbling bats and bouncing rocks. Denise's light disappeared and his ears roared in pain. Oh God, he thought, we're going to die. The cave's collapsing and we're going to get buried!

The noise subsided and Walt reached out across Harley's now prostrate body for some sign of Denise. His hands touched something soft. Cloth. He followed the cloth upward. It was Denise's shirt, but she wasn't responding to his touch.

"Denise?" He felt for her head and recoiled as his fingers came across something slippery and wet. Oh Christ, she was bleeding!

"Denise?" he asked again, rocking her softly, fighting down the panic that had begun to grip him. He was sealed off inside an old mine deep in the desert wilderness and, even worse, his two companions were injured. He was now all by himself. If he did manage to find his way out, which he had no idea how to do in the mine's dark interior, he'd still have to make his way to the Park Headquarters and get someone to believe his assassination story.

On top of that, he'd first brought Harley and then Denise into this mess. It was all his fault. If he had tried to do it alone, Harley would be scooting somewhere on his bike and Denise would be getting ready to do crowd control, but instead they were both lying motionless and bleeding in a hellish cave.

Walt shook her again, less gently this time. "Denise?" No response. He was alone in the dark. He felt completely helpless. He had failed. He had let Katie down.

"Uugh."

The noise, low and throaty, made Walt's heart leap to his throat.

"Denise?" She was alive! There was hope! "Are you okay?"

"I think I'm okay, but Christ, my head hurts." Her voice sounded dull and listless in the oppressive interior of the mine. "And my left leg's pretty banged up." Denise shifted her weight as she inventoried the rest of her body. "I'm cut in a couple of places, too. Nothing major, though." Her voice was sounding stronger with each syllable. "Are you okay?"

"Scared shitless, and a rock must have hit me in the head, but otherwise I'm all right." He probed at Harley. "Harley's seems okay, too. Where's the flashlight?"

"I don't know. I must have dropped it."

"Damn! We've got to find it and get out of here. We don't have long before this air here is going to be nothing but poisonous gas."

Walt patted the ground around him. The darkness was complete, almost palpable. Without a light, they'd get nowhere.

His fingers brushed against something hard and cold. He patted again and his hand struck the flashlight. "I've got it." He tapped Denise with the light.

Grasping the light, Denise rose gingerly to her feet. Her left leg hurt like hell but it didn't seem to be broken. A rock must have dropped on it. She turned the light on and breathed a sigh of relief as the beam sprang out from the tube.

She pointed the light up the tunnel. "Let's go." She helped Walt heave Harley to his feet, took his arm around her neck and then, dragging her left leg behind her, she began to trudge up the shaft as quickly as her injured leg would let her. She hoped it was just her imagination finding a new acidic taste in the air.

Branson stood up from behind a medium-sized boulder, his rifle crooked casually under his armpit. He took a moment to admire his handiwork. A large section of the hillside had caved in, leaving a cloud of dust that was already beginning to drift down towards the desert basin. He'd done a good job mixing his ingredients, but the mine must have been ready to go on its own. Over the years, desert rats had probably scooped out most of its wooden support beams to build their campfires. He looked once more at the crater stretching back into the hill. The tunnel collapse probably went much further back into the mine. If Crawler and his friends weren't dead now, which was doubtful, the chlorine gas would get them soon enough. Branson wished he could see Crawler's body, though. The biologist had proven too tenacious in the past to feel comfortable without seeing his corpse. Unfortunately, that simply hadn't been an option.

He slung the rifle over his shoulder and walked over to the Bronco. Rodriquez' body, missing much of the right part of its head, was slumped in its seat. It really was too bad about Manny, Branson reflected. They'd been together a long time. But war came with costs, and Manny had just paid the ultimate price. Now it was Branson's problem to do something with the body. The best thing to do, he finally decided, was just to make it disappear. It would be gory work, but with some acid to remove the fingertips and a hammer and chisel to ruin the dental plates, it would become virtually impossible for anyone to identify the Texan's body. If anyone ever found it.

The jeep was another issue. He turned on the laptop computer and within moments had run a check on the vehicle's tags. Denise Wallace of Twenty-nine Palms, California. He'd been right about the driver being a woman. Next, Branson tried to locate information on Wallace through a variety of databases to which he had secure access. The search results told him she worked for the National Park Service at Joshua Tree, but not much else. A Ranger? An interpreter? A land surveyor? He couldn't tell. Regardless, she was dead. Had she called for help before she died? He saw the radio in the back of the jeep and picked it up. On a whim he tried to turn it on. When nothing happened, he decided that there had probably not been any last ditch message to headquarters. If there had been, perhaps via Crawler's cell phone, there was nothing Branson could do about it now. He'd just have to take whatever lumps came his way.

The jeep itself had obviously been in a gunfight. The left rear tire was flat, there were numerous holes all over it and Harley's blood was splattered across the windshield. Would he be better off stripping the plates and the vehicle identification tag from the door and leaving it where it was, or towing it to some remote part of the desert where it could stay unnoticed for weeks? Either course of action had its pros and cons and eventually Branson decided to leave it where it was. Even if someone noticed it, which was fairly likely, and the police came, and they figured out who the owner was via the number stamped on the engine, and all that happened in twenty-hours, so what? There was no connection between the jeep and the biosphere ceremony. A Park Service employee's vehicle had been found shot up. When they dug the bodies out of the mine, there would be more questions, but, unless Crawler or Mitchell had some incriminating documents in their pockets, there'd be no answers.

Branson removed the registration from the glove compartment and decided he could leave the rest of the jeep's contents alone. Some nondescript camping gear and a broken jack handle wouldn't tell anyone anything. Using a box of towels he had in the Bronco, he then wiped the windshield, dashboard and cab clean of any obvious traces of blood. Next he folded the windshield down on top of the hood and pulled the Jeep's spare from the back seat. It was flat, too, he noticed, putting some of the pieces together. This woman had had a flat, her radio was broken, her jack was broken. Perhaps Crawler and Mitchell had helped her out and she had rewarded them with a ride. Not that it mattered anymore.

The Jeep relatively sanitized, Branson stepped back to survey the scene. With the windshield down, the blood cleaned up and the extra tire by the rear bumper, it looked like a typical desert breakdown. The bullet holes now were only apparent upon closer examination. There were lots of reasons a broken down vehicle might be shot up out here in the backcountry. The desert was full of them. The scene wasn't entirely clean, Branson knew, but it ought to duck close scrutiny for a little while, at least. And that was all he needed.

He went back to the Bronco and pushed Rodriquez' body aside. It was time to get on the road. It would be a long drive to Flagstaff.

CHAPTER XXXVI

Deep within the bowels of the earth, Walt leaned against a rough-hewn wall. "How much further do you think we have to go?" he asked. Used to the wide open spaces of the ocean, the oppressive darkness of the mine was making him feel claustrophobic.

"I've got no clue, Walt," Denise replied, struggling under Harley's weight. "I've never been through this mine, although some of my friends have poked around it a bit. As desert mines go, this is one of the bigger ones, with spurs and side shafts all over the place. In theory we could wander around for days until we find a way out. I wasn't kidding when I told you about people getting lost in these things. I know there's a second exit to this mine, or maybe even more than one, but I have no idea where. Unless we feel a draft of outside air, we'll have to try each spur shaft until we find a way out."

"Dragging Harley down every shaft is going to kill us. And maybe him, too." Walt had never felt so tired in his life.

"What are you suggesting? That we leave him here?" Denise's voice was sharp. They'd brought him this far, they couldn't crap out on him now.

"No. We're not leaving him anywhere. But it's probably a good idea for one of us to go ahead and find the way out, and the other will stay with Harley. We'll find the exit quicker, it won't wear us down as much and Harley won't get bumped as badly." Although Walt knew this was the best plan, he was partially hoping Denise would disagree. The thought of being alone in this foreign world was terrifying.

"You're right, Walt. This place must have a million dead ends and we'd kill ourselves dragging Harley down each of them. You stay here, I'll scout up ahead."

Walt steeled himself. "No, Denise. That doesn't work. Your leg hurts too much for you to bang it up any more than you have to. You stay here with Harley, I'll go look for a way out."

Denise thought for a minute, the throbbing in her leg reminding her that Walt was right.

When they'd found the way out, she was going to need every bit of resilience she had to shoulder her half of Harley. "Okay. I'll stay. Just make sure you leave a trail behind you at every turn showing you the way back here. Remember, this is a big mine, you could probably get lost forever in here." She handed the flashlight over to Walt. "We don't have any more batteries for this," she said, "so you might want to move around in the dark as much as possible."

"Oh great," Walt sounded as exasperated as he did scared. Dead batteries. They were still alive, but he seemed to have done nothing but go from a bad situation to a worse one for the past week.

"I've done some blind work in mines, before, Walt," Denise encouraged him. "It was part of a rescue training drill. Take shuffle steps and run your hand along the sides of the tunnel. If you can't touch both sides at once, use sticks to extend your reach. When you come to a side passage, shine the light up it. If it looks promising, check it out. Make sure to mark where you've been and where you came from. You can shine the light every once in a while just to orient yourself, but we really want to save the batteries for when we're carrying Harley."

"All right, I'll do what you suggest." Walt picked up two long pieces of wood, then turned the light off. "Take good care of Harley, okay."

"I'll try. See you soon."

"I hope so," Walt said, his voice dying quickly in the dark mine. Then, his sticks making a grating noise as they slid over the tunnel walls, he started shuffling slowly down the shaft.

From the start, progress was painfully slow. Before moving forward, he had to tap gently with his front foot. The air around him was insufferably stuffy and, other than his labored breathing, the light tapping of his feet and the occasional rustle of a bat flying over head, the silence was absolute. Every two or three steps, he'd stop and wave a stick in front of his face to make sure he wouldn't walk into a low hanging rock or support timber. Coming from a completely different world, it was nothing short of a descent into hell.

Time stood still. Again and again he followed spurs off to one side or the other, only to find, after what always seemed like an eternity, that his hopes were dashed by a jumble of rocks blocking the way. Walt's shirt was soaked with sweat and he could feel the dust caking up on his eyebrows and on his forearms. Grit stung at his eyes and he wondered why he bothered leaving them open, but when he tried closing them he lost his sense of balance. He couldn't feel himself sweating anymore and he was afraid dehydration was not far off. His blood would thicken until his heart couldn't pump it anymore and broke down trying.

Finally, after what seemed like a lifetime, Walt could take it no more. The absolute silence, the overwhelming sense of being alone, the frustrating number of dead ends. He needed to talk to someone. Turning around, using the flashlight sparingly to help guide his way, he headed back towards Denise and Harley.

His shuffling feet sounded like thunder in the tomblike interior of the mine and Denise heard him long before he reached her. "Walt," she called anxiously, is that you?" It couldn't be anyone else, but she asked the question all the same.

"Yeah, it's me."

"Did you find a way out?" Hope flooded Denise's voice.

"No, but I found a lot of dead ends. We can carry Harley down a bit, to the point where I stopped. That'll shorten the trip when we do find an exit." That was the logical explanation for his return. Walt couldn't bring himself to tell her that he'd really come back because he felt scared and lonely.

"Are you okay?" She could hear the tension in his voice.

"As okay as could be expected, I suppose," he said, sitting down next to her and Harley and gaining strength by the physical contact. "Give me a minute and we'll take off. It gets bumpy in places, though, and we'll have to get Harley around some pretty rough stuff." Fallen timbers and boulders had turned parts of the shaft into an obstacle course. "It's going to take us a long time just to get to where I stopped."

"Whenever you're ready, just tell me."

Walt sat for a while, knowing that his strength wouldn't return completely until he had something to drink and they were breathing fresh air. "Now's as good a time as any," he said in a flat voice. "Let's go."

They pulled Harley to his feet again and, bent almost double under the heavy load, moved down the tunnel, following the frail beam of illumination thrown out by Denise' light.

They had just reached the point at which Walt had turned around when Denise bumped her left leg against a timber fragment imbedded in the wall. Pain shot through her body and she fell to the ground, cursing as Harley and Walt tumbled on top of her.

"Are you all right? What happened?" Walt's voice was laced with panic. He couldn't move Harley if Denise couldn't help.

"Damn, that hurt." Denise understated the obvious. "I smashed my leg on something. It kills."

"Can you get up?" The thought of staying in one spot in the dark pit suddenly terrified Walt. They had to keep moving. If they stopped, Branson won.

"Yeah, I think so." Denise heaved herself to her feet, only to collapse again, cursing another blue streak.

"Jesus, that hurt. Let's rest here for a minute. When the pain dies down, I'll try again." She turned the light off.

Walt reached towards her voice, waving his hands back and forth to find her. He touched her shoulder and, still feeling his way with his hands, he maneuvered himself around to her side.

He could feel her muscular shoulder pressing against his and he found comfort in the touch.

"We're in trouble, aren't we?" The panic was gone from his voice. It was as if he was discussing a canceled fishing trip.

"I've got to admit I've been in better situations." Walt could hear the smile in her voice. "This doesn't look good."

Walt leaned against her shoulder with more pressure. She pressed back and they settled into a comfortable mutual slump, each supported by the other. Next to them, Harley's breathing was turning into something more like a snore.

"How long do you think we've been down here?" Walt hadn't said anything, but his watch must have been broken by Branson's explosion. For some reason, the inability to keep time was beginning to torment his mind.

"I don't know. I don't wear a watch. What's yours say?"

"It's broken."

"What about Harley's."

"He doesn't wear one either." That neither Harley nor Denise wore a watch pleased Walt. Somehow, he thought, they seemed made for each other, for whatever that was worth in the black hole in which they found themselves. Blacker even, he realized, than the world of his daughter, whose eyes could still, he hoped, register light and dark. Walt pulled the spoon from his pocket and began rubbing it between his thumb and forefinger. Time was so short for Katie, he was failing her.

"Well," Denise's voice brought Walt's thoughts back to earth. "We got in my jeep around seven. It probably took us another three hours or so to get here, so figure it was a little after ten when we got chased inside the mine. Branson blew the entrance about forty-five minutes later, I'm guessing, so it was probably eleven when we really started moving through the mine. It's a different world down here, though. Without any light or outside stimulus, time seems to stand still. You just can't judge it accurately without a watch. We learned that during our rescue exercises, too. We'd enter a mine at dawn, spend what we thought was an hour or two underground and the next thing we knew it'd be sunset. For the hell of it, I tried counting while you were gone, you know, one-one thousand, two-two thousand. Every thousand counts I put a rock in my pocket. But after twelve rocks I gave up. And that was a long time ago. So, basically, all we know is that it's probably much later than we think it is."

"Denise, we've got to get out. There's an awful lot at stake."

"I know, Walt, I know," she snapped. "I just don't know what else to do. No one's going to come looking for us until it's way too late, for both us and the Vice-President and UN guy, as well as everyone else who's out there tomorrow. Or today, or maybe it's already happened! I don't know." Denise's voice was now thick with despair.

Walt said nothing and the two sat in silence. His eyes began to droop and he felt they should get up and start moving before they passed out on the spot, but he couldn't will himself to budge. He could hear Denise's gentle breathing beside him. She was already asleep. Harley shifted his body and Walt tried to focus on his friend, but then his own eyelids closed and moments later he, too, had drifted off to sleep.

CHAPTER XXXVII

14 JULY
FLAGSTAFF, ARIZONA

Adam Branson frowned at the windsock blowing at the far end of the field. He was sitting in the front seat of the Bronco, trying to convince himself that the right thing to do was to get in his plane and fly back to DC before the airport closed at midnight. He looked at his watch. He only had fifteen minutes to decide. He could be back in DC at a decent hour, leaving the Bronco to be disposed of by one of his local contacts. This far away from Joshua Tree, no one would ever track him down. He'd be completely safe.

But, ever since leaving Rodriquez' mangled corpse in a deep hole he'd dug in a remote patch of desert, he'd become increasingly nervous. The thousands of people who would, if all went according to plan, die in a few hours bothered him only slightly. The death of Rodriquez weighed a bit more heavily on his mind, but not much. What was eating at the big man's mind was that he had left a crucial part of his job unfinished. He hadn't seen Crawler's body. Not that he'd had the opportunity to do so, with the mine completely collapsed and the need to leave the area as quickly as possible, but the uncertainty of the biologist's death bothered him immensely. Of course, it had been a good-sized explosion, filling the mine with tons of debris and deadly amounts of poisonous gasses. The odds that anyone could have escaped alive were tiny, almost non-existent. But it was possible. Many of those old shafts, Branson knew, had other entrances or air holes from which egress might be possible.

And if anyone could escape from the underground hell Branson had created, it would be Crawler. He'd escaped in DC, again in Oklahoma and yet again here in the desert. His track record at getting out of tight spots in one piece was too good to discount without seeing the body.

If Crawler got out alone, Branson didn't think he'd have much to worry about. The biologist would never be able to convince anyone that a disaster in the Park was imminent, assuming he could even find his way out of that godforsaken patch of desert before the operation was over. If Mitchell escaped with him, the situation would be a bit bleaker, but still not disastrous. But if Wallace made it out too, she might very well be able to send out an alarm and save at least the Vice President and the rest of the VIPs, if not the thousands of other people by Barker Dam.

The thought of a last minute rescue made Branson cringe. After all of the planning that had gone into setting up these traps, after all the blood that had been shed to get this far, to have it fall apart at the last moment would be a catastrophic failure. It would be an insult to his warrior ethos.

Branson's frown grew deeper, creasing all the way across his broad face as he looked at the windsock floating gently in the nighttime breezes. If he didn't get on this plane soon, he knew he might have trouble escaping the region undetected. Immediately after the news of the disaster hit the air, security throughout the entire Southwest would be ratcheted up to an unbelievable degree. Eventually, Branson was certain, the chemical release would be categorized as a fluke accident with no criminal elements. Nonetheless, at the beginning the authorities would leave no stone untouched in their response. One of the problems with being a big guy, Branson had found, especially one with extra large hands, was that even a good wig, fake glasses and some cosmetic cheek work couldn't hide him from someone he knew. Too many people who'd suddenly be manning roadblocks and pulling extra guard duty at transit hubs like airports would have seen him at some point in their professional careers. Someone was bound to recognize him if he was still around once the security nets were in place.

But the mission came first. Branson knew that as well as anybody. He'd killed for this mission, he was willing to put his own life on the line, too. There was no decision to make. He put the truck back in gear and circled through the airport's empty parking lot to the access road. If Crawler and his companions hadn't died in the mine, then they were still out there someplace, posing a threat to everything Branson had worked for so long. Branson would have to make certain they didn't make good on that threat.

To the west, a full moon hung low in the sky, giving the surrounding desert an eerie glow and outlining some faraway mountains. It was later than Branson had hoped, but disposing of the Rodriquez' body had taken longer than expected. Plus, he'd forced himself to follow the posted speed limit on the long drive to Flagstaff. He was well aware of how a random traffic stop had blown open the Oklahoma City bombing case. Murphy's Law at work. It'd get you every time. He checked his watch again. It was exactly midnight. If all went well, he should be back at the mine site by about seven. If the jeep were still there, he'd circle around the area for an hour or so looking for any possible exit points. He also had his police scanner, disguised as an additional cellular phone, on the seat beside him. If the Feds got wind of his plan, they'd have trouble keeping it off the air, which would give him warning that the game was up and allow him time to shift into the escape and evade mode. If all were still quiet by eight, he'd head up the desert roads towards the mountain resort town of Big Bear. He could loose himself there much more effectively than if he tried to drive back east to Flagstaff or west to Las Angeles. Whatever he did, he didn't want to be on the road after 10:30 AM, by which point the authorities would probably have their nets out in full force.

The early morning air rushed through the truck's open window, reminding Branson of his younger days as a soldier, feeling the wind whipping through the open door of an Army Huey as he set out on a mission. The sensation was the same, the tight feeling in his gut, the wind blowing his hair across his forehead, the knowledge that once more he was heading into dangerous territory, facing a potential foe who would do everything humanly possible to bring him down. He smiled grimly. No one had brought him down yet and Walt Crawler wouldn't be the first.

CHAPTER XXXVIII

15 JULY
JOSHUA TREE NATIONAL PARK, CALIFORNIA

Walt awoke to a gentle but insistent tugging at his arm. "Wake up, Walt. We've got to get going!"

"Huh," his voice was still slurred with sleep.

"Walt, we've got to get going. Now! It's almost sunup. We only have a few hours."

Walt opened his eyes, and then rubbed at them with his grimy knuckles. The view remained pitch black.

"How do you know it's almost sunup?" he asked groggily.

"Don't you hear them?"

"Hear what?"

"The bats."

He held his breath and listened for a moment. He could indeed hear the muted rustle and soft chirps he had heard earlier.

"You woke me up to tell me about bats?"

"No, Walt. Don't you see?" Walt could hear the frustration in her voice even as the tugging at his arm became more insistent. "I told you, I know there are two ways into the mine because I've tracked the bats. The exit we came in is closed so these guys must be coming in from another one. And they feed at night, so the night must be just about over. If we're quick, we can see where they're coming from. Now let's go!"

Walt stood up slowly, the stiffness in his joints reminding him of how much pain Denise must be in with her injured leg. He leaned over and grabbed Harley's arm. As he pulled, the arm pulled back and Harley's voice, groggy and rusty, boomed through the dark air.

"What the fuck's going on?" Harley bellowed, rolling to a sitting position.

"Harley!" Walt almost screamed with joy, "Harley, you're conscious!"

"Walt, is that you?" the biker asked, trying to make sense of his confusing surroundings. "Where the hell are we? What's going on?"

"Can you walk? We'll tell you as we go."

Harley struggled to his feet. "Yeah, I can walk. My left arm is killing me. What happened?"

Denise turned the light on and played it over Harley's body, giving him a feel for his situation. "We're in a mine shaft, Harley. Branson shot you right after I maced you," her voice sounded embarrassed but now wasn't the time for an apology, "and you went into shock. Branson shot out one of my tires and we had to take cover in an old gold mine. Walt figured out that Branson was going to blow the mine's entrance, so we moved deeper into the mine. We were safe when the mine blew up, but now we're stuck inside looking for another way out. Those bats flying over head are coming from that other way, but they're also telling us that it's almost daylight, which means we've only got a few hours before Branson springs his plan. Whatever it is.

"I'm going to turn the light off so we don't freak out the bats too much. If I have any questions about where they're coming from, I'll turn it back on." The light vanished and Denise began shuffle footing down the shaft, followed by Harley and then Walt.

After following the main passage for another several hundred feet, ignoring numerous spur shafts that were empty of bats, Denise stopped and pointed the flashlight up a small tunnel to the right. A torrent of bats flowed from this tunnel, knocking against each other and the three humans.

"This is it," said Denise. "It'll be a tight fit, but they're all coming out of this shaft. There's not even one coming down the main passage anymore. It must be just a dead end further on. This has got to be our shaft. I'll go first. You two follow me." Denise started to move into the shaft and then hesitated. "Can you do it, Harley?" It was a *very* small shaft.

"No problem. I'm a toxicologist, remember?" Harley's made a valiant attempt to appear lighthearted.

"Right, I forgot that part," Denise hunched over and began to ease her way up the tiny shaft. Of all the spurs they had found thus far, this one was definitely the smallest and it wasn't clear how easily the bulky Harley would navigate it, despite his gung ho attitude. There was no other option, though. As she crept through the mine, Denise couldn't even begin to imagine how the old-time prospectors had created these things, working in the flickering lights of a lantern, knocking rocks lose with short handled picks and carrying the rubble back to the main shaft in tiny steel buckets. Of course, they didn't have to worry about people trying to kill them, Denise thought, but their efforts seemed superhuman all the same. She wondered how they had brought their water this far into the mine, wishing that she'd managed to grab some water from her Jeep before she'd dashed into the mine.

Her leg bumped up against a small pile of rocks and she stifled a cry of pain. No matter how much her leg hurt, it paled in comparison with what Harley must be experiencing.

The shaft began to get smaller. The miners must have begun to lose faith in the vein, but still they had dug on, searching for the mother load. Denise hoped that they had found it before the shaft turned into a tortoise hole big enough only for the bats.

Finally, the mine shrunk to where progress was only possible on their hands and knees. The torrent of bats had faded away by now and Denise knew that sunup couldn't be far off. With some luck, the brightening sky would shine down the hole and show them the way out. Denise backed up into the two men following her.

"How's your arm, Harley?"

"It hurts like hell and is useless as tits on a bull. It's probably infected by now, too, with all the bat shit that must be floating in the air. But otherwise, it's fine. Why?"

Denise flipped the light on. "The shaft gets even smaller here. We'll be on our hands and knees for a little while at least. Do you think you can make it?"

"Do I have much choice?"

"You could stay here and we'd come back for you." Assuming of course, that they eventually made it out.

"Denise, no offense, but I'd rather not do that. Walt," he turned to the biologist, "you go in front of me. That way, if I get stuck you and Denise can keep moving forward. That's the important part, to keep moving. Don't slow down for me, don't wait for me. Just get the hell out. I'll go as far as I can, and if I get stuck, you all can come back for me later."

"Harley, I'm not sure I . . ." Walt hesitated, obviously not comfortable with this plan.

"Shut up, Walt. I'm so big that if I get stuck, you get stuck, too. You can't help me, Katie or anyone else stuck behind me in this stupid shaft, so get in front." With his good arm, Harley pushed Walt around in front of him. "Now let's keep moving."

"Okay, guys," said Denise, "I'm going to turn the light off now. The batteries are starting to go. We have to continue as far as we can. This is the way the bats got in, it's the only way we'll get out. Holler if you need to tell me something. Otherwise I'll stop every once in a while to make sure you're still with me. Walt, when I stop, tap my leg to say you're still there. Tug on it a couple of times if you need to get my attention. Make sure it's the right leg, my left one still kills. Any questions?"

"Nope. I'll stay with you." Without an injured leg, Walt was easily staying up with his companion. It was Harley he was worried about.

326 CRAIG A. KELLEY

"Walt, I'm not going to touch your leg for anything," growled Harley. "There's no way I'll be able to keep up with you. You'll know I'm behind you when you see me at the other end of this hole and don't even think of wasting your time trying to learn if I'm okay. Now, both of you, promise you won't worry about me until you've stopped Branson."

There was silence.

"Dammit, promise!" Harley shouted, his voice filling the tunnel like thunder.

"Okay, Harley, I promise," said Denise, turning the light back on and touching him softly on the cheek.

"Walt?"

"All right, Harley, but I don't like it."

"You don't have to like it. Just do it."

Denise turned off the light and began crawling forward. Walt scrambled behind her, unhappy at the thought of leaving Harley behind. Soon, however, his concern for Harley had been overshadowed by a grating agony in his hands and knees. He could feel the pebbles and grit of the tunnel's floor grinding into his skin with every move and his wrists were beginning to cramp from being flexed so continuously.

Inch by inch, Walt crawled through the tunnel, his mind becoming increasingly numbed by pain. He started to lose the last remnants of hope. They'd die down here, unable to stop the disaster that was about to unfold just a few miles away. He was becoming accustomed to that idea and the thought of his own death was not troubling, but the thought of Katie facing the world by herself was pure torture.

The shaft turned a sharp corner and Denise stopped so short that Walt bumped into her. Even behind the Ranger he could feel a gentle breath of fresh air blowing on his cheek. They were getting close! He wanted to tell Harley but he'd long since lost any hope that the biker had stayed with them. He could only pray his friend would make it eventually.

As he moved onward, Walt became aware of a dim gray light glowing through the gloom up ahead, beyond Denise's crawling mass. The shaft began to widen and he forgot about the pain that was consuming his whole body. They had come to the exit! The shaft grew still larger and he rose into a slouching upright posture, his hands and knees proclaiming their relief.

Denise halted and Walt moved up and stood stiffly by her side, bending his legs to work out the cramps. "We've made it," he said simply, his eyes taking in the beautiful sight of daylight, however dim. He had to force himself not to mention Harley. They'd promised to worry about getting out, not about their big friend, and he'd keep that promise.

"Maybe," said Denise. "Let's go see what it looks like."

Side by side, the two limped towards the light. Around them the shaft grew bigger and bigger until Walt realized that they were no longer in a shaft. "Denise, that light's not up ahead at the end of the tunnel. It's above us. We're in a chamber."

She took the flashlight from her belt and turned it on. The dim beam illuminated a long, narrow chamber over twenty feet high. At the far end, a small overhead shaft, braced by a wooden crossbeam, let in the faint daylight they had been following. There was no other exit out of the mine. They would have to go up to get out. Otherwise, they were at another dead end.

"Shit," said Walt slowly, disappointment evident in his voice. "How do we reach that high?" He glanced about the chamber, trying to figure out a way to bridge the gap to the shaft overhead. They had come too far to fail now. There had to be some way to get out.

Denise cast the light around the chamber. A few clusters of beer cans and other random rubbish dotted the rocky floor, indicating that they weren't the first to enter this chamber since the original miners had left so long ago. She pointed the beam towards the opening. Anyone with a stout rope, preferably with knots in it, could have come down through that hole, poked about the mine and then left. If anyone had entered that way, though, they hadn't left the rope hanging.

Walt walked directly under the hole and looked straight up. The clear blue sky overhead looked like an immeasurably valuable jewel to his sun starved eyes. But at the same time he was alarmed at how bright it was. It must be later than he had thought.

"You got any ideas?" asked Denise

"Well, for starters, if your leg can take it, let's see how close we can get with you standing on my shoulders."

Denise got to her feet and looked back up at the hole again. "We can give it a try. We'll still be too short, though."

"At least it'll give us an idea of how far we've got to go." Walt turned and offered Denise his back. She clambered up and hooked her legs over Walt's shoulders. Using his head as a post, she placed her feet on his shoulders and slowly straightened up. Walt extended his right arm which Denise grabbed for additional support as she stood. Even waving her left hand over her head, she was still several feet too low.

"Damn!" she muttered as she climbed back down. "It's still too far."

"Not if you stand on someone else?"

Harley's voice made Walt and Denise jumped as if hit by lightening. They rushed over to their friend as he emerged into the chamber.

"You made it!" they exclaimed.

"Yeah, I did. Did you have any doubts?" His wound had obviously reopened and the biker's entire left side was soaked in blood. His eyes were feverish and even as he spoke he wobbled on his feet. "No, don't answer that. Now, Walt, what if you climb on me and then, Denise, you climb on Walt. That ought to make it."

Walt and Denise eyed their tottering friend. "Could you handle that?" asked Denise.

"I hope so. It doesn't look like we have much choice." He turned his broad back to Walt. "Climb up, buddy. Just try not to hit my arm."

Once Walt was perched on his shoulders, Harley held out his right arm to help Denise up. "Make it quick," he said, "I'm not sure how much longer I can hold you."

Denise leaned forward and kissed the biker on his lips, a quick and unexpected movement that surprised them both. "I'm sure you can hold us long enough." Trying to ignore the pain in her leg, she clambered over Harley's broad back and then climbed up on top of Walt's shoulders, bracing herself with his right arm as she had before. She stretched out her muscular left arm, but the human totem pole was still two feet short of the heavy wooden crosspiece that spanned the opening.

Denise crouched and tensed the muscles in her legs. "Hold on," she yelled to the men below her, "I'm going to have to jump for it." She let go of Walt's right hand and straightened her knees, reaching up with both hands for the suddenly frail looking wooden beam that bisected the entrance. Her fingers brushed against and then encircled the beam just as Walt and Harley collapsed into a swearing, groaning heap.

She swung there for a moment, testing the beam, feeling it flex under her weight. Then she arched her back, swung her legs forward and hooked her right knee over the beam. Ignoring the pain shooting through her left leg, she jackknifed her body so that she lay on top of the beam and, with the agility of a monkey, scrambled out of the hole and onto the desert floor.

Still inside the hole, the two men waited patiently for a minute, Walt back on his feet, Harley sitting down and massaging his left arm. "Denise?" Walt called out. No reply. He looked at Harley and then shouted a little louder. Still they heard nothing and the silence was worrisome. What had happened now? Walt picked up a rock and threw it through the opening. He heard it strike something at the mine's entrance and then jumped back as a handful of stones fell down into the hole, narrowly missing Harley as they rattled to the ground.

"Sorry, Harley," Walt said stupidly. He should have been more careful, Harley was obviously on his last legs. "What do you thing is going on?" Could Branson have followed them this far, killing Denise as she exited the mine? With him, anything seemed possible.

"Don't worry, Walt, she'll be back." Harley fell silent again and continued to work on his arm.

As Walt stared up at the distant blue sky, a thick rope poked its way into the hole. After a moment, Denise stuck her head out over the lip. "You okay down there?"

"Yeah, we're fine. But where've you been? We were getting nervous." Walt looked at the seated Harley. "Or at least I was."

"I had to figure out a way to get you guys out of there. I found this rope lying outside the shaft, put some knots in it and tied it around some machinery up here. Tug on it to make sure it'll hold you, and if it does, climb on up."

Harley stood up and moved over to the rope. He held out his right hand to Walt. "Good luck, buddy. I'll see you in a bit."

"What do you mean?" Confusion flickered over Walt's face.

"I can't climb this rope with one good arm, and you guys can't haul two hundred and fifty pounds of me out of here. And even if you could, then what," Harley swayed back and forth as he spoke, "I'm plumb played out. Up there you're going to have to move quickly to find your way to the Park. I'd only slow you down, at least until the sun cooked me. Down here, it's relatively cool, I'm not moving, I'm in the shade. You guys get out and send someone back for me. But the first thing you've got to do is stop Branson. Then you can worry about me." There were tears on the biker's grimy cheeks. "Promise me, Walt, promise me you'll stop Branson first."

Walt took Harley's hand in his. "I promise, Harley." He dropped the hand and embraced his friend in a gentle hug. "And I promise we'll be back." He let go of the biker and grabbed the rope. "Remember, we'll be back."

Less than a minute later, Walt stood beside a pile of abandoned equipment that marked the edge of the abandoned mine.

"Where's Harley?" Denise asked, even though she knew the answer.

"He's going to stay down there. We'll have to send someone back for him later." It made sense, but Walt didn't like it.

Denise nodded and walked to the edge of the hole. She hung her head over the lip, "Don't get too comfortable down there, Harley, we won't be long," she shouted.

"I'll be waiting right here," the biker shouted back. "Good luck."

The Ranger stepped away from the mine, dabbing at her eyes. After taking a moment to collect herself, she looked up and down the small valley they were in, trying to memorize enough details of their location to make sure she could find her way back to rescue Harley. Other than the ruins of the old mine, the metal equipment streaked red with rust and the wooden shack pitted and weathered by the sun and wind, there was nothing man-made in sight. Not even a four-wheel drive road passing through the valley below. It was a small piece of the desert that time seemed to have forgotten.

She looked up the valley again, concentrating on the bulk of the mountains at the far end. "Walt, I think I know where we are. Given where the sun is, that direction's roughly south." She gestured towards the mountains. "I think that big peak over there is 29 Palms Mountain and that one over there is Ryan Mountain. That would put us somewhere to the west of where we went in. I lost all sense of distance and direction down there. But I'll bet if we keep going east, we'll hit the road we came in on. Then we can either find my Jeep, if Branson left it there, or flag down someone. If worse comes to the worst, we'll hoof it out to the highway."

Denise eyed the steep, stubble covered hillside behind her and remembered how parched her throat felt. If they didn't find help soon, the morning sun would fry them before they could warn anyone of the disaster about to happen at the dam. The escape through the mine, the hellish scrambling on her hands and knees and the throbbing pain in her leg would all be for nothing. And Harley would be left to wither in the dark hole by her feet.

"It's not going to be easy, Walt. These hills are full of cactus that'll poke through your sneakers and make mincemeat out of your toes. They're called jumping cholla. If your feet even brush up against one of them, you're gonna have trouble walking. On top of that, the rocks and boulders are going to be tough on my leg and, even at this hour in the morning, the sun's going to clobber us both. I may not be able to keep up, so you might have to go on without me. The important thing is still for one of us to get to the Park Headquarters ASAP."

"Denise, you're the prophet of doom. It can't be worse than the mine." Walt had already left one friend behind, he wouldn't leave another no matter how bad it got. "Let's go." He began to walk up the hill, keeping his eyes open for the jumping cholla.

Denise followed him up the hill, favoring her injured leg. By the time Walt reached the top of the ridge she had fallen quite a distance behind. He waited for her, sitting on a rough boulder and taking in the moonscape-like view of the high desert in summer. On a distant ridge, an early morning four-wheeler raised a cloud of dust. Walt watched as the cloud slowly drifted down into the valley below and, unexpectedly, the last piece fell into place.

"Walt, you're going to have to go on ahead," Denise called after him. "I can't go any faster. My leg's killing me." Her face was drawn with pain. Between her leg and the dehydration, she was at the end of her rope.

"I can't, Denise, I'm sorry." Walt was worried. "I'm an eastern island boy, remember. I'm used to the ocean. I'll just get lost out here in the desert. You've got to come along. Besides, I know what Branson's planning now."

The Park Ranger reached the ridge, her breath coming in ragged gasps. Walt got up to meet her and she sagged against his shoulders for support. He could tell she was running on empty no matter how lost he might get on his own. "See that cloud of dust?" he pointed towards the distant ridge.

"Yes?"

"You can't see it now, but someone driving a jeep or a truck up that ridge created the cloud. Dust is heavier than air, so it settled down into the valley. I've been watching it drift. That's what Branson's going to do."

"Launch a dust cloud?" She looked at him skeptically.

"No. It won't be dust. That's visible. Branson likes his poisons to stay unseen. You say the ceremony is going to be at a dam, right."

"Right."

"And dams are always located at the bottom of hills because water, just like gas, flows down hill. All those people at the dam are going to be at the lowest point around. Branson's going to let a cloud of poisonous gas drift downhill on top of them."

"Jesus, Walt," Denise exclaimed, "you're right. That's exactly what he'll do."

"I'm not sure how he'll get the gas into the air. An explosion would be too obvious and would allow the VIPs time to escape, but I'm sure he's thought of something. Maybe pressured fogging equipment with a timer."

"No, that's not his method of operation," argued Denise, recharged by Walt's insight. "He makes things look like accidents. He wouldn't be that obvious. Everything he does has some rational explanation if someone prematurely discovers it, plus is easily explained afterwards." She was silent for a moment, then resumed her train of thought in a quiet voice. "I know exactly what he's going to do."

"You do?" For a moment, buoyed by Denise's statement, Walt forgot about Harley and the fact that they were lost in the desert with no more than a few hours to stop Branson.

"I know the dam area like the back of my hand. It's the area's only dependable water supply so it's a natural concentration point for wildlife, including bats. A few months ago, I was checking mines there to determine which, if any, hosted bat colonies. I found one that looked like it had collapsed fairly recently. It's pretty high, too. Anything flowing out of it would fill the valley. It fits with Branson's plan perfectly, at least as we understand it. He found this old hole, stuffed it full of whatever chemicals they're using and then made the mine look like it had collapsed naturally."

"Since he's not likely to use explosives," Walt said after he'd digested this new information, "I'll bet he has a couple of barrels set up to leak on some sort of command. This event's pretty choreographed, so he could probably even use a timer if he could figure out a way to disguise it. When the drums start leaking, the gas they let go will flow downhill and fill up the valley. Branson's probably mixed the chemical somehow so that by the time people start coughing, it's already too late. That way, no one will figure out something's going on until he's already nailed his targets."

Denise looked at Walt with renewed respect. "You're right," she agreed, "that's exactly what he's going to do." Suddenly, her whole body jerked. "That's it, Walt," she cried, pointing with both hands. "We've found it."

"Found what?" Walt looked blankly at the barren landscape, thrilled by the excitement in her voice but unable to understand what had caused it.

"We've found our road! The mine entrance is just below that knob there!" Denise started hobbling down the hillside as Walt stared in amazement at her sudden burst of energy.

He raced after her, catching up as she reached the knoll. Beneath them stretched a long, dusty road, to the side of which was parked her Jeep, glistening brightly in the morning sun despite a thick coat of dust. To the two survivors, tired and sore and dying of thirst, the vehicle looked like the Holy Grail.

"Wait a minute," said Walt, grabbing her shoulder. "What if they're waiting for us?"

Denise shook off his grip and continued downward. "Walt, look at what they did to the mine." A crater stretched from the edge of the road back deep into the mountain. "They think we're dead. There's no way they'll believe anyone survived that. They may have taken my car keys, but I've got a spare set in my wallet and unless they broke something, we'll be out of here in ten minutes."

Walt shrugged his shoulders and moved down too. It was probably safe enough, he reasoned. If there was anyone out there waiting to shoot them, they'd be dead by now, standing out on the open hillside.

Denise stopped short of the Jeep. No need to take any stupid chances here. She circled the vehicle, squatting down periodically to look below its body. There were no clear signs of tampering. She reached into the cab and pulled out a small mirror on a telescoping rod. Extending the rod, she put the mirror under the jeep and slowly walked around it.

"What are you doing?' Walt asked as he watched the ritual. "What's up?"

"I'm checking for booby-traps. Someone like Branson could easily rig this thing to blow as soon as you turn on the engine. He's obviously worked on the jeep-the windshield's down, he's wiped off the dash, he took the key I left in the ignition. Who knows what he's done."

"And you just happened to have that mirror with you?"

"Remember what I said yesterday, Walt. I'm a foot soldier out here. It won't be the first time someone's put a bomb under a Ranger's car. Anytime I leave my jeep in a questionable place, I check it over. I've got some signals that make it easy though." She pulled the mirror out from under the jeep and collapsed the rod again. "See, look here." She pointed to a strand of string in the corner of the hood. "You wouldn't see that unless you were looking for it, but I hot-glued that on. If someone opens the hood, it falls off. So we know he hasn't opened the hood. There's nothing suspicious looking underneath, so we just have to check out the seats, the ignition and the glove compartment. And I've got signals for them, too." Within seconds she'd explained to Walt how she knew the seats and ignition were safe. "But he's opened the glove compartment. Now we have to figure out if he put a go-boomer in there."

Denise fished a bottle of water out of the back of the jeep and eyed it critically. Half full. No telling what Branson might have done to it. She poured it onto the sandy ground and tossed the empty bottle back in the Jeep. She grabbed another bottle. This one was full. Opening the bottle, she heard the reassuring fizz of escaping gas. Unless he had more sophisticated equipment on him than she imagined, Branson hadn't touched this one. She brought it to her lips and drank deeply, feeling the carbonated bubbles cut through the parched crust that lined her throat. It felt like life itself.

She passed the bottle to Walt and swirled the water around in her mouth for a moment before swallowing. "I'm going to have to clear the glove compartment," she said. "It's probably fine, I've never heard of someone booby-trapping a glove compartment instead of the ignition or the undercarriage, but you never know." Denise pulled a pad of paper from under the driver's seat and began to write. When she had finished, she handed the note to Walt. "Now, you go stand over there." She gestured to the other side of the small plateau. "Wait until I've got the jeep moving just to be sure it's safe. If this goes up in a boomer, we don't want both of us to get fried. Someone ought to come check out the fireball. You can let them know what's going on. That note I gave you is directed to Frank Sells, the head of Park security. He'll recognize the handwriting. If you can get it to him, he'll start clearing out the Dam area."

Her tone allowed for no discussion. Walt put the note in his pocket, next to Katie's spoon, and moved across the plateau. He prayed he wouldn't hear a blast instead of the even growling of the engine.

Denise held her breath and opened the glove compartment. Nothing happened. She poked around in its interior and noticed her registration was missing. That was why Branson had opened it. He'd wanted to make it as hard as possible for anyone to track her down. Next, she climbed into the driver's seat, the pistol in her waistband pressing against the small of her back as she pushed in the clutch. Holding her breath once more, she pulled the spare key from her wallet, inserted it in the ignition and gave it a turn. The engine roared to life and she exhaled gratefully. She pulled up next to Walt, her tires raising clouds of dust in the still morning air. "Going my way, big boy?"

"Yes, ma'am. Mind if I climb in?" Walt's smile was so wide it cracked the grime that encrusted his face. He hopped into the passenger's seat and the Jeep jumped forward, its flat tire flopping as it surged down the road to the desert valley below.

"What time is it?" Walt asked.

"What's the radio say? Turn it on and the clock'll come up."

Walt reached forward and turned the knob. The LED display showed 6:31. They had almost an hour and a half to foil the assassination plan. That had to be enough time. "We're set. There's plenty of time to get the word out. How far's the nearest phone?"

"The nearest phone? What for?"

"So we can call up your boss and tell him what's going on. They can pull out the VIPs and clear the Park." It sounded vague even to Walt. He hadn't quite figured out what happened after this point.

"Walt, is that your idea? To call up Commissioner Perkins and tell him what's going on? That's it?" She took her eyes off the rough road and looked Walt square in the face, amazement showing in her strong features.

"Well, yeah. I guess it is. I mean, what else can we do? You yourself said you just wanted me to get to the Park Headquarters if your jeep blew up, so what's the difference if we call first?"

"Walt, the jeep didn't blow. We've got other options now, we don't need to take the same risks that we would have if only you'd gotten out. We can't make any phone calls. We don't know if Branson's got the phones tapped. Right now, he thinks we're dead. He thinks that his plan is safe and he's not expecting anything. If we call up, he might find out that we're on to him. Who knows what would happen then. Maybe he's got a way of sending that poisonous chemical mess down into the valley immediately. That'd be a nightmare. Even if the VIPs got out, there are thousands of other people already at the mine who wouldn't. There's no way we can use the phone."

"You're kidding me, right?" Now it was Walt's turn to look at his companion as if she were a moron. "We've just escaped death at least twice, crawled a million miles through a mine shaft and we know, beyond a shadow of a doubt, that something very, very bad is going to happen in a couple of hours and you want to keep it a secret?"

Denise took the Jeep out of gear and coasted to a stop. Keeping both hands on the wheel, she partially twisted her body to face Walt. She tried to control her temper and then abandoned the effort. She knew from experience that losing one's patience could be useful at times, if the conditions were right. "Listen, Walt," there was a hard edge to her voice, "there are probably ten thousand people sitting in that valley right now. We'll have all sorts of people crushed in a stampede once things start going wrong. And if Branson can accelerate the release, stampeding will be the least of our problems. Plus, he might have backup plans to shoot down the extraction choppers if they pick up the VIPs. We call up and we're basically telling anyone who might be listening to go to the backup plans." Denise took a breath, then rushed on. "Calling just won't work. The only option I see is to go right in and stop the release."

"You're serious?"

"Dead serious."

"What about response gear?"

"We'll pick it up at the Park's response locker. It's right on our way."

"Have you ever worked a response before?"

"No. You'll have to walk me through it."

"Denise, it's not that easy. People spend years training for this sort of stuff. Even without someone like Branson in the picture, you don't just 'talk someone through it.'"

"We've got no choice. I can get you the equipment, you'll have to help me with the rest."

Walt looked at her face, the earnest expression in her eyes. If she, someone with no response experience, was willing to risk it, how could he say no? "Okay," he said reluctantly, but only if we send someone out to pick up Harley first."

"That won't be a problem. We'll run into security elements long before we get to the mine. We'll tell them to get Harley." Denise popped the Jeep back into gear and they sped off across the desert.

CHAPTER XXXIX

15 JULY
JOSHUA TREE, CALIFORNIA

Brian Flannigan finished the last of his coffee and rested his chin on his well-manicured fingers as he looked reflectively at the few drops remaining in the mug. It was probably grown on some former rain forest land now loaded with pesticides and fertilizers, he thought, angry with himself for enjoying such non-environmental pleasures. And the cream probably came from factory-farmed cows loaded with growth hormones. He poured another cup and went back to his speech. His gas mask analogy was all set to go, but the main body of the speech was still noticeably rough. If nothing else, he had to seem to have been prepared to give a real speech and he didn't have time to wallow in self-doubt or pity. The world wasn't perfect and he wasn't either. If he allowed himself to become paralyzed with the specifics of how he lived from day to day, he'd never get anything done.

And there was so much to do today.

A knock on his door indicated that his ride was waiting to take him to the Park for the beginning of the ceremonies. Flannigan grabbed the bag with his gas mask, stuffed his speech into his pocket to work on in the limo and went to the door. In a couple of hours it would all be over, no matter how good, or bad, his speech was, or if he even made it at all.

Putting on an enthusiastic smile, Flannigan stepped out to greet the day.

CHAPTER XXXX

By the time Branson crossed the Colorado River, the sun was starting to crest the eastern mountains. Not surprisingly, the day promised to be another scorcher. The Park Service had been wise to schedule the ceremony before the real mid-day heat struck home. The calm nature of the radio traffic over his police scanner reassured Branson. Clearly the authorities did not know that all hell was going to break loose in the Park in just a little while. He drummed his fingers against the wheel. He was going to arrive at the mine later than he had hoped, which wouldn't allow him much time for a thorough look around. By eight, at the latest, he had to be heading to Big Bear.

Branson turned onto the hard surface road and raced west towards the Park. A tortoise crawled across the road in front of him and he swerved to avoid hitting it. He smiled at the thought of dodging a tortoise but going out of his way to kill thousands and thousands of people. Some things were just not logical.

He turned left onto the dirt road that led up to the mine and sped south as quickly as the washouts and sand traps would allow. Turning the corner where the mine had been, Branson pounded the dashboard in anger. The jeep was gone. He drove to the far side of the clearing looked at the road beyond. Nothing. They'd escaped. Crawler had won again. For a moment, the pain of this discovery made Branson feel violently ill, and he had to struggle to keep the bile from spilling out of his throat. Never, other than at his court-martial, had he let a situation get so completely out of control.

Branson quickly mastered his emotions and considered his options. He could throw in the towel now and head directly to

Big Bear and live the rest of his life on the dodge from the Feds. That would be the prudent thing to do, although life on the lam promised to be pretty miserable. He looked at the police scanner again and wondered at its mundane message traffic. There was no way they could carry on like that if anyone had told them what was going on. The radio would be alive with panicked chatter. The authorities didn't know yet. They couldn't. Branson still had time, he just had to find Crawler and his companions before they could spread the alarm.

So, the question was, where had they gone? Branson unfolded a map of the Park and looked at it carefully, through the eyes of a hunter who knew both his prey and the surrounding terrain. If he took a road that snaked up a ridge not too far from the clearing, he would wind up right by the Park's storage sheds, one of which held all of the Park's hazardous material response equipment. He poked a finger at the map and traced another trail that went southwest from those sheds. It was just an old jeep trail, but it was far from impassable. And it led directly to the hills overlooking Barker Dam.

It was clear now what was going on. Branson felt a wave of admiration sweep over him despite the grim situation. Crawler just wouldn't stop. Somehow, they had figured out what Branson's trap was and were heading there, keeping quiet on the threat until the last moment. He'd have done the same thing himself, to keep the bad guys from picking anything up over the airwaves and going to some alternate, equally destructive plan. Now Crawler and the woman, and maybe Mitchell, too, if he wasn't hurt too badly, were going to pick up response equipment to try and stop the reaction themselves! Unless they really knew what they were doing, they were committing suicide. Regardless of whether they lived or died, though, they would be absolutely successful in getting the VIPs whisked to safety and allowing thousands of people enough time to escape the death zone. And stopping that from happening was all that Branson now cared about.

He gunned the truck into gear and began to bounce rapidly up the hillside.

Denise shifted the Jeep into four-wheel low and jolted her way up a dry gully. "We should be able to pick up the response equipment undetected," she said. "The storage shed with all the gear is just at the tip of this gully. We'll get suited up and then go cross-country to the dam. We ought to get pretty close before anyone stops us. With any luck, it'll be one of the security teams with a Ranger attached to it. If it's just Marines or Secret Service, we'll have to spend too much time explaining ourselves.

"Once we get to the mine, we'll have to dig our way through the blockage. When we're past that, we'll stop the release."

"You make it sound so simple." Walt sounded dubious.

"Unless Branson's rigged up some sort of booby trap, which I doubt, given his penchant for secrecy, it should be fairly simple once we get through the mine's entrance. Digging our way into the mine may be awkward in the suits, but we can do it. After that, it'll be a straightforward response, no? Branson will have a couple of barrels ready to split open or react or release their contents in some fashion. You tell me what to do, and I'll do it."

Walt nodded absently, thinking of what needed to be done. "We'll stock up on drum bands and sorbent barriers and drum putty at the shed. Those things ought to allow us to put a temporary hold on Branson's set up. If you're right, and there are no booby-traps and the barrels are set up like someone just dumped 'em there, maybe it'll be simple. We'll stop the release as best we can and a follow-up team can finish the job."

"A follow-up team?" Denise asked.

"No matter how simple it is, we can't do this on our own. Once we make contact with the security elements you told me about, we'll have to establish backup of some sort. We'll have to use runners to keep the radio chatter down, but the Park's hazardous incident response team shouldn't be too hard to round up. Branson won't learn what we're doing until we've already cleared the mine."

Denise swung the Jeep up the side of the ravine and brought it to a halt alongside a squat concrete block shed. "This is it." Favoring her injured leg, she limped up to the building and punched in an access code on the keypad by the door. She waited a moment and then entered the building, Walt following close behind.

Branson coasted the Bronco to a stop at the end of the gully trail and looked at the group of small storage buildings that ringed the flat, open area in front of him. Next to the middle one he recognized the Ranger's jeep. Otherwise, the space was empty, indicating that his foes were inside the shed. He reached inside his breast pocket and removed his Baretta. Next, he opened up his traveling case and took out a small silencer that he screwed onto the pistol's barrel. The sound of gunshots would be too likely to attract the attention he so desperately wanted to avoid so using his long rifle was out of the question. Gun in hand, he pressed down on the accelerator and the big engine roared to life. He would attack so swiftly they wouldn't have time to respond. In fifteen seconds they'd all be dead.

Denise heard the spin of gravel through the open door and started in surprise. No one was supposed to be here at this time of day, everyone should be right around the dam area. She passed Walt the air canister she was carrying and stuck her head through the door, her hand automatically reaching behind her for the pistol that was still in her waistband. On the far side of the clearing, less than fifty yards away, a vaguely familiar looking Bronco bounced back and forth in an attempt to clear the lip at the end of the gully. Denise had done that before herself. Without enough momentum, most vehicles just rocked back down the trail until the driver gained sufficient speed to keep moving forward. She motioned Walt to the door, "Lousy time to have company."

Walt looked over her shoulder and gasped as he recognized both the vehicle and the vast bulk of the man driving the Bronco. "Shit, Denise, it's Branson! He's followed us here."

At that moment the truck, its driver frantically pulling at the wheel, bounced out of the gully like a mountain goat and raced towards the equipment shed.

With no time to question Walt's explanation as to why a beige Bronco would be driving towards her, Denise drew her pistol, stepped into the doorway and began squeezing off rounds.

Branson swore wildly when he saw the Ranger step into the shed's doorway, pistol at the ready. Fucking Murphy had screwed him again! Those few seconds rocking against the gully's edge had cost him dearly. He'd lost the element of surprise, the most important thing you could have in combat. Now it was just a plain shootout. Branson began to fire the Baretta as quickly as he could, knowing that not all the holes in the windshield were coming from him.

A sharp blow caught him in the right shoulder and the Bronco veered off to the side, smashing into one of the block buildings and slamming his face against the steering wheel. Aware that stopping, even momentarily, during a firefight was courting death, Branson lunged for the passenger's side door, ignoring the searing pain that rocketed from his shoulder and the blood streaming from his freshly broken nose. He thrust open the door, clawed his way over the passenger's seat and dropped to the ground. Instantaneously, with the speed of a fighting man who has done it a thousand times, Branson rolled to his right, and brought himself into a firing position covering the equipment shed's open door.

Nothing.

Were they still in the building? If so, he had them boxed in until help arrived to bail them out. How probable was that? The Ranger had fired from inside the relative cover of the building, which would have kept the noise of her shots from traveling any distance. His own weapon was silenced. The crunch of the Bronco striking the wall may have attracted some attention, but he doubted the sound would have carried all that far. If someone had gotten out of the building, he was sunk, but otherwise, he could keep them at bay until the operation was over, at which point his own survival would no longer matter. There was no hope for escape now. He felt no regret. Violent death was often the way of the warrior.

But he had to find out who was in the building before he decided on staying where he was. If someone were trying to flank him, he'd have to take immediate, although risky, countermeasures. "Hey Crawler," he called across the empty space to the shed, "I'm impressed. You've led me on quite a chase."

Silence.

"I'm really sorry about your ex-wife back in Nantucket, pal. It wasn't part of the plan."

Still no sound. Branson started to sweat, and for the first time he noticed the blood that had spread across the front of his shirt from his nose and shoulder. He was a mess. Where was Crawler? Where was the Ranger? Had Mitchell made it out with them? He had to know.

"We didn't mean to hurt the girls either, Walt. It was an accident. Especially little Katie. It must be tough having a kid a life support."

The silence continued.

"Hey, Walt, you hear from your buddy Detective Tillison recently? I understand he made good fish bait."

Still silence.

"It must have been hard to leave your friend Harley back in the mine. A big guy like that can take a lot of punishment, can't he? But hey, not everyone who gets into a tough spot can get out, right?

"Fuck you, asshole!" came from the building, the stream of profanity ending abruptly as if by command.

Branson smiled grimly. He had his answers. Crawler was in there, losing his temper and the Ranger was telling him to shut up. Harley, they'd left behind. He looked at his watch. Not much longer and he wouldn't care any more.

"Jesus Christ, Walt, shut the fuck up, would you!" Denise was livid with anger. "That asshole's baiting you, and you're letting him do it. Now he knows we're in here." She gestured towards the door with her pistol. "As long as he stays there, we can't get out. He'd drop us before we took half a dozen steps. We're stuck."

Walt looked at the Ranger, the anger leaving his eyes as he saw the blood oozing from her left arm. She might have hit Branson, but he'd scored one on her, too. Just a flesh wound, she'd assured him after she'd picked herself up from the floor, but it was scary as hell all the same. "I'm sorry, Denise. He knows how to push my buttons, though. And he's right about Harley, we just left him there."

"I know that, Walt. That's what's Harley wanted. That's what you and I would want in his shoes. We didn't have a choice. Right now Branson'll say anything to bust our chops. If he keeps us upset, he knows we won't be thinking clearly. That'll make it that much tougher to get out of here. He probably figures he's doomed if we've already called for help, and if we haven't he just has to keep us stuck in here. No need to mess around with any of his explosive concoctions. He'll just sit there and taunt us."

As if on cue, Branson's voice carried into the shed. "Katie's a cute kid, isn't she Walt. Ribbons in her hair and everything!" He had seen pictures of the little girl Walt had brought with him to the SCOT. "Too bad she'll never wear them again."

Walt flinched but said nothing. He looked at Denise with tears in his eyes, "You got any ideas on how to break out?"

"No, but we've got to think of something soon or it'll be pointless, as far as the whole ceremony thing goes."

They waited in silence for a while, the stillness broken only by Branson's occasional taunts.

"Denise, I've got an idea. It might be a stupid one, but its an idea," Walt's voice sounded hollowly hopeful.

"Well, any idea you've got is better than the one I don't. Let's hear it."

Walt pointed at one of the silver air canisters that lined one of the walls. "You know what happens if you knock the top off of one of those things?"

"Yeah. It takes off like a rocket. It'd go right through these walls if it picked up a head of steam."

"What do you think it would it do to Branson's truck?"

Admiration filled Denise's voice. "Walt, you've got a future in front of you. It'd knock the hell out of it."

"And if one us were charging out of here at the same time . . ."

"We could get the drop on him."

"Do you think we can do it?"

"Yes, I think so. I saw one of these things pop once. They fly pretty straight once they get going. We'll aim it from in here," Denise was getting exited. "He won't be able to see us in the building's darkness. You can knock off the top with a sledgehammer and I'll scoot on over around his truck. If the tank flies right, he won't have a chance. I'll pop him before he knows I'm there."

"That sounds like the plan, but you missed something."

"I did?"

"Yeah. You're the one with the sledgehammer. I'll do the scooting on over."

"Wait a minute, Walt. You won't get a second chance on this one. He'll recover from the surprise of the tank pretty quickly, you've got to be handy with a gun or he'll take you out. Remember, he's a pro."

"Maybe. But you've got to be able to scoot pretty damned quick, too, or however good you are with a gun ain't going to help at all. With your bum leg, Branson would have all the time in the world to get a few shots off before you got close. No, Denise, it's got to be me."

"Walt, I can't let you do that. You're not trained in this sort of thing."

"And you are? Charging armed killers with guns blazing. I doubt they teach you that at Ranger school. Besides, this asshole's been chasing me for three thousand miles and I'm still alive. He's not going to get me now."

Walt fumbled with a tank, carefully lining it up with the Bronco. He then pulled a sledgehammer from its rack and held it out to Denise. "I'll trade this for your pistol now, ma'am."

"I don't know about this, Walt. I'd still rather be the one to go."

"Denise, you're too slow," Walt paused for a moment and then pressed on with his strongest argument. "Furthermore, this guy is mine." His voice was steady, full of quiet determination. "He killed my twins and my ex-wife, he's left my poisoned daughter in the hospital, he killed my best friend and he's the reason we left Harley twenty feet deep in some Godforsaken hole. Now he's hoping to kill a couple of thousand more people in the name of some crazy anti-environmental movement. The guy's a monster! And now it's payback time. So give me the pistol."

Reluctantly, Denise handed him the gun. "It's got all seventeen rounds in the magazine, mister. Don't bother saving any. A big man like Branson can probably take a lot of lead and still function. You've got to make absolutely certain he's dead before you stop shooting. You got any questions on how to use it?"

Walt held the gun, his eyes hard and his hand surprisingly steady. "Just pull the trigger, right?"

"That's it, no safety or nothing." She avoided looking into Walt's eyes as she took the hammer and made a couple of warm up swings. "Okay, buddy. You're up. On the count of three, run as fast as your little legs will take you. I'll give you just enough time to get out of the door before busting this cap, so swing to the right once you get outside to let the tank by. Then start shooting as soon as you see something to shoot at. Ready?"

Walt nodded, his throat too dry to speak but the rest of his body set for action.

"One. Two. Three."

His shoulder must be worse off than he had originally thought, Branson decided. It had become painful to the point of distraction and was already quite stiff. Much longer and he'd be in no shape to fight anyone off. He looked at his watch. Time was barely crawling by, but he could stick it out long enough. A scuffling sound caught his attention and he raised his eyes to the shed. Like an insane fool, Walt Crawler was charging across the rocky clearing towards the Bronco! Branson raised his pistol and concentrated on his breathing, just like he taught his team members in their combat pistol courses. One, acquire the target, two, steady the breathing. Three.... Branson was squeezing the trigger when the entire truck rocked back on its axles, knocking him in the shoulder and almost blinding him with pain. What the hell, what were they shooting at him? What had he missed? It was too late to do anything but react now, relying on his professional instincts to pull him through. He tried to bring his pistol back to bear on Crawler, his most immediate threat, but he couldn't move quickly enough, Crawler was already clearing the truck to his left.

A series of quick pops filled the air and Branson felt his body jerk under the impact of the bullets. He tried to roll behind the Bronco's rear tire to get into a better firing position but he couldn't even get his pistol past his chest as he pivoted.

"Don't move, asshole." Through the pain he could hear Crawler bark the order at him. After all this time, to lose the drop to some punk wildlife biologist.

"Tell me, Adam, tell me what's poisoning Katie! What's killing my girl?" Crawler was only a few feet away now, there wasn't a chance he'd miss. "What were those chemicals?"

Branson flexed the powerful muscles in his legs, he wouldn't give up yet. "Fuck you," he screamed, rolling to his right. He rolled faster and faster, trying to bring his gun up, but more pops filled the air and something was hitting him with incredible force, again and again and again. The pistol, he needed to get it across his body so he could get a shot off. But he was moving so slowly. And something kept hitting him.

His eyes were already glassing over when the pistol dropped from Adam Branson's dead hands.

Even in death, Branson was intimidating, caked in gore and blood and with an almost life-like snarl on his lips. Walt stood over the body, and raised the gun again, his desire for vengeance unquenched.

"No, Walt," Denise pushed his arm down. "He's dead. It's over. Don't let him make you do something you'll regret."

"That asshole," Walt was sobbing now, huge tears streaming down his face. "He did it, Denise, he did it all. He killed them, he killed them all. And he wouldn't tell me, Denise, he wouldn't tell me what the chemicals are. He wouldn't help my Katie. He was a monster, a monster."

Two strong hands cradled his head and Denise pulled him to her breast. "It's okay now, Walt, it's okay. It's over for him. It's over." She kept repeating the words until Walt pulled himself away from her.

"It's not really over, is it, Denise?" His voice was calm again, the gambler facing another race. "We've still got the trap he set to deal with, don't we?"

"Yes, Walt, we've got the drums to deal with now, and we don't have much time to do it in. Plus Harley's expecting us to send someone back for him. And we're not giving up on your little girl yet, either." Denise's voice sounded solid and confident.

"Then let's go do it." Walt waved the pistol at Branson's body, "I'm not going to lose to this jerk now."

CHAPTER XXXXI

Five minutes later, half-dressed in over-sized moon suits that made sitting in the Jeep's seats very uncomfortable, Walt and Denise started up the double track road that led to the dam.

"Remember, Walt, when we get stopped, let me do all the talking. You're a hazmat response expert from Massachusetts. We'll use your real name, but that's it. You just sit there and nod." Denise spoke rapidly. They'd had precious little time to put together a detailed response plan and Denise's lack of experience in response operations, combined with Walt's lack of familiarity with the desert environment, was not going to help.

They rounded a corner and Denise pushed in the clutch, letting the jeep coast to a halt. Blocking the road just ahead of them was a Marine Corps Humvee, a large, all purpose military vehicle. Around the vehicle clustered several figures in camouflage utility uniforms, at the center of whom stood a large man in a Park Ranger's uniform. Denise's face lit up with relief. "Stan," she said, recognizing the Ranger blocking the road, "boy am I glad to see you."

"Denise? What the hell is going on?" The Ranger's face was a mixture of suspicion and confusion. "You're bleeding! We heard some distant shots but figured it was folks target practicing over the hills. Was it you?"

"It's a long story, Stan," Denise was all too aware of the picture she presented with her bloodied arm and filthy clothing. "Bear with me a few minutes, but time's absolutely critical. This is big. Don't worry about the blood, it looks worse than it is. I promise."

Three minutes later, Stanley Howlasho, Park Service Ranger with ten years of highly commended service, finished listening to Denise. He looked at her closely and then cast an equally intense look at her companion in the passenger's seat. "Jesus, Denise, you don't screw around, do you?"

"No, I don't Stan. You know that. Now you've got two choices. Let us through, send someone back to the shed for decon gear and start rounding up our HazWhopper team for backup, or bounce it off the higher-ups and hope the bad guys don't find out. If they do, it could get very ugly, very quickly. It's not clear that there aren't other people out here besides Branson, ready to spring some nasty surprise in case their original plot goes south."

Stan thought for a moment, a pained expression on his face. "Christ, Denise, this is crazy. I've known you for years and I'd trust you with just about anything, but I don't know this guy you're with from Moses. For all I know he's got something on you and is forcing you into this." He shot another suspicious glance at Walt.

"Come off it, Stan," Denise interrupted angrily. "Have I ever been the type to let anyone force me to do anything? I'm telling you, we're sitting on top of a disaster and we can't afford to screw around talking about it. Now are you going to let me through or not?"

"I'm sorry, Denise," Stan, caught in a bureaucrat's nightmare, could not look her in the eyes. "I can't go ahead alone on this one. It's all too crazy. Wait here while I bounce it off of Headquarters."

"I'm not waiting, Stan. We've lost too much time as it is." Denise settled back in the jeep. "What's going on is bigger than you and it's bigger than me. I'm going to stop it, or you're going to have to stop me. Think carefully before you screw it all up." With that final, cryptic warning, Denise put the jeep in gear and pulled rapidly around the Humvee, spraying gravel and dust in her tracks.

Before the jeep had gone half a dozen yards, a young man was at Stan's side. Dressed in desert fatigues, he carried an automatic rifle which he brought to his shoulder with the efficiency of a trained sniper. He took a deep breath and held it for a moment, sighting carefully in on the jeep's driver.

"Hold your fire!" barked Stan in a voice that rang with the confidence he'd been lacking just moments earlier. "Lieutenant Russell," he continued to the young sniper next to him, "we've just had a change of plans. I want you to send two of your best men back down this road. There's a one story, white concrete block building several miles up on the left. They need to go in there, take everything from the section marked 'decontamination,' throw it in their Humvee and haul ass back to the dam as quickly as they can. It's up ahead on this road. You stay here and keep anyone else from coming down this way. I'm going to take two of your men and follow Ranger Wallace." He'd send a team to fetch the man in the mine once the initial round of preparations was taken care of. Now get on the landline and tell the Command Post staff to meet me at checkpoint Alpha." Stan pointed to a spot on the map he'd unfolded on the hood of his Jeep. "We'll be there in less than ten minutes. Don't say anything else. Got it?"

"Yes, Sir." The lieutenant would do as he was told.

Stan's Jeep quickly caught up with Denise, who was driving more carefully to avoid bouncing any equipment out of her vehicle. "Don't worry," he shouted as he passed her. "You've convinced me. I've set up a briefing up ahead. I'll meet you there." Denise flashed him a grin of thanks as he sped out of sight around a curve.

By the time Denise reached Stan he was already deep in conversation with a cluster of Secret Service personnel and Park staff. He motioned for her to come over and she coasted the Jeep to a stop behind him.

"Okay, Gentlemen." They were all male. "This is Ranger Wallace. She and Mr. Crawler there uncovered this plot and are prepared to respond. We either let 'em go forward or we don't. I vote we do, but it's not my call."

A thin-lipped man with broad shoulders stepped out of the cluster. "Ms. Wallace," he said in a voice that rang with authority, "I'm Agent Jim Sawyer from the Secret Service." He held up a chunky looking telephone. "We have both the Vice-President and Brian Flannigan from the United Nations on a secured line here. You've got thirty seconds to tell them what you know." Sawyer had been a Secret Service agent all of his life. He was trained to "take the bullet" for whomever he was guarding, in this case the Vice-President. But, as he had risen through the ranks, his job had expanded in scope. Now he not only needed to keep the Vice-President alive, he needed to keep him from looking stupid or dangerously unaware of his surroundings. Sometimes that could take a lot of work. This was one of those times.

Denise took the phone from the Secret Service Agent as if she spoke to such luminaries on a regular basis. "Mr. Vice-President. Mr. Flannigan. I'm Denise Wallace. With me is Walt Crawler, a hazardous incident response expert from Massachusetts." Her voice rang out from behind the cluster of Rangers and Agents and Denise realized she was on a speakerphone. She finished describing the situation and waited anxiously for the response. If either of the two men opted for an emergency extract, it would be almost impossible for the Park Service Police to maintain order by the dam.

Unintelligible noises came out of the speakers, indicating that someone on the other end had turned on an auxiliary scrambler. The noises cleared and a firm male voice came over the phone. To Walt, trying to picture what was happening on the other end of the line, it sounded oddly purposeful, as if the sudden crisis had somehow given the unseen man reason for cheer. "This is Brian Flannigan from the United Nations. The Vice-President and I will stay. We don't want our abrupt departure leading to any unnecessary mayhem down here. We will lead by example and stay here until you are done. Thank you for all you've done so far and may God be with you on this next challenge."

The speakers fell silent and Walt allowed himself a sigh of relief. He and Denise were free to carry out their response plan now. Without surprise, he noted the consternation showing in Agent Sawyer's face. His job had just become much more complicated. If things got out of hand, the Secret Service would snatch the VIPs whether they wanted to be snatched or not, but making such a dicey call incorrectly could ruin an otherwise illustrious career.

Sawyer put the phone away and the men all looked at Walt and Denise expectantly. "We'll know in just a few minutes how bad it is," Walt told them in answer to their unspoken but obvious question. "I doubt it's going to be anything as clear-cut as a bomb. That wouldn't be devious enough to suit their purpose. Remember, they set this up as an ambush, hoping that anyone who looked at it, before or after the fact, would think it was just another instance of dangerous industrial debris." Or, we hope they did, Walt qualified silently. If Branson had set up a bomb, he and Denise wouldn't care how thick their protective suits were. The breakthrough time for flying shrapnel was instantaneous. "We'll take readings at the mouth of the mine. That'll give us an idea of the immediate danger below. On a calm day like this any gas from the mine will flow downhill just like water. So keep the area immediately below the mine clear. If the concentrations are too high, I'll start waving both arms over my head. That means we've failed and it's time to clear the valley no matter what the cost. If I'm out of sight, I'll let you know by radio.

"If that's it, we ought to get going. Ranger Howlasho, why don't you come up to the top of the hill with us? You'll get a pretty good view of the mine entrance from there. Between your visual and good radio communications," he handed the other Ranger a small portable radio, "you'll be able to manage backup operations for us."

Stan stepped up on the Jeep's rear bumper and Denise gunned it up the ridge.

"As long as it remains calm," Walt said in a voice he hoped Stan found encouraging, "the gas ought to flow downhill. If you stay uphill, you should do okay."

Denise let up on the gas and pointed to the side with her left hand. "That's it, that's the mine just below that cluster of big boulders. I know it looks closed, but no doubt Branson set it up so gas'll seep right out of that mess like water through a sieve."

Denise halted the Jeep at the top of the hill, leaving the motor running. "Here's where you get off, Stan," she said with forced cheerfulness. "We'll stay off the air as long as we can, but expect a sanitized comm check just before we go in."

"Okay, and good luck." Stan touched both of them lightly on the shoulder and then jumped from the jeep.

Without looking back, Denise put the jeep back in gear and began slowly bumping down the hill towards the mine.

CHAPTER XXXXII

When the speakerphone was shut off, Brian Flannigan excused himself from the podium. "The call just upset me a bit, is all," he said in response to the Vice-President's unasked question. "I need to stretch my legs and go to the bathroom. I'll only be a minute."

The Secret Service agent in charge of the security detail around the podium raised his eyebrows questioningly but said nothing. He had nothing to gain by crossing such a high ranking VIP even under these circumstances. He gave an almost imperceptible nod and two young men in light blue suits pulled away from the crowd by the podium and attached themselves to Flannigan.

"I'm a big boy," Flannigan snapped, "I think I can go to the bathroom by myself."

"I'm sorry, sir," said the head Agent, "but, under the circumstances, I'm afraid I'll have to insist. There's no telling what else is going on and you might need help getting back here if things get messy."

Flannigan hesitated a moment. "Okay, if you insist." He looked at the two men. "Come on then, let's go." Without looking back to see if they were following him, he plunged into the crowd of photographers and reporters by the podium and then ducked under the security tape and into the crowd of observers beyond. He wasn't watching for his escorts. He knew they were right behind him, wondering what the hell he was doing. The portable bathrooms Flannigan and the other VIPs were supposed to use were all on the other side of the tape. His was not a perfect plan, Flannigan knew, but he'd had next to no time to put one together so his best hope was to move quickly.

The agents tagging along with him would radio back to their boss to get instructions before they actually did anything. The group at the podium would then have a quick huddle to discuss his bizarre behavior, and then the head Agent would instruct his foot soldiers to bring Flannigan back to the safe side of the tape.

If he moved fast enough, Flannigan thought he could be around a nearby clump of rocks by then, out of site of the podium, in as isolated a spot as he was likely to find by the dam. He prayed it would be isolated enough.

Flannigan reached the rocks just as the two young agents caught up to him.

"Excuse us, please, Mr. Flannigan," the taller of the two said, "but could you please tell us what you're doing out here? You're supposed to stay within the barrier tape."

Flannigan said nothing, taking a few final steps so that the three men were completely shielded by the rocks. It was even better than he had hoped. Not only were they out of sight from the podium, the rough terrain provided complete privacy from anyone else also. He hoped that neither agent would be eager to actually initiate physical contact, knowing that touching the wrong person at the wrong time would ensure the rest of their careers were spent guarding foreign dignitaries in Alaska or Michigan's Upper Peninsula. Their reluctance to grab him was the cornerstone of his plan, he'd need that last fraction of a second unhindered.

"Can't you two assholes just leave me the fuck alone?" he asked savagely, turning to face them, his right hand drifting behind his back and disappearing under his coat. While the agents tried to make sense out of this sudden and obscene outburst, his right hand reappeared, the silenced .32 caliber pistol firmly in its grasp.

The four quick pops couldn't have been heard more than ten feet away.

Flannigan tucked the pistol back into its holster and began to run across the rocky ground towards a distant hillside.

CHAPTER XXXXIII

Magnified by the bumpy ride, Walt's nausea rose within him, making his knees weak with anxiety. He wished he better understood what he and Denise would be facing in the mine. He'd been involved with dozens of hazardous incident response operations over the years, but none of them had been deliberately set traps. Further, while he was sure Denise was competent enough as a cop, she'd never been on a response. And how he was going to talk her through anything halfway complicated in the heavy, noisy response suits was one hell of a question. Under the pseudo-battlefield conditions Branson had created to carry out his warped crusade, even working with a veteran responder would have been challenging.

The thought of battle stuck in Walt's mind. What had Laste preached? Chemical response operations were, in their own special way, a type of war. Adam Branson had taken that analogy to a radical extreme, using his position in the SCOT to wage a private war. Like the non-conventional warrior he was, Branson had set ambush after ambush for his foes. Surprise them, hit them, surprise them, hit them again. It was his own little guerilla war, waged against the world with no mercy given. Not even to poisoned three-year old girls.

"Denise," he said cautiously.

"Yes?"

"Let me ask you something that might seem silly at a time like this."

"Okay."

"If you were Branson, what would you have as a backup plan?"

"What do you mean?"

"Well, what would you have as a backup in case the operation started to tank? You know, in case the bubble burst like it has. Would you have thrown all your eggs in one basket and hoped it worked or would you have laid another ambush, just in case?" Walt was speaking more rapidly now, forgetting the discomfort of his suit as his mind started racing. "I've got this nagging feeling that we're overlooking something terribly important."

"But Branson threw everything at us already, back at the mine and at the response shed," Denise pointed out. "The guy's dead. What more can he do to us?"

"But what if he didn't use up everything at the mine? What if he left some sort of reserve somewhere to handle contingencies?"

"You mean if he kept some of his people out of sight? Or maybe put out a booby-trap?"

Walt thought for a moment. "He might not have kept anyone out of sight. Someone else might have done it. I mean, think about it, we don't know if Branson and Rodriquez were working alone, were in charge of things or, maybe, were working for someone. There could be stuff going on Branson didn't know about. We know nothing about what the hell he was doing except that he killed a lot of people. What I'm saying is that whoever was in on this anti-environmental war, be it Branson or someone else, went to a lot of trouble to make sure today's plot went off properly. Branson followed me across the country, for God's sake. They weren't ready to let this go easily."

"So," Denise asked reflectively, "you're thinking Branson's booby-trapped the mine?"

"No, I doubt that," Walt said. "He's been too careful not to leave traces anywhere else. If people figured out that he's laying these ambushes, he'd have lost a lot of his advantages. Once someone understood his war plan, he'd have had much more trouble carrying out these operations. Remember, he planned on being alive when this was through. Who knows what he wanted to do after this, but the guy was crazy. He wasn't going to stop once he realized that he could shape the world with a few well-laid chemical bombs. He would have moved up to gassing NATO, the Congress, the World Bank. Who the hell knows, but he wouldn't have stopped."

"So what's that mean?" Denise stopped the jeep, turning off the engine but leaving the vehicle in gear to keep it in place on the slope leading down to the mine. She looked at Walt and frowned, unable to follow his fuzzy chain of logic.

"It means," said Walt, everything becoming clear to him at once, "that we're not done yet." He reached behind Denise's seat and removed her pistol.

Her face registered surprise and Denise asked in a sharp voice, "We're not done with what?"

"I think there's one more ambush," Walt said quietly, getting out of the jeep. "But this one's personal, not mechanical. They've had someone at every blast so far. The guy on the motorcycle at Lovett. The facilitator in the mountains. I think there's someone here. Or, at least, we have to play it like there is. If we're wrong, we can go on with the response once we've swept the area."

"I'll save you the trouble." The voice came from behind a large rock in front of the jeep. "You've done well, both of you, to get this far," said Brian Flannigan, coming around the rock, pistol in hand. "Now drop your gun, Walt and move over there." The head gestured, but the pistol, held rock-steady in the well-manicured hands, remained centered on Walt's chest. "And you, ma'am," gesturing with his head again but not moving the gun, "moving very slowly and keeping your hands in view, get out of the jeep and move over by Mr. Crawler."

"Who the fuck are you?" asked Walt as he dropped the pistol a few feet away from his feet.

"Who I am isn't important, Walt. It's what I'm doing that's important."

"And what's that?" Walt couldn't take his eyes off the pistol.

"I'm saving the world, Walt. Nothing short of saving the world."

"You're Brian Flannigan," said Denise slowly, still sitting in the jeep. "You're the UN guy who was coming out for the Biosphere ceremony. We had pictures of you all over the office." She blinked as if she could make the apparition with the pistol disappear. "What are you doing here?"

"I'm finishing what Adam Branson started, ma'am." The 'ma'am' was drawn out in an exaggerated show of chivalry.

"But Branson was a homicidal nut, out to kill thousands of innocent people," said Walt slowly, still not comprehending what was going on.

"Oh, there you're wrong, Mr. Crawler. You might think that Adam was crazy, but he was really a warrior in a just cause. From his point of view, he was a wronged man. First he was kicked out of the Army for adversely impacting endangered species, then he was exposed by environmentalists while on a dangerous mission for his country. People he was in charge of died because some environmentalist couldn't keep his mouth shut. He had plenty of reasons to do what he did."

"But what's that have to do with you?" asked Walt. "You're from the UN." Nothing made sense and he wondered if he had finally snapped and was imaging things.

"It has everything to do with me," said Flannigan, inexplicably eager to explain himself to a third party. "I stumbled over his classified resume when I was doing some research on environmental security. On paper, he looked like a dangerous man who had reason to be upset at environmentalists. I was right and, given his naturally short temper, it didn't take much of a nudge to make him a soldier in our struggle to reshape the environmental movement."

"To do what?" Walt couldn't believe what he was hearing.

"You heard me, Mr. Crawler. We're reshaping the world's environmental movement." Flannigan coughed self-consciously. "Or, at least, I am. Adam was just exacting revenge for past wrongs. The effect was the same, though."

"You're the head of the UN's environmental program," said Denise, blinking again. "Why do you want to reshape the environmental movement? And why does that mean killing people?"

"See, you've been bitten by the rot, too," Flannigan said triumphantly, his eyes flashing. "The movement's gotten too soft. The environment faces pressures almost too extreme to understand. Every week millions of new mouths come into our world. China and India alone have over two billion people, and they're getting bigger every day. And all of those people want refrigerators, cars, computers, all the conveniences of the modern world.

"We think we can save ourselves by making this barren patch of earth a Biosphere! That's what all of my peers say. Recycle a little bit here, conserve a little bit there, reduce a little bit someplace else and we'll be fine. They've been selling us that bill of goods for years. You can do all of that ten times over, you can make all of California an International Biosphere, and you won't have done a damn thing." Spittle flew from his mouth as he gave what was obviously an automatic performance, but the gun stayed trained on Walt.

"We need a new environmental vision. Less people, consuming less. I'm sorry, but not every Chinese and Indian can have a car, or a fridge, or even a meat-based diet. There aren't enough resources for that. Nor can they continue to have more babies, either. The world's too small as it is. But the environmental movement isn't willing to take these stands. It's all too tied into the status quo. Its leaders have their own stock portfolios, vacation homes, big cars and big families. They don't want to bring about change, they just want to provide the illusion of working for change.

"They're all too comfortable, and change doesn't happen through comfort. They needed to be rattled, and I am the person to rattle them. When I'm done, we'll be searching through the wreckage for new environmental leaders to step to the plate.

People who haven't bought into the system. People who will have the stomach to promote meaningful changes, not the old hacks we've got today, the deadwood I'm clearing from the forest."

"And then what?" asked Walt, struggling to figure out how his dead ex and children fit into Flannigan's mad scheme.

"And then *I* rebuild the movement. As it should be, with leaders who are willing to take strong stands, who will get things done. Not panderers to the status quo."

"Why in hell would anyone want you to rebuild anything? You're just one more psychotic murderer. Besides, you'd be dead with all the rest down by the mine, wouldn't you?" Walt was having trouble believing his own ears. He was actually having a discussion with a crazed madman who held a gun on him while, just yards away, a chemical stew threatened to kill thousands of people.

"I'll be a hero after today, Walt. I'm not going to die. I brought a gasmask with me today. It's only a prop, though, an excuse for why I, alone, survived. I don't need it. I've got the antidote."

"You've got the antidote!" Despite the gun trained on his chest, Walt took a clumsy step forward. "The same antidote that my girl needs?"

Flannigan nodded. "It's a fairly simple chemical, actually. I usually didn't get down into the weeds with Adam, but, given where I was going to be today, I wanted to make sure I understood that part quite well. No room for mistakes and all that, you know."

"You asshole!" Walt's whole body shook with anger. "You've got the antidote and you're letting my daughter stay in a coma!" He took another step, "You fucking asshole."

"Save the hysterics, Walt. Take one more step towards me and you're dead." Flannigan flicked the gun barrel minutely for emphasis. "It's too bad about Katie, but progress frequently has innocent victims." Flannigan's eyes had a faraway gleam, looking in on a private world where he was the holy warrior. "Amidst thousands of dead, I alone will survive. I'll be a hero, a beacon to those looking for the true path of environmentalism. With its leaders dead, the movement will need someone not incapacitated by shock. I will have survived the holocaust by the dam. I will have the strength to move it forward. It will be my destiny.

"Now get out of the jeep," he commanded Denise, his voice even and his eyes clear once more. "I won't tell you again."

Keeping her hands over her head, Denise clambered awkwardly out of her seat, brushing her knee against the stick shift and knocking the vehicle into neutral. Hoping Flannigan wouldn't tell her to stop, she began to walk slowly around the rear of the jeep, hands held high over he head. "So what's the next step, Brian?" she asked, spitting out his first name. "Are you going to shoot us here? Can't do that, though, can you? That'd blow your cover. Then you wouldn't be able to lead anybody, stuck in prison for murder with some big goon using you as a wife. That's not your vision for this wonderful environmental future, is it? The environmental movement would have to rebuild itself without you, and that would be a crying shame." Her voice was heavy with disdain.

"So you don't want to shoot us." She went on without waiting for a response. "Are you going to expose us to the same chemicals you're killing everyone else with? Make it look like we blew the response and got killed?" She slipped as she walked, knocking her hip hard against the jeep's tailgate and the vehicle inched forward. "Are you going to herd us down where the chemicals will kill us, Brian? Is that it? What if we won't go?"

"If you don't go, I'll shoot you here. I'll put the gun in Walt's hand and people will think he cracked after all that's happened to him." Flannigan's mind raced. Could that explain the two dead agents down by the rocks? He could tell people he saw something suspicious, went to check out the rocks, and there was Walt, gun drawn. Walt had shot the agents, he'd say, and he would be able to fulfill his destiny. He could say they forced him to come up to the mine, where he wrestled the gun away from Walt. In the struggle both Denise and Walt got shot. Desperate to find a way to clear himself, his half-crazed mind couldn't see the holes in his story. It would work. It *had* to work.

"That wouldn't get past the first crime scene analyst who looked at it," Denise snorted.

"Maybe, maybe not." He had connections, he could twist the story however he wanted. But it would still be easier if Walt and Denise died from the chemicals in the mine. He remembered the looks on the agents' faces as he shot them. He'd never shot anyone before. Branson had always done the dirty work. Flannigan had never even looked at pictures of the bodies, and shooting the agents had upset him so badly he'd had to stop to puke twice on his way up to the mine. He didn't think he could shoot anyone again, but he couldn't let the two people in front of him know that.

"You're a sick fucking nut." Denise knocked against the jeep one last time and moved over to where Walt was standing. She kept her eyes focused on Flannigan, praying he'd continue to be oblivious to the slowly moving vehicle until it was too late. "I'm not going anywhere, Brian, you'll have to shoot me. But before you do that, you're going to have to convince me to carry out a communications check with Stan back at the top of this ridge. He's expecting to hear from me now. If I don't call in, he's going to pull out the environmental VIPs by helicopter and start evacuating the whole valley. You'll have missed your plum."

A frown crossed Flannigan's face. He hadn't thought of that. Field operations were Branson's specialty, not his. The gun moved to Denise's chest. "You can call Stan now. Tell him everything's fine."

"And if I don't?"

"Then you'll have ruined my plan. But, in return, I'll make you watch your friend Walt die. And it won't be pretty. Branson taught me a lot of his tricks." Flannigan's lower lip quivered. Things were slipping from his control, despite the gun, and he could only hope that his threat worked. He knew he didn't have the stomach to actually make good on it.

"Denise, what are you doing?" Walt asked under his breath. Why she was challenging Flannigan when he held a gun on her? Keeping the man talking was one thing, but telling him he'd have to shoot her was crazy.

"Quiet, Walt," Denise whispered, "I know what I'm doing." With years of experience in reading people under extreme situations, she'd seen the chink in Flannigan's armor. "You've never done this before, Brian, have you?" she asked loudly. *Look at me,* she prayed as the jeep gained speed, *look at me.* "You've never shot a person in your life. Hell, me and Walt seem to do it regularly. But you've never done it, have you. You probably haven't even been in a fistfight since puberty." Her voice was becoming more confident, challenging Flannigan, keeping his attention off of the jeep. "You haven't got the balls to shoot us, much less torture us. You need Branson and your damned chemicals to do your dirty work. Chicken shit." She faked a stumble in the suit and moved a few more feet towards her pistol, lying in the sand, tantalizingly close yet at the same time impossibly far.

The jeep bumped over a rock and Flannigan noticed its movement for the first time. "What the hell?" he muttered, swinging his body, and the gun, around to face the vehicle.

Already poised, waiting for this moment when Flannigan's attention would be elsewhere, Denise sprang towards her pistol. Encumbered by her suit and slowed by her injuries, she had scant seconds to get the gun and take cover, but it was her only chance. She prayed Walt would react quickly. If he didn't move fast enough, he'd be a dead man when the jeep finished rolling by and Flannigan got a clear field of fire again.

Flannigan shifted his weight and swung the gun back towards Denise, but the jeep was coming much faster than he'd realized. "Shit!" he muttered, squeezing off two poorly aimed shots as he scrambled out of the way of the rolling vehicle. The jeep bounced past, moving between him and the now invisible Walt and Denise, and he readied himself for another shot. How could things have gone so wrong? He'd had them in the palm of his hand. The jeep was almost completely past him when he realized he was standing straight up, fully exposed to what would surely be an armed Ranger. He panicked, firing shots as quickly as he could at the jeep and then, as it continued rolling down the slope, at the vacant dirt and rocks behind it. Vacant? His mind raced, where could they have gone? The gun bucked again and again in his hand, the small cracks of the silenced weapon spurring his panic even more. He'd lost them. The gun stopped responding to his trigger squeezes, the upper receiver locked against the now empty magazine, and he stood motionless, right arm extended like a duck dog pointing towards a downed bird. Slowly his hand descended to his side, the quiver in his hand becoming more pronounced. He'd lost.

As Flannigan lowered his gun, a white blob walked out of a narrow ravine forty feet away. "It's your turn to drop the gun, asshole," commanded Denise bringing her own gun to bear on the now-shaking man.

"Don't kill him, Denise," muttered Walt, coming up behind her, still somewhat dazed by how rapidly the situation had changed, "he knows Katie's antidote."

"I won't, don't worry," said Denise, moving slowing towards Flannigan. "Drop the gun," she ordered again, raising her voice against the desert silence, "I won't tell you again."

Like a man in a trance, Flannigan ignored Denise and began touching his pockets, looking for another magazine.

True to her word, Denise didn't warn him again. Her first shot, a certain hit from thirty feet at a stationary target, shattered his left knee, but Flannigan kept his grip on the weapon. Slowly she began to shuffle towards the fallen man. "Drop the gun," she ordered again, barely hesitating before squeezing the trigger again. Flannigan's pistol flew from his hands as his right forearm disintegrated under the impact of a nine millimeter slug. Satisfied that he posed no further threat Denise told Walt to put tourniquets above Flannigan's wounds. "Don't be gentle about it," she told him unnecessarily, "we don't have time to waste. When you get done with that, put these on his arms and legs," she handed Walt a pair of plastic flex cuffs she'd pulled from her pocket, "and roll him into the shade. He'll live long enough to tell us what the antidote is. I'll do a comm check with Stan and tell him to send someone down to pick up this piece of shit," she nodded at Flannigan, "before we get started." She pulled out the radio. "Stan, can you read me?"

"Clear as a bell. I heard some shots. What's up?"

While Walt secured Flannigan, Denise told Stan what had happened.

"Pulling Flannigan out won't be a problem but can you still carry out the response? Should I start the evac now?" As well as anyone, Stan knew they were walking a dangerous tightrope.

Now standing by Denise's side, Walt shook his head no. They had come this far, they couldn't back off now.

Taking her cue from Walt, Denise spoke confidently into the mike. "My jeep, with all of our gear in it, is still in one piece a bit down the hill. We'll be fine. I'm going to give the radio to Walt for the duration of the response. He'll call you when we get to the mine's entrance. If you haven't heard from him in ten minutes, assume the worst and start the evac."

"Roger. I'll be waiting."

CHAPTER XXXXIV

As she walked to the jeep, Denise could feel the energy draining from her like air from a leaky balloon. The pain in her leg, the confrontation with Flannigan, the struggle through the mine were all taking a toll. She would have to dig deep inside of her to keep moving. She looked back at Walt, moving quickly, alert and full of hope. Through Flannigan, they'd found Katie's antidote, now he just had to get them through the response. "I'm beat, Walt," she said, "but I know more about criminals than you do. You know more about response operations. I'll get us into the mine, but you'll have to take over from there."

"That's fine." Walt smiled at her as they reached the jeep. "You've never worn one of these suits before, so you'll be surprised at how clumsy you'll feel. And it'll be tough to hear me over the noise of your air supply, but we'll stay close together and I'll yell really loud. If you understand me, give me a thumbs up, if you disagree, give me a thumbs down. If you're confused, slide your hand horizontally and I'll explain it again." He leaned against the jeep momentarily as if considering something, then dug into his pocket and pulled out Katie's silver spoon. "Here," he said, almost shyly, "I want you to have this. It's a spoon I bought for Katie. I've been carrying it around as a good luck charm since she went to the hospital. Once we get through this, I'll get her a new spoon, but you've earned this one. After all I've put you through, I want to give you something while I have the chance."

Denise took the spoon, caressing it gently with her fingers before she put it in her pocket. His trust had given her a badly needed boost. "It'll be a good luck charm for me, too, Walt.

And we'll buy Katie her next spoon together, you, me and Harley. Okay?"

"Okay. Now let's get suited up." Walt helped Denise put on the self-contained breathing apparatus, explaining how to work the various parts of her suit. He knew it was a crash course, but, as long as her suit retained its integrity, she should be okay. "One little pinhole, though," he emphasized to her, "and your integrity's gone. You'll be exposed to that methyl ethyl chlorinate and that means you'll be dead. So watch out for anything that might puncture your suit. We'll have about thirty minutes to clear the mine, get in and stop the reaction before we need to back out to decon and get more air. If that's not enough, we'll tell Stan and he can start the evac. Any questions?" After years of carrying out these operations, of enjoying the challenge of pitting himself and his equipment against a dangerous unknown, Walt suddenly found that the thrill of response operations had evaporated, leaving him feeling tired and scared.

"Lots of questions, but there's no sense in asking them now." Denise smiled resolutely, then helped Walt finish suiting up. With each of them carrying shovels, picks and lights, they walked in clumsy, bouncing steps the rest of the way down to the mine. As they approached the shaft, Walt looked at the gas meter he had slung around his neck. Nothing. So far it was still safe.

They swung around a large boulder adjacent to the opening and the meter's peg started to flicker. Walt felt for the dials with his enclosed fingers and for the hundredth time cursed the people who made those suits so unmaneuverable. Not that he'd sacrifice any of the plastic shield that stood between him and the deadly toxins that were spiking the meter, but the thick material did make it hard to work the equipment. He finished adjusting the meter and clicked his radio on. "Stan, can you still hear me?"

"Affirmative."

Walt knew Stan was probably as scared as he was. Heavier than air or not, if this gas made its way up to his position, he'd die a horrible death. "It's clear up to the mine shaft, then we start to get readings of some sort of gas in the air. Not huge amounts yet, they top out at fifty parts per billion, but they're there. This is the right shaft. I'm not going to take any other measurements," he stated. There were always more tests a first responder could do, but he and Denise just didn't have the time. "The next team can do that if necessary. We're going to go straight in."

"Roger. Keep me posted."

Walt let go of the transmitter and indicated to Denise to start digging, then he picked up his own shovel. The non-sparking brass gleamed as he hefted it. The weight of the shovel felt reassuring in his gloved hand, something tangible with which to do battle against the invisible gasses that were swirling around his enclosed body. After years of responding to every type of chemical leak or release imaginable, his mind was moving on autopilot. Stick the shovel in, pull out a load of sand, toss it to the side. Gently stick the shovel back in, taking his cues from Denise as they probed for anything that might hint of danger. The unyielding side of a metal barrel, a rotten beam that was ready to crack, an old nylon rope rigged as a booby trap. Death could come quickly in a situation like this.

Despite the danger, Walt's heart was full of gratitude. A team of Rangers had already headed off to rescue Harley, and with Flannigan, and the antidote, safely in hand, there was hope for Katie. Although this was Denise's first response, he felt they'd succeed in this operation. God couldn't be so cruel that He'd let him get this far only to kill him now. But then, again, Walt reflected sourly, God had been cruel enough to kill Julia and his twins. Perhaps success was not such a sure thing. Even if he died, though, Flannigan and, more importantly, his knowledge of an antidote, were already secured. Katie had a future. Walt prayed he would have one with her. A second chance to be a better dad. He wouldn't let his daughter down this time.

Walt looked to the left, where Denise was shoveling sand away from the shallow opening. Being in a full response suit seemed hardly to bother her at all. Perhaps she, too, was comforted by having a physical task on which to concentrate, no matter how dangerous it was. Or maybe she just didn't know any better. Walt looked closer and noticed that her mouth was moving as if she were singing to himself inside her suit. But the movements of her lips, drawn tight across her face in two narrow lines, seemed too uniform and sedate for a song. A string tugged at Walt's heart. Denise wasn't singing, she was praying.

After several minutes of steady shoveling, Denise reached over and tapped Walt on the shoulder, hard enough so he'd notice her despite his heavy, semi-rigid suit. "Walt," she screamed through the face shield. "I'm going to stop shoveling. You keep digging and I'll feel around at the bottom. There's got to be some gate or something down there."

Walt gave her the universal thumbs up sign. He had to trust her here, just as she would have to trust him later on. Fear of death, fear of losing Katie when he had come so far, anger at Flannigan and Branson for what they had done to his family and friends and thoughts of the future had all been replaced by a professional respect for the danger they were in. There was no room in his mind for anything but the job at hand.

Walt's shovel crunched into something solid. Denise waved him away and dug around with her fingers, feeling terribly clumsy in her oversized suit. Still, even with such a thick suit, she cringed every time she brushed up against a piece of the wrecked mine's skeleton. Walt's warning had hit home. Just one sharp edge hit at the wrong angle could mean the difference between life and death.

Her fingers closed around a heavy chunk of wood and Denise tugged slowly, persistently, at the object. With surprising ease, it came free from the surrounding sand and rubble that filled the entrance to the mine. Another piece of wood, partially charred from a long-ago fire, now stuck out from the shaft. Denise carefully removed that piece, and then another one, studded with square nails that a long-dead miner had once used to hang equipment. Piece followed piece like a large-scale three dimensional jigsaw puzzle. Passing the removed pieces to Walt, pointing out nails or screws that could puncture his suit if carelessly handled, Denise went deeper into the mine. She was glad to have Walt behind her, confident that his abilities were more than equal to the task they had undertaken. As long as there were no booby traps.

Part of her mind, detached from the immediate proceedings, admired the people who had constructed this death trap. Although she knew it was a contrived cave-in, nothing Denise saw looked out of place. To her eyes, eyes that had seen countless collapsed mine shafts, this was just one more case of the timbers giving out and the rock walls and ceiling collapsing during any of the numerous earthquakes, tremors or aftershocks that regularly rocked the high desert. Branson's deception was masterful.

Six feet into the mine, the shaft abruptly cleared. Walt took a plastic coated flashlight from his belt and turned the beam on the small cavern that opened up in front of them. This shaft had been one of many mines in the high desert that had gone nowhere, leaving the hapless prospector with a sore back, a pile of rubble and a worthless hole in the ground.

The radio crackled in his ear. "Walt, Stan here. We've got Decon on site and we're getting backup ready. We'll have a dozer up in just a moment. We can seal the mine if we have to. That ought to slow dispersion down enough to let us evacuate the area safely."

"Roger on the Decon and the backup, Stan." Walt was relieved. Carrying out an operation as complex as this one with neither backup nor Decon was tempting fate. A twisted knee, a tangled air supply hose or any of a myriad of other complications would be the end of the story if there were no backup to lend a hand.

He played the beam around the shaft again. Two plastic barrels, fifty-five gallons each, rested against each other, precipitously balanced on some cracked rocks. Above them, perched on some old wooden shoring, a rusty steel barrel, also fifty-five gallons, lay on its side. Walt had seen setups like this on a score of response operations. People just threw some drums in a cellar, a cave, a field, or simply a wide spot in the road, and then drove away, leaving someone else to deal with their mess. He looked closer and saw a thin stream dripping from the steel barrel onto the plastic ones below. He understood Branson's plan now. The timing of the release was related to how quickly the liquid from the top barrel ate away the plastic containers underneath it. The contents of the two plastic barrels were mixing into a poisonous gas, the reaction accelerating as the barrels disintegrated.

"Keep the bulldozer away from the mine, Stan. We've got three barrels pretty precariously perched in here. A fifty-five gallon one on top is leaking onto two fifty-five gallon ones below. It might not take too much to knock them over." Or it might take a lot. Branson wouldn't have gone to all the trouble of rigging this set-up just to let a local quake spoil it. There was no need to take chances, though. "My guess is that the contents of the two bottom barrels are mixing to form a poisonous gas. We don't want to accelerate that by jostling things with a dozer. There's a box of equipment in the Jeep. Have the backup bring it in. If we can patch the drip from the top barrel, get a barrier between the plastic drums and plug up their holes, we'll be set, at least for a little while. I've handled worse sites a dozen times. No problem." Yeah, right, he thought to herself. His novice partner with the bum leg and hurt arm just made it all easier. Still, Denise had already shown just how tough and solid she was and Walt wouldn't have traded her for the world.

"Okay, Walt." Even with the static on the radio, Walt could hear tension in his voice. "Backup will bring the box right away. Good luck."

"Thanks, Stan, we'll be done in a flash." Walt motioned Denise to come closer to him and handed her the flashlight. "Denise," he yelled, straining his lungs to be heard over the noise of the air supply. "You're going to have to hold the light for me. First we have to patch those drums, then we'll have to move them. It should be no problem. You make sure I can see what I'm doing, I'll do the patching."

Denise took the flashlight. "Okay," she hollered back, seemingly ready for anything. "Just tell me what to do." Sweat was pouring down her face but her voice was cheerful and strong.

Walt checked the meter again. The spikes were over five thousand PPM now. Time was running out rapidly. In moments there would be no choice but to pull the VIPs out even if everyone else by the dam got caught in a stampede as a result.

Stan came back on the air. "Walt, we're starting to pick up readings down below. Still in the low parts per billion, but we're going to have to start evacuations soon if you can't get this thing stopped."

Two huge, suited creatures came around the edge of the mine, one of them holding a medium-sized box in his hands.

Walt took the box with a yell of thanks. "Stan," he said into his radio, "we're headed back in. If we haven't called you back in three minutes, start to evacuate. Give us another sixty seconds to get out. If we're not out by then, block the entrance. Be careful with that dozer, though. Once you've blocked the hole, put down a layer of polly over the entrance and then cover that with more dirt. You can dig us out when the valley's empty."

"Walt, you can't . . ."

"Stay off the air, Stan. We're going in." Walt terminated the transmission.

Followed by a lumbering Denise, Walt turned and moved ponderously into the shaft. If it had been just a regular response site he would no longer have been concerned. This was textbook stuff. But in this particular response operation, all bets were off. It was connected with Adam Branson and nothing could be taken for granted. Bundled up in the bulky suit, pressed for time as he was, there wasn't much he could do about Branson. If he'd booby-trapped the barrels, they wouldn't know it until too late.

"Shine the light on the top barrel," he yelled.

Denise moved the light immediately and Walt studied the barrel carefully. If he overlooked even a hairline crack, the whole barrel might split if handled improperly. He'd seen it happen before, a routine move turned into disaster. Life was like that. Death and disaster lurked everywhere. Against his will, he thought of Julia and the girls. A routine romp in the dunes turned into violent death. With a flash of dizziness, he suddenly felt drained, daunted by the responsibility of carrying out a response operation after all that had befallen him recently. He felt old, aged by fate, and his mind became cluttered with extraneous thoughts. It was paralyzing. He tried to think about the sweat that was running down his limbs and forming puddles in his gloves and boots. He tried, as he always had, to focus on the physical and the immediate, to control his mind again, but he couldn't. He was cracking. He couldn't move.

"Okay, Walt, now what do you want me do?" Getting no response, Denise repeated herself, screaming at the top of her lungs. "Walt, what next?"

Walt remained motionless.

Oh Christ, Denise thought, he's deep-sixed on me. A million possibilities flooded her mind, all of them bad. Her partner was statue still in a mine loaded with poison, where drums full of deadly chemicals were about to rupture and expose thousands of people to their contents. If she and Walt couldn't contain the reaction within moments, she'd have to drag him out of the hole and send the dozer down. Stan would pass the word to start an evacuation and all hell would break loose at the dam. It wouldn't be as bad as Branson and Flannigan had planned, but it would still be a disaster.

"Walt!" she screamed, pushing him gently on the shoulder. "Walt! Can you hear me?" She waved the flashlight in front of his eyes. The biologist's expression didn't change. Denise looked back at the barrels. Could she contain them on her own? In the shadowy ambient light of the mine? With her injured leg? With no one to help her manhandle the heavy drums? Without ever having done something like this before? She knew it would be impossible. If Walt couldn't help, their response was doomed. They had to leave. When she got Walt out of the mine, she'd use hand and arm signals to tell Stan they'd failed, that he should send the bulldozer down. They would have done what they could. Most people would have cracked long before Walt had. It wasn't his fault.

Gently taking Walt by the arm, she started to lead him out the way they had come. Knocking up against him as they walked, she felt something in her pocket pressing against her leg. Katie's spoon! Moving quickly, she wriggled her right arm out of its plastic sleeve and into the cocoon-like cavern of the suit's torso. Reaching into her pocket she pulled out the spoon and dangled it in her visor directly in front of Walt's eyes. "Katie, Walt. We're doing this for Katie!" she screamed. Denise shook the spoon for emphasis and stared at her companion's face, desperate for some sign of comprehension.

Walt's face betrayed no emotions and Denise choked back a sob of frustration.

Then, like a drowning man surfacing for a life-giving breath of air, Walt gasped and a confused look passed over his face, followed by one of concern. "Denise, what happened?"

"You blanked out on me. Are you okay?" They had to decide immediately if they could finish the job on their own. She prayed he would say yes.

"I'm fine. I just snapped for a moment." Walt's recovery was immediate. "Let's finish it up and get out of here." Once again his voice was strong and clear as he turned and led the way back into the mine.

Under the bright glare of the light, Walt traced the drip in the rusty metal barrel to a small hole in one of the seams. Making sure his hands stayed clear of the leaking liquid, he began to apply a small patch to the drum. This was the tricky part. Whatever was in the drum could probably eat right through his suit, exposing him to the deadly gasses that filled the mine. It wasn't a pleasant thought. Condensation formed on the clear shield of his facemask, making it difficult to see clearly and Walt hoped he hadn't missed a second leak as his fingers banged clumsily against the drum.

Several dabs of bonding agent, pressed into place with a long wooden rod, slowed the leak. Walt took the light from Denise and carefully examined the barrel. Other than the leak, now stopped completely, it was sound enough. They would only quick patch it now. Someone else could move it later. He strapped a band around the drum and activated its CO2 capsule to tighten it, reinforcing the plug he'd put in.

Next, Walt turned his attention to the plastic barrels on the ground. It was possible, although less likely, that these chemicals would eat through his suit as quickly as the acid, so he couldn't afford to let his guard down. Even worse than the personal danger he faced, though, was the knowledge that one mistake and the resulting release would be catastrophic. The acid had eaten significant holes in both drums and even a slight jar might split them wide open.

Handing the light back to Denise, Walt took another drum band out of the cardboard box. The band would help keep the barrel from splitting and would also slow down any leaks it covered. He'd put several bands on each drum. Then he'd work some of the barrier tape and sorbent socks in between the barrels. After that, he'd activate the bands' CO2 cartridges and then he would roll the lower barrel across the floor of the mine. The socks and the barrier tape should be enough to contain and separate any remaining leaks in the barrels. After the drums were apart, they'd throw down some booms and more barrier tape and call in the backup to perform the overpack. By that point, the operation would either be successful or it would have failed abysmally.

Walt placed the last of the bands around the drums and, painfully conscious of how quickly the seconds were slipping by, began to pull the tabs. When the bands had tightened, he put his hands on the lower drum and gave it a solid push, his leg muscles quivering as he strained against the mass of the two hundred pound container. Slowly, reluctantly, the plastic barrel rolled away from its deadly companion. Walt pushed harder, feeling the drum give way before him, then his feet slipped on a patch of loose gravel and the drum rolled back towards him, pinning one of his legs against a rotting timber.

"Shit!" he screamed, loudly enough for Denise to hear him clearly. "I'm trapped." Denise's heart sank as she watched the barrel roll back against Walt. Mangled as it was, she couldn't just muscle the barrel away from him without running the risk of ripping the plastic container completely apart. "Are you all right?" she screamed back.

"I'm okay, I just can't move with this thing pinning me. Push here," Walt tapped the barrel with his right hand. "I'll heave too. Once I get my feet under me again, I should be able to move it by myself."

Praying that the barrel would hold and that it wasn't covered with acid that would chew away her suit, Denise pressed her shoulders against the spot Walt had indicated and, grinding her teeth against the pain in her leg, pushed with all her might. The barrel rolled slightly and then rocked back again as Denise slipped on the rubble that covered the mine's floor.

"Try again. We almost had it that time." Walt's voice was steady, betraying none of the fear he felt, pinned under a disintegrating barrel of chemicals in the midst of a hazard-strewn old mine.

Denise put her shoulders back to the barrel and pushed once more, concentrating on keeping her footing. She felt the resistance begin to diminish as the drum yielded and then, like an oversized contortionist, Walt struggled into place beside her, pushing the barrel across the mine's uneven surface with the intensity of a football lineman attacking the practice skids.

When Walt had moved the drum across the mine's floor, he went back to the box of materials he had placed on the ground.

He grabbed an armload of equipment and stepped gingerly into the gap they had just created between the drums, laying down sorbent socks and other barrier materials to prevent the chemicals already released from mixing any more.

"Stan, we've got it." Walt talked calmly into her headphone, a professional to the end. "Send the backup in with three overpacks, drum putty, and some more sorbents and booms. We've got the drums apart and banded, but we're about out of air and we need to exit." He took one last measurement with the meter. The readings were already starting to drop! He waved the meter in front of Denise's face and she grinned enthusiastically. "More good news, Stan," Walt said, "the PPMs are dropping. We're out of the woods."

"Roger, Walt," Stan's voice was full of relief. "Good job. Backup's monitoring this channel, they'll head in now. You two come up to Decon and we'll get you out of those suits and into the fresh air. I'll pass this information on to HQ."

Stan gave a hand signal to the backup responders and they started toward the mine carrying huge plastic overpack containers for the tattered barrels inside. As the backup entered the mine, Walt and Denise exited and began walking slowly up the hill towards the decon line. Stan looked at the two moonsuited creatures and whooped with joy.

He had never seen such a beautiful sight.

EPILOGUE

Walt touched his tie self-consciously and looked at Dr. Bocall, anxiety showing clearly in his eyes. "What if she's different?" he asked, "what if she doesn't remember me?"

"She will, Walt, she will." Doctor Bocall's voice rang with confidence, exhibiting a complete recovery from his own bout of sickness, but Walt was still worried. Soon after his capture, Flannigan had explained what type of antidote would work for Katie. Harley, rescued battered but alive from the mine, had verified Flannigan's information and Doctor Bocall had prepared the antidote. He'd administered it to Katie the night before and was sure it would be entirely successful once given enough time, although it could be weeks before the little girl would be able to walk and run. Nonetheless, her ability to see, speak and listen, he'd assured Walt, should recover relatively quickly. In fact, he said, when he met Walt at the airport, Katie was already responding to the antidote.

Walt hadn't slept during the long flight east, his mind constantly reviewing what had just happened. Harley and Denise had gone to a hospital in Palm Springs where their wounds were being treated. Neither one appeared seriously hurt, but the doctors still wanted to hold them for observation for a few days. Flannigan was in the same hospital, being held under guard for much more than observation. Every few minutes, one of the FBI agents flying with Walt would answer the phone and pass along some new piece of information concerning Branson and

Flannigan. The Agent's news had been nothing but good. All of the remaining SCOT members had been rounded up and were in the process of being thoroughly questioned. None of them, including Laste, seemed to know anything of Branson's activities, although Walt was sure the FBI would shadow them forever. Additionally, news programs and magazines were already filling up Walt's answering machine, offering large sums of money for interviews and talk show appearances. In the space of only a few hours, Walt had become a cash cow. His financial woes were history.

In short, Walt's life had gone from hopeless to brimming with hope in just a few hours. He had wrestled with the devils from his past and had come away stronger, more sure of himself despite the tragedies that had befallen him. The boxes in his mind had become, he told himself, places he would visit frequently, relishing the rich memories and weaving them into the fabric of his present life. Katie might be the only living member of his family, but he would make sure that Sarah, Tracy, Julia, and even Jeff Tillison and Bill Pryor, were never completely dead. Their memories, and the sacrifices they made, would live on in both Walt and his daughter.

They reached Katie's room and Doctor Bocall stopped by the door.

Walt hesitated, scared that his fragile dream of Katie smiling at him would be shattered when he entered the room.

"It's okay, Walt," the doctor said gently, "she's doing fine. Go on in, she's waiting for you."

Walt took a large teddy bear out of the bag he was carrying and fluffed it awkwardly in front of him. "She is going to recognize me, isn't she?"

"Yes, Walt. And she's going to be delighted to see you." Dr. Bocall reached out and opened the door. "Now get going."

Walt stepped through the open door, his fears evaporating as he saw his little girl sitting upright in her bed, a smile on her face and red and blue ribbons in her hair.

REFERENCES

Terrorism threat cited by officials, *The Boston Globe,* 23 April, 1998

Gardener digs up live grenades, *The Boston Globe,* 19 May, 1999

Search for munitions in Sandwich, *The Boston Globe,* 17 February, 1999

Going to bat for bats, *Nation Parks,* January/February 2001

Army Digs Up Old Chemicals from Ambassador's Yard, *EPA,* 18 March 1999

Terrorist Attack, *The Improper Bostonian,* September 23, 1998

Bats take Shelter, *Nature Conservancy,* September/October, 1996

Mines of the High Desert, *Ronald Dean Miller,* La Siesta Press, 1985

One of our H-Bombs is Missing, *Flora Lewis,* Bantam Books, 1987

The Threat at Home: Confronting the Toxic Legacy of the U.S. Military, *Seth Shulman,* Beacon Press, 1992

Police, military team searched base critic's home for munitions, *Cape Cod Times,* February 8, 2001

At Former Military Sites, a Hidden Peril, *The Wall Street Journal,* January 22, 1999

Buried-bomb talk jolts town, *The Boston Globe,* February 11, 1999

BVG